RJ Wat

I JUST WANTED
A BEER

BY: R J WATERS

1

RJ Waters

RJ Waters

I Just Wanted A Beer

Published by Trient Press: 3375 S Rainbow Blvd, #81710, SMB 13135, Las Vegas, NV 89180

ISBN-13:

ISBN-10:

Ordering Information:
Quantity sales. Special discounts are available on quantity purchases by corporations, associations, and others. For details, contact the publisher at the address above.
Orders by U.S. trade bookstores and wholesalers. Please contact Trient Press: Tel: (775) 996-3844; or visit www.trientpress.com.

Printed in the United States of America.

CHAPTER ONE

A cold beer would taste good. Hot and tired from driving all day, I check into a Las Vegas motel. This is a basic motel, no cocktail lounge, no mini bar. Damn. Across the street, a 7-11 sign beckons in the night. It's after one a.m. and traffic is light. The *street* is four lanes in both directions. Sprinting to the median I look both ways, no cars. I start to run; a sudden powerful force smashes into my body, hurling me high in the air. I feel the breath sucked out of me. Crashing to the pavement, I black out.

Beginning to regain consciousness, I feel my face being cleaned with a warm, rough cloth. Am I being washed for entrance into Heaven? My vision begins to clear. A large black dog looms over me, licking my face. *Is God a Dog?*

An authoritative male voice asks, "Can you move?"

I ease up on one elbow. There is only the dog.

The firm voice speaks again, "We have to get you off the street."

Whoever is talking to me is *not* a dog. Head injury… I'm hurt bad. The '*not* a dog' clamps his powerful jaws onto my shirt and starts dragging me toward the median.

"You might try to *help*," he mumbles through clenched teeth.

Managing to push with my legs, I'm pulled onto the median.

"See if you can move anything."

The dog is still the only thing with me. What the hell is happening? I gradually move myself up to a sitting position. We are now face-to-face. The dog is a longhaired German Shepard mix, with soulful eyes.

"You need to get back to your room," the canine orders.

"Why am I talking with a dog?"

"Actually, you haven't said a word. I was getting worried. Now try to get up and I will help you back to your room. We'll discuss the *dog* thing later."

Must have one hell of a concussion, I'll be lucky to make it across the rest of the road. He looks both ways then tells me it's safe to go. I manage to stagger across the street. I hurt all over, but my legs seem to be functioning. The dog is right beside me. After tripping over the curb, I make it across the parking lot, find my room, and unlock the door. The dog pushes me inside.

"Go to bed and get some sleep," he commands.

He shoves the door closed with his ample body, jumps up on the couch and stares hard at me. "Go-to-bed."

Sore, tired, and with my head spinning, I crawl into bed. *If* I wake up, I'll try to make sense of all this. I drift off to sleep.

Swimming toward consciousness, I remember dreaming of ghost-like creatures surrounding me. They seemed worried and waved silvery objects over me. What kind of dream was that? I have dreams all right, more like nightmares. They're a carryover from my black-ops days in South America with the Army Rangers. Bad dreams, scary ones.

My head is throbbing, I ache allover. The sunlight, slamming thru the window shades, hurts my eyes. I throw my hands over my face. I don't recall drinking last night. Beginning to set up, I hear someone speak.

"About time you woke up. It's almost check-out time."

Who the hell is that? I came here alone. Turning my throbbing head toward the voice, a large black dog is lying on the couch.

Dog?

Wait a minute. There was a *dog;* I'm starting to come around. Yes, the dog! He's here in my room. I remember the dog. He appeared after I was hit, when I was trying to cross the street. He was talking to me and dragging me off the street. It's obvious I've suffered a severe concussion, I'm still delusional.

"I need to pee, open the door please."

Dazed I get up and open the door, as instructed.

"I'll be right back."

I close the door and slump down on the couch.

It is warm.

The couch is warm!

RJ Waters

CHAPTER TWO

A short time later, there's scratching at my motel room door. Head still swimming, I open the door. The dog pushes past me and bounds onto the bed.

I am dumbfounded.

"Get dressed, I need food."

I am still dumbfounded.

"You naturally have questions, but first let's check out, then get some food."

I do as ordered. Clean up, get my stuff together, go to the office, and checkout. The dog is waiting by my pick-up.

"How did you know this one is mine?"

"Good, you can still talk."

I open the driver's door and toss my suitcase on the rear seat. The dog jumps in and settles his ample rump in the driver's seat.

"Like I believe you can drive?"

"No, my legs are too short, moron. I call shotgun." He maneuvers to the passenger side. "Now let's get food."

"I imagine you have *food* suggestions. What would be your choice?" Now *I* am being *sarcastic*.

"I prefer meat. Two double cheeseburgers from McDonald's, no sauce. You have the big breakfast. You look like hell. Just a friendly observation."

I drive to the closest Mickey D's and order as instructed. The big breakfast and a large coffee do sound good. We sit in the parking lot and eat in silence. My brain is exploding with questions. I don't know where to start, so I eat. Dog is neat, keeps his food inside the Styrofoam box. Good dog.

When we are done, I start the truck and stare at him. "I am still talking with a dog, and don't understand what is going on. Do you have a name?"

"Yes, thank you for asking. I am Dog." He throws his massive chest out proudly.

"Dog?"

"Dog. That's it. Easy to remember. Now, head north on Hwy 95. I know a good place for us to chill and get everything in perspective."

Chill, perspective? From a dog! I know I'm still suffering from a *colossal* concussion. We pass thru a very nice neighborhood on our way to 95 North. I am just taking it slow, admiring the homes, wondering what the hell happened to my free will.

All of a sudden Dog yells, "Stop." I pull over to the curb and he jumps out the open window.

"I'll be right back."

What the??? Where is he going? He runs behind some bushes, and is MIA for at least twenty minutes, then comes trotting back.

"Sorry. Greasy food."

I reach over and push open the door. His enormous body makes a quick, fluid leap, and he is again seated next to me. Using his massive font paw, he manages to pull the door closed. Dog directs me to head north on highway 95, out of Las Vegas. I don't want to do that! But I do. I can't stop myself... I'm in big trouble.

RJ Waters

CHAPTER THREE

The road is a tedious, strip of highway traversing seemingly endless, rolling, barren hills, hopefully giving me time to clear my head.

I'm in Nevada job hunting. Previously, I had a good position as an investigator in a large California sheriff's office. Then the curse of law enforcement struck-- a divorce. Learning about a small city in need of a chief investigator, I applied and got the job. It was on the coast and I was looking forward to life by the beach. After settling in, the state auditors discovered the city was broke. Seems some of the city council members had been overpaying themselves. They are currently under indictment. The city could not cover payroll, so I am out of work, along with a lot of other people.

Cruising along lost in my thoughts; I notice road signs announcing a reduced speed zone ahead. Coming into view on my right is Creech Air Force base. I know this base trains the pilots who fly drones operating in Iraq and Afghanistan. Utilizing satellites, they fly their missions directly from this base. What technology. Where'd that come from? In South America, our observation planes had pilots *in* them.

Past the base, the speed limit picks up again. I go back to my thoughts. I decided to try my luck elsewhere in *our great country*; having wisely saved some money, and receiving unemployment benefits, I made up my mind to just start driving, and find a new home. I've visited several law enforcement agencies along the way, but I have no plans to look for a job in Las Vegas. Policing in Vegas is a nightmare. I'm not old yet, but I am too damn old for that shit.

We drive onward, the Dog and me.

He has been happily hanging his head out the window and leaving me to my reflections. We come to the road sign for 'Mercury'. I know this is the entrance to the Nevada Test Site, where the atomic bombs were tested, and the entrance to the infamous Area 51. Do not turn off here, or heavily armed guards, who have no sense of humor, will greet you.

After traveling a few more miles the Dog startles me, "Slowdown, we're close."

"Close! Close to what? All of this is restricted government land."

"Pull over here," he gestures with his front paw.

There are some orange cones on the right-hand side of the road, in front of an opening in the fence.

"Pull in there. I'll move the cones, and you drive through." He thrusts his large frame out the window and starts grabbing the top of the cones with his immense teeth, dragging them out of the way.

"Come on, hurry, we don't have much time," His tone sounds anxious.

Stupidly, I do as he tells me. He replaces the cones and jumps into the bed of the truck. Impressive. He is as athletic, as he is impudent.

"Drive up the road, hurry."

The *road* is a dirt path leading away from the highway. The majestic Sierra Nevada Mountains are visible in the distance. By comparison, this horrible brown chunk of lifeless trail, just keeps winding further and further into the desert. I continue to follow the path, avoiding the ruts and bumps, as it winds up and then down between hills.

"Keep going, but not too fast. Don't want a dust trail to give us away."

What am I doing? I don't seem to be able to resist. I *know* this is a stupid idea. We are going into the *restricted area-where deadly force may be used,* according to the sign, *I just passed.*

The path veers down a steep hill and at the bottom I see a small grove of green trees, and what appears to be a shimmering, azure pond. The word *hallucination* springs to mind.

"Pull up under the trees," my guide tells me. I do as ordered, and he jumps out of my truck.

"Wait here, I'll be back shortly. Stay under the trees, you'll be safe."

The Dog races past the pond, around a turn and out of sight. What the hell, what am I doing? A talking dog has led me here. I'm in a highly secret U.S. Government area where intruders are not tolerated, and, I remind myself, *where deadly force may be used.* Deadly force. I still have my personal weapon, from my police days, for protection. No wait. That won't go well if *they* find me. The Dog told me to stay under the trees, and I'll be safe. How does he know that? How could the trees help? With the technology today, I am expecting one of those drones to immediately appear and drop a bomb on me.

For want of a better idea, I stay under the trees.

It's calm here, like a hidden oasis. This spot is surreal, with tall emerald colored trees, and thick grass on the edge of the pond. Must be an underground aquifer nearby that explains all this. I'm enjoying the peace and quiet. My head is clearing; I am still sore all over, but nothing serious, I think. What hit me? I never heard anything coming, and I did look both ways. The dog. What gives with him? He gets me safely out of the street and into my room. He watches over me while I sleep. But he TALKS, and I talk to him. Now he has led me to this place where I know I shouldn't be. I went along with his instructions, even though I knew better.

I hear, "Alright it's time to move on. Get your suitcase and come with me."

I jump at the voice. It's the Dog.

"What do you mean, get my suitcase, and come with you? I am not leaving my truck here. We are not supposed to be here in the first place."

Dog gives me a hard look, and I dutifully get my suitcase, lock the truck, and follow him. What power does he have over me? No one knows where I am.

All this, just because I wanted a beer.

CHAPTER FOUR

Dog leads me down the pathway and around a turn. Ahead of us, is the opening to a cave. He stops at the opening and motions, with a nod of his head, for me to follow him inside.

"I'm not going in there."

Dog looks at me, and I follow him. How does he control me? I don't like this.

I am bent over because the cave entrance is about four feet high, but it's getting higher and wider the further in we go. Within a few feet, I can stand upright. Ahead I see a glow. Behind me, I hear the ominous sound of a heavy door slamming shut.

I look at Dog, "I take it we're staying."

The glow becomes brighter as we walk around a turn. We enter a well-lit room with… furniture? An opening on the opposite side connects to another brightly lit room.

Out of the room emerges a small creature. I freeze. I'm not sure what it is. It's about four feet tall, with a sturdy looking body, two arms and legs, but a large bulging head with two eyes, a nose, and a mouth. There is no hair on the head and small openings for ears. The creature is luminous and devoid of color. My breathing almost stops. Why did I put my weapon in the suitcase?

It's wearing shorts and a polo shirt. Typical Las Vegas warm weather clothing. For some reason, it looks familiar. Looking directly at me, a warm smile breaks across the pleasant appearing face. It extends a hand as if for a handshake and says in English, "Hello, I'm Michael. I am extremely glad to meet you. Dog has told us all about you."

"Hello, I am David, uh, very glad to meet you, I think." I shake the extended pale hand. He has a firm grip for possessing such a small hand.

"Relax David, I know this is very disconcerting to you, but we will explain it all to you. Can I get you a drink?'

"Yeah, I could use a real drink, but I'll take whatever you have." Well that was a stupid thing to say, they will probably poison me.

Michael goes into the other room and comes back with what appear to be two cut crystal whiskey glasses. He goes to a cabinet on the wall and opens it. Inside the cabinet, is what looks to be, a stock of *good* liquor. Now I'm certain I am mentally messed up: a bar-inside a cave-inside a mountain-in a restricted area.

"You look like a Crown Royal man to me. Neat or on the rocks?"

"Uh, you have ice here? On the rocks, please," I stammer.

Michael pours us each three fingers of crown; he has small fingers you know. He opens another door and inside is an icemaker. Putting a couple ice cubes in each glass, he hands me one.

"To the future," he says.

"To the future," I repeat. *What the hell does that mean?*

We both take a sip. I take another one.

"Please sit down and we can talk." Michael gestures to a leather chair in the corner. I sit. My chair is comfortable, first-class furniture, made of quality leather. He sits in another chair, and Dog curls up on the leather sofa.

"Don't let Dorothy see you Dog. You know how she is about your shedding."

As if to defy Dorothy, Dog stretches out full length.

"So, David," Michael says to me. "Why don't you start with your questions and I will do my best to answer them."

"I'm sorry Michael, but why am I here? Inside a cave in a restricted government location, with a talking dog and a small uh, pale man. No disrespect meant."

"None taken I assure you. However, we refer to ourselves as *neutral*. Pale is so, well, so dull." He places both his hands beside his face as if to frame it. His face almost seems to glow brighter. "But, you are here because we need your help."

"You're running out of booze and need someone to get it for you? I'm sorry Michael, but this is very confusing to me." I can't believe I said that. Michael laughs. A hearty, sincere laugh.

"I do enjoy good humor. We are going to get along fine."

"I'm doing my best to hold onto some humor, so why don't you just start at the beginning and tell me why you, Dog and I are here."

Dog looks up from the couch. "I hope you have plenty of Crown, this is going to take a while." He sighs and lays back down.

Michael ignores him and begins to tell me a story that blows me away: Does anyone remember hearing of Roswell, New Mexico? In 1947, there was the reported crash of a flying saucer, with accounts of dead aliens and possibly some found alive. The military swarmed all over the site. Over the years, it has generated a massive number of stories, movies, conspiracy theories, and denials from the U.S government. Some accounts say the bodies were taken to an Air Force base in Ohio for testing. Others say the aliens who survived were brought to Area 51, along with their spacecraft.

Michael states he and his fellow aliens are survivors of the Roswell incident. Fifty-two are still alive and living in this cave. It is their retirement home, courtesy of the U.S. government. The government declares this area is highly radioactive, allegedly from the near-by atomic tests and is off limits to anyone and everyone. This way they can live in peace and safety.

"And before you ask David, yes, back home we were cave dwellers. The external temperature of our planet was too hot to allow us to live on the surface. We had huge cities underground, which is also the reason we have no skin color. This is our normal way of life. We are unable to go back to our home planet, so this arrangement is perfect for us."

The aliens seemingly lack for nothing. The government has set up a complex and convoluted system, enabling the extra-terrestrials to obtain all their needs and wants. The nice furniture, large flat screen television on the wall and Crown Royal. This much Crown being so handy, could lead me back into one of my old bad habits.

The cave, Michael explains, is like the ones used for the atomic tests, in the area north of us. The government had this complex dug under the pretext it too was for testing.

"Were you guys able to help the government rebuild any of your stuff?" I ask.

"Yes, quite a large percentage. And there are bits and pieces of our technology in use, all around the world today." He is quite proud.

"Okay, that explains you guys. But what about Dog?"

"Your turn Dog," Michael waves a small hand at the canine.

"All I know is I grew up here a happy dog, living with a kooky scientist, who worked in Area 51. He would bring me to work every day. I'd hang around the lab and mingle with the other workers. They played with me and gave me treats. It was a good life. Oh yeah, I could talk, but they didn't know. I understood everything the people were saying. The reason I can talk is because my mother was one of them." He thrusts his nose toward Michael. "Well, she was a dog, an alien dog. She had the most beautiful fur. Even prettier than mine." To emphasize this point, Dog tosses his head side to side, like a slow-motion shampoo commercial. He does have a beautiful coat of shiny black fur.

Dog goes on to tell me his mother was Michael's pet, and was on the ill-fated trip. The alien's pets could talk. She was getting older, and Michael wanted to keep her memory. After World War II, our government brought some German scientists to Area 51 to share their knowledge. One of them, Wolfgang, had a male German shepherd. *What else would he have?* He was up for the idea, and they let the two breed. Dog was the outcome.

"It hasn't had any undesirable side effects - except I can read your puny minds and even get you to do dumb things. Like I had *you* do." The dog smirks.

I am just about to ask more questions when in walks a dozen or so glowing, uh, neutral people. All are wearing casual clothes. (From the children's department?) They introduce themselves. They all have normal names. Apparently, they chose the names they wanted to use on earth. There are females as well as males. The female faces are softer looking and cuter than the males. All are outgoing and pleasant to me. Everyone shakes my hand and thanks me for coming.

Like I had a choice.

Wait a minute; I'm going to help them? They thank me for coming. Aliens and a talking dog have kidnapped me.

I just wanted a beer.

CHAPTER FIVE

More of the *little people* keep coming into the room. Everyone is very gracious and seems genuinely happy to meet me. I am now wondering how I will be able to *help* them. What higher purpose am I meant to accomplish?

Or am I dinner?

Michael decides it is getting too crowded in this area and suggests we all adjourn to the family room. More space he tells me. Is this where I get prepared for dinner? My gun is in my suitcase, should I get it? I could take a few of them out before they could overwhelm me.

As if he reads my mind, which I guess he does, Dog comes up to, and me whispers, "Hey man, these guys are okay. Relax. You are the safest you will ever be, in here with them. Trust me. Have I ever misled you?"

"You LED me here," I hiss back.

"Look, this is a good thing, they are nice people. They are not going to hurt you. They need you."

"WHY?" I ask.

Michael comes over and says in a calm voice, "Look David, I know you are confused about all of this. I intended to explain it all before the others came in. Let us go on to the family room, and I will finish telling you what this is about. Please do understand, you can leave any time you wish. You are not a prisoner. You are our honored guest and hopefully our savior."

Savior? I'm an out of work cop. I am looking to save *myself* at the moment.

Dog nudges me forward, and I follow along. For some reason, I trust Dog. He did help me, but how does he fit in all this?

We go thru the adjacent room and into a larger area with *elevator doors*. We enter the elevators; the doors close and we descend. When the doors open, I see huge, well-lit hallways, branching off in every direction. As we walk down one of the halls, I see various rooms on each side. Some look like TV rooms, libraries, and game rooms. We pass a huge dining room that looks like a fancy restaurant. There is even a sign for a swimming pool. A swimming pool underground? Well, why not? They seem to have everything else.

We finally arrive at the Family Room. Essentially, it is a huge living room with overstuffed furniture, sofas, chairs, and tables. Just a big family room for a BIG family. Everyone settles somewhere, and Michael and Dog lead me to a leather armchair.

I sit down.

Dog wanders off to the rear of the room and settles onto a comfortable couch. I hear a high-pitched female voice, "Dog! How many times have I told you not to lay on the sofas?"

"Twenty-seven at last count," Dog replies. The room erupts with laughter.

I now get to meet Dorothy. She is Michael's wife, and they are obviously the leaders of the group. Dorothy is sweet and apologizes for not meeting me when I arrived, but she wanted to make sure everything was neat and tidy for my arrival. I guess alien wives are just as proud of their homes as human wives.

We now get down to business. Michael sits across from me and starts in: "David we do *have it made* here you could say, but there is a threat looming, to our very existence. We have some *gifts*, you humans do not have, but we cannot handle this threat without help from a capable and trustworthy human. We are hoping you are the right person."

Michael goes on to tell me that ever since they were rescued by the U.S. government in the 1947 crashes, the aliens have been secretly living at Area 51 and working with U.S. scientists. Keeping their existence secret was a decision both the aliens and the government agreed to. The government was afraid the public would panic. With the horrors of World War II just over and the rising threat of Communism from Russia, it was best to keep their presence quiet. The Cold War was in full swing. The western world was concerned about the communist conspiracy of world domination. Springing little alien people from spaceships on the public, did not seem wise. Michael and his people only wanted to live in peace. They were stuck on earth.

The mother ship began to disintegrate as they tried to land in the southwest, near Sedona, Arizona. This location was used as a base during their previous expeditions. Michael stresses they never interfered with humans and did their best to stay out of sight. It was a scientific expedition. Yes, they were looking for various minerals they could use back home, but they had no plans to *invade* earth.

"We just wanted to visit occasionally." His face creased into a jovial smile. "We gave up war eons ago. We learned that in the end, no one ever wins."

They put their energies into technology and mastered space flight.

"So, what went wrong on the last trip?" I ask.

"Initially, we weren't sure. The ship was our latest and largest model. It had performed perfectly in testing, all over the universe. It functioned normally on the trip to Earth. As soon as we began to descend into the area near Sedona, our ship just started breaking apart. We hurried everyone into our escape pods and tried to get safely to the ground. The escape pods were not able to get up to full power and, as a result, we all crashed. Our pods scattered over the area between Sedona and Roswell. Most of us made it out alive, but sadly, some did not. I was in the first pod the military found. I was able to communicate with the soldiers and asked their leaders to meet us. The soldiers were so taken aback with us, they did just what I asked."

"You are telling me you actually said, 'Take me to your leader'?" Asking with a smile.

"Yes, in essence I did."

The military, under great secrecy, collected the little people. Michael and his staff met with various high-level government leaders. It was mutually agreed upon, that no one needed to know about the *visitors*. Area 51 was being used as a secret testing facility. Therefore, Area 51 would be the safest locations to hide the aliens, until a permanent plan could be devised.

It turned out Area 51 was perfect for the visitors. They told the government they would be willing to assist them in whatever way they could, using their advanced technology. What else were they going to do?

Once the government realized the aliens were cave dwellers, it was natural to make a home for them alongside Area 51 and adjacent to the Nevada Test Site. The test site area is highly radioactive and is off limits to everyone except a few stray animals who can't read the signs. The government put up more signs and just expanded the *Danger Radioactive Area* perimeter. The cave city was dug, and a supply support system was devised. The supply system is hidden in a convoluted government scheme. One agency receives the orders, another fills them, and yet another delivers them to a warehouse in Mercury. No one knows where the supplies go from there. This system allows the aliens to go to the warehouse using a secret tunnel and go shopping when they need to.

Not all the aliens are technicians or scientists. Some are in maintenance and repair. They have been able to care for their facilities themselves. No human needs to enter. Pretty neat system.

Michael and his people have, for the most part, *retired* from their work with the government. They did what they agreed to do, and now only consult with one or two of the scientists. Only a select few researchers were ever allowed to know of the diminutive geniuses. Dog's grandpa, *so to speak,* Wolfgang, was one of them.

"What is the threat?" I ask.

"Someone inside the Area 51 group wants to force us to develop a particle beam weapon capable of destroying large areas, such as cities. We won't be a part of anything like that and never have. From the beginning we said we would help with science and technology, but not directly with any weapons. You have nuclear weapons. That is already too much."

"Who is this person and why is he being allowed to pursue this?" I am getting anxious to know how I fit in this plan.

"There are only a handful of people inside the government who know about our existence. Most of the original staff have retired or died. We live longer than you humans, therefore, most of us are still here. The original government employee in charge of the project, recently retired and was replaced by his assistant. He is now chief of the project. He aspires to *go rogue,* as you say. One of the scientists told George," Michael gestures to a male sitting close by, "the new chief is talking about stepping up their research into laser beams. He seems to believe we know more than we have let on in the past. Which is true. But we will not help to develop weapons, period. The scientist was warning George to be careful of the chief and asked him to warn me."

"How is that a threat? If you don't cooperate, then what?" I ask.

"The scientist told George he has been keeping a close eye on the new chief since he started this talk. The old scientist is also good at electronics. He has been monitoring the chief's phone and e-mails. How, I don't know, but he claims the chief is talking with an unknown man about forcing the *'damned aliens'* to work with us or *be taken out.*"

"The scientist is limited to what he can do and told George of his concerns, in hopes *we* can do something. He has always been our friend. The scientists usually were. It was the administrators we had concerns about. This new situation is the most severe we have faced. I don't have any idea who he is talking with or what they could do. But any threat to *take us out,* must be addressed. This is where you come in, should you agree to help."

I just sit there listening.

RJ Waters

CHAPTER SIX

I am trying to process what I've just learned, when Dorothy announces dinner. I'm hungry, despite all I've been hearing. We are directed to the dining room. This should be interesting. What do these people eat? Apparently not me.

They drink real booze, so I hope for the best. Michael leads me back down the hall and into the *fancy restaurant* style room. It is huge. There are at least fifty-two of them to feed, plus guests.

I am seated with Michael and Dorothy along with some senior members of the group. They all have what I consider to be human names, like George, James, Bradley. No Zog or Xylu. I ask why they took our names. Back on their home planet, didn't they have different names? George, one of the elders, explains, since they would be working with humans, they all chose names like ours, to make it easier for us. Dinner has arrived. Placed on the table is a platter of prime rib, roasted potatoes, veggies, and bread. There are also decanters of red wine on every table. It all looks and smells wonderful. I could get used to this real quick. Dorothy inquires if this meal is acceptable to me and if not, she will have something else prepared for me. I assure her, this is *my kind of food.*

The chefs and the service staff were also part of the original expedition, so they have just kept doing what they always did. In a sense of fairness, because some of the scientists are not working full time, they are helping with the other chores. Michael says he likes to cook, but the head chef gets annoyed with his interference. The chef tells Michael to "go mop the floors."

Dinner was as good as I have ever had - anywhere.

"What did you eat back home?" I ask.

"We had meats and vegetables. Not like yours but we adapted easily."

"Uh Michael, maybe I shouldn't be asking, but I do remember something about cattle being somehow disemboweled or something. Was that you guys?"

The room explodes with laughter.

"No, no, that was some stupid experiment your military's scientists were conducting. We knew we would get the blame."

"Waste of good meat," one of the others remarks.

"We would *not* get involved with that sort of experiment. We have always maintained a higher ground and would not budge. That is why this new threat is particularly troublesome." Michael asserts.

Now I've eaten and am feeling better, I ask, "What is *my part* in being your savior?"

"Wait until you, Dog, George, and I can be alone in my office. I was the Commander of the mission and George is my deputy. The rest of our party is aware we are under a threat from the outside, but that is all they know. The elders are keeping this on a *need to know basis*, Michael has lowered his voice.

"Dog. He is part of the plan?"

Suddenly, I feel a *not so gentle* nudge in my ribs, "And why not me?"

"Un, no offense Dog, but I still don't, you know, *get it?*"

Dog laughs. Now there's a sound you don't normally hear.

Dinner is finished, so the four of us walk down more of the endless hallways to Michael's office. It is a well-appointed room, dark wood paneling, huge desk, and *small* leather chairs, just what a *Commander* should have.

We all take a chair, and Dog stretches out on the sofa, of course. Michael begins to tell me more. The new chief of the division who oversees the Special Projects, (the stuff no one knows about) has a checkered background. Michael declares this new chief was a leading motivator in some of the worst blunders in the CIA's history. And we all know there have been some dillies. He was sent to Area 51 as a way of getting him out of Washington. In the time-honored tradition of government, he wasn't punished, just moved to another position in hopes he wouldn't screw up anymore. The former chief had managed to keep this guy subdued, but now that he is gone, Mr. John Cranston, the gentleman's name, is feeling his oats. He wants to do something *spectacular*, according to their scientist friend.

The scientist's name is Wolfgang. Yes, *that* Wolfgang, Dog's Wolfgang. He was one of the German scientists we *liberated* after WWII. Although he is getting along in years, his mind is still sharp as a tack, according to Michael. He lives in an apartment at Area 51 and is quite happy. "Wolfgang was not a Nazi and was grateful when the war ended," George adds. "He enjoys working and doesn't care to live in Las Vegas, so he stays here. He loves the outdoors and hikes in the mountains whenever he can."

Cranston has Wolfgang so worried about his *plans*, Wolfgang has tapped into Cranston's computer and reads his e-mails. He is also somehow able to monitor the man's phone calls. Apparently, the computer security system here is no match for Wolfgang's talents.

"Wolfgang has been a good, loyal worker for your government and doesn't want this to develop into what he witnessed in his homeland. He doesn't know how to defeat Cranston by himself, so he is enlisting our help." George adds.

"But just how do Dog and I come into this?"

Michael states according to Wolfgang, Cranston and his mysterious friend have decided Cranston needs some *muscle* on his staff. There are government security officers all over the place, but most are older, and not interested in intrigue. At least Cranston thinks so. Therefore, his unknown friend says he will have *personnel* send Cranston a list of suitable candidates. In other words, ex-black ops agents and Special Forces types looking for employment. You know, someone who has been trained *to do what they are told*, without asking questions.

"You mean there is actually a *personnel* department for those categories of jobs?" I am showing my naivety.

"We know the CIA has always been involved with Area 51. It has been a continuous battle between the military and the CIA as to who is running the facility."

"Wait a minute, the light is coming on. I was an Airborne Ranger in the Army. I was active in anti-drug operations in South America. Would *that* have anything to do with why I'm here?"

"You see George; I told you he would figure it out. Yes, David that is why you are here. Besides, you need a job. Right?"

"But how do you know about me?" I am getting spooked now. Are there no secrets in this world? No privacy?

Michael exhales slowly and sits back in his chair.

Dog gets off the couch and says he needs to pee.

"You are not leaving now Dog. Get back on the couch. We are coming to your part in this, and you stay and face the music with the rest of us." Michael points at the couch.

Dog gets back on it. He won't look at me.

Michael goes on to explain, when I started to apply for police jobs in California my resumes were available online. Seems the little people are quite adept at electronic snooping. Along with Wolfgang, there is nothing they cannot find out.

"Your systems are children's games to us," George replies, not *too* smugly.

"Upon realizing what Cranston was up to, we started to go into offensive mode. Firing up our systems, the ones salvaged from our escape pods, and searching for a human with whom *we* could work. Someone who had all the skills needed and who was available. We did find several candidates, and you were nearby, in southern

California. After reviewing your performance evaluations and other documents in your personnel files, in the Army and the police departments, you stood out as an honorable person. Unfortunately, not all the candidates appeared as respectable. We started to track your movements and observed you were heading to Las Vegas. It was perfect for us."

"Before I run screaming from this room, how did you track me? Cell phone?"

"Cell-phone and your laptop and don't forget your nice truck has a mini-computer emitting a signal, so the manufacturer can tell you to come in for service." Michael states this, somewhat like a father teaching a slow-witted child something new. He continues, "When you checked into the motel, we grabbed Dog and decided to come and see you. Dog has been one of us all along. The plan was for Dog to get to you and start talking. We were hoping he could get your attention, and you would hear him out. Having small glowing people knock on your door didn't seem to be a good idea."

But they thought a talking dog was?

"We had just arrived at the motel when you ran across the street. We didn't know what you were doing. We needed to be able to talk to you. The only thing we could think of was to head you off while you were running, and then try to talk with you. George never was a very good driver, and he used too much accelerator and knocked you for a loop."

"My apologies. I never wanted to hurt you; I was afraid I had killed our only hope." George has his head down.

"We were fearful someone would call the police, so Dog jumped out to look after you and we sped off."

"Fucking hit and run! Damn it! You guys just about had me believing you're super intelligent beings and then you tell me you committed a *hit and run*. Unbelievable!" I'm pissed. Standing up, I look at the door.

Dog jumps up off the couch and comes over to me. "Look David, they aren't used to the outside world. Our world is not *their* world. What they are telling you is true. They came to your room after you went to sleep and used their gadgets to heal you." He looks at the two worried aliens.

Michael looks at me with imploring eyes, "We thought we had killed you. Luckily, you are in very good physical condition, so your injuries were mainly superficial. We did use our advanced apparatus to check you out and give you a tune-up."

"Tune-up, what sort of a tune-up?" I have visions of *alien probes*.

"Nothing major, truly, just assisted the healing of your muscles and tissues, that type of thing." George answers hurriedly.

Dog looks back at me, "They are desperate to save their way of life. Just because they aren't very good at *street work,* for want of a better term, doesn't change anything. That is why they, and I, need your help. You and I together can handle Cranston and the threat. These schmucks need to stay in their caves and help us with their brains."

"I looked both ways. I saw nothing. Heard nothing. How fast were you going?"

"We have a Smart Car we modified so we could control it and still see out the front window. It has blacked out windows, common practice here in Las Vegas, so no one can see us. We can achieve 180 miles per hour in three seconds. We will *never* let George drive, *ever again*. We promise." Michael is pleading now.

"180 in three seconds? You did more than adjust the seats."

"Well, we did use some of the components from our escape pods and improved the performance of the car. Would you like to see it? We know you are a car person."

"Yeah, sure, maybe I can escape in it. Get away from this nightmare." I say out loud.

"David, you can leave anytime you want. But we do need help, and you seem to be the right person for the job. Our plan would involve us intercepting the e-mail messages from the personnel department and inserting your name. We would then discredit or otherwise eliminate any others on the list. You would become a highly paid government agent. When this is over, you would have a great looking resume. Even better than now. Who knows, you might want to stay on after Cranston and his associate are removed."

"I can see getting rid of Cranston with a quick twist of his neck, but how are we going to neutralize someone who is unidentified?"

Dog looks at me. "Quick twist of his neck? Whoa and I'm accused of being an *animal*. Way to go David, I knew we would be a team."

"I was speaking metaphorically," I hastily explain. "I haven't actually done that. Well, not since Colombia, with the drug cartel boss. But that was a life or death situation." Oh shit, I've never told anyone what I did in the Army. I'd had enough of that life, and I didn't re-up. I became a police officer and enjoyed it. No more life in the shadows. Now what am I getting into?

"See he *is* the right one for us." Michael looks at George.

Dog pipes up, "I knew right away. I was so angry when I thought you killed him." He glares at George. George just sinks into his chair.

Everyone is looking at me. My mind is racing in every direction. I gather my thoughts and speak: "Okay. I like you crazy people. I guess I can live with the invasion of my privacy, the hit and run, the kidnapping and all. *I'm in,* with the conditions I am involved in all the planning, privy to any and all information you get, and we make all decisions together. Deal?"

"Deal!" Michael and George both jump up and come over to me and shake my hand. Dog stands up on his hind feet and thrusts a paw at me.

"High five, partner! We're are going to kick ass!"

I high five Dog back.

I just high fived a dog.

RJ Waters

CHAPTER SEVEN

Now it's time to get down to business. Michael goes to a side cabinet and opens it. He reaches in and takes out a large bottle of Crown Royal. He pours a splash in three glasses and gives one to George and one to me.

There is a very audible, "Excuse Me?" from Dog.

Michael mutters, "I'm sorry Dog, no offence meant. I was just so excited."

He opens another cabinet door and behind it is a refrigerator. He takes out a Michelob and pours it into a chilled bowl that was also in the fridge. He sets it down on the floor in front of Dog.

We all toast to the success of the project and take a large sip. Well Dog takes a long slurp, then belches.

"Sorry."

We all chuckle and then start working on our plan. They have already started monitoring Cranston's every move. They have recordings of his telephone calls, cell phone communications, and any keystrokes on his computer. With Wolfgang's help a bug has been hidden in Cranston's office.

"What we haven't been able to learn is the identity of his co-hort. Because of the encrypted e-mail system, we have not yet determined where he is located. But we have some of our best people working on it." George clarifies.

"Why the *need to know* secrecy? If you are *all* threatened, who are you worried about?" I ask a question

41

that has been bugging me. No one comes in here, they have almost no outside contact. What's the worry? Fair question since I am now involved in this conspiracy.

Michael looks at George and then softly begins, "We have a few of our people who want to go public and contact the outside world. They are the youngest ones. They want the human life experience. We have tried and tried to get them to understand it just won't work. It won't be any easier than when we first landed in 1947. We would be a novelty at first, but then humans would begin to fear we were essentially an advance party of invaders. We do have abilities you humans don't. Those would soon be a source of fear, hostility, and violence. Look at your world now. Different races and religions cannot co-exist without major problems. It just would not work. There is another reason for us to stay where we are. We cannot be in the sun for any length of time. We would literally burn up. We would have to be covered somehow. That would just make for more *conspiracy theories*. What do they really look like? Are they reptiles or worse?"

"Hey I liked 'V,'" I admit. "But I see your point. Earth may never be ready for people from *out there*. Especially when you've been hiding here all this time. No, I agree it would be trouble."

Therefore, the plan is…. the trusted ones would continue monitoring Cranston and anyone else they can. When the list of *bad asses for hire* is sent to Cranston, my name will be added, and I will be made to look like the only one evil enough for his plans. I am humbled.

In some way this is exciting to me. I should know better. I've been in the black world a little and didn't feel right about it. This--feels different. Maybe I can save the cave dwellers and stop some bureaucrat's maniacal plans.

If he wants a weapon capable of destroying entire cities, he has no sane reason for it. As the diminutive individuals said, we already have the nuclear capability. What *is* his plan?

Getting rid of Cranston won't stop whoever is behind this. We must find out the whole story. There is nothing for me to do now but wait until I am summoned for an interview with Mr. Cranston.

Michael shows me to my room. I must stay here for the time being. Hey, it's free and the food is good. My *room* is a suite. Quite nice. In addition to a bedroom, I have a living room, a dining area, fridge, and microwave. All the amenities, including satellite TV.

After I settle in with my sparse belongings, Michael takes me on a tour of the facility. The cave complex is *huge*. We travel by electric carts most of the trip. I had only seen a small part of the place. There are research labs filled with paraphernalia I have never seen before. The aliens salvaged some equipment from their escape pods. They fabricated the rest from materials they acquired at Area 51. They have far more capability than the humans are aware of, Michael conveys.

Only a small number of the aliens worked at the Area 51 research laboratories with the human scientists and engineers. The majority worked in separate cave labs underground, away from the human's labs. Therefore, they needed their own equipment. The government was more than happy to give them whatever they wanted. Michael declares, that for self-preservation, they created a safe and secure environment. The cave complex was built just for the aliens. Once the place was set up and the aliens were trained to maintain it, no human has been inside this area, until me and of course Wolfgang.

I should feel special…but?

Next, we enter an immense room comparable to an airplane hangar. I see my truck. To keep it safe I'm told. Sure, but how would I have been able to leave if I had declined their offer? Michael assures me I could have left at any time since I arrived. But he would have tried extremely hard to convince me to help them.

Also, in the room is the Smart Car. It is painted a flat black. Humm? Isn't that the type of coating the stealth airplanes use? Their car has a textured exterior that deflects radar signals *and* police speed guns.

"If you can do 180 mph in 3 seconds there is no police car that could even think of catching you."

Michael takes me to the car and opens the door.

"Let me show you how it works."

Squeezing myself into the passenger side, Michael gets in behind the wheel. But it is not a wheel, it looks more like a video game controller. He pushes some buttons and we rise off the floor. This thing *levitates*! I'm impressed. We then fly around the hanger and land. He says we will go out some night and he will show me what it can really do.

I want one!

If they need to go out in the world they can drive on the roads, Michael tells me. The windows are blacked out; otherwise, the motoring public would think children were driving.

Back at my room, Michael assures me I am free to do whatever I like; they have movies in the theater, game rooms, and all kinds of amusement. I tell Michael I would like to *talk* with Dog. He laughs and using a small cell phone like device contacts Dog and asks him to come to my room. After he arrives, Michael leaves and I ask Dog if we can talk.

"Please, I would love to. We've got plans to make." He utters conspiratorially.

"I need to know more."

We both settle down in the living room, Dog of course on the couch. He nestles back into the cushions and we begin.

"So are your parents still here?" I query.

"No, Mom died a couple of years ago and Dad last year."

"I'm sorry. I just didn't see any other dogs here." I stumbled.

"It's okay." Dog states. "They both had good long lives. Even the little shits couldn't keep them around forever."

"What were they like? Your Dad? You could communicate with him, like earth dogs do?"

"Oh yeah, he was great. Taught me all the male alpha stuff. Miss him. Mom was well, a Mom. Tried to keep me in line. She was just like Dorothy. I was as much a problem to her as I am to Dorothy. I loved her." He blinks and tears up. He wipes his eyes with a massive paw.

45

"Dog, I am still not too sure about all this."

I'm actually having a discussion with a talking dog.

"Look." Dog patiently says." This is all real, just like they told you. I stayed with Wolfgang a lot. He is sort of like family, you know. He has been concerned about Cranston ever since the guy showed up. He told me to avoid him. I have. None of the humans know I can talk. I can go anywhere. The *plan* is for me to be your own personally trained security dog. I will go with you when you work for Cranston and I can be another set of eyes and ears and watch your back."

"The *plan*? I hadn't heard that part. What else haven't I been told?"

"Well, this is *my* plan, I haven't told Michael yet. I wanted to run it past you first. How about a beer?"

The hell with the beer, I want more Crown Royal.

CHAPTER EIGHT

The next couple of days go by with no activity regarding Cranston. I am beginning to become familiar with a world no one would believe exists. Even though my parents have passed away and I have no siblings, a few friends might be concerned about me. I haven't sent an e-mail or called any of them. They know I'm wandering the country looking for a job. How long has this been? Only three days? Seems like a lifetime. I need to e-mail them. I tell Michael my concerns.

"By all means. We don't want anything to be hitting the radar about a missing person. Cranston's people will be checking on you shortly. Send your friends e-mails or call if you want. You have a cell phone."

Yeah, that's how *they* knew where I was. I decide to send e-mails saying I'm checking on a job in Nevada, nothing more.

In the evening, Michael takes me out in the Smart Car. Oh my god! I do want one! *What a ride.* We flew border to border in absolutely no time at all. Completely undetected by any radar.

Since the power plant for the Smart Car is from the pods, I ask why the pods failed when they were landing.

They had figured out why their main ship failed when landing at Sedona. Their pods had encountered the same problem. Michael tells me they felt it best to withhold this information from me, until I was completely on board.

A beam had been sent from Area 51 by one of the *rescued* German scientists. He was trying to develop a weapon. Hitler's regime was already working on this type of beam weapon when the war ended. This scientist was the motivator behind that Nazi project. He was continuing his research at Area 51. The leaders of the Area 51 programs stopped him because he was *too extreme,* even for them. I ask Michael what happened to him. The scientist was *retired* with a substantial pension, Michael informs me

"Michael, this sounds like the same scenario you're facing now, doesn't it?"

"Yes. We have tried to find out what became of him. Initially he lived in Southern California, but he has since disappeared. His name did show on the secret files of a shadow group once loosely connected with the CIA. We think he is somehow involved with the Cranston/mystery man situation."

Chilling.

"I am assuming you guys checked on any of the other scientists who are no longer here, maybe some were friends of his?" The cop in me is speaking.

Michael looks blankly at me.

"I feel like a fool David. We are able to achieve high tech electronics, but we did not stop to think logically, as you just did. You are an investigator and talk to people, develop clues, yes we do need your *puny* human brain, as Dog would say."

"Elementary Michael." I enunciate in my best Sherlock Holmes voice.

Michael then asks how to follow thru with this, in a human way. I explain talking with Wolfgang and any of the other original scientists, who can be located, just might open some leads. I remind Michael they can suck all the data they want out of the atmosphere and still not get what is inside *our* puny brains. *We're special.*

He shakes his head and puts a little hand on my shoulder and gives it a squeeze. "We aren't as smart as we think we are sometimes. Thank you, David, we do need your help."

Michael calls Wolfgang and asks if he would mind coming over to the caves. The pretense is some consultation on a project in case Cranston is watching Wolfgang......as we are watching Cranston. Anyone involved in a conspiracy is super paranoid.

In the past, it was not unusual for a few scientists and engineers to come to the alien's lab areas. Nowadays it is just Wolfgang. The labs are separate from the aliens living complex. There are tunnels and caves all over the site, connecting various testing and research areas.

Wolfgang comes over and we are introduced. He is in his nineties, at least. Healthy looking, with a round pleasant face. Still has a full head of white, wiry hair, the Einstein look. Somewhat stooped when he stands but appears to have a good sturdy body. Must be all that hiking in the hills. Of course, Dog is with us. Wolfgang acts like a grandparent to Dog. Ruffling his fur, scratching his ears and just enjoying seeing him. Dog tries to get in the chair with him.

"He always thought he was a lap dog." Wolfgang laughs, his eyes sparkling.

We discuss the situation. Wolfgang says he is so glad I was located and am willing to help. He stresses the threat is real, and he is quite concerned Cranston's associate is part of a secret shadow government group or worse, an anarchist's movement. We ask him about the original group of German scientists. He tells us he and one other are the only ones still working. He then begins to talk about the others. Some have died, some have retired and are living in various places in the U.S. One scientist even went back to Germany.

Michael asks him about Wilhelm Schultz, the *missing* scientist.

Wolfgang pales. "I was afraid this might be part of his old work. I don't know what happened to him after he was let go."

"Did he have any friends?" I ask?

"No. No friends among the staff. He was a loner. Most of us are. We get caught up in our research and tend to shut out the world. I tried to keep some connections. That is why I had Dog's father. He would make me get out and walk in the open air. Probably the only reason I am still functioning." His elderly arms wrap around dog in a strong hug. gives Dog gives his face a hardy lick with his eminence tongue.

"He did have one regular visitor I remember. He was some sort of government official. He would only visit Schultz. No one seemed to know anything about him. He had to have the special top-secret clearances to get in here. After Schultz was laid off the man never came around again, as far as I know."

"Were there security logs of the visitors at that time?" I ask.

"Oh yes. No one went anywhere in here without passing through several security stations. People who were flown in had to pass through at least three security stations to get to our laboratories. The people who drove here had to pass through even more.

Michael shakes his head. "Who has the *puny* brain now? In ten minutes, you have actually found out information that was right under our noses."

We continue to talk with Wolfgang. He is more than willing to do whatever he can to help. We tell him not do anything to jeopardize his safety. The surveillance the aliens have in place now will keep us apprised of any changes. We leave Dog and Wolfgang to spend some time together. Michael and I go off to search the old security logs.

"Are they actually available?" I ask Michael. "Weren't they handwritten back then?"

"Oh yes they were. But your efficient government had them microfilmed. We can get to them. Conveniently the old records are stored in a tunnel we just happen to have access to."

We enter another of the maze of tunnels. This one leads to the archives of Area 51. Michael assures me the records go back to the beginning. There is a hidden door the clever aliens have constructed. No fools they. The government has no knowledge of the door.

"If we were going to live out our lives here, we wanted to know everything about this place." Michael declares.

We enter the musty chamber. Michael is apparently quite at home here. Not his first trip I gather. He goes to a card index and finds what he wants. Then goes down aisle after aisle of file boxes. He finds the number he wants. I help him pull it off the shelf. He opens it and starts to rummage thru the microfilm file folders. Using a microfiche viewer Michael finally finds the security logs for the time just prior to Schwartz leaving Area 51. After seemly endless pieces of film, he finds a visitor for Schwartz. Then he goes back further and finds the same name about a month earlier. Continuing back on an almost monthly basis the same name keeps appearing, only to visit Schwartz. Michael lets me see in the viewer.

I am looking at the name. Franklin Pierce. Oh my God! Not him!? He was a major player in a past administration. I remember he was a real war monger. Haven't seen or heard much of him since. Has he been a behind the scenes player this whole time? Could he be the mystery man? This is big! What the hell have I gotten myself into?

Michael is having the same thoughts.

"I remember him." Michael says with a frown. "He was considered somewhat of a loose cannon when he was in that particular administration. A lot of people were relieved after the next election when his candidate did not win the Presidency."

"I see you keep up on our politics. Smart move. Our future and yours are intermingled, aren't they?"

"Very much so, I'm afraid. That's why this is so unnerving to us. Your human skills have given us a huge clue. Now we must try and track our newly identified nemesis. I think it will be more efficient if you work directly with our *snoopers,* as you call them. We need your human logic."

"What ever happened to the Vulcan logic?" I tease.

"There are no Vulcans David.... that was television. No Klingons either."

"I take it you watch a lot of TV?"

"Of course, at first it helped us learn how to talk to the scientists and then to gather some history of humans."

"That had to be the scary part. We are not the best examples of a civilized world."

"Oh David, I could you tell you tales of our beginnings. They would curl your hair."

" I guess it is pretty much the same all over the universe, huh?"

"Unfortunately, so."

CHAPTER NINE

I have been spending a lot of time with the pintsized snoopers. They're trying to track down our newest suspect. Until now I have been referring to him as: *the cigarette smoking man* from the X-Files TV show. You never knew who he was.

Now we have a name, tracking him down just got a lot easier. Determining what he is doing these days will be another matter. His politics were definitely of the *bomb 'em* school of thought. He and his colleagues, of a past administration, were always looking for a cause to champion. It usually meant sending American troops and allies into some country to liberate the *democracy deprived citizens*. So far, those actions don't seem to have worked out as planned. Delving into his past in the late 1900s to early 2000s, we find he was actively involved with several poorly run clandestine operations. He is older now but still active with some ultra-right-wing groups. He's kept his ties with associates from that period. Franklin Pierce seems to have political connections and accessibility to plenty of funding and is behind some political action groups with questionable ties to right wing para-military organizations. Money, power, and radical thoughts makes for a scary scenario.

Now it's show time! The e-mail from *personnel* has arrived. Michael shows it to me. The alien's system enables them to re-route all of Cranston's e-mail thru their own equipment first. They will rework it and send it along. I'll be presented as the baddest of the bad. Hands down the only choice, and I already have a Top-Secret Security Clearance. I must say the guys and gals who worked on this are clever writers. Too much TV, I suspect.

It pays off. We can *see* when Cranston reads the e-mail. There is no sound from his office other than the clicking of computer keys. Then he begins tapping numbers on a cell phone.

My cell phone rings, I jump out of my skin. It shows *restricted* for the caller. Michael puts a finger to his lips, indicating everyone in the room to stay quiet.

"Hello." I answer curtly.

"Yes, I'm calling for David Manning."

"This is David Manning, who's this?"

"Mr. Manning my name is John Cranston. I work for the U.S. government and I understand you are looking for a job. I have a position open and would like to speak to you about it."

"Where is the job located? I'm not interested in any out of country assignments."

"It is in Las Vegas Mr. Manning. It is a very stable position. You would be my security consultant. When would you be available for an interview?"

"I was just in Vegas and could be back there tomorrow. Where do you want to meet?"

He gives me an address on the perimeter of the Las Vegas-McCarran Airport. Tells me to go to the address and show my I. D. I will then board an airplane to fly me to his office. He assures me it will be a short flight to where I will be working, should I be hired. I am to be at the airport by 9:00 a.m. the day after tomorrow. That was it. I put the phone down. We all look at each other. We are still listening to Cranston's office using the device Wolfgang hid there.

We can hear tapping on the cell phone again. Someone answerers. Cranston begins: "I got your list and am interviewing a candidate. Looks good on paper. I'll let you know how it goes." We cannot hear the other person, but the conversation is brief. Cranston then calls someone on the land line and arranges for my flight.

Michael high fives me. "We did it."

"Yes, but what did we do?" I wonder out loud.

Time for some real planning. I'll get a room in an *extremely nice* hotel and arrive tomorrow afternoon. If I'm to be a real 'black ops' person, I will be accustomed to only the best, when not in the field. I learned that from my stint in South America. The wee people are paying my expenses. I don't ask how because I don't want to know. Something to do with this open-ended supply chain they have. They feel I should get better clothes. Really, my clothes are being critiqued by aliens. I thought I was looking. fairly good. Hey, I've been traveling.

There are several up-scale shops in or near my hotel. This could work out. At least I'll get a new wardrobe.

I ask Michael how they are aware of the more mundane parts of our lives, like wardrobe. He tells me the women, Dorothy and all, keep up on fashion.

"Why?" I ask. "Not to be unkind but you folks don't go anywhere."

"True, but the world comes to us. Once a month, on a Saturday night, we have *Night on the Town* and we dress up as though we're going to a show or dinner in New York City. We have a grand time. We switch off with the cooks and servers, so they have fun too. This week I will be a bartender." He puffs out his bantam chest with pride.

"Still can't make it as a chef, huh?" I couldn't resist.

The aliens are full of humor and not unlike us in many ways. They're decent and family oriented. Physically, they are on average, four feet tall. Their heads are more like an adult human's in size, but they do tend to be wider at the crown than ours. More room for the brains, I am guessing. Except for their heads, their bodies are in proportion to their height. Arms and legs look fine. The head is rounded like ours also. Not the teardrop, pointy ones you see in the depictions of aliens. Their eyes are like ours too, not all black and creepy. If it weren't for the large heads, you could dress as kids and take them anywhere. Oh yeah, I forgot, no hair, no ears. Their lack of color is a giveaway too.

This will be my last night at the *Cave Resort*. We will have a party to celebrate the beginning of what we all hope will be a success mission. I ask Michael how I am going to get my truck out of the hangar. I noticed there were no roads leading to the outside door.

He cocks his head, "The same way we got it in there, levitation of course."

"Of course. How stupid of me." I've got to get with the program here. I'll be depending on these squirts to watch over me. I'm beginning to sound like Dog.

Seems there is one more item needing to be taken care of; I am told I must have a small transceiver implanted near my ear. Not real thrilled about the prospect of aliens putting implants into me. Haven't we been worrying about this all along? Stories abound of regular people being abducted from their trailer homes and having implants put in them by little green aliens. Well now it's little pale aliens. Michael is about to speak, to reassure me, when Dog pipes up: "Hey no big deal David. I've had one for almost a year. It's cool. They can tell you what's going on and you're able to talk back to them. The base security sensors won't pick it up. I know, I *beta tested* it!"

"You've been watching way too much television too, Dog."

Anyway, I go along with it. With the pass of an instrument, I now have an implant, a painless operation. I have no scar.

Time for the going away festivities.

"Hey do ya wanna parrrrty," Dog howls.

He sounds better than Hank Williams Jr. when ole Hank was doing Monday night football. The party is great fun. Everyone is pumped for the adventure.

"This will be better than those dumb reality TV shows." One of the women says.

They will be able to follow along with me thru their array of devices. "I won't have any privacy?" I inquire.

"You wouldn't have any privacy anyway. Cranston already has a team of his goons checking on you."

"If he has *goons* why does he need me?"

Michael shakes his head. "Trust me, I'm being kind to them. They can follow orders, but they are nowhere near the caliber of agent he wants."

"So how many do I have to kill to prove myself?" I'm joking-I think.

"Actually, your challenge will be his number one and two men. That is why we need Dog there. Your back will need to be closely watched." George pipes up.

"These two are cutting a fat hog as you folks say. They are long time government employees and will not sit still for you taking their jobs. Number two is really going to go ballistic when he finds out he is replaced by a dog!" Michael is chuckling.

"That pussy! I'll just bare my teeth and he'll run." Dog says in a lowered voice. Then he smiles. *Creepy.*

CHAPTER TEN

The next morning it's time to get ready for my job interview. I glance one more time at the list of *horrendous accomplishments,* which fill my resume.

My newfound friends have made a video of the inside of the Area 51 headquarters for me. This way I'll know where everyone and everything is located. I look at it one more time. I know when I arrive tomorrow morning, I'm not supposed to know anything about the place, but if something seems wrong or out of place, I will at least have a heads-up. I won't have a weapon and Dog will not be going with me this trip. I must sell Cranston on the need for my personally trained security specialist. Dog and I have worked out some routines for demonstrating his expertise. It should be fun.

After lunch Michael tells me it is time for me to leave and go check into my first-class Vegas hotel. He, George and Dog walk with me to the cave entrance I first came through. How many days has it been? As we approach the entrance, the wall slides open. Walking into the sun light I see my truck sitting there. It is shinny clean, looks waxed too. I look at the guys.

"Hey, it was the least we could do. You will arrive in style." George says.

I thank them and we say our good-byes.

"Remember, we will be in your ear always, 24-7. If there is a problem the Smart Car will come to your rescue," Michael assures me. God, I hope George won't be driving.

Dog comes over, I kneel, and he licks my face. "Be careful, damn it, I like you being around here. And get me in there with you, quickly, we have work to do."

I drive off the way I came in. Dog runs ahead the full distance to the orange cones and pulls them out of my way. As I drive thru, he thrusts his head upward and howls......long and mournful. Yeah big guy, I'll miss you too.

I drive on toward Las Vegas. I cannot believe my peculiar state of affairs. I've been in some *situations* in the past but nothing even close to this.

I take my time and drive the speed limit. No need to attract any attention. The aliens have disabled the service computer in my truck, I can't be tracked. They adjusted my cell phone so it won't be activated until I arrive in Vegas.

I check into the hotel, which is beautiful. Shame to be alone in such a gorgeous place. I decide to go shopping. I would rather be *sharing* this romantic room, not shopping. However, I do have a job to do. I manage to find some very upscale apparel. Even a suit which fits, no time for tailoring.

I walk the famous Las Vegas Strip in the evening and take in the tourist sights. I will admit, I am wondering if I will get out of this mess in one piece. I want to be able to come back with *someone special* and enjoy this town *properly*.

I find a nice restaurant and treat myself to a grand dinner. After I finish ordering I hear Dog's voice in my ear; "Whoa, chateaubriand! Good choice. You know how to live David. We are going to get along just fine."

I start to laugh. The waiter isn't too far away. "Is everything alright sir?

"Oh yes, I was just reminded of something funny. I'm fine."

Eventually I tire of being a lonely tourist and go back to my hotel. Not that I wasn't offered companionship by a number of attractive females along the way. Friendly town.

The next morning, I am up early and have room service bring a hardy breakfast. I shave, shower, and get on my new suit. Looks sharp. I bought name brand shoes too. Seemed to be the right thing to do. If I'm going to die, I want to be well dressed.

I have valet bring up my truck and I drive to the address Cranston gave me. It is on the backside of the Las Vegas' McCarran Airport, away from the main airport buildings. There are various small hangers and aircraft service companies located here. This would be where casino and other business jets are parked. The address I was given is a large parking lot with a one-story building located on the airfield side. I pull into the driveway. There are a couple of cars ahead of me.

At the entrance is a guard shack. It has several signs posted on the front. Basically, *do not come in unless you have been invited,* said in harsh threatening terms. There are two armed security officers. They wave the cars in front of me through. They must have parking stickers, I surmise. The officers look at my windshield and each raises a hand, signaling me to stop. Immediately I am greeted by one who looks like an older Andy Griffith. Probably retirement job after Mayberry.

I give my name and ID to Andy. "Wait here!" he sternly orders and goes inside the shack, while the other officer is waving cars around me. Busy place. After making a phone call, Andy returns and hands me a visitor pass along with my ID. I am instructed to park in the lot and go to the main entrance of the terminal building.

"It is over there." He is pointing toward the only building on the property.

I can't help myself, "the cream colored one story?" I ask with all the innocence I can muster, while pointing to the structure.

"Yes sir," he says as he points again toward the building. I thank him and pull away. He should have stayed in Mayberry.

After parking, I check out the area. Looks like a normal business day. A lot of cars are parked in this lot. Do all these people work at Area 51? Wow, I wasn't aware it was so busy. Well it is a large place. Other cars keep coming into the lot. The occupants are wearing casual business attire. No uniforms. All exit their cars and walk to the building. They must be the employees who come here to be flown to work. On both sides of the terminal building is a wall blocking any view of the airfield. I can see the tops of three white planes parked to the side of the building. They look like Boeing 737s to me.

Okay, show time. It is 8:50 am and I am *going in*. I continue not speaking to Michael. We have already decided if Cranston is as paranoid as we believe he is, my truck is bugged by now.

I walk to the entrance following the others. More warning signs. Nestled among them is one stating: this building is Operated by EG&G. I have heard Michael and George mention the company in connection to 'operations' at Area 51.

The windows to the building are darkened. But most of the windows in Vegas are darkened because of the heat. Nothing sinister yet. I open the door and enter the lobby area which has a counter, just like most terminals. The people ahead of me all walk toward a door in the rear. The area also has five uniformed guards, all carrying side arms. Two of them are checking the commuters going through the rear door. The one at the desk asks if he can help me. Spotted my visitor badge... he's on it. I give my name. He clicks the computer keys and says, "Your identification please Mr. Manning."

I give it to him, and he gives it a cursory look. He then puts some papers in front of me and tells me to read and sign each page.

This is top-secret stuff which states: You will never, ever tell anyone what you saw or heard at the place you are going to, even if you do not know where it is. It goes on to infer any violation of this oath could result in a long, slow and painful death. Or words to that effect. I sign. I am given my ID back and another officer leads me through a door to another room. Here there are only two armed guards. One of them takes my papers and asks for my ID. I haven't left the sight of the first guard, but this is the game. I give him my ID. He then hands me more papers to read and sign each page. The papers again warn, if I divulge anything I see or hear at this unknown place I could be subjects to the same long, slow and painful death. You can only kill me once whether it is long, slow or whatever, but all right have it your way. I sign, every page.

Now this gentleman hands me off to the other guard who leads me out a door and onto the tarmac of the airport. In front of me is a white Boeing 737 with a red stripe running horizontally down the fuselage. My fellow travelers are walking toward another 737. At this point in time almost everyone in the world knows these planes are flying workers to Area 51 or the Tonopah Test Range. But it is still a *secret*.

The guard points to the stairway, and we go up and into the plane. The cabin is empty. He tells me to sit wherever I wish. Looking around I see the window shades are drawn. This is done so first timers cannot tell where they are going. Again, by now, this is not a secret.

"I would prefer a window seat." I say in a very stuffy tone. I walk halfway down the cabin and take a window seat.

My escort starts to say something official but then just grins, "Even if you haven't been there before you know what this is about. Relax enjoy the flight. It won't take long." He sits across the aisle from me.

"I assume there won't be beverage service?" I say with a grin. He chuckles at my lame joke.

I decide to press my luck, "I know the other plane is probably going to the same place as we are, so why do I get special treatment?"

He looks toward the cockpit and then quietly says, "SOP for first timers. Can't have you talking to anyone."

"Got it, thanks." I say, also quietly.

It is a fast trip. We land and I am met at the bottom of the stairs by an older uniformed officer.

"Mr. Manning, Mr. Cranston is waiting for you," he says crisply. I wonder if he is assistant number one or assistant number two. As if my thoughts are being read, my *ear* says, "He is number two." Thank you, Michael.

The game is on.

RJ Waters

CHAPTER ELEVEN

Number Two points to an SUV near-by. I get in the passenger seat and he drives. "So, what brings you to Area 51, Mr. Manning?" Number Two is in his fifties, overweight and has not taken advantage of the dental part of his health plan. Good job with benefits and he does not take care of himself.

"John asked me to come by for a chat." I am using Cranston's first name as if we were old buds from *the past.* You can almost hear Number Two choke.

In my ear I hear laughter and then, "Good one David," from Michael.

"So how long have you been here?" I ask, further pushing my shadowy status.

"I've been here for 15 years Sir."

"You don't have to Sir me, I'm nobody." I say in a disarming way. "How long have you been with John?"

"Only about four months. The former chief retired, and Mr. Cranston took his place."

"You were with the prior chief?" I inquire.

"Yes, sir, uh yes, I was his deputy security director for over six years."

"So, what is John into these days? Still airplanes or has he branched out?"

"Oh, not airplanes anymore. The other divisions handle them. Mr. Cranston is into weapons and stuff like that now."

As we are driving, I point at some buildings that are quite separate from the main complex. "Why are those so far away from all the others?" I innocently inquire.

"That's Mr. Cranston's latest project. Some kind of a death ray or something. It's not working too well. They are having a lot of developmental problems, I hear."

"Oh, interesting. It never fails to amaze me the things these scientists dream up."

I am just chatting him up now. He is blissfully driving down the yellow brick road. This man has now violated everything in the secrecy oath we all signed. I wonder if he gets one or two long, slow, and painful deaths.

"I can't believe he is telling you so much." George is almost shouting into my ear.

We finally pull up to the headquarters building. A basic no-frills government two-story office building. My new best friend leads me up the stairs and into a lobby. He walks up to the officer at the desk and announces, Mr. Manning to see Mr. Cranston. This guard is unimpressed and asks for my ID. I present it and he checks with his computer and then calls someone. "Mr. Manning to see Mr. Cranston."

He then nods at Number Two and says we may go in.

Number Two leads me thru doors, hallways, into an elevator and then to an office. In the outer office is a pasty-looking male in his forties sitting at a desk. I already know, thanks to the aliens, he is Cranston's administrative aide. He looks up and says we may go in.

I enter the rather nicely furnished office of John Cranston, Chief of Research Division IV. That's what the sign says.

Mr. Cranston gets up, comes over to me and shakes my hand. He is in his sixties, maybe more, looks used up. His face is drawn, sunken cheeks and bags under his eyes. Thinning hair, average build, and height. Needs a good long vacation, I'd say.

"Thanks for coming so soon, David. I appreciate it."

He then thanks Number Two, who almost bows out of the room.

"David, please sit down. We need to talk. I have read your personnel files and resumes. Impressive, I must say. Sometime we must talk about your adventures in South America. Off the record of course. I have never been in those types of situations. I am mainly a behind the scenes guy. You have actually *been there.*"

I'll have to double check my *record*; it must be better than I thought. What did those little resume writers put in there?

Cranston continues, "What I need is a security man who can not only watch over our operations here but can also watch over me, well, be my bodyguard is the best way to put it. You have met some of our staff. Nice guys but basically nine to fivers. They don't have your training and experience."

"Are you under a threat here, Sir?" I ask naively.

"Much more than anyone knows. The government has no clue what is going on here. But some people do, and I have learned they will stop at nothing to shut down our operation."

"Shut down Area 51?"

"No. *My* operation here. I am onto a breakthrough in a new weapons system and there are bleeding hearts in Washington and elsewhere who want it shut down. I need you to be my eyes and ears all the time. I have obligations off base. That is when I am most vulnerable. This is not the paranoid talk of a mad man David. I have received phone calls here on encrypted lines from unknown persons who have threatened me, in no uncertain terms. Whoever is behind this is on the inside. That is the terrifying part. I can only guess who it might be."

"Alright Sir, you have told me some very disturbing information. I am assuming you are not comfortable taking this to any superior in your agency. You feel you must defend yourself from the unknown threat. I can help you. That is my specialty. I will need more information and I have some conditions."

"I'll tell you whatever you want. Yes, I am afraid to say anything to anyone in the government. There are shadow forces, alliances. You know all about that sort of thing, I'm sure. You will be paid well. I can assure you of that. I hold the check book around here. What would your conditions be?"

"This may seem strange, but I must have my partner with me."

Before I can continue, Cranston interrupts, "Whoever you trust and need just tell me and I will make it happen."

"For the present I will just need my dog. He is not just any security dog. He has been personally trained by me and is worth at least two or three humans. He has the usual above normal abilities of extensive hearing, sense of smell, etc. But his true value is the fact he can alert me to a whole world of situations only he can sense, *and* he can make me aware of them. We can communicate almost silently. With a tilt of his head I know someone is approaching, with a slight movement I can send him off to confront the person. He can tell if someone is nervous, angry or whatever. He seems to know what is a threat and what is not. Let me bring him here. He will amaze you. He has saved my ass more than once and that of my client's."

"Could you have him here tomorrow?"

"Yes, no problem. He is used to flying."

In my ear I hear Dog, "Flying, I've never flown, oh yes, I have, in that dammed Smart Car. Okay, as long as George is not flying the plane."

Mr. Cranston then shows me what I will be paid. Holy shit and I wanted to be a cop? I guess this means I'm off unemployment.

"Do we have a deal?" Cranston asks after we talk some more. I do get the picture. He may be in real danger. It may not just be people in our own government who want him out. There may be *other* interests in play here. This could be much more than I bargained for. Police work is looking better again.

"Deal." I say and put out my hand. We shake.

"Come on back tomorrow with your dog. We do have nice apartments here for the staff. You may also live in Vegas if you want but having a place here is necessary sometimes. Bring any weapons you want and your clothes. Check out of your hotel."

He reaches into his desk and hands me an American Express Card. "This is yours. Nothing illegal please." He smiles, then takes my arm and says, "Thank you, I can sleep better now."

Cranston goes downstairs with me and has Number Two drive us both to the airplane. The conversation in the car is neutral. It is obvious he does not want Number Two to know anything. At the plane Cranston walks me to the stairs.

"See you tomorrow. Nine o'clock a good time again?'

"Yes Sir, that's fine. I'll see you in the morning with the dog."

"Call me John, please."

"Okay John, see you tomorrow."

I jog up the stairs and into the cabin. The guard from this morning is still here.

"Did you have to wait, for me?" I ask.

"Yeah, but it's better than sitting around the office with Grumpy and Grouchy."

"Yeah, I noticed there are seven of you."

During the flight back the two of us talk. His name is Thomas, he is a retired Federal narcotics agent. He still retains an air of confidence, a man able to take care of himself. But he comes off low key and not cocky. We hit it off. He is doing this work because he bought a house in Vegas when he retired. When the housing bubble burst, he was underwater in his mortgage. He wasn't about to lose the house, so he went to back to work. He is now able to make his payments and then some.

As we chat, I learn where he worked as an agent. I will have the aliens check him out. After all Cranston, *John,* said I could bring on board anyone I wanted.

RJ Waters

CHAPTER TWELVE

After we land and I get into my truck, the little people will not shut up. My ear is hurting. They are so excited I think one of them is going to pee its little pants.

I'm still not talking to them, but I wish they would just shut up until I am in my room. Once in the Vegas traffic it will require all of my attention, it is the worst.

As I am driving away from the parking lot, I notice a car begins moving at the same time. No biggie probably, but my time in the *other world* has conditioned me to be alert to my surroundings. I pull onto the street and speed up. The car seems to be racing thru the parking lot and comes bouncing onto the street in my direction. Coincidence or has the game already began? Time to find out.

I make a quick left-hand turn onto a side street. Then I take the next right. This is a commercial area. The car follows me at a distance. A couple of right-hand turns and then I am onto a main thoroughfare. I catch a break in traffic and make a quick left-hand turn. The car is stuck at the intersection with the heavy cross traffic. It darts out and is almost hit. Yep, he is after me. I take it easy as if I'm unaware of him and find a Burger King. I pull in and park near the front of the lot. I take my weapon out of the glove box and tuck it in my waistband. My suit jacket will cover it. Then I quickly get out and go inside. As I watch from the restaurant window, the car pulls into the lot and slowly drives to the rear. He then backs into a parking space against a wall at the back of the lot. He has a perfect view of my truck.

I tell Michael what is going on. He is horrified. "Do you want us to come out with the Smart Car?"

"No, not yet. I need to see who this yahoo is." I have been glancing out the windows and can see he is alone in the car. He is sitting and smoking, flipping his ashes out the open window. I devise a plan.

I go out the front door, hidden from his view and to the sidewalk. Next door is a gas station. I go past the front of the station and circle back behind it. I can now see the rear of the Burger King. Crouching, I run to the area behind the wall at the rear of the restaurant. This is a vacant lot. I ease up to where I think the car is parked and peer over the wall. Yep, right on. The driver is sitting low in the car and is hanging his arm out the open window holding a cigarette. The wall is cement block about four feet high. I get a grip and launch myself over and land alongside his left rear fender.

Before he can react, I grab his left arm and bend it back as far as it will go. He yells and tries to turn toward the window. With my right hand, I grab his left ear and pull with all my might. He comes halfway thru the opening. He is now securely wedged in the window frame. I yank open the door and see he has a 9mm handgun on the seat. I take it. I pat him down. Not an easy job with him stuck half-and-half thru the window. He is in his forties, of medium build and probably 5-10 or more in height. Hard to tell with him hanging thru the window and squirming, trying to free himself.

Still twisting his left arm,

I growl, "Who are you and why are you following me?"

He is yelling and crying, but not answering. He dropped his cigarette when I grabbed his arm. It is smoldering at my feet. I manage to pick it up with my right hand while still pinning his arm. I place the burning end of the cigarette against his bare arm. He howls.

"One more time. Who are you and why are you following me?"

"My boss told me to. I don't know why."

"Who do you work for?" I place the cigarette close enough so he can feel the heat."

"I can't" he starts to whimper. I bury the cigarette into his wrist. *"EG&G"* he blurts out.

That is interesting …. EG&G just flew me to Area 51 and is a contractor with the Federal government.

Since we are in the rear of the parking lot, no one has paid much attention. Picture this…. the man is hanging half out of the driver's door window while I am yelling at him. However, this is Vegas. When someone finally does notice, I hold up the credentials Cranston gave me earlier. I mumble something that includes *Drugs* and *Metro*. The Las Vegas Police Department is known as Metro. The person quickly loses interest.

I have impressed upon my friend I am not one to screw with. He tells me his boss called and told him to wait in the parking lot, and then follow me when I came out. One of the guards was to call him when I was leaving the building.

"Which guard?" I demand.

He hesitates; I touch him with the cigarette. He had better hurry because this thing is going out.

"It was Fred, it was Fred." He spits out.

"Which one is he?"

"He sits at the counter, where you co

me into the building."

I *interview* the subject for a while longer but get nothing more of use. He does whatever his boss, a Mr. Ed Benton, tells him to do. He usually snoops on other employees. I then inform him it would be in his best interest to leave town immediately. Since a company under a Federal contract employs him, I will be contacting the FBI and the Department of Defense about today occurrences. I further point out he would most likely go to a Federal Prison or at least never work in the United States again.

I unload his pistol, field strip it and take the firing pin. I leave him to get himself out of the window and walk back to my truck. I drive to my hotel, apparently alone now.

The guys back at the caves are having a fit. I fill them in on everything. We make plans for Dog to be brought in tonight. By Smart Car of course. Not by George please, I need Dog in one piece. Poor George, we will never let up on him.

I ask Michael if they can make up a 'federal looking' badge for Dog, so he can be a real law enforcement service dog. I must be able to get him into my room. I have the official credentials John gave me. Michael says they will do what they can. The plan is for them to meet me just after dark on the access road to the hotel-parking garage.

My room has been made up and all appears to be in order. I always leave some *things* a *certain* way so I can tell if anyone has snooped while I was gone. I change out of the suit and clean up. After dressing in more of my *new* clothes, casual ones, I decide to eat while I am waiting. I go to one of the hotels' restaurants and enjoy another fine meal. I ignore Dog's begging for a *doggie bag*.

It is now dark. I am informed they are ready to deliver my partner. Good, I miss the creature. I go to the driveway which leads to the backside of the hotel's parking garage. It is like being in a dark canyon. The buildings are so high.

Michael conveys to me that they are in the dark space above me. They will ease down and when there are no cars in sight, will drop onto the street. They do, almost at my feet. Impressive, I definitely want one of these cars.

The passenger door opens, and George is there. He jumps out followed by Dog, who was crammed in the back. Dog jumps on me and licks me. "Glad you're safe, David. Now you're in good paws." George shakes my hand wishes me good luck. Michael reaches out from the front seat. "Take care my friend. This has already gone far beyond what we expected. Remember we will be available 24-7 to assist you." They shoot upwards and vanish out of sight.

Dog sits proudly in front of me.

"Well what do you think?" He has on a wide black leather collar with a very official looking gold badge. It has the U.S. government Seal in the center. The words Federal Security Officer-Department of Defense are written around the seal.

"Love it Dog. Better than the crummy card, I got. Let's go in."

We enter the sophisticated lobby. I have already briefed the hotel manager concerning who I am and a special security dog is being flown in tonight. I only needed to flash my new credentials and mention being *flown out* in the morning, to get his attention. The dog is more than welcome. 'Anything you need Mr. Manning, just call'.

Dog and I stroll thru the lobby and into the elevator. We get some stares but again - this is Vegas. I'm beginning to like this town. Dog is at his best. Head up, chest out, and almost prancing. We get to our floor and I start to use the key card on the door. Dog freezes.

"You alone David?"

"Was when I left, why?"

"Someone was just here."

I pull out my gun, unlock the door, and fling it open. Dog bolts in and I follow. The room is empty. So is the bathroom.

"Someone was here recently," says my partner. He is sniffing everywhere. He goes to my suitcase. "He was in that."

I look at the suitcase. It has been disturbed, not left *my way*. I open it and all my stuff is still there, but I can tell it was rifled. He checks the bathroom and goes to my shaving kit. He nods. Things have been moved around there too.

I took any papers I received today with me, so there was nothing in the room to identify me. Twice today, this is not good.

"Hey I'm here. It's good now." He smiles-as only *Dog* can smile.

"No, it is not good. But I'm damned glad you're here." I reach down and give him a big hug.

"Hey, don't tarnish my badge," he jokes.

"You hungry Dog? How about a steak?" I ask.

"I thought you already ate," he says sadly.

"I did. This is for you. What do you want? We have room service."

He orders a large steak, rare of course and two Michelobs. I get a bottle of Crown.

We are convinced there are no bugs in the room, so we chat freely. Dog's senses are acute and if there were any kind of listening devices present, he would know. I close the heavy drapes so sound will not vibrate off the windows.

After a while, there is a knock at the door. Room service of course. I look out the peephole. Looks right to me, but Dog's ears go up. He gives me a look and shakes his head. Does not smell right to Dog. That is enough for me.

I motion him to one side of the room, and I hold my gun behind my back. With my other hand, I open the door and a room service waiter enters, pushing a service cart. His uniform jacket is ill fitting, Humm, not his I bet. I close the door. He reaches under the cloth covering the food, as if to show us our order and begins to draw out an automatic pistol. As soon as the gun is barely visible, Dog launches himself and bites down on the man's wrist.

Dog has him on the floor. I remove the gun and Dog keeps the pressure on.

How much of this do I have to put up with in one day?

"Who the fuck are you and who sent you?" I step on his other arm and frisk him. He has no other weapons. Still no answer. I step a little harder.

"Please, please, don't kill me, I'll tell you," he begs. Too easy.

I tell Dog to *release*. He does. I throw the towel from the tray to the intruder.

"Wrap your wrist. Start talking. Who do you work for?"

He hesitates. I kick his wrist. He falls backwards. Dog is immediately at his throat.

I yell, "I don't know what your game is but where I come from, it's called *talk quick or die!*"

I will admit it is difficult to speak with a large set of very sharp teeth around your throat, but he begins. "I was hired by a group I have worked for in the past. They are not from Las Vegas." I again tell Dog to *release*. The pudgy asshole starts to rub his thick neck and then his wrist.

"Stay on your back and keep talking. What were you supposed to do with me? You were already in here once tonight, right?"

"I had to find out who you were and what you were doing at Area 51 with a guy named Cranston. I couldn't find out anything from your luggage, so I decided to come in and try to get you to talk."

"And if I didn't talk, what then?"

"I would take your identification and give it to the guys who hired me."

"And what would you do next? Kill me?" Dog appropriately emits a low growl.

"No. No, just rough you up and knock you out. That's all. I don't do killings."

I keep him talking. He has contacts within the hotel staff so he can get into rooms when he needs to and when I ordered room service, he paid off the waiter to let him make the delivery. He is a Vegas local. A sort of private eye and what-ever-for-hire thug.

He has some military intelligence background from years ago, but he was bounced from the Army and has been freelancing ever since.

"Vegas is perfect for this," he brags. "You got some money and you can go anywhere and find out whatever you want. I got it made here. Hey, look, you're pretty dammed good at this stuff. I don't know what you're into now, but if you ever want to settle down, I could, you know, help you get set up with the right people."

"Let's talk," I say while sitting down in a chair in front of him. He is still lying on his back on the floor. "You give me the names of the people who hired you and how to find them. In turn I will not tell the hotel about how you have subverted any semblance of security they think they have." I take out my cell phone and take his picture. "I also won't send this to every hotel in Vegas and tell them your M.O."

"Man, that would ruin me. You have to promise me you will not tell the people who hired me how you found them. They would have me killed."

"I don't have to promise you anything. I have all the cards. However, I will not divulge how I found them, and I will find them. In fact, they will probably never know they have been located, until it's too late."

"Who are you? I've met some scary operatives in the past, but you are in a league by yourself."

"Thank you, now *names*."

The poor schmuck starts to reel off his contacts. He does not know much except names and phone numbers. He thinks they are mostly in the Washington D.C. and Virginia area. Sounds right, according to what Cranston has told me. The contact who hired this person is in Arlington Virginia. At least that is where the cell phone is from. That is the home base of the CIA, NSA, and other assorted spooks. I chat with Dwayne, which is his name, for a while longer.

"What are you going to report about tonight?" I ask with raised eyebrows.

"Uh, I got into your room and there was nothing of interest. Just your clothes. I waited all night in the lobby for you to come back to the room and you never did. In the morning, you came in, went to the front desk, and checked out. You had a bellman gather your bags and bring them to the front desk. You left in a waiting cab. I lost you in the morning traffic."

"What exactly where you told about me? Name, anything else? How did you know where I was staying?"

"They knew your name and you were staying here. You'd been to see that Cranston guy at Area 51. They were very worried about who you were and why you went to see Cranston."

"What exact name were you given?"

"David Manning. They just knew you were staying here, not any room number. I had to find that out. They also thought you just checked in tonight. I found out you were here last night too. I was called around four o'clock or so. They just found out about you. Whoever tipped them off only found out today. Maybe just this afternoon."

This information does limit the possibilities of who is behind all this.

"Is EG&G behind any of this?"

"Oh shit, them? No, they have their own people. EG&G does not have anything to do with me. They've gotten in my way a couple of times. Nasty bunch."

"Before we end this conversation by me throwing you off the balcony, any more thoughts on any of this?" I smile, sort of. Dog raises up.

"Look, I'm just a businessman trying to make a living doing what I know how to do. I try not to figure out any of this spook stuff. If I can make a buck here and there, it's all good. I honestly don't know what you are into, man. None of these characters are upfront people. I gotta say be fucking careful. There is something big at stake here if my contacts and EG&G are involved."

I decide Dwayne can leave under his own power. I ask him if he touched the food at all. Was it safe?

"Oh yeah. I had some fries in the elevator. I wanted to take a bite of steak, but someone got into the elevator."

I take the plate with the steak and set it down in front of Dog. He smells it and dives in.

"For the dog, really! I'll be damned."

"I already ate, he hasn't."

I get a card from Dwayne and let him go. You never know in this business. He might be useful again.

As the door closes, I hear my partner, "Uh excuse me but I could use something to wash this down."

"Oh sorry, I could use a drink myself."

CHAPTER THIRTEEN

I settle down with a Crown Royal on ice and Dog is slurping his beer.

"Is that stuff good for you?" I ask. He does seem to drink a lot.

"No worse than that stuff is for you."

"Touché."

The guys at the cave are going nuts with all that occurred tonight.

It has been a constant: "David are you alright?" "Dog what is going on there?"

Both Dog and I told them we were fine but give us a few minutes to just de-stress. God, I wish I could turn this ear implant off sometimes. I told Michael when something is going on please be quiet, I need to keep my wits about me.

Dog was more direct. "Just shut up! I've got so many sensory things going on I don't need your incessant babbling in my head."

Dog and I have settled down and enjoyed a bit of adult beverage, so we begin to talk with the cave dwellers.

Michael has no idea who is behind any of today's occurrences. We all agree there seems to be two separate groups involved.

Michael says Ed Benton is some sort of a security director for the Vegas EG&G office. He is always snooping around Area 51. Michael wonders why EG&G would be concerned about who is visiting Cranston. It's a mystery to him. Cranston is a federal employee. EG&G is a contractor to the feds. A powerful one. They seem to be involved with just about every top-secret project at Area 51. Michael tells me they have been for countless years.

The unknown group that hired Dwayne is probably the one who has Cranston worried. If the individuals involved are in the DC area, then they are also 'well connected'. Are we caught in the middle of a turf war? Could be.

The next morning Dog and I are up and fed early. We check out and head for my truck. Yesterday I parked my truck in the hotel self-park garage since I didn't want anyone to have the keys except me. Dog inspects the outside and then the interior and declares…no intruders have entered. We head for the airport. I enter the EG&G parking lot. Now I have the coveted parking sticker. Andy just waves numbly for me to come onward until he sees the huge black dog sitting next to me. His eyes bug out. I smile and point to the badge on his collar. Andy recovers and continues to wave us on.

I park in an end spot since I don't know when I will return for my ride. It's a newer truck and I don't want it to become a victim of parking lot dents. As I get my suitcase out, Dog takes it all in. He scans the large parking area and watches all the people streaming toward the terminal.

"So, this is how people get to the top-secret place, no one knows about. Understated I must say." He snorts.

We walk toward the Janet Airline Terminal. That's what the EG&G run airline is called. Where that name comes from no one seem to know, but some say it stands for Just Another Non-Existent Terminal.

We enter the front door. Fred is at his computer. He looks up and acknowledges me. I now have *proper credentials,* so he is just nodding at me to go on thru. Instead I go up to him.

"Good morning Fred. Has Grayson come in yet?" I ask.

He is obviously shocked I know his name and the name of the creep he had follow me yesterday.

"Uh, I haven't seen him today." He is perplexed.

I put my closed hand out and say, "Here-give this to your boss, Benton, would you?" He puts his hand out to receive whatever it is I have.

I drop in his hand the firing pin from Grayson's weapon. Then dog and I turn toward the next room. Fred is just standing there stunned.

Stupid expression on his face: priceless.

He recovers and tells us we are to go to the same room as yesterday. We don't get to follow the herd to the rear door. In the next room are the same two officers from yesterday. The one who flew with me, Thomas, smiles and greets me.

"Good to see you again. Whoa, Beautiful dog."

Dog walks up to him and lifts his head. Thomas asks if he can pet him. "Of course," I say. Dog needs to get a good whiff. Thomas reaches down and pets him. Dog wags his tail. Thomas has passed his first test.

Thomas opens the door to the outside and we all go toward the waiting plane. At the bottom of the stairway I make a motion to Dog and he bounds up the stairs. I hear a surprised voice, "Wow, where did you come from big guy?"

I am at the top of the stairs now and I see the pilot petting Dog. The other pilot is just coming up the stairs. We all chat a moment about my handsome big dog and his impressive badge. Then they announce it's time for wheels up. I notice the window shades are now up.

"Thomas," I say in an official voice as I gesture toward Dog. "He hasn't been there before. Shouldn't the window shades be drawn?" Thomas chuckles and we all take a seat. I do take a window seat. Dog goes to the seat across the aisle from me. He looks at me with an: *I need some help here* look.

"Oh yes, Thomas would you mind putting up the arm rests so he can lay across all the seats?"

He assists us and raises the arm rests. Dog settles in.

"I guess seat belts are out of the question. Mind if I sit with you?" Thomas asks.

"Please do. I'm David." I extend my hand.

"Call me Tom," he says and takes a seat.

I ask why we are still segregated from the rest of the secret workers. Cranston ordered it because of the dog, is his answer.

"Okay, but what about the smaller planes around here, like those two King Airs?" I point out the window toward some smaller planes parked in the immediate area. "Wouldn't they be a lot more economical?"

Tom just smiles, "You do remember you are working for the Federal Government, don't you?"

"Yeah, how dumb of me, I know better than to use logic."

He asks a little about Dog but nothing about me. He is smarter than Number Two.

John and Number Two are waiting for me when we land. Dog immediately does not like Number Two. But he is okay with John Cranston. Interesting!

Number Two says Dog looks a lot like the Shepherd the German scientist, Wolfgang, had. I say, "he is a Shepherd and you never know, might be related somewhere down the line."

We go to John's office. No security checks now. I am just waved thru. The officers admire Dog but step back as he passes. As he goes by each officer, Dog gives them a once over.

We enter John's outer office and the admin aide looks up and is visibly shocked to see me. Hmmm? What's that about?

John, Dog, and I go into his office and he closes the door.

John starts to just chat about getting me an office, what I will be doing, that kind of stuff. I stop him.

"We need to talk, alone." I say firmly.

"This is safe. It's my office for Pete's sake. If this isn't safe, nothing is."

Dog has been checking out the room. He alerts and looks at me. I go over to him. He is looking at a picture on the wall. Putting my finger over my lips to tell John not to talk, I gently move it enough to look behind it. On the backside is a *bug,* a listening device.

I say to John, "Why don't you show me my apartment and we can discuss my duties further?"

He doesn't know what I saw, but immediately agrees. The man is not completely stupid. The three of us leave and John tells the admin jerk we will be out for a while.

In the hall, out of ear shot of the officers, John looks at me.

"What was that?"

"A bug. I told you the dog was good. We need to get into one of your vehicles and go for a ride."

John gets one of the motor pool cars and after an inspection by dog, we drive off. I begin by telling John his office is bugged. *It really is.* Because the one I just found was *not* the one Wolfgang put in. The aliens have already taken it out and installed their own system. Whatever that is.

I relay to John, in detail, my two encounters since I was here just yesterday. The man pales visibly.

"I didn't know it was that intense. I mean I knew someone didn't want me to work on my newest project, but who are all these people? How did they know about you?" I tell him I have my *contacts* looking into who is behind this and he has *no privacy*. I ask how long the admin aide has worked there.

"He started just before the previous chief retired. Do you think he is involved?"

"Did you watch the X-Files? Well their advice is still the best: ***trust no one!***"

I tell him he hired me to keep him safe and I will do my very best. He must do as I ask for the present. He has an apartment on the premises also. We go there and Dog checks it out. No bugs according to my partner. John is becoming more and more impressed with *my partner*.

"You use this place much?" I ask.

"No, hardly ever. I have a wife and I go home to Las Vegas most of the time. She's active in charities and other civic affairs, so we are always going to some function in town."

"Do you do much work from home?"

"No, my work is too classified to do from anywhere but my office."

George then speaks in my ear and tells me he is checking on Cranston's wife, just to see what she is into. George, my man. You're a lousy driver, but you are thinking like an investigator.

I explain to John we will *pretend* we don't know about the bug. In the office we will talk about the security of the Research Division, nothing about him or what has occurred. When I get some information on anyone involved, we will take it from there.

The aliens will be able to determine where the bug is transmitting to. That's vital. It can't be far; those things have a limited range.

We arrive at my apartment and drop off the meager belongings I brought. Dog gives me the signal the apartment is clean. No bugs.

"John, you and I must decide what my real job is. At present I'm your bodyguard, also, I'm trying to solve the puzzles we have uncovered".

"My initial plan was for you to be the head of Division Security," John says.

"You already have a person in that position overseeing all the Division's locations and he's responsible for the officers who work there. I don't have the time, if I'm going to be keeping your ass alive, while we stop the threat."

"I agree with you, David. The present Number One is a competent supervisor. Number Two is, in my opinion worthless."

I tell him about my encounter with Number Two. He is aghast.

"He can't stay with a security violation like that. He did not know you from Adam. He told you all that. He has to go."

I agree, but the matter will be left up to Number One when John informs him of Number Two's violations. In the meantime, we decided I will be a Special Investigator, temporarily assigned to the Division, from the Department of Defense (DOD). No one will have any way of knowing any different.

I tell John I would like to have my truck out here. No problem he says, he can have someone bring it out. I look at him. Before I can speak, he shakes his head.

"No, I know better. I have got to get into the game. If we can trust *no one* then we can trust *no one*. You want to go get it and drive it here yourself?"

"Yep."

He thinks a moment then says, "Look I was going to drive back to Vegas tonight anyway. I'll leave early and you come with me. Spend the night at my house and we will both drive back in the morning."

"The dog goes too."

"Oh yes. I want both of you. I'll call my wife and tell her we will be having company."

We head back to John's office. He calls his wife on the way and she seems good with the idea, especially the part about bringing Dog. She is an animal lover. While we are driving Michael speaks in my ear and says they have located the receiver for the bug. Guess where? The admin assholes office.

We walk into John's office and I close the door. Then I begin to talk to John about what we must do next. I am just babbling, making it sound like I have a plan. Then I ease up to the door and yank it open. The aide jumps up; he has an ear bud in one ear with a cord going to his desk drawer. He winces as he tries to get the ear bud out. I grab it along with his ear and open the drawer. Inside, the cord goes to a small receiver. With my other hand I pick up the device and then push him into John's office, still holding onto his ear. I'm getting good at this *ear* thing. Taking the ear bud out of his ear I slam him into the wall. The guy slides to the floor and Dog puts his nose in the guy's face and growls.

I hold the bud to my ear and say toward the picture, "you're busted." I hear the words in my ear. I then give John the ear bud and again speak to the picture. John hears me. He is ready to pass out. I thought he had been in this world before. Apparently not the same world I was in.

The asshole is just whimpering as Dog performs his best, *I'm going to eat you alive* routine. God he's good at that.

John wants to have him arrested and hauled off. I tell him the gentleman needs to talk to us before he leaves.

"I want an attorney," he pathetically wails.

"Oh no dude! This is not a civil matter. This is a top-secret government installation and you have no rights. Remember the oath you signed when you were hired. You may never see the light of day again. Have you heard of *rendition?* Punk." I always liked the Dirty Harry stuff.

With an occasional assist from Dog, he begins to talk.

He previously worked for a security firm in Virginia that had contracts with the CIA. He would review the reports from electronic surveillances the CIA had set up. Someone needs to read and cull the data. The agency hires this out to *trusted* private firms at a cheaper rate than a government employee would receive. I knew this is done from my few years in the covert world. I have never believed giving a civilian company access, to what could be classified information, was a wise idea.

One day the security company offered this guy an assignment as a covert operative. He would be placed at Area 51 and would pass on whatever information he could obtain about the new Chief of Research Division IV, John Cranston. The guy jumped at the chance to be a *real* spy. He was then *hired* by the Department of Defense and sent to Vegas.

"Did you ever think it was odd a private contractor could get you hired immediately at a Top-Secret location?" I ask.

"Yeah, I did ask my boss about how this all could happen, and he said that was how the intelligence community worked. Everything was behind the scenes, he said. Not to worry. The company would still be my contact and I would have a good future if I pulled this off."

"How do you get your instructions and how do you report your findings?" I want every scrap if information I can get out of the guy.

"I have a classified cell phone to use and once I was set up in the Area 51 office, I would sometimes get encrypted e-mails with instructions. They sent me the listening device and told how to install it. Then I monitored whatever Cranston said in his office and reported nightly to my contact. I don't know his name, but it was always the same person. Swear to God, I do not know what they're looking for." He raises hid hand like he is taking an oath. "Just report whatever Cranston was doing."

"What Else?" Dog and I are both in his face now.

"My contact got extremely excited when I relayed Cranston was talking to someone about his new project. I don't know who Cranston was talking with, but it always seemed to be the same person." He's getting really chatty now. "One time when Cranston was on the phone with his unknown friend, he revealed something about aliens and forcing them to help him or be destroyed."

I glance at Cranston; he is shaken by this revelation. He has not mentioned my diminutive new friends to me.

"My contact discounted the information as the ravings of a mentally unstable man." He glances at John and slides even further down the wall.

I get more information out of the chump, secure his cell phone, and make him give me all the passwords to his computer. He has an apartment in Las Vegas and flies back and forth, like the management employees do. Most of the *worker bees* have to ride a *bus* back and forth. I also get the aide's apartment address and key. Then I tell John we need this little slug held incommunicado until I can check on all of this.

After the federal officers come take the aide away, I look at John and say, "Anything you want to tell me?"

John sits down on a chair. He has been blown away by everything that just happened. But then he seems to pull himself together and looks at me.

"I was going to get around to the rest but so much has happened so fast I couldn't even think straight."

He then tells me about the aliens and how they came to be here and where they are now. His story matches what the brainiacs have told me. I am properly amazed and in awe of the whole tale.

I carry it off well.

"All things aside, were you prepared to destroy these people, whatever they are, to get them to work with you?"

I am indigent.

"No, I actually couldn't hurt anyone, but I was under pressure from my *contact,* the person I have been talking with on the phone. He's trying to control me in this new project. I was put in this position as Chief just to facilitate the development of the weapon. The former Chief wanted to kill the project as too dangerous to have it loose in the world. The faction that my contact is involved with forced the former chief to retire, so I could be put in his place, to keep the research going. I didn't realize what I was getting into. I wound up at Area 51, after a couple of CIA operations I was involved with went badly. I was placed here to keep me out of view in case the media got wind of the flawed missions. *I fucked up*, and I can admit it. I thought I was the best mission planner in the world, got cocky and good people died because of me. It was egotistical stupidity on my part! I live with the memory of the unnecessary deaths I'm responsible for. No, I would not hurt or even threaten the aliens. They have held up their end of the agreement with our government. I just spouted that out to my contact because he was putting pressure on me to speed up the development. He believes the aliens have the technology to assist us with this weapon."

"Who is your contact and where does he fit in to all this? Time to clear the air here."

John tells me the man's name. It is the same name Michael discovered in the microfiche when he was looking for Wilhelm Schultz's visitor...Franklin Pierce, former high official in a past administration. John knows him as a behind the scenes figure in the espionage world.

"Ours I hope."

"Oh, definitely ours, but I'm not sure if he is aligned with the standing government or with some people who *want* to be running the country. This is becoming a genuine concern of mine. That's why I truly need your help David. I'm scared of him and his *people*. Ironically, he was the one who suggested I get a former black ops man to be my muscle, to protect the program. When I read your service records, I wasn't sure if you would be right for me or not. But when I met you, I did feel comfortable and decided to ask you to be my bodyguard. If it worked out, then I was going to fill you in on what was bothering me. But things happen so fast. You've already shown me I am in a worse situation than I realized."

"You know John, I am mentally exhausted. It is only two in the afternoon and I feel like I have put in a week's work. Do you guys have food out here? I'm starved. You and I are going to be talking for a long time and I need fuel."

"Of course. We have a nice club. A place that would be considered an officer's club, were it on a normal military base. I don't know if I can eat or not, but let's go."

"Dog has to be allowed in and fed," I say. "Got to take care of my partner."

"No problem. After what I've seen of his abilities, he can go anywhere I go, in fact I insist." As if on cue, Dog gets up and heads for the door.

John looks at him. "It's as if he understands us."

"He does."

CHAPTER FOURTEEN

The restaurant is similar to a military officers' club with a nice environment and good food; a place for the officials and scientists of Area 51. John introduces me to several people, some administrators, and a couple of area scientists. Everyone is curious to know what happened in his office today. News travels fast. He says it was a *security* matter. Everyone knows better than to ask more.

We are seated at our table and Dog is given a placemat on the floor next to us. I am enjoying a good French dip and Dog is devouring a couple rare hamburger patties. He begs for some of my French fries. He does not speak of course, just puts his paw on my knee and his nose in my plate and whines.

"Not good for you." I say as I proceed to put a few in his dish. He looks at me. I can almost hear, *No worse than for you*!

As we are finishing, in walks the German scientist Wolfgang. He is Dog's grandfather, sort of.

John calls him over and introduces us. Wolfgang carries it off as if we have never met. He looks at Dog and comments, "He looks so much like my last Shepherd. May I pet him? Dog jumps up before I can respond. He puts his face up to the Scientist and licks him. Wolfgang playfully ruffles his thick, black fur. "Can I visit him occasionally? I miss my dog."

"Certainly, anytime."

After Wolfgang says his goodbyes, I head to the restroom and leave Dog with John. I need to talk with the cave dwellers. As I am using the restroom for its intended purpose, Michael comes online in my ear and informs me they aren't sure of the security in this place. Great, I can't even pee in private. There is a door to the exterior, near the restroom entrance, so I go outside. Michael says they have not acquired any new information for me.

"Come on guys. You've got all the technology in the *universe*, what is the hold up?"

"We can only work as fast as your sluggish human systems will cooperate. You have uncovered a large amount of information in a couple of days. We will get it all sorted out."

I ask Michael, "Any thoughts so far? This is getting complicated."

"More so than we even imagined." He responds. "I don't know what to make of Cranston. He was very forthcoming with you. I almost believe him. He may be just a pawn in a *behind the scenes* power play. I think your advice of *trust no one* is the mantra for all of us. I know you would like this Thomas, the security officer from the airport, to work with you. So far, he looks suitable. Let us keep checking on him. You could use trustworthy help......in human form."

"The way this is shaping up I might need a trustworthy *army* of my own."

"Don't forget, you have *space troopers* to help you," Michael chuckles at his own joke.

"If I didn't have all of you guys, I would have left last night, taken Dog and gone back to police work. He is still the best partner I have ever had." In my ear I hear a muffled: *Thanks David.*

We go back to John's office. The admin aide is on ice in an isolation cell with no outside contact. I'll deal with him *whenever.* John takes care of some *normal* business and then we're off to his home in Las Vegas. He drives a late model Mercedes-Benz. Of course, it is, what else would he drive? Dog is curled up on the lush leather back seats. He has indicated with a nod, the car is not bugged. Good, one less worry.

We drive down Highway 95 to the north-western portion of Las Vegas. John lives in an area known as Summerlin. We pull into a lavishly landscaped entryway, complete with a guard house. Wow, a gated, guarded community. "Good evening Mr. Cranston," the guard waves John thru as he opens the gate. These places are mansions! John doesn't just live well, he lives amazingly well. We pull up to his house and into a four-car garage. Another Benz sits inside.

We go into the house and John calls out to his wife, "Doris we're here."

From somewhere in this huge house comes his wife. She is probably in her fifties, a little younger than John. An attractive blonde lady, obviously well taken care of by the various spas and cosmetic surgeons of Vegas. She has no wrinkles and very large lips and eyes. Oh yeah, she's been enhanced.

She is pleasant and just goes wild when she sees Dog. "What a beautiful German Shepherd!" She immediately bends down and begins to pet Dog. She is raving about how good looking and sturdy he is. Dog, being the sleaze he is, rolls onto his back and lets her rub his belly. We leave them and John takes me to my room. This is a guest room? Wow, makes the fancy hotel I was staying in look second rate. He leads me to the family room and asks what I would like to drink.

"A beer would go good about now."

He goes to a large bar located on one side of the room, it must seat twenty. He brings a couple beers and we sit down. Dog and Doris are having a grand time in the other room.

"She loves animals." John smiles. "She is on the board of a rescue shelter, among other charities."

Doris comes in and says since we came home early, dinner will be at least an hour or so. I tell her I'm fine where I am.

John reminds me, "You wanted to get your vehicle. Since we have some time, why not go get it? Then we can leave straight from here tomorrow morning."

We leave Dog with his admirer while John and I head to the airport. My truck appears to be as I left it, apparently unmolested. I tell John this would be a good time to check on the admin aide's apartment. I have his keys. John agrees and we drive to the apartment; it's nothing fancy but in a decent area. I knock on the door. He said he lived alone but I'm being cautious. No answer so I use the keys and enter. Typical bachelor pad. Minimal furniture and a large flat screen TV and a laptop. I toss the place. Nothing of interest. Some bills and mail but nothing that seems to be connected to the *plot*. I do take his laptop and mail to scrutinize later. I wish I had brought Dog along to give the place his ultimate scan test, but I'm satisfied it's clean. I lock up, jump in my truck and follow John back to his house. We find Doris on the patio setting the table, while Dog is enjoying a roll on the lush lawn.

"It's so nice out I thought we could eat out here." She smiles.

"That sounds wonderful," I say. "Did Dog behave himself?"

"Oh, he is such a lovable dear." She gushes. "He just followed me around as I tended to dinner." Good boy. That's exactly what I wanted him to do.

John goes to help her with dinner. I wander out into the huge yard. I find a bench in a secluded area. I sit down and Dog comes up and sits in front of me.

"You aren't going to believe this Partner," he says.

"What ya got, Partner?" I ask.

"Sweet ole Doris is having an affair. That's what. As soon as you two left she gets on her cell phone. She calls someone named Eddie. Tells him John came home early with his new assistant. Eddie seems to be interested in you. She told him you're a very nice man who is going to be helping John with some problems at the base. He was asking *what problems,* but she said she didn't know anything else. Just work stuff. John has been stressed lately and David is going to help out. Then she raved about me. They are going to meet for lunch tomorrow somewhere. He will call her in the morning."

"Excellent job." I high five him.

George comes on in my ear and says they have not tracked her cell phone yet, but they are working on it. "We weren't counting on that little tidbit. Remarkably interesting. Boy do we have a can of fat worms in this whole mess." Good way to put it George.

John comes to the yard and announces dinner is ready. We all go to the patio and enjoy a great meal. Doris did all the cooking. I'm somewhat surprised. From the looks of the neighborhood, you would think everybody here had servants. Apparently, there are housekeepers and landscapers, so no one has to do too much work.

We have a pleasant evening just chatting and enjoying the outdoors. It gets blistering hot in Vegas at times but tonight is just balmy. Makes me think of the beach I had to leave.

The next morning when we get up, Doris has a nice breakfast ready and waiting. She may be having an affair with Eddie, but she is still holding up her end at home. At least it appears so. I follow John out Highway 95 to the Mercury turnoff and then through several checkpoints on the road to Area 51. On the way, Dog tells me John's house was clear of any bugs. He was pampered by Doris and probably will get fat if we go there too often.

The little folks tell me I'm invited to the *-Night on the Town-* party Saturday night. Michael says hopefully, by then, they will have managed to get some answers concerning the recent events. At this point any information would be helpful. Do we have interconnecting events being played out or are these just separate non-related incidents?

CHAPTER FIFTEEN

Arriving at the headquarters building, I decide it is time for me to display my presence. I will occupy the currently incarcerated admin aide's office. John calls in Number One and introduces me. I am a special investigator from the Department of Defense and will be working independently on DOD matters. John tells Number One to give me any assistance I require. Number One is of course more than happy to assist in any way he can. He has already fired the old Number Two.

Now down to business. I have been talking with Michael and George about our jailed spy, the admin aide. What do we need to do to find out who is behind this? That is the question. We have the names of a couple of his former bosses, but no hint as to who this jerk was reporting to. If we turn him loose and track him, his bosses will avoid him like the plague, since he has already been caught. He is useless to them now. For the moment we need to keep him in custody. The aliens will be dumping his cell phone and computer. I will give them his laptop to peruse.

The next issue is Mr. Benton at EG&G. Why did he have me followed on my first day at Area 51? I need to talk with him, *in person*. I ask my fellow agents if they have anything on him. George says Benton has been at EG&G for several years. He hasn't done anything to grab the alien's attention.

"What information do you have on him?" I'm asking. "You know, full name, age, where he lives, all that cop stuff."

George is bringing him up on whatever data base he is into, probably EG&G's.

"Let's see-Edward L. Benton…Oh, good heavens, Edward, do you think?" George asks.

"Edward. That could be *Eddie,* couldn't it?" I respond.

"Could explain why he had you followed." Michael chimes in.

I have to talk with him, for sure now. I know *Eddie* is having lunch today with Mrs. Cranston so maybe later this afternoon I can pay him a visit. Dog did not hear any location mentioned, when he was listening to Doris and Eddie.

I wait until 11:45 and place a call to Benton's office. He is at lunch I am told. Not suspicious, most day workers are. He is expected back after 2:00 p.m. I am also told. I ask how late he usually works. Until around 5:00 p.m. is the answer I receive. The receptionist is now trying to get me to leave a message, but I tell her I will get back to him.

I tell John I need to go back to Vegas to follow up on something.

"You do what you need to. Do you want to spend the night again?" He asks.

"Only if it isn't an imposition on you and Doris."

"No. Not at all. Let me call her, she's having lunch with a girlfriend today." He dials her cell. Doris answerers and tells him she would be delighted if I stayed the night again, as long as I bring along my black beauty.

I go back to my office.

"George could you get a location on Doris from the call?" He has her cell number in his tracking system now. These guys have scary abilities.

He checks and tells me the address she's at. I go to Google and find it is a restaurant called Henri's. That is all I need.

After 2:00 p.m. I call Benton's office and actually get to talk to him. I say my name is Walt Brzezinski and I am from the DOD zone office and I am in town for a couple of days. I would just like to meet him to introduce myself. Just a quick face to face. He says he will be in the office until five and to just 'come on by.'

That worked nicely.

I work a little longer and now I must get Dog rounded up. Since we have moved into the HQ building, he has been *visiting* all the offices. He is a big hit. He has been in every office in the building. He has not found any more bugs, but the chow hound has found out where all the treats are. The staff loves him. He has only been here a few hours but is welcome everywhere. I have also discovered that I don't need to worry about his being let out to do his business as he just goes to the security officer in the lobby and paws the door. The officer jumps up and lets him out. When he is ready to come back in, he barks at the door. Life is tough for Dog.

"This sure beats the cave," he tells me on the way to Las Vegas. "The little squirts were always good with me but some of them were a little intimidated. It's a size thing I think."

"Dorothy isn't intimidated a bit." I remind him.

"Yeah, but she is a pushover. She puts on the tough girl show for the others," he snickers.

We pull up to the EG&G office. It is about a quarter to five. I want to visit with Benton alone. His office is a small distance away from the airport. This building is the main Las Vegas office for EG&G. I park and go in the front door. A guard calls Benton's office and Dog and I are sent upstairs. No one says a word about my partner. He has himself pulled up to his full height and with that big, bad ass, gold badge hanging from his collar, no one is going to question us.

Benton's office is near the end of the second floor. No secretary, just a sign on the door. I knock.

"Come in," a male voice says. We enter and I close the door.

"Mr. Benton, my name is David Manning. Brzezinski asked me to take his place."

Benton's face looks stricken. He definitely knows who David Manning is.

'Un…. Glad to meet you Mr. Manning." He stammers.

"How was lunch at Henri's, *Eddie*?" I ask. If he hasn't peed his pants yet, he did now.

Benton becomes a babbling idiot. He is in his fifties, in passable physical shape but no Mr. America contender. Certainly no better or worse looking than John Cranston. A round, red face, which shows the effects of years of stress and probably too much drinking.

I sit down in front of his desk and Dog takes a stance facing Benton at the side of his desk.

"Okay, now that I have your attention, I don't give a shit if you are banging Doris or not. I want to know why you had your goon follow me. And by the way how is Grayson? He didn't look too good when I last saw him."

Benton continues to stutter and stammers a bit and then begins to make sense. He was told about a guy who went to see Cranston. He was told I was a civilian but looked like a cop. Benton said he was afraid Cranston had hired a private investigator to follow Doris. After I told Grayson I was a DOD person, Benton decided he and Doris had nothing to worry about.

"How did you find out about us? Did Cranston hire you? Are you a PI or what?"

"I am, in fact, a DOD special agent and could care less about your private business. After you sic'd Grayson on me, I had reason to delve into *your* life." I lean across his desk and stare hard at him. "I'm involved with top secret matters and when I am followed, I need to know why." My deep, scary-cop voice always works.

He is apologizing and begging me not to tell Cranston. I assure him the *affair* is safe with me.

Benton settles back into his chair obviously relieved. Dog backs away from him and begins to roam the room. He alerts and points his nose at a picture on the wall. Not again.

I put my finger up to my lips and go to the picture. Yep, there is a bug behind it. I take it off the back of the frame and drop it into the coffee cup Benton had been drinking from when I walked in. He is speechless.

"How long has that been there I wonder?" I ask him. "You know it is transmitting to some place in this building."

"Has to be, but who?" He is sweating.

"Let's find out." I stand up and open the door to the hall. Dog goes out. "Who else is up here?"

"Probably no one at this time of day," Benton says

Dog wanders down the hall and then turns and goes in the opposite direction. He stops at a door at the end of the hall. He looks at me.

"It's the Las Vegas director's office." Benson says." The director is in Washington DC this week."

"Can we go in?" He opens the door. There is the secretary's office and then the director's office beyond it. No one is there. The secretary left early too. Dog goes to the director's office and then to a hutch on one side. He looks at me. I open the door. Sure enough, there is a receiver with a tape recorder.

"That Bastard!" Benton is not amused. I examine the set up and see there are four wires going to the unit. Each wire has a name taped to it. *Ed* is on one. I show this to Ed Benton. He says the other names belong to the deputy director, another top executive and the financial manager. The director definitely wants to keep tabs on his people.

I tell Benton he can do what he wants with this information. I am not interested in *internal* matters. He thanks me profusely for finding the bug. He doesn't know how he will handle it. He asks about Dog.

"I didn't know a dog could hear those things," he says. I pass it off as a matter of training.

"They have many more senses than we humans are aware of."

Dog looks at me and smiles--that creepy smile of his!

CHAPTER SIXTEEN

The evening with the Cranston's goes well. I am assuming Benton didn't say anything to Doris about me being aware of their love life. He said he wasn't going to. She was just as bubbly as last night and lavished Dog with attention all evening.

The next day back at Area 51, I am in my office and learning what John's division is actually doing. The top-secret project Wolfgang and others are working on is my top priority. John takes me to the lab where the research is being conducted. The building is nestled up to a hillside. I noticed it when I first arrived. Inside are various work areas and testing rooms. The testing is done using caves dug into the side of the mountain. This way the work is hidden from satellite surveillance. I am learning a lot of what is done here at Area 51 is *hidden* from aerial view. Any project involving airplanes is usually conducted at night. Needless to say, the place is active around the clock.

After the tour we go back to the office. John goes about his work and I check in with the guys. I am reminded tomorrow night is the big *Night on the Town* party and I am expected to attend. Not a problem. It will be Saturday and a day off. I will be at my apartment on base. When it is time to attend the soiree, Dog and I will ease over to the alien's lab entrance.

While I'm talking with Michael and George, on my imbedded device, Dog suddenly interrupts and says he needs me outside the HQ building.

"What's up? You okay?"

"I'm fine. But you have got to see this."

I run downstairs and slam out the door.

"Where are you?"

"Come over to the west, across the road."

There is just an open field in that direction. I run around the building and look toward the west. Then I see the reason for his interest. There is an Air Force 'Air Police officer' and a security dog in the field about 100 yards out. The dog is a German Shepard, a soft tan and black.

"Isn't she a beauty?" Dog is breathing heavily.

"No lover boy, I don't think this is going to work for you," I laugh at my partner.

"David, the handler is a female. From here she looks pretty cute. I think to be neighborly you should introduce us. What have you got to lose?"

"She is armed, you know."

"So are you. You got your badge, you're just one of the boys. Come on, let's go talk with them."

Oh, what the hell, why not. We do have the dogs in common. "Behave yourself," I admonish him.

I walk across the road and into the field. I wave and keep walking forward. The officer does not seem to be planning on shooting me, so far so good. My badge is on my belt, so I do look official.

Dog drops in alongside me and *we* look official, I hope.

The officer is indeed a beauty. Even though she is wearing cammies and has her hair pulled into a ponytail under her cap it's obvious she is attractive. The dog's not bad either.

Given my present job with John, the aliens and an unknown number of conspiracies, I don't see how this will work out for me. But what the hell.

As we approach, she has her dog sitting by her side. I put on my best smile and say, "Hi. Hope my beast wasn't bothering you two."

"No not at all," She says. "I was just about to call in a loose dog report when I saw his badge. You two stationed here?"

"Yes, for the time being. I'm with DOD," I reply. Dog stops when I do and sits properly next to me. He can be good when he wants to. "Your Shepherd is beautiful," I add.

"This is Griselda," she says with a straight face. "I call her Grizzie."

"You named her Griselda?" I ask with unmasked amazement.

Not a good move David. It may be a family name or something. It has been so long since I actually talked socially with a woman, I forgot myself.

"No, she was named before I was assigned to her. That's why I call her Grizzie."

Whew, I got away with that one.

"What is your guy's name?"

"Dog," I say proudly.

"Dog! Really? That is the best you could do?" She is at least smiling.

"Uh, same reason as you. He was already named when I got him."

She moves closer and Grizzie stays by her side.

"He is gorgeous." She says. "What is he beside Shepard?"

"I don't actually know. He is just listed as a German Shepard. But I agree, there is something else in there." This is going well.

"His coat is so lush. May I pet him?" She asks.

"Yeah, it's good with me but what about her?" I am worried about Grizzie. She has moved right up in front of us, along with her handler.

"Oh, she's fine. The only time there would be a problem is if I were in danger." She reaches down to Dog. He stretches his neck and looks up at her. Good boy.

She reaches down and pets him. He does his Doris thing. Let's her pet him, rolls over and she scratches his belly. This dog has no shame. Wonder if that would work for me, just thinking.

Grizzie just sits next to the officer. She is leaning forward and smelling deeply. Her tail begins to wag. The officer asks if they can meet. "Yeah sure," I tell her. She

lets her leash slack and Dog goes over to the female. They
do the usual dog greetings and then bounce around a little,
rub noses and both behave themselves.

"My name is David."

"I'm Pamela, Pam," She extends her hand. We
shake, good solid shake.

I ask, "Where do you stay, here or back at Creech?"

That's the Air Force base just outside Area 51.

"when we are on shift we're here for four days and
then back to Creech. There are pretty nice billets for us
over there." She points to an area near where my apartment
is located.

"When are you off shift?" I am now thinking like a
man, not an investigator.

"At 1700 hrs. Then back to Creech tomorrow
morning."

"Well, if you don't have any other plans how about
we four have dinner and you can enlighten me on this place.
I would appreciate an insider's input."

"The four of us?" Pam looks at the dogs.

"Yeah, all of us." I make a sweeping gesture.

"You planning on a picnic? Where can we all eat?"

"At the club." I gesture toward the area where the
facility is.

"I can't eat there, I'm not an officer."

"You are off duty and my guest."

"They let dogs in there?"

"Yes, they do…. after Mr. Cranston told them Dog would be allowed. We even have our own table in the corner, with a place mat for Dog on the floor."

"Oh hell, why not," She says with a grin. "I've got to see this."

Pam says she will be ready by 1830 hours or 6:30 p.m. in civilian terms. I will pick them up at her quarters. As we are walking back to the HQ building, the little people are whooping it up and giving me a bad time.

"Wow, great job David."

"Didn't let any grass grown under your feet."

"Proud of you my man." Stuff like that.

I ask Dog what he thinks. "It's good. She seems like a nice person and I like Grizzie. So maybe the four of us can hang out once in a while, right?"

I can't believe I am having this conversation with a dog. Unreal.

CHAPTER SEVENTEEN

Dinner goes well, Pam and I hit it off. We talk, laugh and enjoy each other's company. The dogs each have their own place mats and devour their meal of rare beef. They just settle down next to each other and seem happy to be there.

Pam is single, like me and divorced, also like me. She is wearing a white top and tan slacks. Her auburn hair is down around her shoulders. Her hazel eyes are sparkling. She looked good in her cammies, but she looks great in her *civies*.

We mutually agree this was a good idea and on her next assignment to Area 51, we should do this again. We linger over dinner and have a couple of drinks. By then the bar is receiving most of the action and we are by ourselves in the dining area. Suddenly, we hear loud angry voices in the bar. Two men start shouting and getting into each other's face.

This is not the place for that kind of stuff, guys.

They have squared off and are ready to go at it when Dog, followed by Grizzie, jump up and intercedes. The two dogs put themselves between the combatants and let out low growls. The men wisely back off. The manager of the club tells the men to leave and not to come back. The dogs watch them leave and then return to our table. The manager comes over to Pam and me.

"Can I hire them? That was great. You bring them in any time you want. They eat *on the house from now on.*"

When the manager leaves, after getting us another round and the two 'hairy bouncers' a few choice meat scraps, Pam says that she has never seen Grizzie do anything on her own.

"But she's not working. She is off duty and relaxing with you," I say. "And at this point she's just being a pack animal, following the Alpha. I think it was great."

"Yes, I must admit I was pretty proud of her," Pam acknowledges, giving Grizzie a big nuzzle and hug.

After a while we leave and I drive the ladies back to their quarters.

Pam opens her door and then leans over to me and gives me a kiss on the cheek.

"Let's do this again, soon." She smiles sweetly at me. Then she jumps out and opens the rear door for Grizzie.

"You boys take care," She says as she closes the doors. Dog lets out a low whimper and Grizzie answers.

"That went very well, thank you for behaving," I say to Dog as we drive away.

"No problem, I actually enjoyed just hanging with her. I don't have any dog friends you know." Dog is looking out the rear window.

"And I don't want to hear a thing from you guys," I say loudly to the aliens who I know are listening.

"David that was sweet. I hope it works out for you two. She seems to be a nice person, like you," Dorothy answers.

"Uh, sorry Dorothy, I didn't expect you to be there," I splutter.

She just laughs. "See you tomorrow night."

Tomorrow night, yes, it's *Night on the Town*. That should be interesting. I do not have any real dress up clothes, wait, I do. I have the suit the aliens got me, so I will dress up.

Saturday morning Dog and I go to the office just to see what goes on when most people are not around. The security officer at the entrance was surprised to see anyone on a weekend. Probably figured: *new guy* he'll get over it soon enough.

Basically, *most people are not around*. Good for me. I just roam around the building. Dog knows it inside and out. I get familiar with who is where and the lay-out of the place. I go to my office and then into to John's. I poke around his desk and filing cabinets. He has already given me access codes. Nothing unusual, all kinds of reports on the various projects from the past. That is to be expected. All marked *Top Secret-Restricted Access*. I keep digging and digging through the files. They look like they should to me, but what am I missing?

Then it hits me. There are no reports on the *present* projects. Where are they? All the old ones are from the time John's predecessor was in charge. Nothing since John's tenure. Maybe they are all kept at the project site?

I call out to my unseen listeners. "Anybody there, hello."

"Yes David, how may I help you?" it's Michael.

"Michael, I thought you would be prepping for tonight. Still going to be bartender, aren't you?"

"I'm ready, trust me," Michael asserts.

"Is Wolfgang coming tonight, by chance?" I ask.

"Yes, he is. He genuinely enjoys the parties. You have questions for him?"

"Yes, I do."

"Good we have some information that should help you also."

"About time. Dog and I've been doing all the heavy stuff here."

"And your work is appreciated. Tonight, we all will sit down and hopefully solve some of these mysteries."

I roam around for a little longer and then get Dog and wish the lone officer a good night.

"How much longer are you stuck here tonight?" I ask him.

"Just another hour and then it's back home to Vegas."

I chat with him a while. Never hurts to make friendly contacts with the unnoticed but always present staff. They see what goes on.

Back at my apartment I get cleaned up and put on my *finery*.

Dog is looking in the mirror. "Does this badge look too ostentatious or is it proper for dress-up night?"

"When did you start talking like that?" I ask.

"I've been watching some of the fashion advice shows on TV. I may have a social life now, beyond you and the little shits." He is serious, I think. I may still have a concussion!

CHAPTER EIGHTEEN

At the appointed hour, Dog and I make our way to the cave entrance. One of the aliens lets us in. I don't remember his name, but he smiles and welcomes us. There are fifty-two of them after all, I can't remember everyone's name.

We get into an electric cart, travel to an elevator and then finally get to the floor where the party is. I thought it would be in the dining room but *no,* these guys have a huge *night club*---tables, dance floor, stage and of course a bar.

The guests are beginning to file in. They are all dressed in formal evening wear. Men in tuxedos and the ladies are in quite fancy evening gowns. Michael is at the bar and waves us over.

I can't help myself, "Michael, where on earth did you guys get these clothes? They aren't exactly off the rack stock." I am of course referring to their short stature.

"David, we are in *the entertainment capital of the world.* There is all manner of merchants who supply the shows with their costumes. We order custom tailored clothes a few at a time. We have built up quite a wardrobe for our theme nights," he smugly states. "Next month is Country-Western night. You won't want to miss it."

Yeah, I will not want to miss that! Stocky, glowing children in ten-gallon hats and cowboy boots. Maybe I'll bring Pam. *I laugh inside at the mental picture of her face.*

During dinner I am sitting with George, his wife, and Dorothy. Michael is dutifully tending bar. I notice Wolfgang come in and he is immediately called over to another of the tables. He seems to be popular.

Honestly, the night is a hoot! We have a wonderful dinner; lobster-tails, steak and all sorts of salads, breads, desserts and of course wine and whatever you want from the bar. I am stuffed.

Now Dorothy takes the stage and announces the evening's show will begin. A curtain behind her opens and there is a huge screen. It's displaying a world-famous female entertainer who just happens to be playing in Las Vegas. The show begins with an opening act and then continues to the star herself.

I lean over to George, with whom we are seated and state, "Tell me this is not live."

"Oh, but yes, it is. We can link into all the big shows. Wonderful isn't it. No lines, no high-priced tickets, just sit back and enjoy."

Damn, and I was feeling sorry for the little ones. They can take care of themselves quite well. Hell, when they had a threat they went and found me.

After the show is over, the partying begins. The aliens have a D.J. of their own and he plays requests and they dance. The D.J.'s name is *Sammy the Slammer*. Why I don't know and neither did the others, but he is funny. Quite an entertainer in his own right. He starts to play music and the little revelers start to dance.

I am sitting talking with everyone when I see a smile on Dorothy's face. At the same time, I feel a tug on my sleeve. I turn and look.

Standing next to me is one of the *ladies*, all four feet of her. I turn and smile. I say "Hi."

"Would you care to dance?" She asks me.

I shoot a glance at Dorothy. She nods quickly and keeps smiling.

"I, uh, sure I would love to." I say and get up. We walk to the dance floor. She reaches up and takes my arm.

"I'm not much of a dancer so please be kind," I say.

We do dance, sort of. I feel like I'm dancing with a child but then again, I am, sort of. But she is having a good time and so am I. the dance is over, and I thank her. She smiles and says I did wonderfully. While we were dancing, I saw Wolfgang also dancing with a wee lady. Apparently, this is accepted by all.

I go back to my table. George is laughing his head off. Dorothy leans over and says, "I should have told you this would happen. You are quite a… specimen to them." I take a drink of wine and feel another tug on my sleeve. Yep, another little lady wants to dance. And so it goes the entire evening. I have never been the center of attention before. It was fun. I'm getting tired and my back is starting to ache. I must lean over a little for them. It was a kick.

Dog is ribbing me all the time in my ear. "I'm going to tell Pam."

As things begin to wind down Michael comes over to the table. He says since we are all full, tired, and probably a little inebriated, we should conduct our business in the morning. Yes, an excellent idea. My *room* is still available, so Dog and I will spend the night. Dog certainly won't mind; he is treated like a king here. We agree to meet for breakfast.

The next morning, we meet in a small conference room. A hearty breakfast is supplied, plus plenty of coffee and juice. These guys know how to eat. Present are Michael, George, Wolfgang, and me. Also, Dog of course. He does consider himself the brains of the outfit.

He probably is.

CHAPTER NINETEEN

Michael and George confirm what we already know. John's *contact,* Franklin Piece, is obviously a warmonger, as demonstrated during his time in our country's administration. Since then he has been outspoken about the United States not being the world power it should be. He has all but stated, certain countries should be made into *parking lots,* by using the *nuclear option, of course.* Franklin Pierce is associated with several like-minded wealthy and influential persons. Michael says this group includes some former Pentagon officials who may be behind un-official para-military organizations. This is scary stuff. George adds this group of former military leaders were always the ones who wanted to *push the button.* I though those guys were old and decrepit by now. Apparently, they may be older, but still feel this country should be *taking names and kicking ass.* They are basically endorsing a dictatorship rather than our democracy. They feel the public doesn't know what is going on in the world and since *they* do, they should be the leaders.

I know it is breakfast time but after hearing this frightening revelation I just want a drink and a stiff one. You see movies and TV shows about this stuff, but you just don't want to believe it could be real. Well, my fellow Americans, it is.

George agrees, Cranston does seem to be between a rock and a hard place. He has his job because of his contact, Piece, but does not want to be a part of *this* scheme. On top of that, he is apparently getting threatening phone calls on the encrypted phone line in his office. No idea who is making them. It appears the caller wants Cranston to stop the project. Stopping a project concerning a horrendous weapon by using death threats does not seem logical. The guys are stymied by this one. We talk for a while longer. They need to find out who is making the calls. The threatening calls don't last long and so far, the pint-size hackers have been unable to trace them.

I inform Michael and George I have a concern and a demand.

"What, David, whatever we can do we will," Michael says obviously concerned.

"I want to be able to turn off this implant when *I want to*. I don't need you guys monitoring me 24-7. It has been of great value to me in this job, but I do want some private time."

"Of course. I'm so sorry. We did not even think of that. Yes, you do not need us in your head or your private life all the time," Michael says. "We can add an off switch which you can activate. It will be your choice *when* to activate it."

"How about me? I get tired of your babble too." Dog speaks up.

"I guess we could do the same procedure for you too, but I'm not sure how you can do the switching."

"Yeah, no opposable thumbs. I know. You *brains* figure it out." Dog is feisty.

George asks Dog and me to just hang out for a while and they will get to work right away on the updated units.

Dog looks at me and winks. He trots off. Michael takes me to the Control Room, as the aliens call it, to wait. This room is the heartbeat of the caves. The entire underground living area can be run from this room. Ventilation, lights, security, and everything in between. This is apparently my monitoring station also. Now I really do feel naked.

All their computers, which link to the human world, are in here. This is where they can monitor Cranston's office, as well as the shows on the Vegas Strip, and pretty much anything else they want. The little technicians on duty show me how it all works. Impressive.

In talking with these guys, I learn they are younger than Michael and George and are considered middle aged by our standards. They say there are younger ones also. They were born after the aliens' ship crashed. The crew was mostly made up of married couples so having a child was normal. Because of the uncertainty of their status here on earth the group quickly decided not to produce anymore offspring. I ask what the *youngest* ones are doing. I am told they are being trained to take over the jobs of the older ones. One of the techs says some of the new generation want to go out into the real world. Bad idea he feels and has tried to reason with them.

"Besides there is the sun to consider, we may be cave dwellers, but we are not vampires. We can't live covered up all the time," He says.

He goes on to tell me there are also some activists among the younger ones, who feel the aliens should come out and be assertive in the Earth's politics, since they believe they are mentally superior. He tells me he is worried about this group. There is only a handful of the younger aliens in this bunch, but he considers them worrisome.

"Are Michael and George aware of them?" I ask.

"Yes, but I don't think they believe the younger ones are serious. I have mentioned them to both George and Michael, but they seem to dismiss them as just *children* with childish ideas. That's why I'm telling you about them. I know you are street wise. I have listened to you when you are dealing with people. You are in the real world. Michael and George are great leaders, but not of the outside world. Your world is not our world. You understand what is truly going on." He is talking quietly so the others in the room can't hear him.

Shit. Why not complicate this whole thing some more.

If only I hadn't wanted that dammed beer.

CHAPTER TWENTY

Dog and I get summoned to the medical suite. We are to get our new devices. I go first and just like the last time it takes only minutes. Out with the old and in with the new. A wave of the *healing wand* and I'm good as new.

Michael says I can turn the device on and off by pressing a certain spot behind my ear. I use Dog as a test. He can't hear me through his device. It works as advertised. Then it is Dog's turn. Michael says they made Dog's on/off button larger so he should be able to activate it with a paw. We are both cautioned to be careful when scratching behind our ears or we would be continually turning ourselves off and on. "More of a problem for Dog than me," I joke.

We then go to lunch and just enjoy the cavern life for a while before we need to head back to the apartment. I go back to the control room and play with the button in my head. I call Dog and then we both take turns switching them on and off. I am doing this for two reasons. I want to make sure they work correctly, and I also want to be sure when we switch them off, the *little ears* can't continue to hear us. I didn't get this far along by trusting, without verifying. Satisfied all is proper, I wander off to see what is on the big screen in the sports bar. Oh yeah, they have one of those too.

About an hour later Dog calls for me. I tell him where I'm at and he trots in.

He looks at me and hits his *off* button. I get the hint and do the same thing.

"Come with me. There is someone you need to meet." He whispers conspiratorially.

I follow as he leads me to one of the lounge rooms. The only one inside is a female alien. She seems to be one of the younger ones. Determining age is difficult with them as they do not wrinkle or show the usual signs of aging, we humans do. Maybe from staying out of the sun, I don't know. As I said before the females have cuter faces than the males. The males aren't *cute at all*. But the females are. She is dressed in a popular teen idol's tee shirt and shorts. Trendy running shoes complete the teenage style outfit.

"David I would like you to meet Michele," Dog says formally.

"Hi Michele, I'm pleased to meet you." She puts her hand out and shakes mine.

"I have been wanting to talk with you." She says somewhat shyly. "I talk with Dog a lot and he said we should meet."

"Uh, okay, what is this about?"

Michele tells me some of the younger males are much more rebellious than the elders believe. She basically tells me the same thing the tech in the control room told me. However, being younger, she is around these dissidents more and hears a lot more of what they are saying.

"They scare me," Michele says. "I have been telling Dog about them and he says you are the only one to talk with about this. I didn't know just how scary they were until the last few days. Dog has been gone with you and I was so glad you both came back last night. The elders won't listen to me and I don't know who to trust among the other kids. Everyone calls us the *kids*." Her voice is higher pitched than the males. Softer than Dorothy's though.

"When were you going to tell me about this, partner?" I look at Dog.

"Think about it, Sherlock. I am amazingly talented, but I can't write. My paws don't work a keyboard to good either. So if we had these devices in our heads, how was I going to talk to you, off the record? When you asked for the on-off switches I saw my chance. About time you carried your weight. I can't be the brains all the time." Dog blows out a large snort.

Michele giggles. Then puts her hands over her mouth. "I'm sorry but sometimes he's so funny."

"Yeah, he's a laugh a minute. But he makes a valid point." I acknowledge. "Michele, I appreciate your concern. Do you know anything specific these guys are planning? Or are they guys?"

"Yes, they are. There are six of them. They are extremely smart and have huge egos. They believe they can become a power in the outside world. They want to take over Earth and be the rulers."

She's got my attention now.

"Just how do they plan on accomplishing this? They may be smarter than earthlings, but we are not pushovers either."

"Something to do with a horrible weapon. Some kind of a force field or beam. It has something to do with how our ship was brought down when our parents first landed in Arizona. They call themselves *The Conquers*, and are careful not to say exactly what their plans are but after drinking, they will slip a little. I just listen and try to remember. They don't ever pay attention to me because one of them is my brother. I'm just a kid and not even there as far as they are concerned."

"Do these guys have any outside contacts?" I ask.

"Yes, someone who use to work here. A scientist, one of the Germans I think."

Holy Crap. Wilhelm Schultz I'll bet! While their parents were working on Area 51 projects these *kids* were reading the files.

"Michele, you have given me some explosive information. What you have just said meshes with things I have already learned. Are you in any danger being around them? Have you said anything to anyone else?" I am concerned now. If *The Conquers* are discussing these ideas, then what are they *capable* of doing?

"No, I haven't told anyone. I don't think any of the other kids would get it. My brother and his friends are loners. The others don't like them but probably don't think of them as actually being dangerous. I'm not in any danger as long as I just play dumb and don't ask questions."

"Now, Michele, be very honest with me. If they were to implement the sort of plan you are talking about, then innocent people would be injured or even killed. Are your brother and his friends capable of that kind of action? It goes beyond dreaming and making big talk. Would they follow through?"

She looks at me, tears starting to well up in her big eyes.

"Yes, I do believe in my heart they would do whatever they needed to do to make their plan work and they would have no pangs of guilt or remorse. I know they have snuck out at night into the desert and killed rabbits and other small animals, just to see how it felt. They would laugh about it when they came back."

"And they aren't aware you know about any of this?"

"No, I'm not right with them, usually I'm in another room or off to the side. I have exceptional hearing, you know, the *little shits* as Dog calls us." She smiles at Dog.

Dog starts to stutter, "Uh, well you know I just am joking and all, uh I like all you guys...."

Well, well, the brazen canine has embarrassed himself.

"Oh, it's okay Dog, I know you are just playing." Michele hugs the sputtering pooch.

"Look, Michele, I do not want to put you in any danger, but any information you learn would be vital in helping me stop *The Conquers,* along with stopping the weapon. It is a real project and it is being worked on right now, here at Area 51." I tell her.

Her eyes get even bigger.

"I thought it was something your government stopped a long time ago. Or so the elders have told us. Until the other day when my brother and his friends started talking about the German scientist. I didn't take them too seriously. It was not stopped then?"

"Yes, it was, but someone involved with *our* government now wants it completed. They can't do it without the German, Wilhelm Schultz is his name. He was the one who brought down your spaceship. Our government at the time fired him and closed the program. No one knows where he is now. Are you saying your brother's group has found him?"

"Yes, my brother has talked with him somehow. He was very excited when he told the others about it. We are not allowed to have any contact with anyone on the outside. I don't know how he did it, but his friends are all truly clever when it comes to electronics and computer stuff."

"Michele, you are a cute girl, don't any of his friends have any interest in you, as a, well, a friend?" I'm curious because the age difference here seems to be close.

"No. They are all, well, as you say here on Earth...gay. No interest in females at all." She says very matter-of- factly.

"Well, takes out the option of you infiltrating the group."

Now I'm faced with pale *skin-head* anarchists, who want to take over the world, using an old Nazi scientist. I *know* I still have a concussion.

Michele is more than willing to relay to me and Dog whatever information she can learn. I tell her she needs to have a code name so her real identity won't be known.

"Mickey, I want to be Mickey." She says.

"Have you ever been known as Mickey? That's close to Michele."

144

"No, I have always liked the name, but didn't tell anyone."

"How about your friends?"

"No, we all just use our given names. I haven't told anyone."

"Okay, Mickey it is! Agent Mickey please be careful. This is potentially dangerous stuff we are getting involved with. Please understand just how dangerous," I implore her.

"I know! I knew we needed help. That's why I told Dog about what was going on. We can stop this, can't we?" Her eyes are tearing up again.

"Yes Mickey, we will stop this," I say with confidence.

Please let it be true.

RJ Waters

CHAPTER TWENTY-ONE

We leave and Mickey heads back to her family. I've given her several ways to contact me or Dog if she gets any more information or if she thinks she is suspected by her brother's group.

We stay and have dinner with the cave people (trivial name for such a highly advanced species). I have decided not to say anything to Michael or George about what I learned today. Besides, we have no proof any of this is true. However, the circumstantial evidence is piling up.

After we finished dinner and are starting to leave the room, the tech from the control room comes up to me. His name is Brian. He was the one who said he was concerned about some of the younger aliens. He pets Dog and acts like he is just playing with him. He says quietly, if I need any help from him, he would be willing to assist. He tells us he is younger than the other techs. He works night shift a lot and can do some snooping on his own. Apparently, the control room has the ability to eavesdrop on the caves much more than the residents are aware. Only the leaders and a few techs know of this. And we thought *we* invented this.

"Brian, you are the NSA of the caves. All right, I could use some inside help".

"I consider it my duty to help my people; anyway I am able to assist."

I ask Brian just how secure my voice link to the control room is. He says the room has the only receiver and all six of the techs are very trustworthy. He says the young rebels have no connection to the room or with any of the techs. The security of the caves rest with them. They all take the responsibility very seriously. Michael and George are the only other personnel allowed inside the control room.

Dog and I make our way back to my apartment on the base. I need to put all of this in some sort of order. I pour myself a tall Crown and a Michelob for Dog, in a chilled bowl of course. Dog goes over and take a big slurp. "You know David, since I'm going to be hanging out with you maybe I should start drinking Coors Light. I've got to watch my waistline you know."

"Would Grizzie have anything to do with your sudden concern with your physique?" I reply as I take a sip.

"Smart ass." replies the canine. "You might want to think about your bulging gut yourself."

Making sure our buttons are in the *off* position, we discuss all we have learned and what resources we have available. I am a spymaster now. I have covert agents working for me. They may be short in stature, but they are definitely a big step up from what I had to work with in South America.

There is of course good old Eddie Benton, the EG&G Security Director. He owes me. Thomas, the EG&G security officer, and former DEA agent may also be helpful if needed. Then there is Pam. Ahhh, yes Pamela. She is another pair of eyes when she is on base. Also, a pleasant diversion from this mess. I hope she comes around often, I enjoy her company.

The immediate problem is to locate Wilhelm Schultz. If he has been contacted by Mickey's brother, then we need to find him... fast. Michael says they can't find him, and Wolfgang says he had no friends, so how did the geeky teens locate him, if they actually did?

Then there is the problem of John's *contact, boss or whatever* the hell he is. We know *who* he is now, but not exactly how he fits into all this. He seems to be able to pull strings to get research projects worked on by U.S. government scientists, but he is not in the listed chain-of-command for this division at Area 51. But then again *Area 51* doesn't officially exist either. I am mulling this mess over when there is a knock on my apartment door. Being the cautious type, I pick up my weapon and go to the peep hole. It is Wolfgang, the scientist and sort of grandfather to Dog. I open the door.

"Hi, I saw your light on and wondered if I could visit with Dog. I miss mine." He asks somewhat loudly.

"Yes, of course, come in. You are always welcome." He enters as I glance in the hallway and close the door.

"Actually, I need to talk with you. These days I am getting pretty paranoid so that is the reason for the ruse." Wolfgang utters.

"You mean you didn't want to see me?" Dog is indignant.

"Of course, I always want to see you, big guy. But I needed an excuse for my visit." He kneels and begins to pet the pathetic looking creature.

"I know Doc, I'm just teasing you." Dog says as he bounces around the scientist.

"What's going on Wolfgang?" I ask.

"This afternoon I received a telephone call here at my apartment. I don't get many. As I told you before, all of us scientists were pretty much just loaners wrapped up in our projects. I am still a member in some scientific societies and my home phone is listed as a contact. No address of course. The call was from one of the German scientists we all worked with during the war. He was one of the unlucky ones the Russians kidnapped." He takes a breath; he is obviously agitated.

"Wolfgang, can I get you something to drink?" I ask.

"Ya please, that would be nice. What are you having?" he points at my glass.

"Crown Royal, but I also have beer, cola and water."

"The whisky looks good."

"Neat or on the rocks?"

"Neat please."

I hand him a good pour. "Danke." He slips into his native tongue, now and then. With glass in hand the scientist continues to tell us about his phone call.

The German on the phone told Wolfgang he had recently arrived in America. He had been working for the Russians throughout the cold war and then was allowed to leave. He had been living in Switzerland, but now he has moved to the U.S. and he is trying to locate any of his old friends.

Wolfgang snorted: "He had no friends! He was possessed! He was a Nazi, through and through! Most of us worked for the German war effort because of fear for our lives and threats against our families. Friedrich Hoffman loved his work for the Fuhrer." Wolfgang takes a large sip of the whiskey then wipes his bushy mustache. "I'm sorry for the outburst. I haven't gotten so emotional for years. Hearing his voice brought it all back."

"Understandable. Apology not needed." I say. "If you two were not friends then why did he call you?"

"He was asking what I was working on now. I told him "Nothing important, besides, you know I can't tell you." He asked if it was the force field research Schultz was developing with him when they were in Germany. He said he had *heard* Schultz had been working on it in the U.S. I told him Schultz blew up the equipment and the project was closed. That was partially true. After he brought down the alien's spaceship, the power gird he used literally melted down."

"Was he trying to hit the aliens' ship?"

"Nein, he did not even know about it until later. He was fascinated by the magnetic fields concentrated around Sedona. Schultz was trying to use the beam from here to deflect the magnetic fields. He thought if he could deflect them then he would be able to use the magnetic field for a super weapon. All of Area 51 was shut down for over a week because he had somehow been able to tie all the electricity from miles around into his giant generator for his force beam. The generator also exploded. Thank God. Schultz wanted to rebuild it, but he was eventually fired.

He brought attention to this place the government did not want. It was covered up by saying the power outage had something to do with the atomic testing the government was doing at the time. We were able to blame a lot of our mistakes on the Test Center." He smiles and takes another sip of his drink.

"Hoffman said he wanted to get together with his old associates. He asked about a couple of the others who had worked here at Area 51 with me. I told him they had died. Which is true. What I thought was interesting, he did not ask about Schultz. He did give me a telephone number if I wanted to get together sometime." Wolfgang reaches into his shirt pocket and pulls out a piece of paper with a telephone number on it. He hands it to me. "I looked up the area code." He says and gives me a wink. "It is in Sedona, Arizona. And I will bet he is with Schultz, that's why he didn't ask me about him."

I take a long pull on my drink.

CHAPTER TWENTY-TWO

Wolfgang stays for a while and relaxes. He has moved to the couch so Dog can be *a lap dog*. Dog just rolls around and squirms in his lap. The German scratches Dog's ears and ruffles his fur. Dog loves his *grandpa*. My big fierce partner is still just a puppy. Kind of cute.

Wolfgang is profoundly serious about helping to stop the project and the two other Germans. He says he will do whatever I ask. Even if it means putting himself in danger.

"I know what it is to not have freedom. I may be old, but I will fight to save it. My people should have resisted when Hitler started his rule. I was young then and did not believe in his flaming rhetoric, but I did nothing." He says. "This is a threat to our society and Schultz and Hoffman are as evil as they ever were during the war. Probably more so now, with what you have told me about them connecting with the younger aliens. The aliens do have superior brains compared to us. I have always been in awe of them. Until now, I had no worries; the alien scientists we worked with were very ethical. Sadly, sometimes more so than us." Wolfgang takes another long drink. Then he looks imploring at me, "Are Michael and George oblivious to the young ones or maybe just don't want to believe their children could be so warped?"

"I'm not a history expert here but I think all societies through the ages have experienced their youth's rebellion and desire for change. Look at the world around us today. Why should the aliens be any different? I bet Michael and George were rabble-rousers in their day." I say chuckling at the thought of staid old Michael and George being troublemakers.

Speaking of the *leaders of the alien pack*, I need to get them involved in the latest information regarding the two scientists. I'm not ready to tell them about *The Conquers*. That needs to wait until I have convincing evidence. Wolfgang agrees not to say anything.

After Wolfgang leaves, I hit my *on* button and Brian answers. He says he is alone. I ask Brian to get Michael for me. He does. When Michael comes on the line, I tell him about the two Germans and the possibility of their being together in Sedona.

He is noticeably upset by this news. I give him the phone number Wolfgang got from Hoffman. Michael will hopefully find out the physical location. He says he will have his Brian get right on it. We discuss what to do about this new twist. I say I must go to wherever the phone is located and see if I can confirm the presence of the Germans. While we are still talking, *NSA Brian* gives us our answer. That was fast.

The phone is a landline from a house in Sedona, Arizona. Almost too easy. But if they have no idea anyone is aware of their plans, why would they hide?

George has now also joined Michael and they suggest we take the Smart Car and fly down to the area at night. We can get a close-up view without being noticed.

"Who's driving?" I ask.

"Not me." George sighs. "One little miscalculation and they never let you live it down."

"Miscalculation my ass." I say indignantly. "You almost killed me."

"My bad, I am truly sorry." George says.

Michael says he will drive and since space is limited it will be just me and him.

"Dog too." I demand. "If I have to get on the ground, I want him along. I know you can stuff him in the back."

"Stuff *your* ass in the back, it's not comfortable." gripes my furry partner.

Ignoring the whining dog, Michael asks when I want to go.

"Well since you're driving and it's after dark, how about now? I've had a little adult beverage, but I feel good."

Dog snorts. "A little adult beverage? How many did you and the Doc put away? I'll bet you *feel good!* Hey Michael, have you been drinking tonight? I got to look out for myself you know."

"I'm fine Dog. One wine with dinner. I could go now."

We agree and Dog and I slip out of the apartment and make our way toward the cave entrance. It is quite dark; the moon is barely coming up. Then I hear, "Over here."

It's Michael. He has the Smart Car sitting on the ground right in front of us. I was about to walk right into the damn thing. I'm barely able to make it out in the darkness. Dog squeezes into the back grumbling the whole time, I get into the passenger seat and we take off.

Dog is complaining as we reach altitude. "Take it easy man, I've got nothing to hold onto back here."

"Dog, quit your complaining, I've got my knees in my chest, at least you can stand up." Damned short legged driver.

It only takes minutes to reach Sedona. Michael has programmed the location of the house into some sort of GPS-like device he has in the car. We find the house and hover over it. Then Michael slowly eases the car downward. We are now about fifty feet above the building. It is a simple A-frame type of cabin, Located on a narrow road on the outskirts of Sedona. No near-by neighbors. There is an older Mercedes-Benz in front of the house.

"My God." Michael exclaims. "It is the same car Wilhelm Schultz had at Area 51 when he worked there, I'd swear to it."

"Hey, Benz's are built to last," I remark.

We continue to scan the house and yard. There is a concrete block building in the rear. It is about twenty feet by sixty feet, single story. The last twenty feet look newer than the rest. There are windows in the older part and none in the newer part. The rear yard is quite neat. Flowers, bushes, a stone path, nicely done.

Michael says Schultz was also into horticulture while at Area 51. He kept a tidy garden outside his apartment.

"I'd say from the circumstantial evidence in front of us, we have found Schultz, my professional opinion." I declare with authority.

"You never cease to amaze me, Sherlock!" Dog says sarcastically. "Can we go now?"

Michael is fiddling with some of his gadgets in the dashboard.

"I am able to use our infrared scanning and have found two life forms in the house. None in the rear building. The persons I would say are watching television. That is what my readings say. There is an electronic device emitting waves consistent with a television." Michael says.

"So, what are they watching, hotshot?" Dog is on a roll tonight.

I ask where the *life forms* are in the house. Michael says they are in the front portion.

"I'd like to try and get a look at the rear concrete building. Can we land to the back, in the open area, so Dog and I can sneak up on the building?"

"Oh sure, stuff the dog in the back, jostle him around and then decide he is useful. I didn't hear 'I could use your marvelous talents. Please Dog.' Did I?"

"Just how much beer did you have tonight fuzz butt?" I tease.

Despite the bickering of his crew, Michael lands us to the rear of the German's yard, in a large field. After we get out, Michael will rise and keep watch on the *life forms* for any movement. It is pitch black out. I do have a flashlight but don't want to use it. It would be a like a beacon in the darkness.

Dog and I ease up to the building. There is a door in the older part along with the windows. I look in one of the windows. I can see the glow of electronic devices. Nothing seems to be moving but there appears to be a lot of equipment of various sorts. I try the door handle, it's locked. Damn, I didn't bring my *Mission Impossible* lock picks and I don't see anything I can use to *MacGyver* the door open. He always found some item to use, why can't I?

Wait; if Schultz is a gardener then he must have garden tools somewhere. There is a small shed on the far side of the yard. Worth a look. It is not locked. We go inside and I find some garden tools. I pick up a couple which might work.

I whisper to Michael and ask if he can determine if there is any kind of alarm on the building. He says he does not have that capability from the car.

Okay, so here goes. I use a tool with a tine on it and manage to push the bold open on the door. Not a high security lock. I ease the door open just a crack. Nothing, no sound. Michael says the two life forms are still not moving. I open the door and let Dog and myself in.

Cupping my now useable flashlight I look around the room. It is crammed full of electronic gadgets, along with computers and printers. It is a lab for serious work. In the middle of the room is a device which looks menacing. It has a large barrel-like tube pointing toward the far end of the room in the newer area. The area in-between is open with nothing in it. At the end wall area is a pile of twisted and melted metal.

That bastard Schultz is still trying to develop his beam weapon!

Then Michael excitedly shouts, "One of the persons is moving toward the back of the house."

I turn off my light and move to the door. I ease it open. I see a light come on in the back of the house. It looks like a bathroom window to me. I wait. In a couple of minutes, the light goes out. Michael says the person has gone back to the front again. Must have been a commercial pee break.

I take out my cellphone, turn on the camera, and take a few quick photos of the room. Hope no one in the house noticed the flashes. Now it is absolutely time to leave. Dog and I slide out, replace the bolt, take the garden tools back, and place them exactly where I found them. Then back to the field and into the waiting Smart Car.

Michael is breathing heavily. "I am just not use to this kind of tension. How do you do it?"

Before I can answer Dog speaks up, "**He** uses booze. **Me**, it's just who I am."

CHAPTER TWENTY-THREE

After arriving back at *cave international airport*, we immediately head to the control room. Michael takes my camera and downloads the photos I took inside the rear building. He puts them up on a large computer screen.

"Well." Michael exclaims. "The bastard has built a small version of his force beam. He has been testing it on those pieces of metal at the end of the room. If he and Hoffman are together then heaven only knows what they can build."

"More like *hades* only knows. They are both depraved." George pipes in.

While we were out playing ninjas, Brian has been busy doing what he does best, snooping. He checked the assessors' lists for Sedona. Wilhelm Schultz purchased the house two years ago. The car we saw parked in front of the house is registered to Schultz.

Friedrich Hoffman legally entered the United States one month ago. He came in on a business visa from Switzerland. He listed Schultz's Sedona address on his paperwork as the location he would be visiting. His visa is only good for six months.

Even though we have travelled to Arizona and back, it is still early, eleven-thirty. The Smart Car is truly amazing, astonishing speed, fully pressurized and stealthy. What is not to love? I need to question Michael. Why did they chose the Smart Car over some other model of automobile? Michael replies the structure allowed them to install their own power plant and equipment. All this without effecting the appearance of the exterior, so it is useable on a public road. No one would notice the difference. The wheels turn while not providing any power. The seat can be adjusted for height and moved forward so the diminutive driver can see out. There are no pedals, only controllers like a video game. With the seats moved forward, there is *Dog* space. Okay, makes sense.

The big guy and I head back to our apartment. Even after all this, we still have to go to work in the morning.

First thing the next day I call Wolfgang at his apartment and offer him a ride to his workplace. I want to fill him in on what we found last night.

The good doctor looks at my photos of the beam gun or whatever it is called.

"It is just as Michael said. Schultz, probably with Hoffman's assistance, has built a small version of the force beam. *Dies is nicht gut!*" he says with a harsh Teutonic accent. "With a portable power source, they could do a lot of damage. If more weapons were to be made, then the potential would be terrifying. They must be stopped!" He is highly agitated.

I tell the old German we *will* stop them... Just how, I do not know, yet.

He looks out the window and then at me, "I may know someone who can help you."

"I'm all ears."

"I have been going over all of this in my mind. You need to speak with Charles Renshaw."

"Who is he? Wait is he Cranston's predecessor?"

"Yes, he was a good administrator and had the country's best interest at heart. Which is why he tried to block the project. Pierce had him forced into retirement. We have kept in touch. I do not know if he can assist but I'm sure he would be willing to talk to you, in private, of course." I agree to talk to Renshaw. Wolfgang will give him my cell number. This should be interesting. I thank the German and drop him off at his workplace. I go to my office. John is already there. Early for him.

"David, thank God, you're here. I need to talk with you. Let's go for a ride." Seems like all I am doing lately is riding somewhere.

We get into my truck with Dog in the rear seat….Hey, he didn't call shotgun. I can tell Dog feels John's stress too.

"What's up John?" I ask.

"I received another threatening phone call on my government cell phone last night at home. It was much worse than the others. This male voice said if I did not shut down the project and padlock the building my wife and family would suffer a horrible death. He emphasized the building should be locked down with the atrocious equipment left inside, so no one would have access to it. The threats have never been specific before. He said I had until the end of the week or they would be killed."

"You have family John? I don't remember you or Doris saying anything about kids."

"No. We do not have any children. Our parents are both dead, Doris has a sister who lives in Florida, but that's all."

"So, the person making the call doesn't have true information on you. He is using a bluff assuming you have more family than just a wife. A reasonable assumption for someone your age."

"Yes. He called me *Mr*. Cranston."

"How did the person speak, good English, slang, accent?"

"There was no accent, seemed to be a younger voice, not a kid, just young. He spoke English, but more casual not formal. He did seem cocky as well as threatening. And I may be wrong, I was getting upset, but I swear I heard a male voice giggle in the background."

In my *device,* I hear George saying they will be checking to see if any information can be obtained from John's cell. The control room was not monitoring him last night; but there will be a recording they can recover. George will get back to me.

I tell John I will do some checking on his phone and try to find out where the call came from.

"You can do that? It showed as a *restricted caller*."

"I have some sources," I say. "In the meantime, I think it is time to add to our team. We need another body on board."

"Whatever you say. Tell me who you want, and I will make it happen."

I tell him that I need to see if my man *wants* the job first. I take John back to his office, and I go into mine. Dog goes treat hunting, after he thoroughly checks our offices.

I know this case has its twists and turns but one at a time, *please*. The threatening caller was not either of the German scientists, Hoffman or Schultz. They both have distinct accents, I am told. John's *contact* wants him to push the project, so he does not seem to be a likely suspect either. Besides, from the voice on recordings, he is older sounding. Who can it be threating John? The caller wants the project shut down and padlocked. Hmmm. I wonder. He is acting as if he is against the horrible project but does not ask it to be destroyed. I need to talk with my NSA greenie, Brian. Not on shift yet, I will get hold of him later.

Next item is to talk with Thomas, the ex-DEA agent who works for EG&G. I place a phone call.

"Benton," a voice answers.

"Eddie. Hi, it's David Manning, remember me?" I say in a genuinely friendly voice.

"Please don't call me Eddie. Yes, David I remember you. What can I do for you?"

"How's everything going?" I ask.

"Quite well in fact. I do thank you for your *insight* when you visited." He seems to mean it.

"I would like to speak with your security officer Thomas, you know, from the airport. I enjoyed his company during my flights. I wanted to ask him about something he mentioned when we were talking. Could you tell me when he will be on a flight landing here so I could chat with him for a couple of minutes?" I ask in the most nonchalant way I can. I could go to the airport myself, but time is of the essence here.

Eddie checks the schedules.

"He will be on the flight landing there at 1400 hours today."

"If it's all right with you, I would like a minute with him."

"Sure, no problem, the plane will be on the ground for at least thirty minutes."

"Thanks, Ed. I appreciate it."

"Hey why don't you stop by when you're in town, maybe we can have lunch? My treat," he says.

Excellent, that means he made good use of the *bug* that Dog found in his office. I tell him I will call him next time I'm there.

1400 hours is 2:00 p.m. in civilian terms. I will go ask Thomas if he wants a career change. My clandestine associate's background checks on him came up clean. He was a field agent, not a desk jockey. Good reviews, a couple of minor incidents. If you do not ruffle some feathers in that type of job, you are not doing your job. Just look at my record. No! Let's not.

At 2:00 p.m. I am sitting at the landing strip with Dog, as the red-striped 737 pulls up. After the passengers (employees) get off I send Dog up the stairs. I hear the crew calling to him. "Hey where have you been big guy?" I go up the stairs as Thomas is petting Dog. We shake hands. I ask him to come on down to my truck.

"Good to see you again, David." He says. "How's it going here?"

"I'll cut to the chase. I need some good help here. Would you be at all interested in leaving the Seven Dwarfs and becoming one of the Three Musketeers?"

"I'm assuming you are not talking about standing around in a uniform checking ID's?"

"I need an assistant. This job is more involved than I expected. Your experience would be just what we need. You would be a DOD agent, like me.

Dog looks at me and shakes his head causing his badge dances around.

"Yes, and like Dog. We would be the three Musketeers." I shoot a look at the sassy shepherd.

Thomas laughs. "It's like he understands you. Hell yes, I would give anything to get out of the rent-a-cop game."

I tell him to be careful what he asks for. Then I give him a *brief* overview of the job. The death threats against Cranston mainly. I leave out the aliens, talking dogs, death rays, trivial stuff. I will ease him into those things along the way.

Thomas asks some questions and says he will have to talk it over with his wife.

"I would like to leave EG&G. I feel I am wasted in this job. If I have to work, it should be at something I have been trained to do. I will get back to you tomorrow. If that's all right?"

"Absolutely, I need you to be sure. Talk with your wife. Could be some nights and weekends you know." I caution.

I leave Thomas and head back to the office. Michael comes on and says we need to talk as soon as possible. Michael says he only wants to talk in private and in person. I wonder if he listened to the recording of John's phone call and recognized the voice. We agree to meet after dark at the cave entrance. He does say we should be in the *off* position. He is truly worried if he does not want our *devices* to be *on*.

Back at the office, I tell John I will have someone else for our team soon. I am confident that Thomas cannot resist the call to duty and maybe some action. After having a career in law enforcement, he must be dying a slow death at EG&G. I know I would be. John seems to be somewhat relieved. I tell him he is safe for the week anyway. Small comfort I know.

CHAPTER TWENTY-FOUR

After dinner, Dog and I go to the entrance to the cave. As we approach, I hear Michael, "over here David."

He is standing away from the cave door.

"Jeeze Michael. Do you *always* have to be hiding in the dark?"

"I need to talk with you, completely alone. Let us walk." He is speaking very quietly, and his voice is strained.

Dog pipes up: "Wow shorty, take a breath, I've never seen you this uptight."

We walk away from the cave door and Michael stops and takes a seat on a large rock. "I'm sorry but when I listened to the tape of the threat to Cranston I almost fainted. I know who called him." He takes a breath and continues, "It was Brandon, one of our own."

"You sure?"

"I am positive!" He says with conviction. "I should know his voice; he is my nephew. His father was my older brother, who died a few years ago. I check in with my sister-in-law and the two children all the time. Brandon is one of the young ones I told you about who want to go out into the world. My brother was able to keep him in line. His younger sister, Michele, has told me before she was worried about Brandon and his friends. She said they were scary and were talking about doing crazy things. I admit I did not worry. Young adults, you know, they get ill-advised ideas, and then they grow out of them. I did."

"So, what do you make of this?" I ask.

"I just don't know. Why would he make such a call, to Cranston, to anyone for that matter?" Michael says.

"How was Brandon able to get into Cranston's government phone or even find the number? Do any of them have access to the control room? What was your brother's function here?" I need answers. Nothing is secure here now.

"My brother was a research scientist like George and me. We all worked on the various projects at Area 51. No, the security of the control room has always been very tight. My brother was never allowed in there. George and I, as the leaders of the expedition, were the only ones allowed in, along with the technicians who were assigned there. The technicians are starting to get older so we brought Brian in a couple of years ago to be sure security would remain intact. He is the youngest."

"So how did they get access to Cranston's phone and who knows what else?" I am pressing hard.

"I know our children are every bit as intelligent as we elders. Possibly more so. We have always emphasized technology in our schooling. The children are always building robots, various other electronic devices, for fun. We encourage it. These are very bright children, well actually, young adults. I can see it would be a challenge to them, especially if they were unhappy with their potential future here in the caves. We do have strict rules. They are not to attempt to make any outside contacts. But apparently they did."

More than you know Michael.

"Have you said anything to them?" I ask.

"No. I haven't even told George. I listened to the phone call with earphones. The techs in the room didn't even hear. David, I have to ask you, do you think this has anything to do with Schultz and Hoffman?"

Even in the darkness I can see his eyes, they are wide and imploring.

"Michael, why would you think this has anything to do with the Germans?" I am curious as to his thinking here.

"Because Michele told me her brother and his friends wanted to go out into the world and be a powerful influence. I dismissed the idea then, but now with the Germans showing up, building the weapon, I am worried too. My brother worked on various projects. At that time, we would allow our children to come along while we worked. They were smart and absorbed what they saw. We all worked at one time or another in the building where Schultz's project was housed. We aliens never worked with Schultz because we objected to the nature of his project. The notes, plans, and results of his experiments were still in the files. Our children being children would look through the files. We adults were not aware of their snooping at first. When we found out what they were reading we stopped allowing them to come with us." He relates.

"The top-secret files were just open and available for anyone to read?" I ask incredulously.

171

"Yes, because the entire building was under such tight security only a very few people were allowed in." Michael says.

"But your children could *come and go*? Doesn't sound like *tight security*."

"We had our own tunnel entrance from our caves and there was no other check point. We were responsible for our own people. We thought it was a good learning experience for the children to go to work with the parents. In hindsight, not such a smart idea." He is shaking his overly large head.

"Why didn't you tell George about Brandon? You two are the power here." I'm curious.

"I was afraid to say anything inside the caves. I have to wonder just what else Brandon and his friends have tapped into. I'm getting paranoid. I wanted to bring George tonight but if someone saw us both leave, I don't know, David I am afraid like I have never been afraid before. Including crashing our ship into Roswell. I did ask George to stay in the control room until I came in. I don't know what to do now. I'm the leader of my people and do not know what to do!" He is in tears.

Good old Dog, he nuzzles up against Michael, trying to make him feel better. "Hey Michael, we'll work this out. David and I will get this handled for you guys. Trust us. I trust David, I've seen him in action, and we can do this. Right David?" Dog says with conviction.

"Yes, we will handle this Michael. It may not be pretty, but we have to handle it. There is too much at stake for all our peoples." I answer. "Michael, are you going to tell George?"

"Oh yes, he has to know. Right now, I think our whole groups' future depends upon George and me, along with you and Dog." Michael reaches out to Dog and pets him. "David what do you suggest we do next?"

"I think we need to *bug* the Germans and try to learn exactly what they are up to and with whom. Can you make something we can attach to the outside of their house, so we don't have to enter?" I ask. My mind is racing to keep all this in order so I can stay ahead of the developments.

Michael is thinking.

"Yes of course we can. Probably the best would be several devices so both buildings are covered. We can do this." Good he is back on his game. We need him and so do his people.

I must ask. "So how secure do you think you are now? Have these kids compromised your security and communications?"

"No, I certainly don't believe so. I was just getting caught up in the moment, finding out it was one of ours, *my* nephew made the call. We have enough encrypting and safeguards the control room would detect if the main systems were breached. As far as them going to the outside, to Cranston's phone or to the Germans, yes, they could do that, with the proper equipment. Your human *hacker* kids have already done similar stuff."

"All right, then we will proceed with the assumption your *kids* are unaware we know what they have done, namely calling Cranston. We will put the listening devices on the Germans and see where that goes." I don't want to tell him I know the control room can eavesdrop on

173

the cave populace. I'm not going to *burn* Brian. I have good feelings about him, and I have stayed alive in the past by listening to my *inner feelings*. I ask, "Michael, is it possible for your control room system to perhaps *check in* on Brandon and his friends at times, to see what they are up to?"

Michael goes for the bait.

"Yes, we can monitor our people much more than they are aware of. I am not proud of it, but with our situation here on Earth, George and I agreed such a system should be put in place in case we needed it. I have noticed Brandon and his group are more active in the later hours and even at times all night. I'll have Brian, I think you met him, he works nights in the control room, check in on them."

"Yes, I met Brian, appears to be a conscientious guy. I agree that would be a good idea, Michael."

That worked out perfectly. I love it when a plan comes together. I feel like I should be puffing on a cigar at this moment, but I do not smoke.

CHAPTER TWENTY-FIVE

The next morning when John arrives at work, I tell him to call his *contact*. I want him to tell this person about the attacks on me, the spying admin aide, and the threatening phone calls. John does not know his wife's lover was responsible for one of the calls and he doesn't need to know. Would serve no purpose. However, if John tells his man about everything that has occurred and it all seems to be linked back to the CIA, NSA, Arlington Virginia area, the *contact* might have some idea about who is behind it. After all, he is the one who suggested John hire some *muscle* for protection.

John's usual procedure to get hold of the gentleman is to send an encrypted e-mail, then wait for a phone call on his supposedly secure phone. Within ten minutes of the e-mail, John's phone rings. He answerers and begins to tell the party on the other end what has happened. It is obvious, from where I am sitting, the man is outraged by the incidents. He is loudly ranting and raving about someone. I can hear the words: *bastards, sons of bitches* and others I can't quite make out.

He and John talk for a while and after John hangs up, he looks at me. "I've never heard Frank so upset." This is the first time he has used his contact's name in front of me. Franklin happens to be the first name of the man the *aliens* identified as being the *contact*. So far so good.

Frank told John he knew who was behind the troubles. It was someone from another one of the un-named black ops groups which seem to breed in the D.C. area. Frank said this other person was trying to find out what Frank was up to now at Area 51. He had to be responsible for the admin aide and the attacks on me. Frank also said EG&G would work for anyone who paid them off. Therefore, as far as Frank was concerned, everything is coming from his competition in the sleazy world of government contracts, secrets, etc. Frank told John not to worry, he would *take care of it.*

For the moment that takes care of one segment of my problems. I am going to assume Franklin Pierce is probably correct. This is a spy vs. spy turf war.

My next move is to get the *bugs* into the Germans *lair.* Along with Michael condoning the eavesdropping on the teen rebels, should allow us to take control.

I leave John to do whatever it is he does and go into my office. Dog has already given me the nod of approval for the privacy of the room. Can't be too careful. Things change quickly around here.

About 10 a.m. my cell rings, it is an unlisted number, but so is mine. I answer, "Manning"

A muted male voice says, "A mutual friend says we should meet."

Okay, here we go, is this Wolfgang's friend? "Go on, I'm listening."

The voice is hesitant, "I must be certain no one will follow you."

"Not a problem, that's how I spend most of my days," I assure him. "Where would you be comfortable meeting?"

"There is an old bar on Sahara, west of the strip, Rocco's. It is quiet this time of day. Could you be there at 1500 hrs.? And please bring Dog; I'd like to see him again."

"1500, we'll be there." The phone disconnects.

If this is Wolfgang's friend, the former director, why is he so paranoid? I guess I will find out.

Dog look at me from the couch he has now claimed. "Was that Charles?"

"Yes, he wants to see you. Does he know you talk?"

"No, he just liked me. Always brought me treats every morning. Nice guy."

I tell John I have a lead in Vegas I need to follow up. Then I call Michael. He answers and tells me George is there too. "You guys hear all the call?"

"Yes, be careful David. Charles was our friend when he was here. However, there is some reason he is so cautious. We never got to say good-bye to him. He was just abruptly---escorted off the property."

"I'll be my usual paranoid self, besides Dog will be along. Now to the present business, is the tunnel to the Schultz project still there?"

"Yes, it is. Both entrances have been sealed off, but the tunnels remain." Michael apprises me.

"Checked them lately?"

"George and I went there last night. All appears in order. No sign of tampering. We had the same thoughts."

"Can you place a camera with a motion sensor to cover the entrance?"

"Already done. Are we starting to think like humans yet?" George is giggling at his own joke.

"I'm proud of you two. Good work. Now how about the bugs for our friends?"

"Ready when you are. Tonight good for a trip?" Michael inquires.

We agree to meet after dark. I ask Michael not to *suddenly appear* in front of me in the dark as he seems prone to do.

I want to visit Wolfgang at the lab. I will have time to make my clandestine meeting if I hurry. It is the same building where Schultz worked. I need to see the *sealed* off tunnel for myself.

As I am driving over to the worksite my cell phone rings. It is Thomas. My new recruit, I hope.

"Thomas, what's going on?" I ask.

"I talked with my wife and even with the possibility of nights and weekends she gave her blessing. My wonderful woman knows how much I hate my present job."

178

"Bless her. Thank her for me Thomas. I'll do my best to keep the hours reasonable. Welcome aboard *The Titanic*, no just kidding. When can you start?"

"I owe EG&G notice, they have been fair with me. I'll talk with Benton and see what I can work out."

Thomas is a good man, hates his job, but wants to do the right thing.

"How about I call Ed for you?" I ask.

"You know him?"

"More than he is comfortable with. I'll call and let you know what he says."

I immediately call Eddie and outright tell him I want to hire Thomas and how soon could he let him go, as a *favor for an old friend*.

"How much longer is this *favor for an old friend* thing going to go on?" He is actually laughing. "I suspected as much when you wanted to talk with him. Yeah, you can have him; he is way overqualified for this job. Let me have him for one more day and he's yours. I happen to be in good shape staff wise. I know you will want him to be able to take the flights to Area 51, so I'll put him on the list"

"Yes, and thank you, Ed. I see no further favors in the near future, but you never know."

"I'm still buying lunch."

I call Thomas back and tell him to be on the 8:00 a.m. plane to Area 51, day after tomorrow.

"What do you have on Benton?" He probes. "Never mind David, I probably don't want to know."

"See you when the plane lands, Tom."

I arrive at the lab. Dog jumps out and makes a quick perimeter check. I know there is security inside, but the way this job is going, you cannot be sure of anything. We go inside and up to the security desk. I engage the officer in small talk to give Dog time to get the feel of the place. We've been here before, but Dog will know if anything has changed. He seems comfortable and we go in to see Number One, the security chief for Cranston's project. He is relaxed and we chat a bit. I ask for another tour of the place.

"I know you showed me before but now I'm more settled and want to take it all in," I offer as an explanation.

Number One tells me he is happier since I came on board because he can stay over in the project building and not have to go back and forth to handle things for Cranston in the main office building.

"How's he doing?" Number One asks. "He was getting kinda goofy there for a while. Seemed to think everyone was after him."

"He's a lot better." I answer. "We straightened out a couple of problems, so he has settled down." I lie.

"Good. Cranston was pretty mellow at first but after he became chief, he seemed to get stressed a lot."

We make the tour of the project. Wolfgang is working with two other scientists. Dog of course goes over to Grandpa. Soon the three scientists are fawning over the beast. He loves it.

I ask Number One about the tunnel entrance. He looks blankly at me. He doesn't know about any tunnel he says. In my head I hear Michael telling me Number One was not working in this part of the area when the tunnel was being used. It has been sealed for several years.

"I was just wondering, I heard there were tunnels all over Area 51," I cover. "Since the building is set into the side of the mountain, I just was curious."

"There were several used for the nuclear tests, but they were way over to the west." He explains patiently to me

I tell Number One I will get Dog and chat with the scientists before I leave, so I won't take him from his work. He gets the hint and goes back to his office.

Back in the lab I get Wolfgang's eye. He leaves the others and comes over to me. I act like I'm asking about the project and lead him off.

"Do you know about a tunnel into here from the caves?" I ask quietly.

"Oh yes. Follow me." He leads me to a back portion of the lab; behind some drapes is a large dark area. I follow him into the space. It goes back into the mountain quite a way. He switches on some lights. The end of the area looks a lot like the rear of the building at Schultz's place, only much larger and deeper. There is a lot of melted metal lying on the ground.

Wolfgang looks at me: "Yes, this is what Schultz is trying to do in the pictures you showed me. We do not use this area. We also don't seem to be *able* to further develop the machine he had here. On purpose! I have dismantled what was left of it. There is nothing of use to anyone here." He smiles proudly.

"What about the tunnel?"

"It is over here." He leads me to a place on the left side of the area near the back. You can clearly see there was an opening, at one time. It was about five feet in height. It seems to be permanently sealed and has not been disturbed. I call for Dog to leave his audience and come. He does and declares the area seems undisturbed to him.

"No pasty ones have been here, for a long, long time." He wiggles his nose.

"Glowing, radiant, even pallid, but not pasty, please." Says Michael in our heads.

"Whatever." Replies the sarcastic canine.

Now we rush down to the Las Vegas Strip for our meeting. Dog is happily hanging his head out the window and processing all the wondrous odors the desert has to offer.

The bar is not in the best of areas. 'Off the strip' means mostly old. Mixed in-between various commercial and retail buildings I find Rocco's. It has been here a long time. Could use some paint but probably couldn't stand the extra weight. If it looks bad on the outside, wonder what the interior is like. Well, time to go in.

I pull open the door and then remove my sunglasses. It is a typical dark, dingy bar. On the left is a long bar with two customers seated halfway down. Booths run down the right side and across the back. The bartender looks up startled, and then looks toward a gray-haired man sitting in a corner booth at the far end of the room. The man nods to the bartender and waves to me. Dog walks slightly ahead and I can hear his deep breathing as he is processing the odors. The two men at the bar do not even look up. They are in deep conversation about baseball. Also, deeply into their beers as the words are not coming out well.

The man motioned me to have a seat. Dog sticks his head under the table and then winks at me. 'It's clear.' I motion Dog to jump onto the seat and go toward the man. I then take a seat. Charles Renshaw reaches out to pet Dog and give him a hug. "How you doing big guy. I heard he's taking good care of you." Dog gives him a big lick.

The man then extends his hand across to me, "Glad to meet you Mr. Manning. Wolfgang has nothing but praise for your work." Firm solid grip. His face shows the results of years of governmental service. Sagging jowls, bags under the eyes. He is tired. Also appears troubled, keeps looking toward the door.

"I wasn't followed, I can assure you. Mr. Renshaw."

"Call me Charles, please. I am worried Mr. Manning."

"David. Why are you worried?"

"Franklin Pierce... he is out of control. I used to think I knew him, but when this project began, Pierce became obsessed with it. He used to be just in the background and never seemed to care what went on here. Then after we fired Schultz, he came at me with this beam project. My God, Schultz almost took down all of Area 51s electrical power and could have killed himself. I went straight to the Director and demanded we get rid of Schultz. Pierce was furious. I later found out he was visiting Schultz on a regular basis without even a courtesy checking in with me."

"Wasn't Pierce your boss back then?"

"Not really, he was only an advisor, I thought. After the Schultz incident, there were some behind the scenes changes in D. C. Pierce suddenly became my superior. Never explained to me."

"How did John Cranston play into this?"

Charles sighs, "John was here because the CIA needed to find a place where he couldn't do any harm. He screwed up a couple of big operations. One night over a few too many drinks, John told me Pierce was the driving force in those ops and he pushed John into making hasty decisions. By saving John it gave Pierce a puppet for later use. Turns out John did not want to cooperate either. He played the game much smarted than I did. He just kept giving Pierce lip service. Project was online, had a delay, unforeseen problems, etc. Lucky for him you came along."

"So why do you think Franklin Pierce changed into the apparent war-monger he has become?"

Charles is quiet for a minute, then shaking his head says, "The whole group running the government back then, never gave up, and kept planning for their *place in the sun*. I heard them talk, but I didn't think they meant a government takeover."

"Why do you think that now?"

"Franklin Pierce basically said so. He hastily changed his tone and laughed after he realized I was there."

"Why are you so worried about Pierce, Charles? You are gone, retired."

"Before I was escorted off the property, Pierce came up and whispered in my ear, 'Enjoy your retirement, Charles. Keep your tongue or I'll have it cut out. The man was stone faced as he spewed the threat. I nodded and left."

"Have there been any threats since?"

"No, but I do keep my eyes open. David, you do realize the sort of monsters you are dealing with, don't you?" His sad blue eyes are imploring.

"I do. Right up my alley. So, we have never met, and I wouldn't recognize you if I saw you on the street."

We talk a little more and then I leave. This poor bastard gives years to his country's service and has to retire in fear. That will end, I will see to it.

RJ Waters

CHAPTER TWENTY-SIX

Nightfall comes and Dog and I head out to meet with Michael.

I hear a soft, "Over here." Michael is trying to be funny.

"I still can't see you. Dog where is he?" I ask my partner.

Says the alien jokester... "About twenty feet over your head."

He lands and we get in the car.

"Very funny." I say.

Michael is laughing. "You were worried about walking into the car, so I made sure you didn't."

Now the fun and games are over, we get down to business. Michael shows me the listening devices the aliens have made to be placed on Schultz's property.

They are to be placed so they will face windows and pickup voices from inside and transmit the sound to a transmitter which will be somehow be linked to the control room.

"You can do that?" I ask. "It's like two hundred miles."

Michael just looks at me.

"Yeah, okay, of course you guys can do that. Why would I ask?"

I have embarrassed myself.

"Puny brained human." Scoffs Dog.

We soon arrive over the German's house. The Mercedes-Benz is not in front. Michael's sensors show no one is in either the house or the workshop. Based on our first visit, Michael has already picked out the best places to mount the devices. This requires me to hang out the open window and attached the units to poles and a tree. These are fifteen to twenty feet off the ground. I manage to do the task. Michael is handing me the devices and Dog is ready to grab me if I slip.

Dog is ready to grab me-uh huh.

Since I'm halfway out of the car, I'm not sure where he will grab so I make sure I don't slip.

With the attachments done, we check in with the control room and Brian says he can hear electronic buzzing from the workshop and a refrigerator in the house.

High tech shit these space-travelers have.

On the way back I ask Michael how secure the Smart Car is. My thought is Brandon and his buddies might hijack it to meet with Schultz.

"Way ahead of you." Says Michael with confidence. "We have completely changed the codes and security for it. It will only respond to George or myself."

"Not George." Moans Dog.

"Just for security, if anything happens to me."
Lectures Michael.

"Heaven forbid." Utters the canine.

Back at the caves we go to the control room.
George is there with Brian. George says Schultz, and he is
assuming Hoffman, have returned to the house.

They went to dinner, how nice.

They are speaking German. Since George, Michael,
and some of the older aliens worked with the Germans they
quickly learned the language.

After listening for a while, Michael says it is indeed
Hoffman and Schultz in the house. Also, they are without a
doubt talking about the beam weapon. Michael say they
seem to be anticipating some coming event.

While Michael and George both keep listening on
headphones, I take the opportunity to talk quietly with
Brian. He has been trying to listen in on Brandon and his
cohorts. They have been keeping to themselves and for the
most part, away from any place Brian can eavesdrop. He
does say the group seems to be getting more excited about
something they are planning.

Brian thinks he has isolated a device Brandon may
have used for outside phone calls. While he was trying to
determine where the threatening call to Cranston came
from, he discovered it was linked to the old Area 51 secure
phone lines from the early days. It seems in their infinite
wisdom the government has not disabled the old system,
just added in the newer ones. Probably did that in case there
were problems in the new system and then just forgot to
disable the old system. Here we are looking for Brandon's

group to use alien high technology to contact the outside world and instead we just left them the old way. Without monitoring.

I love this country, but we sure do some dumb things.

Brian now has the device monitored so if Brandon uses it again, we will hear the call. I ask Brian about Michele. He says he knows her, and she is Brandon's sister, but she does not seem to be involved with the gang at all. Brian does know she has told Michael of her concerns about her brother. I ask him if he would mind if she came to him if she had any problems or any information about what her brother is up to.

"Absolutely, she is a nice kid. Yes, tell her she can call me anytime. On shift or not." He says. "You don't want Michael to know?"

"Let's just keep it this way for now. We have a lot going on. Tell me right away if she has any problem, please. By the way she will use the name Mickey." I tell him. "If she uses Mickey then it relates to her brother."

"Code name. Wow, this sounds, uh James Bond like." He looks at me curiously.

"I just don't want her in harm's way, and she is genuinely worried about what her brother is up to. She can learn things even you can't." I tell him.

"I understand, I'll keep watch over her." He says.

Michael and George are still listening to the Germans. George says they are watching TV and not talking too much. I leave the control room.

I call for Dog. He says he is with Mickey. Good, she was my next stop.

They are in one of the lounge rooms as they call them. Family rooms to us mortals. I hit my off button and Dog does the same.

"Why are you guys both scratching your ears?" Mickey asks.

"I had an itch, he has fleas." I say.

Dog glares. Mickey giggles.

I ask her if she knows Brian and what she thinks of him.

"Oh, he's really cool. He's one of the control room techs. They have the best job. I would love to be able to do that. They are the elite." She gushes.

Maybe this isn't the best idea I've ever had. This sounds like the *girls love cops'* thing on an alien level. Well I started it and Brian seems to be professional. I have to go with this now, but I'll kill him if he steps out of line. Dog will beat me to it though.

I tell her if she has any trouble or if she finds out anything new about her brothers plans, she should contact Brian. I tell her to call me first but to get hold of Brian if I don't answer right away. I tell her to use the *Mickey* name if it is urgent.

I know each family has an apartment in the cave complex. I ask Mickey if her brother Brandon has his own room.

"Oh yes, we all do. His is full of tech stuff, computers and weird gadgets." She says. I ask if Brandon locks his room when he is gone.

"He does now. He didn't use to. He is real fussy about his privacy these days." Mickey says. "He doesn't mind if I wander in and out when he is in his room but as soon as he leaves, he locks the door. Us kids are responsible for cleaning our own rooms so Mom isn't bothered about him locking it."

I ask her if the *boys* have found a way to go outside again, since the security has been tightened.

"I'm not sure but they may have. The caves are huge, but sometimes I notice one or more of them seem to disappear from time to time. I don't follow them, so they won't get suspicious, but I am thinking maybe they have found some secret way out or at least some hidden place to meet." She tells me.

I wonder which of the elders might have been involved with the construction or design of the caves. Mickey doesn't know, she was too young. Maybe there are plans somewhere. Time to visit George and Michael. I tell Mickey to keep her eyes and ears open but *please* be careful.

I go back to the control room. The guys are still listening to the Germans.

Michael says they are still watching boring television. I ask him about the construction of the cave complex.

"George and I were working with the human engineers on the design. The humans never saw us. We just

192

talked with them over intercoms. We both had sets of plans and the engineers were told we were people in Washington D.C. who were planning to use the caves for some secret purpose. In reality we were in another building in Area 51. Our two groups would talk back and forth about the designs. At night when the workers left, we elders would go into the work area and see all was as correct. It went well," Michael says. "All things considered."

So yes, there are plans for the complex. Michael says he has a set in his files, so does George. Michael thinks a moment. Then his face darkens: "My brother was also involved. He would have had a set of the plans. Oh Lord, Brandon could have seen them." He is noticeably upset.

We decide Michael will go see his sister-in-law, Mickey and Brandon's mother, and ask about the brother's files. He will do this when Brandon is not in the apartment. His concern is the mother does not say anything to Brandon. He decides he will just ask to see the files. He cannot find some old meeting minutes he needs.

Aliens keep minutes, how human of them.

RJ Waters

CHAPTER TWENTY-SEVEN

Busy day, I'm tired. Dog and I go back to the apartment. I need sleep.

My mind won't calm down. Today I have possibly derailed the unknown spooks who want to cut in on Frank, John's boss; hired Thomas; bugged the Germans and learned our small visitors have not only a way to the outside world electronically, but possibly an escape route from the caves. What will tomorrow bring?

"If you don't shut up and go to sleep, tomorrow will already be here." Scolds the also tired dog.

The next day is quiet. John seems to be more relaxed. The cave dwellers have been quiet so far. No news is good news…for the moment.

John has made the arrangement for Thomas to be allowed on the plane and for his official papers to be drawn up. I wonder if they will have to close the window shades for him, it is his first time as an Area 51 employee. Rules are rules.

In midafternoon, Mickey calls me and says she was able to take a picture of her brother's room without him knowing. I tell her I will be over tonight and see her. Ballsy kid.

A couple of hours later, Michael calls and says he was able to get into his brother's files. He can't find any cave plans. Bad news, I will see him tonight also.

Shortly after, Brian calls. He just came on shift and says Brandon's bunch are off the grid. He cannot locate any of them. In addition, he cannot find Mickey. Now I am worried. I ask him to get me Michael.

In a few minutes Michael comes online. I ask him if Brandon was aware of his searching for the plans. He says no, the mother said Brandon had gone off with his friends about an hour before Michael arrived. He told his mother they were going to study at some place quiet. Mickey was not around either according to Michael.

I tell him Brian can't locate Brandon, his group or Mickey. Michael is worried now too. I ask him if the plans show any secret escape exits. His silence tells me they do. I am going to have to make clear the meaning of *full disclosure* to Michael. I tell him I will be right over. He says he will get George and meet me. Dog has heard the conversations and is ready to go.

We enter the cave and meet George and Michael who have their copies of the plans. They are old, hand-drawn blueprints. Not the computer aided work of today. There are four escape exit tunnels in the plans. The aliens had them put in just in case anything went wrong with their agreements with their hosts: the U.S. Government. A smart move at the time. George has Brian in the control room scanning for the missing aliens and the other control room techs out checking on the secret exits. Only one of the present techs knew about them. They're so well concealed none of the aliens ever found them. According to George they are out of the medieval castles of human history. Hidden switches and all.

196

Then one of the techs says he has found some debris near one of the exits. We rush to the location. The exit is on the end of the complex, not far from Brandon's apartment. We arrive and the tech shows us some dirt on the floor near where the door is hidden.

Dog goes up and declares, "They have been here. Mickey too. Her smell is fresher than the others."

We discuss entering the tunnel and are about to trip the hidden latch when the door makes a *thunk* sound. We all back away and duck into a nearby hallway. It curves away from the main hall so we can stay out of sight. I take out my cell phone and put the video on. I set the camera on the floor near the wall. I am lying on my stomach watching the tiny screen. The others are behind me.

The door makes a creaky sound, it is opening. We hear a male voice, "It's clear, let's get back to the main area before anyone notices we are gone."

Michael whispers, "Its Brandon."

The door shuts with a thud.

In the cell phone I watch as all six of the boys walk past and down the main hall.

We look at the video again. Just the boys. No Mickey.

"She was there, I know it. Her sent is still strong! We got to go inside and find her." Dog insists. He starts to move forward when we hear, "No, I'm here, behind you. I never went in; I've been trying to follow them and every time I would lose them right here. So, I hid behind this hall and waited until they came out... just like you." She

197

proudly says. "Oh Dog, you were worried about me, how sweet." Dog is all over her, licking and nuzzling.

Needless to say, the adults are flabbergasted. For a moment we don't speak then all at once we all start to scold her. Then Michael goes over and hugs her.

"Oh sweetie, you are so brave. Your Daddy would be proud of you. Nevertheless, do not do this sort of thing again. Please, I'm an old man, I can't take much more of this."

She looks up at Michael and says, "If you had listened to me in the first place, I wouldn't have had to do this." Mickey smiles sweetly at him. The little shit looks at me and winks. "I did good, huh?"

We all go back to the control room, except for Mickey and Dog. We send them off to the TV lounge. Mickey doesn't need to be seen with any of us. She did show us the photo she took of her brother's room. Michael and George study the equipment in the room. Nothing unusual they say. What is inside the gear is what counts. We'll tackle that later.

Michael lays out the plans for all of us to see. No secrets now.

The hidden door we just saw opens to a tunnel leading to the outside. It is on the west side of the main Area 51 complex. At one point, the passageway is not far from the tunnel leading to Schultz's old lab, I point out.

"You don't think they are trying to break into *that* tunnel, do you?" George says. "Well of course they are. How dumb can I be? It's right there in front of us."

I give my cell phone to Brian and ask him to put the video on a big screen so we can see the boys better.

Sure enough, they're dirty.

George has recovered and says there are *dirt areas* where anyone can play different sports. The younger ones go there all the time.

"Even I do." Says Brian. "But I've never seen them there. That group doesn't exercise."

For the moment we decide to put a camera on the exit and watch it. We need to go in there but don't want the conspirators to know. I wonder if there is a time when we could be certain where they would be. So we could get in the tunnel without any chance of them coming in.

Michael says there is a periodic meeting of the residents which is mandatory for all and they cannot leave until it's over.

"We haven't had one for some time. I think it is time. The problem is, we all must be there. The only exception is one tech in the control room. Therefore, you and Dog would be the ones to go in the tunnel. Are you okay with the plan?"

"Not a problem, in fact I prefer it. I would like Brian in the control room please."

"Done." Michael says. "How about tomorrow night at 7:00 p.m.?"

Well my quiet day has gone to hell. Tomorrow will be Thomas's first day. I don't think he is ready for any of this mess yet. I'll spend the day getting him up to speed on

John and show him around then put him on the plane by 5:00 p.m. Then I'll grab a bite to eat and head over to the caves.

I get Dog and we go back home. He says Mickey is pretty proud of herself. He told her not to be too bold. Let us handle it now. He did promise to tell her what we find in the tunnel.

Who is Dog, really? I share my life with him now. He is very much a dog part of the time and then at other times he is so human it is scary. Or is he *alien*?

Glad he's on my side.

CHAPTER TWENTY-EIGHT

The next morning Dog and I meet Tom at the airstrip. No, they did not put down the window shades for him. In fact, he didn't even have to have another officer on board. *Edward* Benton said Tom could go by himself.

After he lands, I introduce him to John, who is pleased to see him. He is feeling safer now he has the two of us and Frank has said he will take care of the threats.

I haven't told him the real threat has nothing to do with the D.C. crowd. Ignorance is bliss.

I introduce Tom around and then show him the layout of the area, including Wolfgang's lab. I do not go into exactly *what* is being done there. Mainly because I *don't know* exactly what Wolfgang's doing in there. I know he is not working on the death ray of Schultz's. Hell, he may be building his own secret weapon for all I know.

I do fill Tom in on the death threats John Cranston has received. I tell him about Frank, of the old D.C. bureaucratic crowd, and his competitors in the spy vs. spy game.

"Man, sounds like the world of drug enforcement. Don't let the FBI or any other agency know we have a case, they will want in." He's shaking his head at the similarities.

Boy, it's great to have someone I can talk to who has been in my world. He will be good to work with, but he's still not ready for *the rest of the story!*

I get him on the 5:00 p.m. flight back to Vegas. Dog and I get some dinner and head over to the caves. George lets me in. Michael is in the meeting room and checking off each resident as they arrive to be certain no one plays hooky from the big meeting.

George communicates with Brian in the control room and says the hallways to the secret door are clear. George will take us to the door, show me how to open it and then he will beat it back to the meeting.

While we are in route, Michael informs us the last of the Teen Conquers has arrived at the meeting. Good. Now Dog and I can go about our mission.

George shows me how to open the door. Simple if you know the trick. Pull down on a chunk of rock in the wall and push on another. Both are at least five feet above the floor. No small children could reach them. Good safety factor. With the slight scraping sound of solid rock, a door opens into the tunnel. We go in and George shows me where the opening and closing switches are, then leaves. I close the door which is a genius of engineering. The heavy rock smoothly glides back and seals off the tunnel, which is now inky black. I switch on my flashlight.

"Don't do anything stupid superhero because I could be stuck in here." Dog warns.

Brian then speaks in our *devices*: "Don't worry Dog, I'm here. You won't be trapped."

With that settled we begin to walk the tunnel. I have the map of the caves so I can sort of tell where we are. After about five minutes we see something ahead of us in the tunnel. Turns out it is a stack of tools, pickaxes, shovels, pry bars, digging implements. Where did they get them? Brian clears up the issue by saying there were a lot of similar items left inside the complex by the human workers. Closer checking shows the boys are trying to dig their way into the near-by tunnel leading to Schultz's old lab. They haven't made much headway. The rock is dense.

Dog starts to snicker: "Sure smells of sweat in here."

At the rate they are going, the boys will be old men before they get through. They must be aware of that by now. They will have to come up with some other method. Blasting would be noticed.

We start walking the rest of the tunnel. Nothing of interest along the way. Dog senses the boys have been here recently. They may have already given up on the idea of breaking through to the adjacent tunnel. Finally, after a ten-minute walk we come to the end. My map indicates there is a door to the outside. Dog is all over the wall.

"They have been touching here." He points with a paw at a protruding rock.
I look at the map. It indicates the rock must be turned 90 degrees to open the door. I turn it and sure enough the door slides inward and swings to one side.

Through the opening I see desert landscape. We are on the western side of Area 51 away from the main complex. We look around outside. There are multiple footprints in the sandy soil. Small footprints. Dog senses it is the boys.

"Are you guys outside?" Says an excited Brian. "I don't have any alarm sounding. That door should have an alarm."

I go to the opening. Checking around the cave opening I find a round hole with a metal peg in it, which should have popped out when the door opened. However, there is something jammed into the hole, so the peg won't move. I tell Brian.

"How long has the alarm been disabled?" He wonders.

We check the surrounding outside area. The boys have been out here a lot says the four-footed nose. He starts to go further out into the desert.

"Come on, they go out here." Says my guide.

We go out at least a hundred yards. It is dark so we would not be seen by anyone. There are no security sensors out here. We are well inside the high security boundaries. The tracks keep going in the same direction. My map shows nothing out here. Brian says there is an old bunker on his map about 300 yards out from the caves. It is unused from what he can tell.

We find the bunker. It is a large mound of dirt with a huge door up against a small hill. The area in front of the door is covered with little footprints. No way to open the door. No handle. Dog cannot find any hidden levers. No keyhole. How do the little bastards get in there? Dog cannot tell. He does say these tracks and smells are very recent. Maybe they *don't* have a way in, yet.

Brian interrupts and says he is getting word from George. Michael is running out of things to say to stall the meeting. Okay, we're done for the night. Dog and I backtrack into the tunnel and close it up. Then back to the hallway and make our way into the control room. Brian gives George the *all clear* and the meeting is ended.

Michael and George come into the control room. I fill them in on what we found. "What do you know about that bunker?" I ask.

"They both are trying to remember. "It has been years since anyone worked in there," they say. The aliens themselves never did any work there, so their knowledge is limited.

"Oh my god!" Exclaims Michael. "Schultz worked there; I remember now. When we first arrived, when the cave complex was being built. Schultz was working there. Then before he was fired, he was moved to the building where Wolfgang is now. My brother did go over there after Schultz was moved to see what was in there since it was close to our new home. My brother did a lot of the planning for our complex. He was an engineer. So long ago, I had forgotten all about it."

"By any chance did Brandon go with your brother during this time?" I have to ask.

Both Michael and George nod in the affirmative.

"He went everywhere with his dad in those days." Michael adds. "It was just in the last few years, before he died, my brother started having trouble with Brandon."

Apparently, Brandon and his friends began to push to get out into the world. They felt they were smarter than humans and wanted to show the earthlings how to run the planet. It was Brandon and his friend Calvin at first. Then later they picked up four more followers.

"They were what you people would call activists today." George said. "We leaders were concerned but didn't think they would go to extremes. Where do we go from here? Do we just watch and see if they are looking to harm Cranston or contact the Germans? I just don't know; we haven't had a problem like this before."

I tell the two leaders for now we need to keep a close watch on the *activists*. We are already monitoring Schultz and Hoffman. Brian says he can put a night vision camera outside to see what they do out there. In the meantime, he can still monitor Brandon's *outside* phone calls.

I tell them the bunker outside the caves interests me. Brandon would have known something about it from his trips with his father.

"Not to open old memories, but how did your brother die?" I have met many older ones here," I have to ask. The more I learn about these folks the more questions I have.

"He did die unexpectedly." Michael says sadly. "He was apparently bitten by a poisonous snake. He liked to walk outside in the desert at night and look for unusual rocks. When he didn't come back one night, his wife called us. We went out and found him, he was already dead. There were two puncture wounds in one of his wrists."

"What do you do with the bodies of your people when they die here?" Always the cop.

"We preserve them in hopes of someday getting them back home for proper burial."

"I thought you had accepted the idea you were stuck here?" I ask.

"We are able to communicate with our home planet. Since we discovered our ship did not fail but was shot down by Schultz, we have told our people back home the design was a success and if they build another one, we could be rescued. We are told the engineers back home are in fact doing that right now. It will take a few years to complete and to travel here. We have told no one. So, they won't get their hopes up." Michael says.

Wow. Will the surprises never end with the *mighty minis?*

RJ Waters

CHAPTER TWENTY-NINE

I want to know the history of the bunker we located. Michael and George say it hasn't been used since Schultz was moved out of it years ago. In the morning I ask John what he knows about it. He says it was already closed when he arrived at Area 51.

"Who would know?" I ask.

"EG&G, they know just about everything going on here. They handle all the logistics for any of the government operations." John answers.

"EG&G again. A private company knowing way too much much of what happens here?" I am surprised.

"Yes, they are sort of the *property managers* of the place. They are not involved with what we do, but the supplies, maintenance and all, are up to them." John says. "I must say they do a good job. The buildings are kept up and so are the grounds. If you want to know anything about the bunker, then that's who to ask. Do you want me to call them?"

"Uh, no, thanks. I already know who to contact." I rapidly sputter just as Tom comes in. "Good morning Tom, we have work to do, come on." Tom just waves at John and follows me out.

"Did I miss something?" He asks.

"No, well yes, but I'll explain. Do you have any knowledge of the various buildings EG&G handles here in Area 51?" I ask.

"No, I've just been the guard on the plane. Uhh, what does EG&G do here anyway? I do know they have a large presence. A lot of EG&G employees come out here."

"From what I can determine… just about everything, short of pushing the buttons on the atomic test blasts and designing the stealth planes flying here."

We go into my office and using my supposedly secure cell phone I call my old friend *Eddie* at EG&G. He is as thrilled as ever to hear from me.

"What do you want now? You have terrorized one of my men, hijacked another, so what's left?" He is laughing I think or maybe he's crying, hard to tell.

I ask him about the bunker. He says he will have to research it, but as far as he knows, it has not been used for years. He says there are a lot of old buildings here no longer used and they just sit. I tell him I need to get inside.

"What the hell for? It's just an old shack up against a tunnel of some sort."

"How do you know there is a tunnel?" I ask.

"Quick education, city boy…you don't build a structure into the side of a hill unless you are planning to use the hill for a tunnel for an experiment of some sort. Take a look around Area 51, all you see are buildings set against hillsides, right?" He patiently informs me.

"All right Dad, I get it. Now may I please get inside this ingenious structure?"

"I'll see what I can do." He says flatly.

"How's Doris?" I inquire sweetly.

"I said I'll see what I can do, damn it!" He slams down the phone.

Tom looks at me. He has only heard my side of the conversation.

"I still don't think I want to know." He laughs.

Now Tom and I go back to see John. I know the week is about up the *mysterious caller* gave John to close down the project. I want to prep him in case Brandon calls again. I don't know if Brandon actually has a plan, but we need to take the offensive.

I tell Tom to just play along with whatever I say.

I tell John if he does get another call, he is to be calm and keep control of the conversation. He is to say, *the project being developed now is not a weapon and the one the caller was referring to has long since been disabled.*

"That is all you will say to him." I direct John. "Let him rant, rave, or make whatever threats he will, but continue to repeat what I have told you to say, no more. We have a tap on the phone and the longer you keep him on the better. Understood?"

He looks at me and then at Tom. Tom just nods.

"Yes, I'll do it." He is dumbfounded. "How can you do these things? Who do you know?"

"The good guys." I reply.

"Why do I feel I'm really not needed here?" Tom asks as we go back to my office.

"You really are, I need you here." I tell him. "Things have been moving fast on several levels. I don't want to scare you off, but it is time for you and me to sit down and get you *more* up to date."

Tom narrows his brown eyes, "*More* up to date? That's comforting David. At least tell me why I can't be *completely* brought up to date."

I sit back in my chair, sigh and look at Tom.

"Okay, here goes. What if I told you there is a colony of little aliens living in caves on Area 51, and a splinter group of them want to take over Earth using a death ray devised by a German scientist who came here after World War 2 and the German scientist has recruited another old buddy, who was taken by the Russians, to help him rebuild the weapon?"

"Look David, if you don't want to fill me in now, just say so."

"I just did."

"You mean you don't want to fill me in now?"

"No! I **did** fill you in. **That's** what is going on!"

Tom sits back in his chair and stares at me. He is looking for a smile or some sign I'm pulling his leg.

"Come on, *you're shitting me* man, I know you are." He is staring intently at me.

"Remember the secrecy oath you signed when you were hired, yesterday?" I ask.

"Yes of course, but what has it got to do with this B.S. you are giving me?" He asks.

"It is not B.S. Tom. It is real. All of it. It is time for you and me to take a trip to the caves." I tell him.

"Can I come too?" Asks Dog, who has been quietly laying on the floor.

I wish I had a camera on Tom at that moment. His expression was priceless.

He just looks at Dog and then at me.

"You're a ventriloquist, right?" He says.

Dog stands up and puts his face right in front of Tom's.

"No Tom, he is not a ventriloquist. I'm just a really talented dog." Then he licks Tom's face.

I am laughing my ass off. Tom has probably peed his pants or worse.

"He really talks?" Tom asks me in a whispering tone.

"Hey, look at me. Yes, I really do talk." Dog is still in his face. "Take a deep breath, relax, you'll get used to it. You should have seen David the first time I spoke to him."

"Come on you two, let's go over to the caves and get Tom a drink." I say, getting up and heading for the door. Tom slowly gets up, Dog pushes him. We all go down to the parking lot and get into a vehicle. Tom is not saying anything. I have left my device on so Michael is aware of our arrival. We pull up to the entrance and all get out. The cave door opens, Dog trots in and I motion Tom inside. He steps in tentatively and Michael steps out, extends his hand and says:

"Welcome Tom. I am Michael. Pleased to meet you. David speaks highly of you."

Tom recovers and shakes Michael's hand.

"I'm glad to meet you too, I think."

Michael and I give Tom a quick rundown of how the aliens came to be here. Then we get in a cart and go to Michael's office. We go in and Michael immediately pours a round of drinks. Tom would have probably drunk anything put in front of him, as long as there was *alcohol* in it.

We sit and just talk. Tom has all sort of questions, just as I did. Finally, he is beginning to believe all this is real and not a bad dream.

"I'm blown away. We have all heard about aliens at Area 51 and the Roswell incident but most people, including me, though it was just the conspiracy theory of some crackpots. The talking dog though is a new twist, I never heard that one before."

"That's because I'm unique, one of a kind," proffers Dog. "I do accept petting, but ear scratches are the best."

Tom reaches over and scratches Dog's ears. We all laugh.

"Welcome to the family Tom." Michael says.

CHAPTER THIRTY

Tom, Michael, and I talk for a while longer. George comes in and meets Tom. So far so good. He hasn't tried to run out of the place. George suggests we give him a tour of the complex. Tom is quite impressed, as was I on my first trip here.

I ask the guys to show him the Smart Car. He has to see that. On our way to the hangar, as I refer to their engineering shop, we pass two of the younger aliens coming out of the area. Michael says they are part of Brandon's gang.

"Why would they be in the shop area?" He wonders out loud.

George says we need to talk to the chief of the shop.

We go in and while Michael shows Tom the Smart Car, George and I go talk with the chief of the shop. He says the two boys in question have been taking classes in engine development.

"What exactly is engine development?" I ask. Being part of Brandon's group anything they are doing must have an ulterior motive.

"They are the power supplies we use to move anything, like our spaceships and the escape pods." The shop leader says.

"Do you have any engines around?" I ask.

"Sure, one powers the Smart Car, another is mounted on a frame and used for general lifting around the complex. That is how we were able to move your truck around. We have two other complete engines and I am using the various parts from the rest of the escape pods to assemble as many as I can. I am also teaching some of the younger ones the basic technology." The chief says. "You know it's funny you should ask about those two boys. It was only recently they joined the class. They showed no interest in anything but computers and complaining in the past."

I look at George, he nods. He's thinking just what I am. The *activists* are suddenly getting an interest in engines, systems that can move and fly. I suggest an inventory of all the parts would be in order. The chief says, "Already done, on a daily basis."

"These engines are our lifelines. If we ever need to get out of here, they are our only hope."

George looks at the chief and says with an authoritative voice: "If even so much as one part turns up missing, I want to be notified, immediately!"

The chief gets a concerned look on his face. "Something's up, I take it,"

"Something's up, yes and say nothing to anyone, understand?"

"Understood." The chief responds.

Michael has regaled Tom with the antics of the Smart Car and we all go back to Michael's office. We tell him what we have learned about the *new students*.

"What the hell are they up to?" Says a frustrated Michael.

"Looks like they are trying to get out of here, one way or the other." Tom suggests.

"We have to keep all the engine parts locked down. Classes must go on; we need to have skilled people in all fields. But we must watch the inventory, just to be safe." Michael says.

"How about the completed engines and this lifting frame you have?" I ask.

"The engines? They are already secured but the frame; I never even gave it a thought." George is saying.

"It is just as capable as the Smart Car, right Michael?"

"My heavens." You can almost see Michaels' brain spinning, "With a body of some sort and seats, why yes it could go anywhere. Not as fast or high as the car but it could be taken…."

"To Sedona to meet Schultz and Hoffman." I interrupt.

Everyone just sits still and contemplates the thought of the *boys* fleeing and meeting up with the Germans.

We agree, until the group makes some overt move, we cannot do anything. This is just still circumstantial so far. It is obvious they are trying to do something but exactly what we don't know. From our monitoring of the Germans, we know they have been busy working in their shop and not saying much. But, from what we hear, they are waiting for contact from someone who will help them… proves nothing. Yet.

Tom, Dog, and I leave the caves and drive back to the office.

"Well Tom, what do you think? You going to stay?"

"Oh hell yes! I've got to see this through. DEA was never this crazy. Aliens, international espionage, death rays and on top of it all, a smart-ass talking dog. Yes, I'm in!"

"I prefer witty, if you don't mind." Dog pipes up.

"You know Tom; I don't have to tell you, no one can be told about what you just found out, including your wife."

"My wonderful woman has put up with my entire career, never knowing exactly what I was doing. She is so happy I have a safe job now. Retiring from DEA was a big relief for her. She is willing to put up with a few nights or weekends now. I'm happy and she's relieved." Tom says. "But where do *you* think this is going to lead? Do we have amateurs or professionals involved?"

"I think we have both. Call it a feeling, I don't know. I think we are still missing a piece of the puzzle here."

"Wise, this one is." Says the Dog.

"And Yoda, not are you." I reply.

Back at the office John is still somewhat nervous about his threatening caller. I don't want to tell him we know who it is, but I do try to reassure him we have it under control. Tom offers to be available during the weekend for John.

"I do live in Vegas, you know, not here in Wonderland like David. I will keep my cell with me all weekend."

"Thank you Tom, yes that does make me feel better." John says. "I was thinking of spending the weekend somewhere else but if you two are sure the house is safe then I'll be there."

"The house is safe, believe me." I say.

At the end of the day John and Tom are ready to leave. Dog and I walk out with them. As soon as we are out the door Dog lets out a bark and runs off towards the parking lot. I see an Air Force vehicle sitting there next to mine. Pam gets out and Grizzy follows. The two dogs meet up halfway, they nuzzle and jump around each other, stuff dogs do when they meet. Pam waves. John and Tom look at her and then me.

"I can drop Tom off at the airplane if you'd like." John smiles.

"I'd appreciate it. See you guys on Monday. Let me know if anything happens. You are in good hands John." I say as I walk away.

"Looks like you are too." Tom laughs.

I walk up to Pam. She gives me a big smile.

"Care to go to dinner when I get off shift?" She says.

"Yes ma'am, I sure would." I gaze into her eyes. "What time should I pick you two ladies up?"

"Seven would be good." She says coyly. "I got this shift at the last minute, I hoped you would be here." She reaches and squeezes my hand and then gets into her vehicle. "Let's go Grizzie, we'll see them shortly."

I go to my truck and as I get in, I notice John and Tom are still in the parking lot, staring. I drive over to them.

"Don't you two have someplace to go?"

They both give me thumbs up and laugh.

The most secret place in the free world and I have no privacy.

CHAPTER THIRTY-ONE

Pam and I are having a pleasurable dinner. She is looking enticing in a beige silk blouse with the top two buttons open and a pair of extremely nice fitting jeans.

The dogs eat *on the house* as promised. Their placemats now have *Bouncers* written on them…Cute. The manager sees we are well taken care of and then leaves us alone.

Pam is telling me more about herself. Seems her dad was an Air Force pilot, and the family moved around a lot. She has an older brother, an orthopedic surgeon in Southern California.

"So, he could put me back together, if your father doesn't like me and takes me apart?"

She laughs, "He would probably help my *father*, but don't let that worry you."

"Okay, enough about your family, what about you? How'd you wind up in the Air Police?"

"I saw so many messed-up kids in the various areas we were stationed, I decided to become a social worker, counselor, just someone to help them." She looks down at her drink, then with a sad look on her face continues, "College, made me realize I wasn't cut out for that type of work. I would help anyone, but I couldn't coddle someone just because of their situation. People need to put effort into helping themselves.

Pam looks up at me, "Does that make me sound cold? Because the instructors would expound: *the poor things deserve help, it's not their fault, etc. We must do our part within the system to help them, even if they do not try to help themselves.* Standards and the value of hard work were part of my upbringing, waiting for everything to be handed to me, was not. Maybe it's because I'm an Air Force brat, but I just couldn't go along with the social worker mantra. I switched majors and took up criminal justice. I felt much better with those courses. I would still be helping people, just in a different way."

"Somewhere along the way you got married."

"Yes, I already told you how my marriage ended. My senior year, set to graduate, and I come home early and find him---well you know. I did graduate and then I enlisted in the Air Force. Best decision I ever made. Went to Air Police training and then off to the Middle East. I spent a year in Iraq and then back to the states. I wanted to get into the K-9 program, so I went thru the training and was given Grizzie. We were immediately sent to Afghanistan, Bagram Air Base. After my *second* tour, Grizzie and I landed here. We may still be stationed in another gigantic desert, but it beats the hell out of the Middle East."

"So how was it in the combat zones? Bagram was in the middle of it all."

"We didn't do external patrols, like the Army and Marines. Our duty was within the bases. It had its moments. Shelling, infiltrators and always the threat one of the Afghan soldiers would be a jihadist and try to kill as many of us as he could." She pauses, swallows hard; I can feel her disconnect. Then Pam blurts out, "It was bad, extremely bad! I am *so glad* to be here. Believe me."

224

Leaning toward her I touch her arm, "What happened? If you feel like talking about it."

She looks at me with emotion welling up in her hazel eyes, takes a deep breath, and begins: "One evening after duty, Grizzie and I were in our room. I had just gotten my laptop out to Skype my parents. I tried to e-mail or talk with them after each shift. I was sitting on my bed, and Grizzie was on her bed, beside mine. The rooms weren't very big. My bed, Grizzie's bed, and a footlocker, that was about it. I heard yelling down the hall, then gunshots. I dropped the computer and lunged for my gun belt hanging on the other side of my bed. I was just pulling my weapon out when a heavy kick smashed my door open. Standing in the doorway was an Afghan soldier, his dark eyes glowing with hatred. He was pointing his pistol at me. Grizzie instantly attacked and her jaws locked onto the wrist of his gun hand. Her attack knocked him onto his back, and into the hallway. Grizzie kept her hold and started dragging him into the room. He wasn't able to do anything but scream. She kept her teeth clamped deep into his wrist. I had my gun on him but suddenly, with his free hand, he reached for the knife on his belt. I fired three times into his chest. Blood gushed from him, splattering me, drenching everything. Then the knife dropped from his hand, and his body went limp.

Hanson, one of the people in my unit, was suddenly in my doorway shouting, "Pam, you all right?" He was holding his side. Blood was oozing out between his fingers and dripping onto the floor, mixing into the pool of blood already there.

"That bastard burst into the break room and shot at all of us. Jackson and Ski are down. Looks like you took care of him. Good job soldier."

"Everybody came pouring into our building. On duty, off duty. I realized Grizzie was still holding onto the guys' wrist, the gun still in his hand. I reached down, took the gun, and told her to release. I'd be dead if it wasn't for her."

I pull Pam to me and wrap my arms around her, holding her close and tight. Trying to soothe her and make her feel safe. With my face against hers, I can feel her tears. Then she raises her head and looks at me, "I haven't been able to tell my parents about it. You're the only person I've told since I came back. You've probably had to make that decision many times, but I've never had to kill anyone. I was prepared to do it. It was part of my job, but off duty? I knew it could happen over there, but it was still surreal."

Dog, bless his heart, nuzzles Grizzie and licks her face.

"Look at Dog. How sweet. It's like he understood what I just said." Pam kneels down to Grizzie and hugs her. "I am so grateful for her." Then she gives both Dogs a kiss. She sits back down at the table and pulls herself together.

"Thank you, I needed to tell my story." She puts her hand on mine and squeezes. Her eyes are smiling again. "Now, you are up to date with my story. Your turn."

"Uh, well, dysfunctional family as a kid, went into the Army after high school. Just to get into a settled environment, I guess. Nothing patriotic, just self-serving. I didn't know what I wanted to do with my life. I made good grades in school, and the teachers told me I belonged in college. I just wanted to get out of Dodge."

"You didn't actually live in Dodge City, did you?"

"Bakersfield. Just as bad."

"So, from the Army, then to California as a police officer, right?"

"Yeah, that was it."

"How long were you in the service? You've mentioned the Rangers and South America."

"Eight years." I mentally reflect. Yes, it has been that long. Flew by, just a blur now, except for some of the more vivid memories.

Pam still has my hand. She gives it another squeeze. "There is something there; I can feel it in you. Do *you* want to talk about it, I'm all ears?"

"You have ears?" I joke as I look up from the table, taking in her blouse and up at her beautiful face.

"Jerk!" She slugs my arm and then reaches over and kisses me.

"You want to tell me about South America, or another time?"

"No, now is probably a good time. You opened up to me, so here it comes." I take a deep breath, and the memories start flooding my brain.

"Like I told you before, we were sent there to do some drug interdiction ops. It was one of those top secret, nobody knows where the hell you are, kind of things. The Army's part was well organized. Two of us were inserted into the jungle in the middle of *somewhere* and found what we were looking for: the coca fields and the processing

227

plant. They had been located by our surveillance planes. The processing plants were just sheds, but that's where the coca became cocaine. All local labor, of course. We kept out of sight and just observed.

There were a couple of head honchos with automatic weapons, AK-47's, in charge of the workers. In the afternoon, a Land Rover pulled up, escorted by two pickup trucks full of armed men. The guy in the Land Rover was known as La Piranha, the major drug lord of the area. He was small in stature but deadly, like his namesake. We recognized him from the photos we carried. His presence confirmed we were in the right place. We radioed in our information. Our HQ was excited. The plan was, the rest of our unit would be air dropped in that night, and we would attack in the morning. My buddy and I had nothing to do but stay hidden, keep watch, and wait for our guys.

A couple of hours later The Fish, as we referred to him, got a cell phone call. He had a satellite phone. No cell towers out there. Immediately he yelled at his men, and they got into their vehicles and sped off. The bosses at the facility looked dumbfounded. They had no idea what was happening. Eventually, they went back to work possessing the coca.

We advised HQ what happened. They were pissed to say the least. Everyone wanted to nail La Piranha. Finally, HQ advised us the mission would go ahead as planned. The difference was, less of our people would be brought in for the job. HQ said since The Fish had left the pond, and there were only a couple of dozen workers, with only a few weapons, we could easily wrap it up. I bitched like hell. In this area, you never know who is around the corner.

I was told, follow *orders*.

My C.O. said, "The CIA is here, and Agent Worthington tells me he knows where the bad guys are. You just seize the plant at daybreak. Understood, Soldier?"

"I was furious. I felt the hair on the back of my neck stand straight up. How'd the CIA get into this? I knew it was going to go bad."

"What did you do?" Pam is on the edge of her seat, well almost on top of me, hanging on every word.

"We were two guys in hostile territory and could only hope they would send us enough help to pull this off. Then we could get the hell out of there, and with any luck, we would all still be in one piece. When their day was over, the workers all headed in one direction. No one was left at the plant. We followed them and found the workers huts in a clearing not far away. They were cooking dinner and drinking beer. We ate MRE's and watched.

Later that night, we were notified our troops had been inserted and were making their way toward us. We made contact with them. All six of them! God help us. Eight Rangers against maybe twenty or so locals. Not bad odds normally, but we didn't know how many weapons they had stashed. We hoped they drank *mucho cerveza*.

"It was still a while until daylight, but we made a mutual decision to attack immediately. One Ranger went back to the plant and was to set off an incendiary grenade on my signal. With the coca, cocaine and chemicals they used, there would be no more processing plant and a hell of a distraction. The rest of us set up a perimeter around the huts. It was pitch black except for the glow from the embers of their cooking fires. At my signal, the grenade went off. The workers came running out of their huts. *Every damn one of them* had an automatic weapon! They began shooting everywhere into the darkness. We immediately returned fire. It didn't take long to dispatch them. Then, just as the last shot was ringing off into the now still jungle, a new round of automatic weapons fire poured into the area. This attack was coming from the far side of the clearing. The pickups from the afternoon pulled into the clearing; men were jumping out and firing toward our positions. As I motioned everyone to move back, I saw La Parana's Land Rover stop at the far edge of the clearing. I signaled my guys to take up defensive positions. I cut into the jungle and made my way toward the Land Rover."

"By yourself, of course. Go on." She is barely breathing now.

"There's not much more. I managed to get to the Land Rover and The Fish is sitting there like a fucking general, smoking a cigar, and watching his troops in battle. His driver is outside the vehicle watching. One shot and I take him out. La Parana tries to jump into the driver's seat. I get to the open door and grab him by his head as he is coming across the front seat. We tumble onto the ground; he is reaching for the pistol in his holster. I still have his head in a solid grip, so I give it a quick snap. He goes limp and just stares at me.

"That CIA bastard set me up. He said you would attack at daylight." His voice was weak and gravely, but his eyes were wide open, glaring at me. He blinked, then exhaled his last breath."

"Realizing the firing had ceased, I eased around the vehicle, keeping low. I turned my radio back on. I had it off while I was creeping thru the jungle. I heard one of my men quietly calling, 'Dave, Dave, are you there?'

"I'm here, what's the status?"

"We are all okay. The bad guys are dead."

"Roger that."

CHAPTER THIRTY-TWO

We sit close together, quiet, having just poured out our souls to each other. It is time to take the girls back to their quarters. The time has flown by. It's getting late and Pam has an early shift. I enjoy her company and she seems to feel the same way. We had verbally agreed on the *let's take it slow* concept, but her eyes tell me she is feeling the same way I do.

On the way to her quarters, Pam asks me who the two men were at the office. I tell her about John and Tom.

"I've seen Cranston before. At Creech. He comes at lot in the evenings and sometimes on the weekends. He is seeing Major Andrews. Kate Andrews is the base intelligence officer."

"You mean *seeing* as in *dating*?" Says the somewhat surprised me.

"Yes, that would be putting it mildly. Patrol officers *see all* you know. They don't see us-*but we see them*. Is he married?" She asks.

I nod my head. "Yes, but his wife is also having an affair and I've felt torn about not telling him, but now it's a moot point."

She laughs, shakes her head and then leans over to me and says softly, "I like you David, let's make a promise - we will be better to each other than we have both experienced in our pasts. We've shared our stories; we know what it is to be hurt. Deal?"

I am at her barracks now. I stop the car and look at her.

"Deal." I start to say something else, but her face is right in front of mine. I lean over, our lips meet, and we kiss, long and passionately. Then we just look at each other.

"I've got to go." she says. "Come on Grizzie," she leans over and gives me another kiss. She jumps out and looks at me

"Would I be too forward if I asked about tomorrow night? Same time?"

"I would be heartbroken if you didn't, because I was about to ask."

"See you at seven." She and Grizzie head into their barracks.

Dog and I watch them safely enter the building, "She likes you," says Dog. "I know, Grizzie told me."

"Well I like her too. How are you with Grizzie?" I ask.

"You know, I really enjoy being with her. This could be good for both of us."

I still can't believe I have such personal conversations with a dog.

After we get back to the apartment, I get a cell phone call from Brian. I've had my device turned off during my date.

"Yes Brian, what's going on?" I ask.

"Brandon just called Cranston. He is yelling at him for not closing the project. Cranston is telling Brandon exactly what you told him to say. Brandon is saying Cranston is a liar and he knows the project is still going on. Cranston is being calm and keeps telling him the project was destroyed. Oh, Brandon just slammed the phone down. He's pissed. I'll keep checking on Brandon and get back to you."

Then Cranston calls me. I answer and say, "Hi John, I know you just received another call. We're on it. You don't have to worry. The person is nowhere near you and is being watched."

"How do you know this? I just hung up and called you. You were already listening to him?" John is taken aback.

"Actually John, I have a source monitoring your phones. I was notified as soon as he called you. We have him located and he is being watched. Trust me, you have nothing to worry about. Apparently, Frank didn't get the problem solved on his end. We will handle it from here on out," I tell him very professionally.

"David, I'm impressed. I've worked with some top-notch agents in the past, but you just blow me away. I'm very grateful you agreed to help me. I don't know what I would have done on my own." He's becoming emotional.

I talk with him for a little longer and then tell him I will update him on Monday. I ask if he called Tom. He didn't, just called me first. Good, no reason to spoil Tom's weekend. I'm sure he is still trying to digest all he learned today.

I have my *device* on now and Brian says Mickey wants to talk to me. I'll be right there, I tell him.

"Come on Robin, to the Bat Caves!" I say to Dog

"What are you talking about? You didn't have that much to drink tonight, and there's no bats at the cave," says the new generation pooch who never watched Batman on TV.

"I'll tell you about it sometime."

Mickey tells us she just heard her brother yelling in his room. She says Calvin was in there with him. She stayed near the closed door and heard Brandon yelling at someone like he was on a telephone. Then she heard him tell Calvin *"It is time to get the Germans up here, one way or another!"* Then they started talking quietly and she couldn't hear anymore.

I thank her and again tell her to be very careful and not to make her brother suspicious.

Mickey pulls herself to her full height of three feet nine inches or whatever and says proudly, "I am going to do whatever I can to protect my people and yours. And hopefully stop my idiot brother from making a big mistake. He is messed up, but he is still my brother. Dad would want me to help,"

"Your Father would be immensely proud of you. But please, be careful!" I say in my best father-like tone.

I check in with Brian and he tells me all is quiet. The boys are still in Brandon's room or at least in the apartment.

I ask him about the Germans, Schultz, and Hoffman. He says the day shift heard them planning to go on a camping trip to visit the magnetic vortex locations in the area. Sedona is a biggie with the new age cult types. People go to the vortex areas for whatever healing or mind-altering effects they think come from those places. We already know Schultz is interested in the magnetic fields for his own reasons.

It's now Saturday and I don't have any plans. John is home or somewhere other than here and Pam is working. I am just enjoying a little relaxation when my cell rings. It is *Eddie* Benton from EG&G.

"Good morning Ed." I am cheerful. "How's it going?"

"You still want to get into that building?" He asks briskly

"Yeah, I would appreciate it."

"Be there in twenty minutes. I will have a crew open the building for you, then you're on your own."

"On a Saturday? Thanks Ed but a *crew* to open it. Won't a key do?"

"No, it was welded shut at the order of the Defense Departments. I will have a couple of welders there to open it up for you. I don't know what is in there. I located a retired EG&G manager who handles the logistics for all the federal lands up there. That's what we do, you know. We have no idea what is actually being done at any given site. Our job is to bring in supplies and take care of building maintenance. Before you ask, I don't know why it was welded shut. But DOD ordered it shut and since you are DOD then, as far as we are concerned, you can open it.

"Thank you, Ed, lunch is on me now."

"Just be careful. There was some reason it was sealed shut," Ed says.

"Oh Ed, I didn't know you cared."

"I don't. But I'm holding you to lunch." Ed hangs up.

"There goes my quiet Saturday," groans the Dog.

We go to the bunker and as promised, the EG&G work crew shows up. They look at the front of the building. There is nothing but a steel wall. No door. We didn't see a door the night Dog and I checked it. No sign of a weld either.

"I was told this place was welded shut," declares the foreman. "I see no welds. You sure this is the right place?"

In the meantime, Dog has climbed up the earthen sides of the bunker. He is on top of the place over our heads. He whines and paws, looking at me.

"Hold on," I tell the workers. I scramble up the side of the bunker and make my way over to Dog. He is pawing at the dirt.

Quietly, he says, "There is an opening under here, I can tell."

Sure enough, he wipes enough dirt away a metal plate can be seen. I have the workers toss me up a shovel. I start to clear away the remaining dirt. Yep, there it is, a metal plate about four feet square, welded in place, onto a metal roof.

I tell the guys I have found the opening, and they bring up a cutting torch.

"How did the dog find it up here?" one of them asks. "How did he even know what you were looking for?"

"He special." I say scratching his ears.

They make short work of cutting and removing the welds and help me pry up the plate and set it to one side. Underneath is a hatch. I reach down to the handle and pull, it lifts up. The guys help me get it open. There is a ladder leading down into the building.

"This is as far as we are supposed to go, and frankly, this is as far as I want to go," says the foreman.

"No that's good guys. I appreciate you getting this open. Can I buy your lunch at the club?" I ask.

"Oh, you don't have."

"I want to. Just keep quiet about what you just saw." I take out my cell and call the club manager. I tell him to put their lunch on my tab.

They say thank you and head off for lunch.

"You're actually going down there, aren't you?" Dog inquires.

"Of course. You?"

"I don't do *down the ladder* real gracefully you know. But since someone has to watch your ass, if you get a rope and hold on tight, I might try it," declares my four-legged partner. "I can't let you have all the fun."

I go to my truck, get some rope and flashlights. I am tying a harness onto Dog when Michael talks in my device.

"For God's sake David, be careful. I wish we could help you. Why don't you wait until nightfall and we can be there?"

"Tempting, but now since it's open, I have to at least see what's in here."

I lean into the dark space and shine my light around. It looks like a control room of some sort. There are panels with gages, switches, levers, and some TV screens. There are two chairs in front of the equipment. Definitely a control room. I start to climb down the ladder. Dog is still on top. As I look around, I see a switch panel on the wall next to the ladder. Gingerly I pull one switch up.

The room suddenly lights up. I almost lose my grip on the ladder. I didn't know what to expect but certainly not that the lights would still work.

"Dare you to try the other switch." Dog smirks.

Just to spite the Dog, I do. I hear fans start up. A ventilation system! After all these years, no one has turned off the power. Just like the old phone lines Brandon taped into.

Gotta love the efficiency of our government.

"Get me down there," my partner hollers.

I climb back up. I attach the rope, like a harness, to Dog and he backs into the hole as I let out some rope. He tries to guide himself on the ladder.

There's a picture.

"No more seconds for you man, you're too heavy," I grunt.

He reaches the floor. I climb down. I get the harness off him and he goes around the room.

"No one has been here for a long time," he declares.

At the back of the room is a heavy solid metal door. It has a wheel handle like you see on a submarine hatch. I try the wheel. It starts to turn. Slowly I turn it all the way until it stops.

"Well you going to open it or not?" Dog asks. "Here let me sniff first. Never know."

He smells deeply around the edges of the door. "Nothing but a brunt smell, electrical odor of some sort."

"Okay, you stand to one side."

I pull gently on the handle. The door won't move. I pull harder. Nothing. Then I get a brilliant thought. If this is a safety door then it would open inward, if there was a problem with what's inside, it would not blast into the control room. I scare myself sometimes.

Sure enough, a solid push on the door causes it to move inward. I can see the lights are working in there as well. Pushing it open further, I find the cause of the electrical smell my partner detected. The room is blackened with soot. In the far end of the room, which is in fact a tunnel back into the hill, is a twisted mass of metal, wires, and just blackened stuff. The ventilation is working so I can breathe well, considering the heavy odor. Something blew up in here-that's for sure. The lights are recessed into the walls and have protective cages around them.

We ease further back into the tunnel and find a large tube-like structure lying in pieces around the floor. There are wires and coils and insulation material all over. I look up at the ceiling. There are large doors up there.

I know what this is. This is the beam machine Schultz used to take down the alien's spaceship. This is the tube that shot the beam. There are hydraulic cylinders on the floor, some attached to the tube and some to the floor. This sucker was able to rise through the opened doors and shoot its deadly beam. There are compass like marks on the floor. The son-of-a-bitch could aim it. No wonder this place was sealed up. This thing could take out Las Vegas and who knows what else. What the hell was that crazy kraut going to do with this?

I take pictures for Michael and his crew to look at. With a lot of pushing and shoving, I manage to get Dog back up the ladder and I close the hatch. I shove the metal plate back in place and cover it with dirt.

As Dog and I are making our way down the side of the bunker, up drives Pam and Grizzie in their patrol vehicle.

"Pardon me sir, but are you authorized to be over here?" Man does she sound sexy when she is being official.

"Hi girls, we were just getting some exercise," I lamely say. "Do you ever see anyone over here?"

"No, never. There is never anyone here. It's not on our beat but I saw your truck and had to check on you. So, what are you *really* doing?" She asks.

"Uh I'll tell you later, right now I think I need a shower, I have a date tonight."

She looks at me. I am covered with dirt and soot.

"I'm sure whoever your date is will appreciate the shower." She smiles and they take off.

On the way to my apartment, I discuss what I've found with Michael. He totally agrees with my theory, I have found the original beam weapon. He says they never knew where it was located.

"Was it all destroyed?" he asks.

"Oh yes. Wait until you see the photos. Even the equipment in the control room appeared to be fried. I see why they closed it, too much work to clean it up. There is plenty of open land here to build another lab. Which is, of course, what they did," I say. "That would be the lab where Wolfgang works now, right?"

"Yes, I had though they built it there so we could work with them using the tunnel to our caves. I always wondered why the government closed the bunker behind us. Now I know," Michael says.

"If you want to see the mess inside the bunker, the metal plate is just setting on top of the hatch," I tell him.

"I'll look at your photos and see. From what you say there would be nothing of use to anyone." Then Michael adds, "Like Brandon's bunch."

Later at the appointed hour, Dog and I go on our date with the ladies. Another fun evening. Yep, I like this lady. We decide we need to leave Area 51 and go places, like Las Vegas, shows, etc. Scheduling is our only problem, but we will work it out. Dog and Grizzie can hang out at the caves. Mickey and the other kids would love Grizzie. And Grizzie won't be able to tell Pam where she's been. I just need to figure out a cover story. Something other than…. I'm going to put them in a cave with aliens.

I know - *Tom can offer to baby-sit.* Yeah that should work. I hope. In the back of my mind I hear the haunting words: *"What could go wrong?"*

CHAPTER THIRTY-THREE

After Dog and I get back to the apartment I check in with Brian at the control room. He tells me Brandon placed a call to Schultz in Sedona, but the Germans had already left for their camping trip to the vortexes. Brandon left a message saying it was time for them to move forward. He said he would call again as he cannot leave a phone number for *security reasons.*

Brian says he told Michael and George about the call. They were mystified about how the *boys* can *move forward.* Are they bluffing or are we missing something they have done? Brian thinks they are bluffing and trying to get their hands-on whatever weapons they think Schultz and Hoffman have developed. Do the Germans even know who they are dealing with? The *boys* may be older in years, compared to humans, but they are just teenagers, emotionally. Teenagers with huge brains. Now there's a scary thought.

I am turning all of this over in my mind. We believe we have shut down any access the plotters have to propulsion systems, but have we? They are smart and have plenty of time to outthink the elders. They're motivated, it's damn frightening.

Wait a minute, weapons. I haven't even asked about what, if any, weapons the aliens possess. Come in peace, *my ass!* I can't believe you would travel across the universe without some protection. Michael says they gave up on war a long time ago but that doesn't mean they don't carry a big stick, just in case.

I call for Michael and ask if we can talk. Come over he says.

"You coming Robin?" I ask my sidekick.

"What is this Robin thing and there are no bats in those caves!" Snaps back the pooch.

"You mean you have never seen any Batman movies? I know you are too young to have seen the TV show but Batman Returns, the Dark Knight series, none of them?"

He looks at me and sighs, much like a parent would to their child:"I don't go to too many movies you know. No dogs allowed. You've seen those signs."

"But the aliens have *movie nights*." I respond.

Apparently, Brian has been listening to our conversation.

"Uh David, the elders do not allow us to see all the movies available. They are concerned about the violence and some of the seamier stuff you humans watch. They preview them, before we are allowed to watch."

"Okay. I can go along with that." I say. "Batman movies were not exactly bedtime fare for children."

"So, who's Robin?" Asks Dog.

"I'll tell you on the way."

We go to the caves, Michael meets us, and says we are going to George's office. Never been there before.

"Wow, George, this is really great." I exclaim as we enter his office. "I love it. Just like a mountain lakeside cabin."

It is. He has murals of pine trees, lake vistas and huge overstuffed furniture. Above our heads is an open beamed ceiling, with large hand carved beams, just like a real cabin.

"There is a refreshing feeling in here. I can almost smell the pines." I say taking a deep breath.

"I have a subtle pine odor infused in here." He says proudly.

"I though you all lived in caves back home. Where did this come from?" I ask

"Sedona wasn't our first visit to Earth you know. We dropped in on Lake Tahoe once and I fell in love with the whole scene. Mountains, lake, and the pine smells. When we settled here, I created this." He sweeps his hands around the room. "It took a while, but it was worth it."

"It's beautiful George." I sink into a huge chair. (George must just about *disappear* into this one)

"All right guys, down to business. Tell me what kinds of weapons you have, how they are secured and were there any weapons on the downed spaceship?"

They both look at me, somewhat startled. Michael says, "You never cease to amaze me David. You sure you don't have alien in you? Yes of course we have weapons. We have personal defense weapons that would compare to your handguns and rifles. They are kept in our armory which is located alongside the control room. We have not kept up with the training we previously did because there has been no threat, until now. At this point we are not sure if we have a real threat or just our rambunctious youth. The Germans have not shown to be a direct problem to us, but we are obviously watching the situation, just as you are. Yes, there were defensive weapons on the spaceship. We had a particle beam. It would cause another object to literally beak apart when struck."

"Just like your ship when Schultz hit it with *his* beam?" I ask.

"Yes, exactly. We were lucky he did not have any more power than he did, or we would not be here. Still, from the distance of around 200 of your miles it did the job. We were very vocal with your government about the dangers of his experiments when we learned about them. He had not discovered how to create and store the needed energy. That is why it blew up. Let us see your photos, please." George says.

I show them the shots I took inside the bunker. The two aliens shake their big heads.

"Look at this George" Michael says. "It is a wonder it even got off one shot. It looks like it started to blow up at the generator and continued to the fire tube. My God, it would had destroyed us all if so much power had come through the tube."

"Not to change the subject fellas, but we haven't discussed religion or such things before. I notice you all use the God word. May I ask if or what your people's beliefs are on the *greater power* subject?" I have to ask the question I have been wondering about.

"Well, our people are pretty much like yours, divided on the subject. I think most of us do believe in some *higher power*. We do have a couple of what you would call religions. A minister was on the ship, but he was killed in the crash landing of his escape pod along with the others in it. In all our space travel we have seen wondrous sights but, who knows?" Michael says.

"Back to your weapons. What happened to the particle beam weapon from your ship? Was it destroyed or is it out there in the wilderness of Arizona or New Mexico?" I ask.

"We were able to go to the debris area of our ship. This was several months after the crash. We had settled here at Area 51 and agreed to assist your scientists in various research projects. Your government flew some of us there to search for any useful equipment. We did find quite a lot of salvageable materials. Your soldiers helped us gather up anything of possible value." Michael says. "We did manage to get our personal defense weapons which were in lockers. The soldiers and scientist who were there did not know what they were looking at so they helped us get anything we said could be used. Would they have assisted us if they knew there were weapons inside, probably not?" He smiles. "But the majority of material was what you would call electronics, for communication and control of the ship. Those items were invaluable to us and your government has benefitted from some of the technology as well."

"We were generous with our knowledge as long as it was *not* going to be used in a destructive manner." George adds.

"As far as the particle beam and its components, they were in the portion of the ship hit by Schultz's beam.

Ironic isn't it? We did locate a lot of the components of the weapon but never the storage device, capacitor is the scientific name. It holds the charged particles until the weapon is discharged. It is like the magazine of your pistol. That is where Schultz failed. He did not have a device sufficiently sturdy to contain the charged particles. From your photos it appears his machine blew up in his old laboratory.

We searched for any sign of our capacitor unit at the scene but never found any sign of it. I still think it must be out there somewhere. I would feel better if we found it or some remains of it." Michael says. "Especially now, since we know Schultz is active again."

"That was one of the reasons we built the Smart Car." George says. "Michael and I have taken some night trips to the area, but even with our advanced sensors, we have not yet located it. The debris field covers quite a large area of mountainous terrain."

"Did you ever talk with Schultz about his weapon and the fact he hit your ship?" I ask.

"We did talk with him when we first started to work on projects with the scientists. He wanted to discuss particle beam technology and we were agreeable, until we realized he wanted to use the information to fabricate a weapon. Then George and I told our people not to discuss any of our technology with the humans unless it was first approved by George and myself. I did find out later that one of our scientists had already told Schultz about the beam weapon onboard our ship. That was just before we went with your military back to the crash site to look for usable equipment. Schultz never told us he made the device which ultimately shot us down. We learned that from the other human scientists after Schultz was discharged."

"You said one of your people told Schultz about your beam weapon *before* you visited the crash site, right?" I ask. "Was Schultz one of the humans who accompanied you?"

"No, he had already been let go." George says.

"I'm playing cop now, how about Cranston's friend Franklin? Was he there? We found out he was visiting Schultz on a regular basis, remember?" I ask.

"I don't know, there were a few men in civilian clothes I had not seen before. George, did you know who any of them were?" Michael asks.

"No, I knew they were from Washington."

"Was Wolfgang there at the scene?" I ask.

"Yes, he was." Michael says excitedly. "Because he was younger than most of the other scientists, he helped carry some of the material we found"

"I'll ask him in the morning, maybe he will remember."

"David, are you thinking Franklin Pierce was involved in this all along?" George asks.

"Think about it." I say. "He was Schultz's *mysterious visitor* and he has been pushing Cranston to continue the beam weapon project. In fact, he probably forced Cranston's predecessor to retire because he would *not* continue the project. Makes sense."

Michael stands up, he is visible shaken. He goes over to a side cabinet and pours himself a drink. George looks at him, "Excuse me, but if you are going to be free with my liquor at least pour me one, as well as our guests."

Michael looks sheepish. "Oh sorry, I was just so blown away by all this. Of course, everyone want a round?"

CHAPTER THIRTY-FOUR

In the morning I call Wolfgang and tell him I have more questions for him. He invites us over for coffee. I ask if he remembers anyone who was present when the aliens went back to the crash scene site. He looks at me: "A lot of people, David, a lot of people. Soldiers, some of us from Area 51, of course the aliens and a few men from Washington."

"I'm sorry, Wolfgang, I was up late. Let me try again." I have now embarrassed myself.

"He needs more sleep and less to drink." Quips the dog having his ears scratched by the scientist.

"Be still." I reply. "I could have left you back at the apartment."

"Oh please, then I could sleep in for a change." Dog snorts. "By the way whatever happened to *we need to keep in shape and workout every day*? The only time your heart rate rises is when you're around Pam."

Ignoring the canine, I rephrase my inquiry.

"Was the man, who use to visit Schultz regularly at his lab, also there?"

"Yes, he was. In fact, he was quite interested in what was being found. He was looking closely at everything, asking questions: "What is that? What is it used for? Lots of questions. The other men didn't seem as interested in the equipment as he was. I wondered why he was so curious. It had something to do with Schultz's work didn't it?" the German asks. "Of course, it did!" He answers his own question.

"I'm sure it did. Were you aware the aliens had a particle beam weapon on their spaceship?" I ask.

"Oh my heavens. No! I have never heard that before. Did Schultz know?"

"Yes he did." I reply. "Michael and George told their people not to say anything, once they realized Schultz wanted to make a similar weapon, but the cat was out of the bag. One of the aliens who worked with him had mentioned it. Schultz was discharged shortly after. Now that I know of Franklin Pierce's association with him, it all begins to make sense. Franklin Pierce was the name of the man who visited Schultz."

"And he is still in the political power structure somewhere in the background, correct?" Asks the scientist.

"Very much so I'm afraid. What Peirce was looking for that day, in the debris field, was fragments from the particle beam weapon. Michael says it was all pretty much destroyed, but they never found any sign of the storage device."

"Yes, the capacitor would be the key to making it a good weapon. "Wolfgang says. "Schultz's problem was he could not devise a strong enough capacitor to store the energy he wanted to use for his weapon. That is why his machine destroyed itself."

"You were at his lab when it happened?" I ask.

"No, we all ran over there when it exploded. Schultz and Hermann were the only ones inside. We helped them get out. I went back in there later and looked at the device. The capacitor could hold only so much energy and electrons. Schultz, the fool, overloaded it and it blew apart. Hermann told me Schultz had just discharged the weapon as it exploded. If he had waited another second, they both would have been killed, I am sure of it."

"What happened to this Hermann?"

"He retired a few years ago and decided to live in Las Vegas. After he survived the explosion, he decided he must be naturally lucky, so he took up gambling. He died a year or so ago." Wolfgang tells me.

"What did he die from?" Hey, I'm a cop, my mind works this way.

"Cirrhosis of the liver." Said the German. "He loved to drink. But he was 92 at the time, so I still drink. I have a few years left the way I see it." He laughs.

I thank Wolfgang and go back to my apartment. "Hey smart ass." I say. "What say we go for a run; you know *keep in shape*? I'll change and let's go."

"Oh man, me and my big mouth." Dog replies.

We go out and start down the road to the North. We head out into the desert and I get a good pace going. Starting to feel nice and comfortable. Dog has been poking along, stopping and smelling every so often. Suddenly, I hear him coming up behind me. He races past me and then cuts in front of me and makes circles around me, all while I am trying to keep a steady pace going. I stop.

"Jerk! Show off! What are you trying to do? I know four feet are better than two, but are you trying to get me hurt? You can't drag me back from out here." I'm pissed at the canine.

He just snorts and races off. "Come on candy-ass, try and catch me."

I do make a valiant effort, but two feet cannot catch four. Finally I stop, out of breath. Dog trots back to me.

"Had enough? Let's go back. I'm hungry."

We start to jog slowly back when I see a familiar Air Police SUV coming across the desert toward us. Great, now I am all sweaty and dirty again.

Pam pulls up besides us.

"Impressive guys. I've been watching you." She looks at me. "Don't feel bad, I can't catch Grizzie either. Want a ride?"

"Yes, thank you ma'am, but the dog will have to get back on his own." I go around to the passenger side and get in. "Let's go."

Pam looks at me. "Really, you wouldn't do that, would you?"

"No, but he is a smart ass and a showoff." I say as I open the door for him to jump in. I forget she does not know the verbally abusive dog I live with. She thinks he is just the sweetest thing outside of Grizzie. The two dogs jump around in the back seat. Glad *he's* still got energy.

"What are you doing after your shift?" I ask charmingly.

"Actually, I have a date with a DOD agent, after he has a shower, I hope." She answers.

"Hope you have a date or hope he has a shower."

"Both actually." She giggles.

We get together in the evening. As we are relaxing after dinner, she looks at me with those beautiful eyes. She leans over toward me and says quietly, "So what exactly are you doing here? I know it is probably *classified* but I must ask. You are out of place here. You are more than a security guard. You are here for a much more important reason than is apparent. I know you cannot tell me anything but if I can help, ask me. Remember *patrol sees all*."

"I was going to ask if you would keep an eye on the area where you saw me and Dog, by the old bunker. Any movement there would be of interest to me. And since you are offering, *anything* out of the ordinary you see, here or anywhere in Area 51 or even at Creech. It would be appreciated." I reply.

Pam sits back in her chair.

"Wow, I didn't expect that. David, what the heck are you involved with? I know, I know, you can't tell me, but just what the *hell are* you involved with? Maybe you can't tell *me* anything, but I can tell *you* a couple of things, I have seen. I don't think this is a good place for us to talk. I do want to run a couple of things past you. Is your apartment secure?"

"The apartment is secure, but I'm not sure I can guarantee your safety though." I say, with a lascivious smile.

"I've got Grizzie. I'll be fine. I do want to tell you what I've seen. You mentioned Creech so I think you are the right person to talk to."

Interesting turn of events. This sexy lady is inviting herself over to my place to discuss business. Well, what the hell.

We leave the club and the four of us go to my place. The dogs have been stuffed by the staff at the club, so they just settle together on the carpet.

I get Pam and me each a glass of wine and we settle down. She takes a big breath and begins, "I've been thinking of saying something to you ever since you told me who Cranston was. The affair or whatever it is doesn't matter to me, but since I now know he is a big shot here, I have been wondering about what I've seen."

I'm leaning forward, looking at her eyes and listening intently.

Pam narrows those eyes and scolds me, "Are you listening to me or just looking for a kiss?"

"Both actually," I say.

She leans into me and we connect.

"All right, back to business." I say. "What have you seen?"

"I told you I had seen Cranston with Major Andrews and they were definitely fooling around. No big deal by itself but, Major Andrews has another visitor regularly. He is from Arlington or D.C., somewhere back there. She is single so that's fine. But one of the gate officers, a girl friend of mine, told me he only comes to the base to see Andrews, no one else, he goes to her office and then after a while they leave, each in their own car."

Pam continues, "Major Andrews has her own place off base in Las Vegas, as do the rest of the officers. Still no biggie, but then my friend tells me the guy always asks if Cranston is on base. My buddy knows who Cranston is and asked me what he did at Area 51. She said this other guy obviously did not want to see Cranston or for Cranston to see him. Being girls, my friend and I are wondering what's going on. So, we start to compare info. I just say Cranston is a director of something at Area 51. She says the DC guy is DOD but only seems to come to Creech to see Andrews. I ask her his name." Pam looks intently at me.

"You interested, Agent Manning?" She puts her beautiful face right in front of mine. Before I can answer she leans in.

"Damn you." I say, "Who is interviewing who here?" I reach for her.

Dog groans with disgust and Grizzie covers her eyes with her paws.

"Not in front of the children." Pam says.

"Okay, name please Officer."

"Franklin Pierce." She says. "Know anything about him?"

I don't answer. Franklin Pierce is Cranston's contact, his boss. Franklin Pierce is coming to Creech to see the same woman Cranston is having an affair with. My mind just went into overdrive.

"I take the silence and the rolling back of your eyes as a yes, you do know something about him." Pam brings me back to earth.

I grab her.

"Baby, I love you. You are the best patrol officer ever." I give her a big hug and then a long kiss.

"You know you could have had the kisses for free but I'm glad you're happy. Now do you want to let me in on any of this? Come on, you have to give me something." She implores.

I swear her to secrecy.

Pam says, "You know, we are already under what I would call, *death threats* if we tell anyone what we see or hear in Area 51. You're covered."

I begin to tell her what I feel secure in sharing. I leave out the cave inhabitants, the fact Dog can talk and a few other items. I tell her about Schultz and that he was developing a device and how it exploded, but not what it was, that Franklin Pierce was visiting Schultz on a regular basis before the explosion and his dismissal. Much like he is now visiting Major Andrews. I explain Cranston's predecessor was the one who fired Schultz and tabled his project, then Franklin Pierce somehow leveraged the predecessor to retire and put Cranston in his place so he could get the project restarted. I take a breath.

"This is all for real, right? Not just some gibberish you are making up to pacify me, so you won't tell me classified stuff?" Pam eyes me carefully.

"No bull, this is for real." I say. "The best is yet to come…. Cranston is **not** in favor of the project but goes along with it because Pierce saved his butt and his career when a couple of black ops Cranston ran went sour. As time went on, the remaining German scientist, Wolfgang, was dragging his heels on the project because he did not want this particular device to be developed. He is originally from Nazi Germany and saw firsthand the evil empire in action. Cranston was caught in the middle. He didn't want the project developed either but had to try to placate Pierce. Then he started getting threatening phone calls. From whom we are not sure. Enter yours truly." I take a bow and continue.

"Schultz has resurfaced in Sedona and is again working on his pet project. In fact, he has what appears to be a functioning model. He has also teamed up with another scientist from the Third Reich he formally worked with on the project in Germany. That chap's name is Hoffman. He is visiting Schultz on a tourist visa." I take another pause to let it soak in.

"Holy shit." Says the lovely listener. "And I just thought it was a couple of jerks involved in a lover's triangle. How do you know so much about all of this, you haven't been here that long?"

"I have a little help from my friends in low places." I smile.

"I can only imagine, and I don't want to go there." She continues, "So as I see it, Franklin Pierce and Major Andrews are working together to keep an eye on the project and Cranston. Did she start an affair with Cranston just to get inside information out of him? Yes, of course she did. That's perfect."

"That is my thought." I add. "What do you know about Andrews?"

"Not much, she hasn't been here long, a few months maybe. I don't know where she came from. She is in her mid-forties, somewhat attractive and can be quite personable, especially to males. Charming, but very manipulative, just my opinion. Not so friendly to females." Pam answers.

"I am hearing… *good looking bitch who gets her own way*…right?" I smile.

"You got it." She says. "Wait a minute, Cranston has only been in charge a few months, you said. He does not want to go along with Pierce's project and then Andrews suddenly appears, to soften him up or at least spy on him. You know my dad was in that same office until the Major came on base. He was just putting in his time until retirement, doing some type of intelligence analysis. He was a pilot and then decided to just take a desk job until he had his time in. They settled down in Vegas mainly to be around me. They wouldn't admit it, but that's what I think."

"He was in the Major's office? "My mind is whirling.

"Until she came on base. He had to give up his office to her. He does not want to discuss it. One day he told Mom and me it was time to pull the plug, retire."

"And what do you think?"

"I truly don't know what to think. He was not happy about leaving. He seems alright now, but he sure quit suddenly. He had his time in, so it was no financial burden. Mom was unquestionable happy. He won't talk about it with me,"

Unfortunately, Pam has to work tomorrow, and we have burned the midnight oil already. I drive the two ladies to their quarters.

Back at my place I reflect on it all.

I feel something is fermenting somewhere. I think the active ingredients are in Sedona and the catalyst is in the D.C area. Major Andrews at Creech is possibly one of the extra ingredients, if needed. There may also be something here in Area 51. I am not sure how Brandon's bunch will be mixed in.

"Can we sleep in tomorrow, please?" Whines the pooch. "This burning the candle at both ends is getting to me."

"Definitely!" I say.

And we do.

CHAPTER THIRTY-FIVE

Whinny the pooch and I just hang out on Sunday. Nice for a change. No one has threatened anyone, the Germans are still in the wilderness doing who knows what, and by evening I am bored. The aliens must be psychic; Michael calls and invites us to dinner.

So, off to the caves.

After dinner, we go to George's office, my new favorite place. George looks at Michael and asks, "Since you are now a true bartender, do you mind if I have a drink?"

Michael smiles good-naturedly, gets up, and pours drinks.

I tell the little ones about Wolfgang's visit.

"He might be able to spread some light on things," Michael responds. "Certainly worth the time."

"Do we have any idea when Schultz and Hoffman will be back?" I ask.

"No." Says Michael. "But from what we overheard they should return in just a few days. I will be anxious to hear their reaction to Brandon's voice mail."

The guys have no knowledge of Major Andrews. Michael calls Brian and asks him to find information on her.

"How does she fit into all of this?" George wonders. "Why hasn't she shown up in our monitoring of Cranston if he sees her so much? Another round fellows?"

"More imbibing of alcoholic beverages?" Lectures Dog. "Is that the only way you folks can talk?"

"It helps sometimes." I reply. "Want another beer Dog?"

"Yes, if you don't mind." He answers. "Oh crap, I fell for that one."

The next day is Monday and John and Tom show up on schedule.

John says he had a quiet weekend. Tom just looks at me and shakes his head. He is still not sure what he saw and heard last week. But he came back to work, so he is hooked.

I have Tom working with John, acting as if he were John's bodyguard. Which he presently is, even though I don't think it's necessary. Tom will go with him any time John leaves the office. Should keep them busy until the main event, whatever that will be.

I take Tom aside and fill him in on Major Andrews and her connection to John and to Pierce. He doesn't know her. She wouldn't have flown on *Janet Airlines*. Air Force personnel *drive* out to Creech.

I tell Tom I am weighing whether to talk to Cranston about Major Andrews. He thinks it is too soon. John might say something to her and blow our lead. I agree. Then Tom says, "Give me her info and I'll use some of my old sources and see if she comes up on their radar."

266

"Brilliant, of course you would have *old sources.* Welcome to the team."

Yep, I have a real partner. Now we're rolling.

I make a call to Michael, who tells me Brian has come up with the Major's service record and is researching further into her past. I take the information and pass it on to Tom. He goes to his cell phone and calls his contacts.

We finally have info we can follow up on ourselves. Much better than waiting around for intercepts from the *cave control room.*

Now this is my case. The aliens may have gotten me involved in this mess but now, I'm in. I intend to do it my way, using anyone's help I can get. Besides, I am a bona fide government agent, and this is my country being threatened.

I call Pam's cell. I know she is working out of Creech today.

"Hi handsome, what's up?" Her cheery voice answers.

"How did you know it was me?" I ask.

"Honestly think you're the *only one* I call handsome? But you're the only one who would call me from a *restricted* number and you're the only one I've given my number to, except my parents."

I ask her if she could discreetly find out the dates and times Cranston and Franklin went to Creech.

"You don't want much do you? She responds. "Let me talk with my girlfriend and see if it can be done, discreetly."

We talk a little longer and then she has to get to work. Five o'clock comes and John and Tom leave. I go to the club for dinner, along with the now well-rested hound.

"We need some action, partner," he says. "Let's go to Sedona and roust those trouble-makers."

"Nice to have you back. If it weren't for your snoring, I wouldn't have known you were around for the last two days."

"Come on, I've been listening. Sedona is where it's going to happen. Those two Germans are the key to what's going on. Schultz is wacked out, but I think the one that was in Russia, Hoffman, he's the real instigator in the renewed interest in the beam weapon."

"Well listen to you. You *have* been paying attention. You may be right about Hoffman. Good Dog." I say with a smile and pat him on his head.

"Don't patronize me, two- legged." He snorts.

Later George calls and notifies me Brian has been able to develop some background on the Major. I tell him I'll be right over.

As we are entering the control room, I see Michael is listening on headphones. George says the two Germans have returned to the house in Sedona.

Good. We have been waiting for their response to Brandon's message. While Michael is eavesdropping, we talk with Brian who has discovered quite a lot about Major Andrews.

Brian informs us, "Major Katarina Anna Andrews was born in Russia to Alexander and Anna Antonovich. She attended the Moscow State University. When she was 26, she immigrated to the United States, where she enlisted in the U. S. Air Force and became a U.S. citizen. Because of her fluency in Russian and other Eastern European languages she quickly rose in the ranks and now is a Major in the intelligence sector of the Air Force. She changed her name to Andrews prior to enlisting. Further digging indicated her father was a Colonel in the GRU, the Russian military intelligence service."

We not only let her into this country but also made her a citizen and an officer in the Air Force, the intelligence section, no less. There is a story here. There better be! We may be sloppy sometimes, but this just does not sound right. Brian was able to dig deeper into the files than I would have thought possible. This guy is amazing, glad he's on our side. Wait, is he? I sure hope so because he is one smart alien.

The original immigration papers Brian located show our government not only knew who Katrina was, but also knew her father had defected. He became a source of information on Russian military intelligence. His present location is not divulged. That's a no brainer. There is no mention of mom. Did she come too, or did she stay in Russia? Unasked questions bother me.

We have the daughter of a Russian intelligence officer working for the U.S. in an intelligence position, getting chummy with a U.S. intelligence official--Franklin Pierce and even chummier with the head of a secret project to produce a terrifying weapon-- good old John Cranston. I think it all stinks…. just my opinion.

Finally, Michael puts down the headset and relays what he has learned listening to Schultz and Hoffman.

They were quite interested in Brandon's message. Schultz said he knew Brandon was the son of an alien scientist, from the Area 51 days. Brandon had contacted him previously and offered to work on the beam weapon Schultz tried to develop. The only help needed from Brandon, is to find the particle storage unit from the alien's spaceship. Apparently, the reason for the Germans trip to Sedona. They did not find it. *Thankfully.* From listening to the Germans conversation, it sounds like they knew where to look, in the vast wilderness east of Sedona, where the ship went down.

"Schultz had already been fired when all of you went out to the crash site. How did he find out where to search?" I ask.

The little leaders all look at each other.

"That is a good question, David," says George. "He knew he shot us down, but as to exactly where, no. We didn't know until the Air Force searched for our debris and finally located it. We landed to the east, in New Mexico, in our escape pods."

"Someone else had to be in touch with him." Michael says slowly. "You don't think Franklin Pierce, do you?"

Ever the earthling, I say, "Duh, do you think? Who else? Pierce visits Area 51 regularly and then stops coming after Schultz is fired. I bet the bastard has been in touch with the German the whole time and arranged for him to move to Sedona. He probably got Hoffman involved also. We know he wants the weapon. We know Pierce was present during the recovery efforts at your crash site."

"How does my nephew Brandon fit into this, is he also connected to Pierce?" Michael asks.

"I'll guess he is a free agent. He was able to locate Schultz, when you guys couldn't and is trying to work his own deal." I answer. "What else are the krauts talking about?"

Michael says they are interested in what Brandon could offer in brain power but are unsure of his motives. Michael gets the impression they are waiting to hear from someone else. No name is used. More mystery?

I bet it's Pierce.

CHAPTER THIRTY-SIX

The next morning, I fill Tom in on the latest information we have on Major Andrews and the Sedona Germans. He absorbs everything I say.

"So…Hoffman was taken by the Russians after World War Two, then shows up to work with his old compatriot Schultz. Major Andrews' father is a defecting Russian intelligence officer, she is now a US Air Force intelligence officer and somehow U.S. spymaster Pierce is involved. I agree David, this stinks. I haven't heard back from my old contacts but with this new info I'm going to call in an old debt. I saved an FBI agent's ass once. He owes me. Seems like a good time to call in my marker."

"Impressive Tom. Hey while you are at it, see if he knows anything about Herr Hoffman. Worth a try. My best old contact is doing life for murder, drug smuggling and jaywalking. He's no help anymore."

"Jaywalking?"

"Hey, gave them *reasonable cause* to stop him."

There is not much to do until Brandon, the Germans, Comrade Andrews, or Pierce make their next move.

I remember one item which has been in the back of my mind ever since I learned about it…. the death of Michael's brother. They didn't do an autopsy. They assumed, from the two holes in his hand, he died from a snake bite. I get George on the line. He says they do have medical staff and could do an autopsy if requested.

"Why do you need an autopsy done?" George asks. "Did you find a body?"

I tell George my thoughts about Michael's brother. Michael did say the aliens preserved the bodies of their deceased so hopefully they could be buried back home, someday.

"Honestly, we never even gave it a thought," George says. "It seemed obvious with the bite marks. He was outside at night in the desert when the snakes are active. What are you thinking?"

"When we were listening to Schultz last night, he said he knew Brandon's father. I remember you said *none* of you worked with Schultz. How would he have known Brandon's father?" I ask.

"Only by sight. Since we refused to work on his type of project we were never in his lab. He ignored us once he realized we would not help him." Then George asks, "So are you thinking Michael's brother's death may not have been caused by a snake bite? That Schultz was involved? Well, Schultz was still here when it happened, it was just about the time he was leaving. My god, David that is horrible. Why would he kill him?"

"I'm just being a cop, George. I like all the loose ends tied up and this is one I would like to tie up. How would Michael take to the idea of the autopsy?"

"I'll talk with him. He was terribly upset his brother died so young. I do remember talking with our doctor. He told me he thought our metabolic makeup should have been able to fight off the venom. I'll talk with Michael. At the time we had no reason to think anything but the obvious." George is clearly upset.

Tom comes back from calling the FBI agent and has heard the tail end of my conversation with George. "Okay, tell me why Schultz would kill Michael's brother? Because they wouldn't work with him?"

"He was found close to the bunker Schultz used. It was at night. Schultz knew his time was limited and just maybe he wanted something from the bunker. I don't know. Maybe the brother came along at the wrong time. I don't like loose ends."

My cell rings and it is Pam.

"Hi beautiful." I answer.

"I'm not even going to ask how many women you call beautiful." She jokes. "I have some information for you. How about dinner tonight?"

"You're on. I didn't think you were here today."

"I'm not. It's an off-duty day. I'm at my parents in Vegas. I stay here when I'm not working. My folks would like to meet you. Don't worry, I can hear the gears turning in your conspiratorial brain. I just told them you had asked me for some help on a case you were working, but since I won't be back to Creech for several days, I was going to call and meet you somewhere. Mom said she would make dinner. We can sit and talk afterwards, and they won't bother us."

"You often bring your work home with you?" I tease.

"Do you want this information or not?" she answers testily.

"Yes Ma'am I would appreciate it, Ma'am." I say.

"That's better. It'll be fine. Don't worry. They are great people, you'll like them. My Dad was a pilot in the Air Force. He just retired."

Oh great. A cocky, *don't even think of looking at my daughter like that you pervert*, Air Force pilot. I really do like Pam, but my conspiratorial mind says this is a ploy to get me to meet her parents. I'll give it a try. Won't be the first set of tough parents I've met. Besides, I'm armed, I can fight my way out if necessary.

She gives me the address along with a gate code. Gated community, hum, they are doing well. I tell John I need to leave early for a meeting in Las Vegas. He asks if I would like to spend the night at his place. Yes, that seems to be a good idea. Please bring Dog he says, Doris is always taking about him. In fact, he says he would be happy to take Dog home with him so I won't have to worry about him. Even better idea.

I go back to my office and Dog looks at me.

"You could have at least asked if I minded. Small gesture but it would have been the proper thing to do." He lowers his head and gives me a look that only Dog can give.

"I'm sorry buddy but he just offered, I wasn't even thinking of it." I am apologizing to a dog. Well I do have to admit he is much more than *just* a dog.

The canine laughs out loud. "Gotcha! Of course, I would love to go and see Doris. She will pamper the heck out of me. What's not to love?"

Later in the afternoon I take off for Pam's house. Her folks live north of where John does. I pull into the entry gate. Punch in the code and enter the area. Nicely landscaped drive leading to a park. The houses are not as ostentatious as John's. This looks like a place where I would like to live.

I find the house and pull into the driveway. As I'm walking up through a courtyard, Pam opens the door and runs out to me. She gives me a quick smooch and leads me into my fate. Her Mom is in the kitchen. She's about Pam's height: hair, nails & make-up nicely done but not showy like Doris. She comes over and greets me warmly.

"So nice to meet you David. Pam has told us all about you."

How much is *all*, I wonder to myself.

Then Dad comes into the room. He is a quite pleasant and jovial, a regular guy. Five-ten at least. He was not a fighter pilot. He's not the *Tom Cruise little shit, I walk on water type,* that most of them are.

"Welcome David. Can I get you a beer?" He says while shaking my hand. "Where's your dog? Pam says he is quite a beauty."

"I left him with my boss for the night. His wife loves my dog." I reply. Just then Grizzie comes into the house through a doggie door. She comes right up to me, wagging her tail. Then she looks around as if to search for Dog. Not seeing him she promptly goes back outside.

"I just assumed you would bring him." Pam says. "I should have told you he would be welcome."

We sit and talk a little. Turns out Dad was a bomber jockey. We hit it off. Once she sees we are going to be okay, Pam helps Mom finish dinner. When dinner is ready we all go into the dining room.

"Wonderful dinner." I tell Mom when we've finished. "Thank you for having me. That was great."

"Well thank you David. Now I know you two have business to discuss, so we'll leave you alone."

"Can I help clean up, clear the table at least?" I ask. Ever the gentleman.

"No, no." Dad says. "You two go on to the living room. We've got it."

In the living room Pam sits on the couch and pats the cushion next to her. I sit like a good boy.

"Dinner wasn't so bad, was it?" She says.

"No actually I enjoyed talking with your Dad. Interesting guy. Your Mom is sweet, just like her daughter." I feel like I'm pandering but I do mean it, she is a very nice lady.

Pam looks at me and rolls her eyes. "Always full of it aren't you.

She then takes out some papers and shows them to me. "Cranston comes at least once or twice a week. He arrives at the gate around five-thirty or six. He will go to the officer's club and meet with the Major. They will drink and eat and then will leave in the same car and drive toward Vegas. I told you she has a place in town. The next morning around eight a.m. they return and in a few minutes Cranston leaves and heads toward Area 51. Draw your own conclusions, investigator." She leans over to me; I smell the heady aroma of her perfume. I start to reach for her and then remember where I am. She takes advantage of my hesitation and pulls me to her, gives me a big kiss then says, "Back to work."

I can hear the parents in the kitchen. They are chatting away and cleaning up, I guess.

Next Pam shows me Pierce's visits. He comes at least once a month. He arrives around six p.m. and stays for approximately an hour, sometimes more. Then he and the Major leave in separate cars at the same time. Both head toward Vegas.

"I think they go to her place also." Pam says.

"Why? It sounds like she gives him a report on Cranston's activities, and they leave, going their own way." I reply.

"Because, as a diligent patrol officer, I have gone past her office while he's still there. I've seen them hugging and kissing and sometimes more. At night when you leave the blinds up, anyone on the outside can see in. You were a patrol officer, don't tell me you never looked into an open window." She says.

"Only to ensure the safety of the citizens." I answer.

"Of course." Pam smiles. "Me too."

We talk some more and then her Dad announces desert is ready. I am sitting next to my desert, oh yeah, at her house.

We all get together for home-made peach pie. Yeah, I'm being softened up, as if I need to be. Finally, I say I should be getting along.

Dad says, "We have a guest room; you are welcome to stay you know."

I wonder how close her room is to the guest room. Don't temp me. No not yet, this is going too well.

"Oh thank you very much, but I have to go to my boss's house, he's expecting me. Dog will be worried if I'm gone too long." I smile.

"Well next time and bring your dog along. I understand Grizzie just loves him." Mom says.

Pam walks me out to my car. We have several long embraces, etc., etc.

"I'm glad you came. Now maybe we can go see some Vegas shows and do other things we've talked about." She says between kisses.

I'll be back.

CHAPTER THIRTY-SEVEN

I drive over to John and Doris Cranston's house. If I had known of the availability of the *guest* room, I would have made different plans. But it is just as well I didn't know. I have enough stress building now and I am getting along great with Pam's parents, best to keep it that way.

The Cranston's are still up. As I walk up to the front door, I hear Dog barking loudly. John opens the door and my furry partner leaps at me, tail wagging and licking my face.

"Whoa, I'm happy to see you too big guy, but don't maim me." I laugh as I try to keep my balance.

"Oh, look how happy he is to see his daddy, John. That's sweet." Doris says as she comes to the entry.

I sit with them and we talk for a while, then Dog and I go to our room.

As soon as I close the door to the room, furry butt turns and snarls:

"My Daddy! My ass! I figured once you were with Pam, I'd never see you again. So, what happened, the dad throw you out?" Then he laughs as only Dog can laugh. "Missed you *Dad*, so how'd it go?"

"It went quite well, I will be going back and spending the night in the guest room and so will you. They thought you were coming and were looking forward to seeing you. Pam has praised you."

"How about Grizzie, did she miss me?" He asks softly.

"She did. She came into the room, came up to me, looked around, saw you weren't there and went outside, pouting I believe." I tell Romeo.

"Good. Now down to business." Dog says conspiratorially. "I know how John contacts the Major." He then just looks at me, goes to the couch, jumps up and settles his immense form comfortably.

"Are you going to tell me or just keep it your secret?"

"Keep your voice down, David. You don't want them thinking you are talking to yourself, do you?"

I go over to the couch, sit next to him and whisper in his ear.

"Listen, *Shit Head*, I could leave you here. Doris would love to adopt you."

"Hey don't get bent out of shape. I haven't had anyone to talk to all night. I got to give you some static. All right, I'll tell you, besides Doris would get on my nerves after a while."

"So?"

"John has a *burner* phone." He says.

"A *burner* phone?" I say.

282

"Yeah, a burner phone, *hot shot cop*. You know-like the drug dealers use so they can't be traced." His highness says condescendingly.

"I *know* what a burner phone is. I didn't think you would know." I snap back. "Oh yeah, television, right?"

"Of course. Before you came along, I didn't get around much you know."

"What did he say to the Major?" I ask patiently.

"He said, 'Hi Babe, how's the love of my life? I'll be down tomorrow night.' Stuff like that."

"He really said *Babe* and *love of my life*? You sure he was talking to Major Andrews?" I ask. I can't picture John Cranston talking like that.

"Yeah it was her. He did call her Kate and said he would be at her office around 1800 hours tomorrow. He also said he was missing her and wanted to spend more time at her place, not just a night here and there. He's serious David. I could sense his rising emotions while he was talking to her." Says the canine psychologist. "You know, just like when you are around Pam."

"What do you sense about Pam's feelings? Oh great wise one." I inquire.

'Hey, that's not fair, you got to ask her yourself." He says piously. "But, you're fine."

"Thanks, now any more about John?"

"Yeah, he called Pierce, while we were still driving. *On his burner phone.* Told him he is getting the project back online. Said hiring you, David, was the best thing he could have done. He thanked Pierce for suggesting he hire someone. He said you are getting the staff back on track. After he hung up he said out loud, "That should hold the bastard for a while." Then he looked over at me and said "I don't know how he does it, but your master is something else. I know he's going to save my bacon." I just looked at John and gave him a soft whine. Then he reached over and gave me a couple pets. Fool! If he only knew!" Dog shakes his head. "Master, indeed."

"Bud, you did a great job. Thank you. Best partner ever, without a doubt." I give him a big hug. He gives me a big lick. Only time a partner ever licked me.

CHAPTER THIRTY-EIGHT

The next morning my partner and I head back to Area 51. John is behind us. In a way I wish Dog could be with him now that I know about his burner cell phone. But he didn't offer. I will have to see if the cave hackers can tap onto it.

When we get back to base Dog goes socializing in the building. After a night with Doris he doesn't need more treats. I huddle with Tom and update him on what we have learned.

"I'm assuming John isn't aware of the Major's relationship with Pierce," Tom says.

"Doesn't sound like it to me," I reply. "Poor S.O.B. I started out believing he was the enemy and now I feel bad for him. He can't even have a real affair."

"So how do John and his wife get along when you are there?" Tom enquires.

"They seem fine. In fact, Dog says they are quite at ease with each other. Almost like roommates rather than a couple. She has her charity work, social clubs, and those kinds of activities. He goes along sometimes, probably for appearance's sakes. The have been married for some time. No kids, family living elsewhere. Sadly, I think it's the way of life for too many couples. Not what I want."

"My wife and I have what I consider the best marriage." Tom says. "We were there for each other while we were working and raising the children and now, we are enjoying our retirement. I do have to work for a while longer, but this is fun, chasing drug dealers was not fun. My wife is relieved I have something I enjoy doing, rather than sitting around all day or babysitting passengers on little red and white airplanes. I come home in a much better mood. We still have our nights and weekends together. It's all good. And *no,* I haven't said anything to her about aliens or a talking dog. That would blow her mind. Did mine at first."

Just then George calls me. Pierce has called the Germans in Sedona and is still talking with them.

"Ha! I knew it. Come on Tom to the bat caves!"

"Haven't heard that in years," Tom chuckles.

We get Dog and rush over to *cave command central.* Michael and George are inside the control room with one of the techs. Michael is listening on headphones.

Shortly he puts them down and tells us what he has heard: "Schultz referred to his caller as *Herr Pierce* and said he had been waiting for his call. He informed Pierce they did not locate the particle collector unit while they were in the Sedona wilderness. Then he asked if the aliens could have retrieved it. Pierce was sure they had not, so either it has not been found or Schultz vaporized it with his beam. Schultz seemed to take offense to this conjecture on Pierce's part. He was adamant he was not responsible for destroying the necessary part. Pierce continued mocking him saying Schultz didn't even know he had hit the alien spaceship so how could he be sure he hadn't destroyed the very part they now needed. Then Pierce got very tough sounding and told Schultz if he had built one machine--he could build another. Schultz told him the aliens held the key to the collector unit, so he needed to get them to work with him. Pierce told him the aliens don't want to work on his device. At the end of the conversation, Schultz said to Pierce, *"They are here at your pleasure, you make them work with us."*

As Michael repeated the German's words, he looked at George and then at Tom and me. "This is what we were afraid would happen. This is why we asked for your help."

"We're on top of these guys," I say with all the confidence I can muster. "We are one step ahead of them and we have to stay that way. How did Pierce answer?"

"He told him he would do what he could, but if Schultz and Hoffman couldn't do the job, he would have Hoffman's visa revoked and send him back. The threat angered Schultz. He said he needed Hoffman. Pierce was cold and told him 'then you two better get busy.' He hung up on the them. Schultz was livid and swore in German words I haven't learned yet," Michael added. "He and Hoffman were yelling and arguing and then Hoffman asked about the young alien who called Schultz, why not see if he can help. Michael said Schultz got quiet and said he was afraid to use him. Hoffman kept after him, asking why. Finally, Schultz answered."

"Because I killed his father. He might know."

Michael pauses. We all look at him. He looks at George.

"That is why you were asking about an autopsy, isn't it?"

I speak up. "I started it Michael. I had the feeling something wasn't right with the circumstances of his death. I'm sorry."

"No, we must know. George please get our medical team together and have them remove my brother's body from the burial vault. David and Tom please stay with us, you are more acquainted with crimes than we are. We require your help." Michael is fighting tears.

George goes to summon the medical staff and Michael continues to listen to the recording of the Germans.

"Does he say *why* he killed your brother?" Tom inquires.

Michael rewinds and listens again.

"Schultz says he needed some notebooks from the bunker where his device exploded. Your government had closed it for safety and told him he could not re-enter. So one night after mid-night he snuck out and went to the bunker. He managed to get inside and retrieve his books. As he was climbing out, my brother, apparently on one of his rock hunting quests, saw Schultz. There were words between them. My brother knew, as we all did, that Schultz was responsible for the destruction of our ship and the death of several of our people. My brother was going back to the caves and intended to report Schultz for entering the bunker. Schultz said he reached for my brother as he was walking away but my brother resisted and tried to get away. Schultz said he held my brother's head as he turned to away and heard a cracking sound. My brother fell to the ground, dead. Schultz told Hoffman he must have broken his neck."

"How about the snake bite marks on his hands?" I ask.

"Schultz knew he had to cover up what he had done. He pulled my brother closer to the rocks near the caves and used a pocketknife to make the two marks that would appear to be a snake bite. Schultz then left and told no one what had happened."

Michael puts the earphones down again. This is too much for him to hear. He begins to sob. Then he becomes angry and jumps up.

"We do not have violence back home. We live in peace with each other. Disputes are settled with an arbitrator. *NO violence!* We only have weapons for defense if attacked and that has not happened in eons." He is clenching his fists.

I've seen Michael worried and emotional before but never has he shown anger. He gets control of himself.

"I am truly sorry for the outburst. I suppose it shows no matter how civilized we think we are, our true nature is not far beneath the surface."

We all go to him and try to comfort him. Between Tom and me looming over him, the techs hugging him and Dog trying to lick his face, it is a wonder we didn't smother poor Michael.

"I think we should let George do the translating for a while, Michael."

We all agree it would be best not to take any action until after a cooling off period. Michael agrees and he has calmed down, but I can feel his heartache. You can see it on his face.

George now has the medical staff ready and the body of the brother has been brought from the storage area. We all gather in their medical facility. The alien physician goes over the body very thoroughly. He has not been told anything except to do a complete autopsy.

He turns toward Michael and softly tells him, "His neck was broken. Death would have been instantaneous. If we had done an autopsy initially, we would have seen it. As I recall, we were all so grief-stricken the bite marks on his hands was as far as we looked. How did this happen?"

George says he will tell the doctor later. We all leave.

On the way back to the office, Tom asks, "We have a homicide or at least manslaughter on a U.S. Government facility. However, the evidence was obtained from an illegal surveillance. Where the hell do we stand on this?"

"I haven't got a clue." I answer. "To further complicate it, an alien *was* killed but their existence is denied by our government, which is unofficially allowing them to live here. But do they have any protection? If Schultz had an attorney, he would have a field day with the murder of someone who doesn't exist. I am also afraid our little friends may have their own rules for such a circumstance."

"You mean they might *handle it* themselves?" Tom asks.

"Yeah, but that would only solve part of our problem. We still have to sort out just whose side Pierce is on, as well as what Major Andrews's part is in all this. Then there is Brandon and his bunch. We must keep our extra-terrestrial friends from blowing this up by offing Schultz. Haven't heard from your FBI guy yet, I take it?"

"No, he said it would take a few days. As usual he was in the middle of some *big* deal. You know how they are." Tom scoffs.

When we left Michael and George they had agreed to hold off on any action until emotions calmed down and reason could prevail again. I know if they wanted to, they could scoop up Schultz and bring him back, strapped across the fender of the Smart Car, like a deer.

I'd like to see that.

Behave yourself David. All things will come in due time.

CHAPTER THIRTY-NINE

George calls me later that afternoon. He says Michael is going to recluse himself for at least a day to be with his wife. George says Dorothy will be a big help in keeping Michael in the proper frame of mind.

"She can handle him, she's my sister." He says. "I'll be there too if needed. Michael and I have been best of friends since childhood."

George adds usually in their culture the whole family will huddle together in times of turmoil but with Brandon's possible part in this, it will be just Michael and Dorothy.

George adds nothing will be done until they meet with Tom and me. He and Michael are fully aware of the scope of events and don't want to interfere with solving the *whole* problem. I tell him that makes me feel much better.

"What did you think? We would go down to Sedona and bring him back?" George asks.

"The thought had crossed my mind, to be honest with you George." I say.

"Ours too, to be honest with *you*. But no, that is not our way of handle things." He replies. I feel somewhat relieved.

Tom, Dog, and I are now in my office trying to determine our next move.

"I told you Sedona was where it's at. Didn't I?" Dog pipes up. "What are we going to do about Brandon? He hasn't done anything really wrong yet, has he? A few rabbits, I can relate to that."

"He didn't eat them; it was just for the thrill. To see what it was like to kill. Not good, Dog. You don't do that, do you?" I ask.

"No. I have chased them, for fun, but I wouldn't just kill them unless I was hungry. But I'm so spoiled now they would have to be at least medium-rare. Not raw."

"Go back to sleep, you're not helping." I glare at him.

"He does make a point." Says Tom. "Brandon has grown up in a very strange world. He never knew his homeland. He is basically trapped in a cave knowing a whole world is outside he can't be a part of. He grew up with television and movies showing our way of life. I think once he learns the man he was sure would help him join the world, actually killed his father, it will make a difference in him."

I sit back in my chair.

"Tom, I am impressed. Where did such deep insight come from? The jaded, hardened DEA agent? No, but you are right. Thank you. I do see your point. We had our rebels who turned out to be solid upstanding citizens. Sometimes I do have to stop being the hard-ass cop and try to be human. You two are the best partners for me" I say with all humility.

Dog looks at Tom and then at me; "We'll be there for you, Boss. You have a way to go yet, but we'll keep trying."

I look for something on my desk to throw at him. Fortunately for him there is nothing suitable.

Then as if on cue, Tom's cell phone rings. He answerers, then mouths the letters, F-*B-I* and we keep quiet.

After he hangs up, Tom takes a big breath and starts in: "My contact has done some digging. He has talked with the *handler* for the Major's father, the Russian defector. All *high-value assets* have a handler. A Russian intelligence officer is a high-value asset. The handler told my friend the father was of little value to the U.S. He gave up some supposedly top-secret information, but it was basically useless, according to his contact. At first the government just believed the father really wanted out of Russia and to bring his daughter to safety. So, his lack of good Intel was just basically blown off as a father's attempt to get himself and his daughter out of Russia. My friend says the handler is getting the feeling dad wasn't actually being all that noble. The present handler took the father over less than a year ago. The original agent retired. The new agent started to familiarize himself with his new charge and is troubled by what he finds. Basically, a lot of holes in the *facts* of the file. The father did have a daughter. He also had a son and a wife, who the agent has discovered, are still living in Russia with the *daughter!* My friend's contact says he thinks U.S.A.F. *Major Andrews is* a Russian planted agent who the *father* was able to pass off as his daughter."

"Has the handler reported his findings to anyone?" I ask.

"My friend says he's hitting a brick wall. Possibly because the original agent is a close friend of the present supervisor. It could make a couple of agents look at best careless, and at worse possibly implicated. The handler was grateful to speak to my friend as he fears retaliation from his supervisor. Unbeknownst to me, my friend is now at FBI HQ in the Office of Professional Responsibility unit. *Him* doing *OPR*? Well who better? But that's a story for another time, over beers." Tom says.

"What happens next?" I ask.

"My bud will start his own investigation and if those facts are true, then the Major and Dad will be become *guests* of a different kind with the U.S. government. It won't happen overnight, and he will keep me informed.

"I guess we still just sit and watch, or rather listen and wait, for the next shoe to fall." I say rather dejectedly. I have so much information at hand and no clear move. It is like staring at a chess board with various pieces in play, but no obvious move.

"That's what the DEA work was like." Tom says. "You put surveillance in place, see this person buy drugs from that other person, then try to find who he buys from and so on up the ladder until you get to the top. The problem is, the longer the chain gets, the more convoluted it becomes. A lot of it becomes circumstantial and even if you know who is behind it, you can't prove it in court. Sometimes the process takes so long the chain is broken along the way and you lose the top dogs. It sucks. You have developed a lot of information in a short period of time, David. We know what they want: to locate the capacitor device or learn how to build one."

"Yeah, the German boneheads can build the gun but don't know how to make the magazine for the bullets." Dog interjects.

"Dog, where do you come up with this worldliness?" Asks Tom.

"Television." I say. "Basically, the same as Brandon and his cohorts. The tube and movies are all they know about our world. Dog at least has been out, they have not. Which reminds me, Dog. I've been meaning to ask you; how did you know about McDonalds' double cheeseburgers and big breakfasts? That's where he wanted to go the first day we were together." I explain to Tom.

"I lived at the caves with Mom, but Wolfgang would always come and visit. Sometimes he would take me to town for a weekend." Dog answers. "We'd get a hotel room, like you did, and then he would put a *Guide Dog* harness on me, and we would *do the Strip*. Boy did he get service. We went to all the big clubs, ate anywhere he wanted, and I always got treats. We ought to try it sometime David, you would have a ball."

"That is just not right Dog, and it's also probably illegal."

"Yeah, well you have a girlfriend to go places with. He didn't. But he liked to play slots a little and just get away from here. He did the same with my dad when he was alive. With my dad or me along Wolfgang had protection. Its Vegas you know. It wasn't all bad, he paid his way. Well maybe he got a few free drinks."

Tom is laughing so hard he almost falls out of his chair. "Wolfgang, who'd a thought? Why did he stop?"

297

"He's getting older and after Mom died, he thought I should stay with the cave dwellers and out of sight. He was getting worried about Cranston. He feels a lot safer ever since you came David. He likes you too Tom." The fraudulent Guide Dog nods at each of us.

"You know, David, you are probably right about the young alien's view of our world being formed by TV. Maybe we can use it to our advantage, if and when a confrontation comes. Something to consider." Tom says.

"Man, I'm sure glad I got you for my flight out here. I like how your brain works."

Speaking of flights, it is time for Tom to go back to Las Vegas. "Might as well, nothing happening here for now."

We put Tom on his flight and decide to go eat. I am frustrated, I want some action. I *want* one of the chess pieces to move. I have always heard you should be careful what you wish for.

Just then Brian calls and says Brandon is calling Schultz. One of the chess pieces just *moved!*

We now go to the alien's control room. George is already there.

"You go ahead, I'm going to find something to eat." Dog says as I enter the room. "You want me to bring you something?"

I thank him and say I'll get something later. How is he going to bring me food? Carrying it in his mouth? I don't think so.

"Fine, don't say I didn't ask." He says as he trots off.

Brian hears the exchange and is laughing. "You know we can have something brought in here. What would you like?"

"Let's just see where this call is going first." I say. Everyone is worried about my stomach.

George has been listening to Brandon and Schultz's call. He has a worried look on his round, pale face. After a few more minutes he puts the earphones down. He lets out a sigh and shakes his head.

"I really am worried about Brandon now. Schultz has told him if he can help them develop a particle collector, Brandon and his group can become a part of the new world order. A shadow government is forming. He tells Brandon he and Hoffman have strong ties to the leaders of the new world movement. Brandon tells them he can develop it with the help of his friends. He said his father worked on their unit on the spaceship and he has his father's notes. Schultz is elated. He asks Brandon if he can do the design work at Area 51 and then send it to Sedona for the two Germans to build. Brandon then tells them he can do the designing but would need to be there when it is actually built to fine tune it. Schultz asked him how he would get out of Area 51. Brandon said they could pick him up on the road outside of Area 51 on the east side. He will have a transporter made by then. It will get them to the road. Schultz seemed to agree to the plan. He wanted to know how long it would take Brandon to complete the work. Brandon said hewould start immediately. He would update Schultz on his progress. Brandon did ask Schultz why he needed help to build the unit. He said his people were told Schultz shot their spaceship down with a particle weapon. Schultz says he can

299

make the weapon, but the capacitor or storage unit was his problem. He didn't make it strong enough for all the energy. He discusses it with Brandon and mentions he had the device located in the bunker behind the caves. Brandon says he knows about the bunker but has not been in it. Schultz says it was destroyed anyway." George pauses and looks at me.

"David, he is serious about this. He believes he can pull it off."

"Can he design the collection unit? Does he have the technical knowledge? Would his father have enough notes to enable him built one?"

George thinks deeply. "Brandon is a very bright person. But I don't think he has sufficient technological training to properly design it. Even with the help of his *friends,* again all bright boys. But they haven't been doing any real developmental type of work. They fiddle around with the computers and other electronics but the science of particle physics is way beyond their training. I would guess his father's notes, if any, would only be regarding the maintenance of the unit, not the design. The notes would help, but only if the person reading them had a solid grasp of the science. I'd say the boys do not. What do you suggest we do now, David? Is it time to tell him Schultz killed his father?"

"We definitely need Michael in on this." I answer. "Brandon is not the big threat here. We need to snare the Germans, hopefully Franklin Pierce and anyone else we can, to stop the *behind the scenes* plotting. Your people won't be free from a threat until we do."

George agrees. He listens to the recording some more. Schultz and Hoffman discuss what Brandon has offered. Hoffman says they could use the alien's help and if he is technically advanced he could be an asset for them in the future. Schultz says he feels better about Brandon as he does not seem to be aware of how his father died. The German scientists are also quite interested in the transporter Brandon mentioned he was making. They apparently believe Brandon is much more learned than he is.

My mind starts to go into high gear. If we could get the Germans to think they are picking up Brandon, the particle device plans and a transporter we just might be able to scoop them up right outside Area 51 and bring them in. That would be a lot neater logistically than trying to capture them in Arizona. No outside agencies involved. I like that.

Brian says he has not yet been able to locate Cranston's burner cell phone. He is not using it enough for Brian to get the fix he needs to tap into it.

"Maybe Dog can help. If he leaves it on his desk while at the office, Dog could bring it to you or Tom. Then we could get the number."

"Good idea, I'll tell the pooch when he has his stomach full. Speaking of food, I'm hungry now." I say.

George says he needs dinner too, so we go to the dining hall. Dog is there holding court with the children of the caves. They just love him. The *children* are in reality teenagers. Dog is fun for them. He sasses, jokes, and plays games with them. He is apparently quite good at soccer, alien version. Good for all involved.

Agent Mickey is sitting next to her biggest fan. He leaves the kids and comes over to George and me.

"Mickey says Brandon was talking to someone earlier in his room and is pretty pumped up now. He and his friends are all jumping around and high fiving. I didn't tell her it was the German scientists. He is going to work with them, isn't he?"

"Yeah, he thinks so for the moment. Make sure you tell her to be careful and thank her. When you get a chance, tell her we can listen in on his phone calls, so she doesn't have to take any risks."

He winks at me, conspiratorially and trots off back to the kids.

CHAPTER FORTY

The next morning I meet with Tom and fill him in on the phone call.

"Everything happens at night around here," he complains.

"It is *not* for *naught*-they call it Dreamland,"

John comes out of his office and says he has to go to a meeting downstairs. After he leaves, Dog comes in and shoves John's cell phone at me.

"Yuck, it's wet."

"No opposable thumbs, remember?"

I get his number and check his call log. I recognize the number he uses for Pierce and there is a local cell phone number. Aha, the Major I bet. He makes no other calls. Good! I do not need any more scenarios at this point in the game. I write down the numbers and after wiping the phone off, I put it back on John's desk.

Dog coaches me. "No, more to the left, now down a little, there, perfect. You can follow instructions, *good boy*!" The damn dog smiles.

I give the phone numbers to the tech in the cave control room. This will help us get the complete picture, I hope. In the afternoon, Pam calls. She is working the four to midnight shift.

"Mind if I drop by your place after shift, for a night-cap," she asks softly.

"I'll be there, pretty woman," I answer quickly. I am not completely stupid.

Thankfully, the rest of the day is uneventful.

George calls. He hasn't told Michael about Brandon's phone call to Shultz. "Tomorrow will be time enough."

"I was thinking about the transporter Brandon said he was building. Maybe you should *double check* with your shop manager about the parts inventory."

"Way ahead of you David. I talked with him earlier and nothing is missing. He is going to keep an extra close watch on the *new* student. The student appears motivated and wants to learn all he can. Asks for extra work. The manager is keeping him off base, giving him some meaningless busy work."

"Good work George. We'll talk tomorrow." That taken care of, I just have to wait until mid-night and hope nothing happens in between.

In the evening Dog and I are just sitting around watching TV and waiting for our ladies to arrive. Around 11:30 p.m., my cell rings. It's Pam. Before I can say anything, she starts talking rapidly, I can tell she's distraught.

"David, are you at your home? I need to see you. Something terrifyingly weird just happened."

"Pam what's going on? Are you all right? Yes, I'm at my place." I've never heard her like this.

"Yes, I'm fine, I think. I'm pulling up to your apartment now."

Dog and I run outside just as Pam speeds into the parking lot in her patrol vehicle and screeches to a stop. She jumps out followed by Grizzie. I run to her and she throws her arms around me.

"Hold me, tell me I'm okay, I'm not going insane!"

"Baby, baby, calm down, you've always seemed normal to me. What on earth happened?

She takes a big breath and looks around.

"Let me lock my vehicle and we can go inside. I'm going to need a drink."

"Uh, don't you need to be off duty first?" She *is* stressed.

"Oh, duh, thank you, I'll take my radio inside and call in."

The four of us go into my place and I pour her a large glass of wine. Before I drink, I need to hear what happened to rattle this normally cool, composed woman.

Pam takes a large drink and then a big breath. "Okay. I'm ready: As I'm finishing my patrol, I decide to take a closer look the bunker you mentioned. Driving up I see things scattered on the ground. Tools, a shovel and a pickaxe, but no one is nearby. I get out of my vehicle and leave Grizzie inside... *won't do that ever again.* I'm shining my flashlight around the area and Grizzie starts barking. Then I hear a little female voice yelling: '*Pam, look up.*'

I look up to the top of the bunker and there are, I swear David, 5 or 6 boys with ghostly white masks on, standing above me on the bunker. One of them has a shovel raised over his head, as if he is going to throw it at me. I jump back. Grizzie is barking furiously. I command the boys to '*Get down here, now*!' "They all run down the side of the bunker and then *keep running toward me*! The one still has the shovel. I pull my weapon and demand they stop. Grizzie is going crazy growling and barking. I'm too far from my vehicle to get to her and I don't want to turn my back on the boys. They are still coming toward me. Then I hear the door of my vehicle open and Grizzie comes snarling past me and takes a stance in front of me. The boys drop everything and run away into the darkness. Grizzie wants to chase them but I hold her back. Then to my side I hear the same little voice say: *Hi Pam, I'm Mickey. David's right, you are pretty.*'

She is also wearing a ghost mask but hers has a cute face. Then she turns and runs to the side, toward the hill. I shine my light and see a hole in the side of the hill, and she runs into it. As she gets to the hole, I heard her yell: "*I'm going to tell Mom.*"

Then I catch the boys in my light as they are running toward the hole. They go in and I *swear* the hole in the hill *closes*!"

Pam pauses and takes another long drink of wine. "David what was that? Who were they? No children live here, do they? They were only four feet tall at the most. Their heads were larger than they should have been for their size. I did see them, didn't I?"

"Yes my Dear, you did see them. You have witnessed something as *Top Secret* as it gets-*here or anywhere.*

I tell Pam it is essential I notify my people about this interaction immediately. I call Brian and advise him Brandon and his group tried to attack an Air Force Police Officer. I make it clear to Brian he is to give George this information, now. My recommendation, the *boys* be secured. I ask him to check on Mickey and make sure she is alright and her brother hasn't retaliated against her.

Pam says she should report this to her command. "I called you first David because your apartment is close, and I was so damn rattled with what just happened. I would have called for backup, but it was over so quick. I had nothing to show anyone! The mountain closed behind them. I would have looked like a fool if I called everyone out and had nothing to show them. I'm not a beginner at this patrol stuff, but this was unreal." Pam looks at me, "Tell me they are not the product of some horrible medical experiment."

"No. They are aliens from another solar system. You've heard of Roswell? They are from that incident. They are real. No masks. That is how they look. Large heads, no hair and pale almost luminous skin. I agree you should not have said anything to anyone, because the government would deny there were strange, small, pale people out here. They would sacrifice you, to protect their secret."

Pam finishes her wine. She looks at me.

"I understand you could not tell me about them David, but how do you keep something like this to yourself? That is the weirdest, most amazing thing I have ever heard of. Oh, right, we have our oath not to divulge anything we see in Area 51 or at Creech for that matter. Still how do you deal with it? Well, now, how will I deal with it?"

"Together, I hope."

Pam snuggles up to me and puts her head on my chest. I put my arms around her and hold her tight. We stay that way for a long time. She is processing it all.

Meanwhile Dog and Grizzie are also curled up together. He looks at me and seems like he is going to say something. I shake my head no. One shock at a time, please. The aliens are more than enough for one night. The talking, four-legged beast, can wait.

Pam stirs a little and looks at me: "The little girl, Mickey? She told me you said I was pretty. You obviously know them and talk to them. Mickey warned me and she had to have let Grizzie out of my patrol vehicle. I don't know what I would have done if she hadn't let Grizzie out. I did not want to shoot children! They were not stopping! What are they like? Why were the boys going to attack me? Or were they boys?"

"Well, since you have had the *alien experience* now, I think you deserve to know what it is all about."

I pour us both more wine and begin to tell her *most* of the story. I leave out being hit by a flying car and, of course, the talking canine. Despite the wine, I have her full attention. She asks questions and soon she is almost fully briefed on the situation. I was the one who asked her to check on the bunker, so I feel she has earned the right to know what is going on. She's up for it. She wants to help and do what she can.

"What's the extent of the duties for the Air Force Police at Area 51? I know they patrol Air Force projects in the sector. There are so many different projects going on in Area 51 I have no idea who is doing what. Which is the idea in a top-secret place, but still I see so many different security and police vehicles up here I wonder if anyone is overseeing the whole picture."

Pam laughs, "EG&G runs the place. Isn't it ridiculous? A private company basically operates the most secret place in the world, which no one will admit exists. Well, I guess the government has finally admitted it exists, but still look at how many people work here and have for years. Each entity, which has a project here, manages its own work. But, all supplies and logistics are handled by good old EG&G. The security for each project here is handled by the agencies' security people and the perimeter of Area 51, itself, is handled by Wackenhut Security, probably under contract with EG&G."

"Wackenhut! They were door-shakers where I came from. You know, just private security, like Burns and the others."

"They handle the perimeter security for most Federal buildings and properties."

"I know about EG&G, but what do you do if you find a problem in your area of responsibility? You told me before there is usually only one officer here at a time."

"We call it in to our office at Creech. If it's serious enough, the other security units here will come over to help. With the tight perimeter security already in place, I think we are more of a 'fire watch' than a crime suppressant force. We do not have crime up here, like we do on the base. That's why I was caught flat footed tonight. I know better than to get out without Grizzie in an unknown situation. I'm embarrassed David. I know better."

Brian has texted me saying Mickey is fine. He has also notified George, who called Michael. He agrees to place the boys in separate holding rooms.

Michael then calls me. He spoke to Mickey and received the same details Pam gave me. Michael is livid at what the boys did-- unauthorized contact with a human, the attempted assault, and being out of the caves.

"How is your girlfriend David, Is she all right?" No secrets here. Everyone from the littlest alien, to their big boss, knows I'm dating Pam.

"She's fine, thanks, Michael. Just taken aback at what she saw. However, she is extremely concerned they kept coming at her, especially after she drew her weapon. I do not understand it either. They do know they are mortal, don't they? Do they think life is a video game where you can hit *reset* and start over again?"

"I'm deeply disturbed also," admits Michael. "It is one of the questions I will have for them. I would like you to be here when we talk to the boys. Also, I would appreciate it, if I could talk with the officer; Pam I believe is her name. I want to apologize to her and ask her what she saw. Wait, George just came in, he was overseeing the lockup of the boys." I can hear George in the background talking. Then Michael shouts: "They are what?"

I can hear George say, "They are high, Michael. They are on some kind of drugs."

Pam is still with me and overheard the conversation. She nods in the affirmative. "I'm in this already so I want to see what is over there. Can Grizzie come? I don't have any place to put her."

"Oh sure, she'll be a big hit.

Pam has relaxed and we curl up for the night like the dogs, just not on the floor. We can talk more in the morning.

CHAPTER FORTY-ONE

I share all of the late-night happenings with Tom and ask him to keep a watch on John while I go to the caves.

"Damn it, I've said it before, and I'll say it again, the good stuff always happens at night around here."

"Want to work nights?"

"No thanks, but still I wish something would happen when I'm here."

"Be careful what you ask for."

I take Pam and the dogs to the alien's caves. George and Michael meet us at the entrance. When she first sees them, I can almost feel her amazement, *my god they are real.* To her credit she does not show any reaction.

Michael is falling on his sword, expressing to her his regret for what happened.

Pam is very tactful and speaks somewhat nervously: "*Teens are teens* everywhere, apparently."

We go to Michael's office, and Dog takes Grizzie and goes off to find Mickey and the other young ones. Two other leaders of the colony are already in the office. Pam officially relates to them, exactly what she witnessed last night. They are appalled and visibly distressed by what she has described.

"Thank you for not shooting them, my dear, though I probably would have, if I had been there," one of the men admits.

George says the boys were under the influence of some type of drug when he got to them.

"They were as you human would say '*higher than a kite*.' I don't know what they took or where they got it," George says. "We don't have anything like that here. At least we didn't before this."

Pam speaks up: "I feel much better now. You have explained a great deal. I have seen our kids and adults high on drugs. That clarifies their irrational behavior. I'm sorry but with their size and coloration, I just had no idea what I was into. No offense intended."

"None taken Pamela, believe me. We all understand," Michael states. "In fact, I am quite impressed with your demeanor. Here you are, inside a cave with several diminutive, monochromatic people, some of whom have attacked you. You show a maturity beyond your young years. David is incredibly lucky to have found you."

I am shifting around uncomfortably in my chair.

"Uh, not to change the subject, uh, I agree she is handling this amazingly well, but what about *the boys?*" I am trying to gain some control here or assert my authority or something. "Exactly how are they acting?"

"From watching your television shows, I would say *stoned*, and others, especially Brandon were combative, aggressive, not their selves," George relates. "The way he was behaving when we got to him, I'm surprised Brandon ran when your dog charged them. He was quite a handful for four of us to subdue."

Michael says in a soft tone, "I checked Brandon's room. There were some pieces of what appeared to be a plant from the desert, laying on a table. There were some round button-like flowers. Does that make any sense to you two?" He looks at Pam and me.

"Buttons? I would say peyote," Pam says immediately. She looks at me.

"I thought peyote was from Mexico, does it grow here?" I am *really* looking good now.

Not to be deterred by my apparent ignorance of the area in which I live, Pam looks back at the aliens and says, "It is still used by some Native American tribes in a ceremonial way. It is illegal and can cause hallucinations and other behavioral problems. This entire area," Pam sweeps her hands in a circular motion, "was once inhabited by the indigenous tribes. No, it doesn't grow naturally in Nevada but *who knows what you will find out here.*" Then, realizing she is gesturing at a room full of aliens, she blushes.

The extra-terrestrials break out in sincere laughter.

"Ah Pam, you are quite charming. Please do not be embarrassed. It is we who should be embarrassed," Michael says. The others nod in agreement.

We discuss how to handle the *boys* and what they should be told. Pam feels strongly they be informed we are aware of what they have been doing. She stresses Brandon needs to be informed Schultz intentionally killed his father.

315

"Maybe it will shock him into the reality he is being used by an evil person."

Michael looks at her and then at the rest of us, "I agree with Pamela. It is all out in the open now. They need to know they have no secrets and more importantly, Brandon needs to know the truth about his father's death."

We all concur. Michael says the boys will all remain in lock down in separate cells until Brandon is told about his father. George says Brandon is not yet among the lucid, so that will have to wait.

Michael states," Depending on his reaction to the revelation of his father's demise, the elders will decide how to proceed with the boys."

"Since you don't officially exist, there is not much we can do," I state in an official tone. "However, I do trust you to keep them under tight constraints." All the elders nod agreement.

"Let us know what his reaction is," I say as I stand up. Pam follows my lead and gets to her feet.

George comes over to her and says, "Please do not judge us by the actions of our youth. We are good, decent people." His eyes are imploring.

Pam leans down, puts her arms around the little gentleman, and gives him a tender hug. "Hey, I know kids, we were all young once. Maybe not that wild, but these boys are in unusual circumstances. They do need to be hit with reality though. Now!" She smiles at George and the others.

We leave the meeting room and are met at the door by Dog and Grizzie. Dog has of course been following our meeting with his implanted device. He knew it was time to leave and gathered up Grizzie and waited at the door. Grizzie has a pink bow attached to her collar.

Pam laughs, "I imagine this is from Mickey?"

"Probably, she loves to play with Dog, so she would take to Grizzie immediately."

We leave and, on the way, back to human-land I look at Pam, "I am impressed. You are one cool lady."

She smiles demurely, "How do you think Brandon will react to the news the German scientist killed his dad?"

"I have no clue. Can only hope he has fond memories of the time he spent with his father and gets angry about what he was going to do. And maybe come over to the good side."

"Very Yoda of you David, but I agree. His brain needs to be on the side of the force."

We both laugh, but silently hope it to be true.

We take the ladies to their vehicle so they can make it back to Creech for their next shift. Before she gets out, Pam reaches over, grabs my arm, and pulls me toward her, "David Manning you have some *interesting friends.* Despite that, I actually want to see more of you." Then she kisses me firmly on the lips. I reach for her, but she hops out followed by Grizzie, "No time, we have to go." Then she looks at me with those come-hither eyes and says, "See you soon."

317

The ladies roar off in their Air Force patrol vehicle. Dog lets out a low moan.

"Yeah, me too Buddy."

CHAPTER FORTY-TWO

Back to the real world. Or what most people think of, as the *real world*.

Some of us know different.

Thomas tells me, all has been quiet at the office. "So how did it go?" He inquires with raised eyebrows.

I fill him in on what transpired.

"Wow, what the Hell is next?"

"Your guess is as good as mine."

While we are speculating on the *unknown*, my cell phone rings. It jars me back into the present.

"Manning!" I growl into the phone.

"And a good day to you too, my noble friend Davey."

"Eddie, I'm sorry, I'm kind of involved in something here. What can I do for you?" Eddie from EG&G! What does he want from me? Cranston's schedule so he can meet up with Doris?

"I am, one more time, here to help you," he chuckles. "Seriously, I had a visitor just now and he was asking about you. He was one of *your government types,* the kind I don't like. Present company excepted."

"You got my attention," I say as I switch my phone to speaker so Tom can hear.

"He said he heard you were working at Area 51 and wanted to hook up with you. Served together somewhere in the past, he said. I played dumb. Told him I vaguely knew the name but didn't have any contact with you. He definitely wants to locate you."

"What's his name?"

"Howard Worthington, the third. Sounds like a CIA spook to me."

"That Bastard!" A rage swells up in my head and my body tightens at the sound of his name.

"I take it you do know him."

"Put him on a one-way flight here. I'll bury him out in the desert up to his scrawny neck and leave him for the coyotes." Dog immediately comes over to my side and tries to get into my lap. He is licking my face.

"No, Dog, it's okay, I'm okay."

"Calm down Pal, I'm here, it will be all right." He is still licking my face.

"Who was that?" Eddie asks. "Not your dog?"

"Uh, no, Ed. Ah, Tom is here too and my dog. When I get upset the dog comes over and licks me."

"Just as long as it wasn't Tom. Hi Tom, miss me yet?" Eddie asks.

"No Ed, it has been really interesting here, I'm quite happy." Tom smiles as he answers.

" What's the deal with Worthington?" Eddie inquires.

'South America, few years ago, I was with a drug interdiction team of Rangers. Worthington was CIA and sold us out to curry favor with a drug cartel boss he thought he could flip to work with him. We fought our way out of the trap carrying two wounded Rangers; we never leave our people behind. We reported him to our superiors. Nothing happened to him. Later we found out his father and grandfather are big Washington DC movers and shakers. The bastards have the money and clout to get done, or to cover-up, whatever they want. So little Howie couldn't be touched."

Tom is on the edge of his seat; you can see the questions forming in his head. Eddie beats him to it.

"Why would a CIA agent sell out his own government's men? I know they are known for stupidity, but that's criminal."

"He was a new case agent and needed to prove himself, probably to dad and grandpa, more than to the CIA. He was way over his head with agents, double agents and was desperate to make a name for himself, even at the expense of others. I heard this later, from some other CIA guys I knew. He was such a piece of crap, other agents refused to work with him. One even retired early because of Worthington. Apparently, we were expendable or at least collateral damage in his eyes. He did get sent back to Langley HQ afterwards, I was told."

"That's why DEA wanted nothing to do with any of their operations," Tom adds. "Bad news."

Eddie clears his throat, "So what do you want to do about him? I told him I would ask around and he gave me his cell number and said he was staying at The Bellagio. *The Bellagio.* On taxpayers' dollars, no doubt. I didn't like him. I'll help you bury him in the desert."

"Let me mull this over and get back to you Ed. I need to figure out which team he is on. Also, why he, of all people, is asking about me. Give me his cell and I will check it out, if you don't mind."

Ed gives me the phone number and pauses, "Look, Dave, we started off rough, but be careful. I'm willing to help if I can."

"Thanks Ed, I appreciate it. I'll be in touch." I hang up.

Tom is on his feet, "You are not going to handle this by yourself, you know. I'm your partner."

Dog who still has his front paws on my lap adds, "I'm the one who got you into this mess. You are not going anywhere without me."

"Thanks guys, but I'm not sure what to do yet. First, we need to see what he is up to, then have the little snoops check out his phone and whatever else they can find."

In my ear comes George's voice, "Already on it. We'll let you know as soon as we get anything." Whoa, they are good. I forgot about the earpiece. I should have used a kinder term than little snoops.

"Thanks for being there George. We must determine just which group he is with. Hopefully not a new player. We have too many bogies in this already."

"We do have your back, you know." George declares.

"You'd need a chair to reach his back Shorty," Dog adds sarcastically.

After a good laugh we all start to offer suggestions as to our next move. Dog wants to grab Worthington by the neck and toss him around until he talks. Not a bad plan, I like it. Tom favors something similar involving pain. Tough group I have. Love 'em.

After only a few minutes, George advises the cell phone is from the Virginia area, no surprise there and Worthington is still listed as a CIA employee. These space travelers amaze me. Even the NSA couldn't work so quickly. Unfortunately, they can't learn any more about Howie Worthington. Knowing he is still with the Agency is enough for the moment.

I get a thought. My old pal Dwayne. Yes, Dwayne the P.I. who tried to accost me in the hotel room after my first visit to Cranston. He has the nefarious ability to get into hotel rooms. I give him a call. Always ready for new work he picks up on the first ring or beep or whatever his phone does.

"This is Dwayne," he says anxiously. Business must be slow.

"Dwayne. David Manning. Remember me?"

A not so upbeat Dwayne answers, "Yes Mr. Manning, what can I do for you?"

"I want to hire you, Dwayne. Interested?"

I can almost hear his mind saying 'Shit, this guy and his dog nearly killed me. What could he want?'

"Wh-what do you want me to do, Mr. Manning?"

"Call me David and I need your special abilities. Do you have your typical connections at The Bellagio?"

"The Bellagio, yeah, I do a lot of work there. Good connections. What do you need?" He's excited now.

I tell him he will be well paid for his services. He says because of our past relationship he will give me a break. How nice, I still might let Dog have him.

I don't know if Worthington is using his real name or not. I tell Dwayne what I do know. He will check and call me back.

Now it is sit and wait. I hate that.

CHAPTER FORTY-THREE

The three of us, Tom, Dog, and I are sitting in my office talking with George and now Michael. Poor Tom can't hear the cavemen, but we keep him filled in. No more information on Worthington but they have managed to tap his cell phone. Then my cell rings, it's Dwayne.

"Your man is registered under his own name. Comes here a lot, I am told. Big money, likes to gamble. Hotel knows his family too. Comes from the D.C. area." Dwayne cautiously asks, "Are these the same ones who hired me to check on you?"

"I can't say, Dwayne. There are several players in this game. You still in?"

"Oh hell yes. A job is a job. Besides, I do kind of owe you for not killing me."

"I wasn't planning on killing you," I pause, "but the dog was."

"That fucking dog. I've never seen a shepherd so large. He could have bit my head off."

Dog looks at me and smiles, as only Dog can. Tom stifles a laugh.

I tell Dwayne to determine if Worthington is in his room. It's where I want to confront him.

"There will be two of us plus the dog."

"There are cameras. How can you do that?" he moans.

"You will find a way, won't you Dwayne?"

"I'll see what I can do, no promises."

"We'll be there in two hours. Do it Dwayne. Call me when you know what he is doing."

"Yes sir."

You still in Tom?"

"Try and keep me away."

"Good. Better tell your wife you will be home late tonight."

After partially briefing Cranston, the three of us leave in my truck for the Bellagio. Dog in the rear seat with his head out the window.

Tom asks, "If his mother was from their home planet, why does he have such thick long fur? The aliens have no apparent body hair and lived underground, so the temperature must have been mild."

The pooch turns his head inward and says, "Long story short, their pets did have the ability to speak like I do. Years of living with the puny ones, I guess. Actually, we have different tongues than earth dogs." He sticks out his tongue at Tom.

Tom looks back at the tongue. "It *is* more human-like than our dogs. I'll be damned. Never noticed before."

326

"That's because I don't go around with it hanging out all the time like the earthling dogs."

Dog continues, "Mom could go outside the caves because her thick fur insulated her from the heat. Mom's ancestors were the outside eyes and ears for the cave dwellers. At least, until the advances in electronic gizmos put them out of a job. Then they became pets."

"Fascinating." Tom looks at Dog. "How do you keep all the fur so neat? You are always well groomed." Then he looks at me, "Or is that your job."

"Not mine, he takes care of himself. You ought to see all the shampoo, conditioner, and blow dryers he has."

"Shithead!" Growls Dog. "All this beautiful fur is naturally self-cleaning, as nature intended it." He then does a complete body shaking starting from head and winding up with is furry tail.

"I don't shed much either, to answer your next question."

Tom gets a perplexed scowl on his face, "How'd you know what I was going to say?"

"Get used to it Tom. He can read our puny minds, or so he claims."

Just in time to pause our lesson in Dog-ology, Dwayne calls.

'It cost me, but I got a way for you guys to get into the room. The damned Dog too. Your boy has dinner reservations at seven in the steak house. That should give you an hour or more in his room. The time frame work for you?"

"Perfect. We will be there in about thirty, forty minutes. Where do we meet you?"

"Park in the garage and I'll meet you at the hotels' rear service entrance." Dwayne hangs up.

Tom asks, "What's the plan?"

"I don't have one, just going to play it by ear." I look over at him and smile.

"He wants to throw the jerk out the window." Dog offers.

We park and casually stroll up the alley behind the hotel. As casually as two men can, with a huge black dog at their side. Dwayne is waiting. He motions us to follow him behind some storage containers. There he hands us two hotel maintenance uniforms. We slip into them. They are the *one size fit all* style. Then he points to a service cart with a white sheet draped over it.

"The cart is for the beast. Hope he will fit." I lift the sheet. There is a shelf near the bottom. Dog looks at me with a *No way in hell am I getting in there* look.

I say sternly, "Get in, you can do it." He looks right at Dwayne and glares, but he crawls on the shelf, lays down and tucks in his tail. We lower the sheet and it is good.

Following Dwayne, we enter thru a delivery door and into a service elevator. Any checkpoint has already been paid off to overlook us. We stop on Worthington's floor. Dwayne checks the hallways and motions us to follow. He stops at a room door and swipes a card in the lock. The door opens and we all enter.

Dwayne is calling out, "Hotel maintenance." No one is inside. Good so far.

"What do you want me to do?" Asks Dwayne. "I can call you when he leaves the restaurant and goes to the elevators."

"I would appreciate that Dwayne. Thank you."

"You're not going to try to roll a body out of here, are you? No of course not." He asks nervously.

"No, I'll just throw him off the balcony." I stare deadpan back at him.

Dwayne pales.

"Just kidding. I'm not planning on killing him, just a polite conversation is all."

"Now I am worried." Dwayne says as he leaves. "I'll be on my cell."

As the door closes, Dog emerges from his shelf. "I'd like to gut that fat bastard."

"Settle down. At least you did not have to push your lard ass, like we did." Tom says.

Dog glares. "He needs to go back on airplane duty."

We decide on a plan. When Dwayne calls, Dog will lie behind the sofa, out of sight and Tom will be in the bathroom. I will be behind the door so when it is opened, I can slam it shut and confront Worthington.

Now it is sit and wait time. Worse part of any operation. Nothing to do, adrenaline is pumping, you listen intently, jumping at every sound.

CHAPTER FORTY-FOUR

After an hour and thirty-seven minutes (who's counting?) my cell vibrates. We all jolt upwards. It is Dwayne.

"He is on his way up alone. Let me know if you need me."

We take our positions. In a few minutes, I can hear someone outside the door and take a quick look thru the peep hole. One male. I step back as the electronic lock beeps and clicks. The door opens and in walks a male. I slam the door shut and spin the male around. He is about five-eight, pudgy build with ruddy complexion.

"Hello Howie. Long time no see." Worthington turns completely white.

Tom is on him quickly and pins Worthington's arms behind his back. I thoroughly frisk the bastard. He has a SIG .380 caliber auto in a shoulder holster. Nothing else. We pull up a straight back chair from the desk and put it in the middle of the room. Tom shoves him down.

"What the fuck is this, do you know who I am?" He is finally able to speak.

With that, Dog who has remained behind him, now moves in front of the chair, jumps up and plops his front paws in Worthington's lap, sticks his massive muzzle into Howie's face and growls. A long, low growl. Worthington whimpers and begins to cry.

"What do you people want, I have money, don't hurt me, I can pay whatever you want."

Now it is my turn to stare into his pitiful face, "Remember Operation Fish?" I say with a low calm voice.

Worthington blinks and stares at me. You can almost see the thought processes flowing thru his brain cells. Then a light comes on. He blurts out, "Manning! You are Manning. The son-of-a-bitch who almost got me fired from the CIA."

Before I can respond, Dog leaps and knocks Worthington and the chair to the floor. He wraps his jaws tightly around Worthington's neck.

"Dog. No, Release, let him up."

Tom yanks Worthington to his feet and sets him back on to the chair, not so gently.

"Wrong response, rich boy. Your family connections may have saved your pathetic ass then, but you are mine now." I am still using a calm, controlled voice.

"What do you want from me?" He is beyond scared. The crotch of his expensive, wool navy-blue slacks, is now darkening.

"All these years, I have wanted to ask you why you were willing to sacrifice American lives. Just to make yourself look good? Why Howie? Why?" I am still keeping my voice controlled but am putting an edge in it.

He is sweating profusely, stammering, trying to come up with words.

Tom steps in front of him and with both hands, grabs his lapels, pulling him to his feet. "Listen you piss-ant punk. I don't give a damn what or who your family is. What you did was the act of a coward and you're a traitor. How many other good men were sacrificed during your career?" Tom shoves him back down on the chair.

Wow, Tom, my man. I sort of expected Dog's reaction but not Tom's. But, as a DEA agent, he has dealt with the same cross and double-cross intrigue I have. It was time for the years of the controlled restraint, that law enforcement personnel must maintain, to break.

My turn again, "Look Worthington, I want to know why you were snooping around asking about me."

"Look, I just ride a desk most of the time now, thanks to your complaint. My section chief asked me to investigate what you were doing here. I do not know why. He knows I come to Vegas a lot to gamble and asked me to check up on you. That's all I know."

"Bull shit!" I take a step toward Worthington. So, does Tom and Dog again lands painfully in Howie's lap.

He nervously looks back and forth at each of us. He is shaking again. I think he has now completely relieved his body of all waste matter, liquid and solid.

"Okay, Okay. My boss showed me a file and I saw your name. He wanted to find out about you and why you were here. I offered to come to Vegas. I wanted to settle up with you. At least to find out some dirt so I could pay you back."

Between his sweating and the other stuff, he is reeking now. We all back off. No Dwayne, we won't be removing this miserable creature from the room. Getting him to the balcony now even seems problematic.

"What was the case with my name on it about?" I inquire with the same emotionless measured voice.

He is beaten down now. He just starts to babble and spills his guts. Apparently, good old Frank Pierce, John Cranston's' boss, has stirred up the shit in the intelligence community. He has been shaking the trees to scare off anyone targeting Cranston. This raised the hackles of Howard Worthington's boss, who has had bad experiences with both Frank and Cranston in the past. So Howie's section chief starts to check out what Franklin Pierce is up to and finds John Cranston, at Area 51. Then of course my name shows up as his assistant. Worthington tells his boss he knows me and offers to check out the Vegas angle. He even admits a trip to Vegas is a perk for him and if he got the chance to even the old score with me that would have been a plus.

"I just wanted to get out of the office and back in the field, even if was not a real operation." He looks up at me with pleading eyes, "Manning, as far as that operation went, I never intended anyone to be hurt. I thought by warning La Piranha he would just leave and be grateful to me. Then I would have an *in* with him. I told him you would not attack until daylight and he could be safely away by then. I never thought the bastard would lay in wait for you. Swear to God, Manning, I was not trying to get anyone hurt. I just wanted him to trust me so I could maybe turn him or at least get some useful information about other drug lords. That's how it works you know. They will do anything to kill off the competition. The Agency wasn't too pleased with me. My performance evals already were poor. I had made some mistakes. Some bad ones. Egotistical stupidity. That's what my section chief called it. He was right, I knew it. Yes, I hid behind my family's influence. I'm not proud of it. The family did not want me in the CIA. I was supposed to enter the family tradition of getting into some position of influence in the government. That's how our family's wealth was made. Insider information and back-door deals."

Howie takes a deep breath, exhales and looks me in the eyes, "Manning, I do apologize to you. I am grateful no one got hurt. The Fish was killed, wasn't he?"

"I killed him personally. Snapped his neck." I say this with a deep, stone cold, slow voice.

Worthington swallows hard. Fear comes rushing back into his eyes as he keeps looking at me.

"Relax, I'm not going to kill you."

He closes his eyes and seems to utter a silent prayer. "Thank you for that. I …"

I cut him off, "Now let's get down to the real issue here. Does your CIA section chief have any interest, in any project, at Area 51? Is he only checking into Frank Pierce and John Cranston?"

"We aren't involved in any of this black stuff. Our section monitors Eastern Europe and Russian Intel reports. My boss was involved in a couple operations with Pierce and got burnt by him. He has been waiting for Pierce to fuck up, so he could repay him."

"Just personal vengeance? That's it?" I ask with raised eyebrows.

"Yeah, there is a lot of that going on in the *Company*."

"And I thought the DEA was the only place like that. What do I know?" Tom says.

"Alright Howard, here's how it is; I am doing *my job* of keeping the project at Area 51 and its participants, safe and secure. I know nothing of politics or personal history. Not my problem unless it interferes with my job. *You did*. So now, we have had our little chat. I accept your apology. You tell your section chief if he has any questions, he can talk to Franklin Pierce. We are going to leave now, and I would suggest a shower and change of clothes. Sorry about the slacks, they look expensive. Any questions before we go?"

Tom is pushing the cart toward the door and lifting the sheet for Dog.

Worthington sits upright, clears his throat and then actually smiles, "No, just thank you again, Manning. Uh, I don't even remember your first name. I am sorry. I truly am. I don't belong in the field. The analysis desk work is better suited to me and probably safer for other agents. I'm going to tell my boss all I could find out is... you are at Area 51, somewhere, and no one seems to know where. Is that all right with you?"

"Perfect. Howard, take care." I make a gesture toward him. I certainly am not going to touch that smelly mess of humanity. "Oh yes, I almost forgot."

I take his Sig out of my pocket, strip the clip and eject the round in the chamber. I then take all the cartridges and walk into the bathroom. I flush the bullets. On my way past him I toss the weapon on to the sofa.

336

"You really ought to have more fire power than a .380."

With Dog now back in his table, we all exit the room.

I call Dwayne as we hurry down the hallway. He meets us at the main floor elevator door. He is sweating almost as much as Howard.

"How'd it go? Is he, uh still alive, hurt?"

"He will be fine, after a shower." I smile. I think my smile is getting to be as creepy as Dog's. I'm around him way too much.

"I would say that went quite well." Dog comments as we leave Dwayne, we walk back to my truck.

Tom and I both look down at the loquacious canine and laugh.

"Dog, you are something," Tom says. "But I agree. I would say Howie Worthington has *seen the light* and will no longer be a problem. Sounds as if his boss is just playing the game all government administrators' play--watch your back and keep an eye on your competition. Glad I'm out of it." Then Tom gives me a quizzical look. "Or am I?"

"You know Tom, what he said has got me wondering about something else. He works the Eastern European and Russian desk. We have a concern about a couple of Russians, don't we? Do you think this must be more than Howie Worthington's boss's history with Franklin Pierce? What if he has some inkling about Colonel Kate and her *father*?"

"Whoa, that opens up a whole new area. Is it a coincidence or not, Worthington's boss wants this checked out? Over the years in this business, I've learned coincidences are rare."

Brian comes on in my earpiece. "David, George was wondering about the same thing when he was listening to Worthington. He has me trying to investigate. Will not be easy, CIA and all. They are tough to penetrate."

"I got faith in you Brian." I respond. Then I tell Tom what Brian told me.

"Now Tom, it is time to get you home to your tolerant wife.

CHAPTER FORTY–FIVE

The next morning, George advises me they have not been able to find a tie between our Russians and the CIA. They will keep checking.

Tom says, "If this gets any more convoluted, I'm going to need a spreadsheet to keep it all straight in my mind."

"Make me one too."

George then advises us they have already started one. "It is becoming almost too complex for us." He chuckles.

"If all is quiet with Cranston, let's plan on putting our heads together and see if we can make some sense of all this. That good with you guys?" I ask.

"Come over whenever you are ready." George responds.

"I'm in on this one too." Dog pipes up. "This shit is getting too complex for your *puny* human minds." Ah, Dog…always the wise ass.

After we check in with John, we go to the caves. George has-yes-a spreadsheet, on his flat screen TV. Tom just shakes his head. "You are too much."

"I'll take that as a complement," says George.

I must admit, having it all down in black and white, does help to put this mess into some perspective:

Franklin Pierce--a former administration official, now somehow associated with the Dept. of Defense. He is a hawk of the first degree. Rumored to have links with *shadow government* types who want to establish a *new world order*. He is John Cranston's boss.

John Cranston--poor bastard, was a CIA figure who botched some past covert operations which cost the lives of American allies. Pierce plugged him into Area 51, to run a secret research project that would produce a mega powerful particle beam weapon. The prior director was forced to retire, by Pierce, when he refused to be a part of this type of a weapon development program. Cranston does not want the weapon developed either, but he is trying to walk the line between his conscience and his boss, Pierce. He has been giving Pierce lip service on the project.

Major Katrina (Kate) Andrews--Air Force Intelligence officer, who was enlisted by Franklin Pierce, to initiate an affair with John Cranston. Andrews's *father* is a Russian turncoat, from the GRU, the intelligence agency in present-day Russia (Think old KGB.). He asked for asylum for his *daughter* in exchange for giving what turned out to be useless information. With some help from inside our government, Pierce maybe, she was allowed to become a citizen. She changed her name and joined the Air Force. Because of her ability to speak Russian and other Eastern European languages, she rose quickly in the intelligence section of the Air Force.

Her *supposed* father has a real family still in Russia, including Katrina, his real daughter. The whole thing was bogus, and it certainly appears there is complicity within our government.

At this point I need a drink, is it too early? Yes, keep the mind clear.

Eddie Benton--Security Director at EG&G. That would be EG&G, the *civilian* property managers for the entire Area 51. Oh yes, and he is having an affair with John Cranston's wife, Doris.

Wilhelm Schultz--the German scientist. He and his former Nazi buddy, scientist Friedrich Hoffman want to produce a particle beam weapon. But who is behind them? They wouldn't do this at their advanced age without some enticement, would they? If Franklin Pierce and his cohorts are looking to take over our government and maybe the world, then a weapon of that magnitude would certainly be an asset. It could destroy selected areas without the radiation hazard of nukes. It all sounds *insane* when you say it, but then, these people are *insane.*

Brandon and his buddies--Alien teenagers who are in cahoots with the German scientists. They want to conquer earth and run it themselves.

Everyone we're dealing with seems to be up for that job.

RJ Waters

CHAPTER FORTY-SIX

I ask the elders if they have done anything with Brandon and his friends.

"They needed a dose of reality," Michael says. "And while you three were enjoying Las Vegas, we elders gave them some."

"What did you guys do?" This should be interesting. The aliens are basically low-keyed, especially with *the children.*

"We sat down with each of them individually. Brandon was first. He had come down from his overdose and was alert.

"In fact, he was very agitated and demanded to be let out of his cell. 'I have not done anything wrong. Why am I here?'"

"I looked straight into his eyes and told him to sit there, be quiet and listen for once. He was startled. None of us parents ever speak harshly to our children or to each other for that matter. Never had to."

Michael takes a deep breath and continues, "I told Brandon that we elders knew about his activities, his threatening phone calls to John Cranston and his connection to the Germans. He was astonished we doddering old folks were smarter than him and his pals. Then I sat down next to him and said he needed to hear a recording of his German friend, Wilhelm Schultz.

"I placed a small player in front of him and let Brandon hear Schultz's admission to killing his father."

"How did he react?" Tom asks.

"He was quite stunned. Just sat there for a minute or so, with a blank expression on his face. Then he burst into tears. He looked at me and for the first time in years, threw his arms around me. "Uncle Michael, what have I done? My God, what have I done? All of you told us to never contact the humans. That no good would come of it. I knew we were smarter than any of them, they couldn't hurt us, and we were superior.' He looked at the other elders standing in his cell. "I am so sorry to have done this. Tell me I haven't done anything to bring harm on the colony.'

Michael continues, "George told Brandon there *is* a threat from the outside world and his contacting the Germans increased the threat. The elders, with assistance from certain trusted humans, are in the process of handling the danger."

"Brandon just slumped backwards and started weeping. 'What can I do? Anything to help. I have been an embarrassment to my father's memory and to my family.'"

Michael goes on, "we informed Brandon he and his friends would continue to remain in solitary confinement until the problem was resolved. Then it would be decided what further was to be done with them."

"And how did he take that?" I ask.

"He just sat there blubbering, 'my friends are not to blame. I am. I talked them into this.'"

"No matter, they are just as guilty as you are... for treason to the colony," Michael told Brandon.

"You *left* them in their cells?" I inquire.

"Yes we did." Michael declares with a somber countenance, "All of them. We went to the rest of the boys and had the same discussion. They heard the recording also. They will sit in their cells until the current threat is over."

I read the pain in his eyes.

CHAPTER FORTY-SEVEN

The elders have spoken. Now we continue to try to put the other pieces of our puzzle together.

Tom sits straight up, like he was just hit by an electrical shock, "How about this one: just say Howie Worthington's section chief, who oversees the CIA's Eastern European and Russian desk, *is* aware that Major Andrews and her so called father are Russian plants. He then finds out John Cranston is fooling around with the Major. So he arranges for the wimpy admin aide to spy on Cranston."

Tom looks at me, "When *you* show up, seemingly referred by the section chief's old nemesis, Franklin Pierce, Dwayne is hired to check you out. That plan didn't work out for them.

"Then you catch the aide spying on Cranston. Franklin Pierce gets wind someone has been checking on Cranston. He gets stirred up and raises hell with the intelligence community to *leave his project alone.*"

George leans forward excitedly: "And... and.... the section chief then shows Howie Worthington a file he's working on. Howie says, 'I know that SOB' and he dumbly offers to come to Las Vegas to further check on you and to have some fun at tax-payers expense. By the way, we all enjoyed listening to the encounter between you and Howie." He smiles.

I jump in now: "I like this line of thinking. It makes sense. Tom, could you push your FBI buddy and see if he has any more information on Major Katrina and her *father*? I will contact Howard Worthington and see if he would have his boss call me. I'm wondering if his boss and we are on the same team. Then, again we may not be, but it's time to find out." I look at everyone in the room. All are just staring; wheels are turning but the mouths are not opening.

"Come on guys; opinions, comments or anything." I implore.

Finally, Dog, who has been quietly lying on the floor, slowly rises up, stretches ever so unhurriedly and says: "I don't know what took you guys so long. Of course that is what is happening. Do you want me to go and talk with Howie?" He looks at me and cocks his head. Everyone is stifling a laugh.

"No, thank you. I will just phone him."

That bit of levity has broken the intensity and we all settle down and discuss the pros and cons of my idea. It is agreed I will reach out to Howard and seek his assistance.

"I can reach out to Howie."

"Dog, no!

CHAPTER FORTY-EIGHT

I place a call to Howard Worthington. He guardedly answers with a faltering, "Hello."

"Howard, how are you feeling today?" I ask in a chipper voice. "David Manning here." I swear I can *feel* the color drain from his fat face.

He blurts out, "How did you get my phone number? Leave me alone. Didn't you mess with me enough last night?"

"You messed yourself, Howie. I never touched you. I got your cell number while we were chatting. Probably when the dog landed in your lap. You remember the dog, don't you?" I pause, "Seriously, Agent Worthington, I need you to have your boss call me. After thinking about what you told me last night, I believe he and I may be working the same case, just from different angles. I won't mention the details of our meeting... if you don't."

"You actually expect me to have my supervisor call you? Are you crazy? I haven't decided what to tell him yet." He whines.

"Listen to me Howard. From what you said about the file he showed you, I think he and I can help each other. You can be a hero by passing this on to him. If you don't, then I will find him thru other means and cut you out of the glory. Got it."

"Alright, I'll tell him when I get back to Arlington." He angrily responds.

"No. You call him *now*. This is a *national security* issue, Howard. You don't need ignoring this issue going on your record too." I give him my cell number. He says he will call his supervisor right now. *What a pathetic POS.*

Leaving the cave dwellers, Tom, Dog, and I head back to our office. The little people have a lot weighing on their huge brains right now. I don't think they have any idea what to do with Brandon and his bunch. They have not had a problem like this for eons. Bet they have regretted coming to Earth more than once.

As we pull into the parking lot, my cell rings. *Restricted number*. That was quick.

"Manning," I answer.

"Agent Manning, I'm Howard Worthington's group supervisor, Brad Young. He tells me you think we are on the same case. What exactly did Worthington tell you?"

"He said you were interested in the activities of Franklin Pierce and John Cranston. I am also concerned with Pierce's involvement. Cranston is about as much a threat as your boy Howard."

Young bursts out laughing, "You do have his number, don't you? Some day we will have to have drinks and you can tell me about last night. Howard won't say much. Tell me your concerns with Pierce and I'll tell you mine."

I ask Young if he is aware of Pierce's connection with an Air Force Major.

"Okay, we are on the same case. Yes, I am aware of Major Katrina Andrews." He answers. "Do you know about her father?"

"Yes, he was a Russian turncoat GRU who got his supposed daughter into the country."

"Man, how did you discover that, way out there in the desert?"

"I have friends in low places."

"Damned good ones. We do have to meet for drinks—you've been there a short time and it took us years to find out about those two."

Brad and I continue to exchange what we know and suspect about Pierce, Katrina, and her father. I ask him if he knows about the German, Friedrich Hoffman. He doesn't have any clue about him or Schultz. Without mentioning the aliens or talking dogs, I give him an outline of what is happening, sort of. Cannot give it all away.

"Particle beam weapon? That large? No way. We can't even make one work in an airplane. They built one?"

"Herr Schultz did, but it blew up. It did have the mega power needed for that kind of weapon. Now Hoffman has joined him, they are trying to harness it."

"Holy shit." He exclaims, "I thought we just had run-of-the-mill spies here. What is Pierce's place in all this? That bastard can't be the brains of the plan. Can he?"

"Brad, you know him better than we do. If it goes higher up than Pierce, we don't know it, yet. He was well connected in prior administrations and has extremely right-wing associates, so who knows who else might be involved. Scary huh?"

"Diabolically frightening." He quietly replies. I can hear the concern in his voice.

"While we are exchanging info about our cases, Brad, you wouldn't know anything about a certain admin aide who was placed in Cranston's office a little while back, would you?"

Brad sighs. "Yeah it was me. When I heard, Pierce had arranged for the old department head to retire and put Cranston in, I smelled a rat. I called in an old favor from someone I know at DOD personnel to have my man placed into the office. I had the prior aide moved to a higher paying position so there would be no suspicion."

"How decent of you."

"Hey, tell me you wouldn't have done the same, if you were in my position."

"Of course I would. You want him back? He is on ice right now. Otherwise he is alright."

"I would appreciate him being released. No charges?"

"No charges. You can tell him whatever you want. The rent on his apartment is still paid so I'll get him back to Vegas."

"Thank you. Give him my number and I'll get him back here and put him to work. Thank you, Manning."

"David. We are all on the same team. We need to work together to stop this crap."

"Agreed"

CHAPTER FORTY-NINE

Brad and I agree to keep each other informed of any new information.

Tom shakes his head, "Poor guy, who did he piss off to get stuck with babysitting Worthington?"

"Somebody had to get him." I offer. "So…. George, Michael, whoever is listening," I call out. "We have to dig deeper into Pierce's background and his associates."

George answers back. "We've tried, but we have not been able to penetrate his private life. We will keep digging."

"Good, thank you." I look at Tom and Dog, inquiringly, "So what do we do now?"

"I don't know what more we can do from here." Tom offers.

"Let's get in the Smart Car and go to him. I can make him talk!" Dog snarls.

God he can be downright frightening at times.

"Overall, not a bad idea, but not a smart one, I'm afraid."

Thinking out loud I say, "If we could get his cell phone and dump it, the content might give us some pay dirt."

"Great idea, but how are we going to do it?" Tom asks. "I'm sure he doesn't have to hand it over at Creech when he enters."

"No, not there. But if he flies into Vegas, thru McCarran, when he leaves the next day, he will go through TSA inspection."

Tom brightens up, "Yeah, we could get his phone in the x-ray machine, we could have it stop and dump it quickly. Behind the machine the passengers cannot see what you are doing. We could get TSA and Homeland Security to go along, couldn't we?"

"I think it takes some time to properly extract the information." I offer. "Plus, I've never done it. It takes a special device."

Dog rolls his big eyes. "What do you think we have the cave people for? Entertainment? They can do that stuff, right shorty?" He yells out loud.

There is a long silent period with no response. "Yes Dog, that is what you have us for, we can do *"stuff."* In the background George's laughter is apparent.

"Hey guys, please excuse the ill-mannered pooch. But can you dump a cell quickly?" I ask.

"Child's play. You don't have to even touch it, just be ten or twenty feet from it."

"No shit?" Tom spurts out. "You fellows are something else."

"Thank you Thomas." Michael answers.

"That opens all sorts of possibilities. Hey if you could do that all along, then why didn't you save us all that trouble when we needed Cranston's phone? Taking the slimy thing from Dog was not pleasant."

"To be completely honest with you, David, we have just now *almost* perfected the device." Michael admits.

"Almost perfected?" Dog growls. "Almost perfected? We don't need 'almost' Shorty, we need perfected."

"Because of this case, we saw the need for such a device and have worked diligently to develop it. Remember we had no need for cell phones and such before this threat arose." Michael sternly answers.

"Yeah well, I'll give you that one, but when will it be *perfected*?" The ill-mannered canine responds.

"Probably by tomorrow. We wanted to surprise all of you."

"Thank you, Michael, and please excuse the beast. Wait a minute, why should I apologize for him, he was yours first, remember?"

Dog jumps up and says indignantly, "I am not going to sit around here anymore. I am apparently not appreciated. I'll be visiting the offices of people who appreciate me for who I am." With that, he grabs the door handle with his massive jaws, opens the door and leaves.

"He's going for treats." Tom offers. "Probably going through withdrawals."

"I heard that!"

When the laughter subsides, Michael begins instructing us. The device will be slightly larger than a normal cell phone. We will need to be close to the subject's cell phone and activate one button on our device. It will require twenty to thirty seconds to download all the information from the other phone. Fascinating.

We start throwing around ideas. How will we get the device close enough to Pierce? He doesn't know any of us, but the only location we know he visits is Creech.

"That's it," I say. "Perfect. We don't have to be there, just the device and maybe a helpful Air Force Police Officer who will push the button for us."

Tom looks at me with raised eyebrows, "Pam I suppose."

"No, she doesn't work the gate, but her friend does. She can talk her into it, probably." My voice drops off, yeah, that may not be the best idea. Another person in the plan. Too many can cause a leak.

Tom offers, "Maybe Pam can offer to work the gate? She'd do it for you, right?"

"She probably would. But as a patrol officer, with Grizzie and all, she is too qualified to do gate duty. Beside we don't know exactly when Pierce visits Creech. Once a month generally, no specific date."

Dog prances back into the office, kicking the door closed.

"Look you mindless morons, Pam is the answer to this. David, you ask her out on a date, someplace real, not dinner at the club. Then you tell her your situation. Let her comes up with the solution. She's a smart cookie. Pam will know how to get close to Pierce. Besides, I miss Grizzie."

"You've been out there the whole time? Jerk. I'm going to have the flip handles on the door changed to knobs, so I can have some privacy. You're probably right though, I have to admit."

Tom quietly says, "Take some advice from a happily married man. Don't spring this on a date. Ask her outright if she can think of a way to help us. Then ask her out on a real date. Voice of experience here." He smiles.

I agree. Don't ruin my best chance for future happiness on a mission.

CHAPTER FIFTY

I am trying to decide how to approach Pam. Tom has gotten me thinking. Thank you, Tom. Experience counts in these things, matters of the heart. I talk every day with Pam, but we have no *next date* planned. She has a crazy shift schedule right now. We both want to spend as much time together as we can, but with my current case and her schedule, it is day by day. I decide to call her and ask outright: can you think of a way to help me?

I chase the guys out of my office and reach for my cell. It vibrates in my hand-- text message from Pam. 'Give me a call when you can, handsome.'

So I do.

"Hi Beautiful, I was just dialing your number. I really was. You go first."

"Sure you were," she laughs. "I know you are up to your, well you know, in this case but could you get away for a night? One of the officers has two tickets for a show tonight in Vegas and he just got duty." She tells me the name of the star and where and when. Caesars Palace. Glad I've still got the pricey suit the little guys bought me.

"Interested? You could bring Dog. He can stay with my parents and Grizzie while we go to the show and you can stay the night," She lowers her voice and adds in a sexy tone, "If you dare."

"Woman, woman, you are incorrigible, one of the many attributes I love about you. Nothing could keep me away."

We are to meet at her parents' house.

Well that worked out well, I hope. She called me first, right? So if I ask her to help me, it isn't like I planned it, right? Time will tell.

I leave work early, put on my fancy suit and make my way to Pam parent's house. Dog won't shut up the whole way.

"Come on. You are driving like an old man. 75. That's the best you can do?" He is anxious to see Grizzie again.

"The speed limit is 65 here Dog. Just stick your head out the window and be still."

We arrive and Pam's parents, Don and Helen, welcome us. Grizzie is beside herself with joy at seeing Dog. They run outside and romp around the yard.

"Aren't they cute together? Dog is so beautiful." Helen says. "So glad you could make this David. Pam is excited about getting the tickets. Don't you look handsome! Nice suit."

"Thank you. Uh, aren't we missing someone?" I ask looking around.

"Oh, Pam is getting ready. She just got here a little while before you."

Don says. "Care for a beer while you wait?"

"Sure, it's been a hectic week."

Dad and I sit down with our brews and Mom goes to check on Pam. Dad turns toward me with a serious look in his eyes. Oh boy, here it comes, 'what are your intentions toward my daughter young man?'

He leans forward and says quietly, "David, I know whatever you are doing out there in Area 51 is secret, but I can tell from Pam's mood she is quite worried about you. She doesn't say anything, but I know my little girl. I mean, we only just met you, but Pam likes you, well to be truthful, *really* likes you. I can tell. She is afraid for you. She knows more but can't tell us. Are you safe Dave?"

Well that took me back. I didn't expect this. I'm trying to come up with a reasonable sounding answer when he says, "I know you two have been seeing each other for only a short while but Pam cares a lot for you. She has been careful with dating in the past. Well, you know about her ex-husband, the asshole, but she has fallen for you. Dad knows. I know you care a lot for her too, from the things she has shared. I know there is nothing this old flyboy can do for you out there, but I am here if I can be of any assistance. Just know that." He nods his head toward me.

"I don't know what to say except-thank you. I am certainly in less danger now than when I first took this crazy job. I can honestly tell you. I have people I can trust with me now. We know what we are up against and I can say I am fairly safe now."

"You have a team working with you?"

"Actually, a *small* army, so to speak." I smile to myself.

"I feel better now. But remember what I said, I am available if you need something, well you know, you can't do on your own. Pam and Helen don't know, but I was in Air Force intelligence most of my service career. I have done my share of digging around the seamier side of the world. I told the girls I was transferring into the Intelligence Office at Creech just to finish out my tour. They have no idea I have been doing this for many years. It is just a paper shuffling job here, kind of a reward for the more active years."

Losing my composure, I respond, "No shit. Air Force intelligence. I had no clue. Wow, uh, there just may be something, no! I don't want to involve you. You are Pam's father. You are retired and should enjoy your time. I'll be just fine. Have a great team to help." I know I am babbling. I am overwhelmed.

He reaches over and puts his hand on my knee. "Son, this old warhorse can still do the job. Retirement is boring. Sure we have golf, grandkids and such but I don't like the pasture much." Don looks deep into my eyes, "What do you need? I have contacts you know. Tell me, I just might be able to open a door or two."

I absorb this revelation: my girlfriend's father used to be an Air Force intelligence officer and I am investigating an Air force officer/ Russian spy, in intelligence. I take a deep breath and ask, "Do you know anyone at Creech in the intelligence office?"

"If you mean, presently, stay away from her. Major Kate Andrews is the Intelligence Officer now. She is the reason I retired when I did. HQ slid her in and made her top dog. I became just a flunky. A Lieutenant Colonel Flunky, but a flunky just the same."

"In my Army a Lt. Colonel outranks a Major, I thought it was the same in the Air Force." I'm sensing the hand of Franklin Pierce here.

"Not when you are told by unseen powers 'because of her special expertise', she is in command of the office. My CO told me the decision was way above him. He didn't like it one bit, but he was informed it was a 'national security' matter. He thought it was bull shit. I was eligible for retirement but was enjoying myself and it was nice to relax with a desk job after all the time I spent in the dark world. Like you are doing now I suspect." For the first time since I've met Don, he has a sadness in his eyes.

"I think you and I need to talk, at length." I say quietly.

"I thought so. I peeked at the papers Pam was going to show you when you came here last time. Old spies want to know. When she said she was helping you, I knew it had to be off the record. I needed to see what my daughter was getting herself involved in."

"you saw the papers before I came?" I ask.

"Yep. If you had spent the night, we would have talked then. I didn't want to scare Pam or her mother, so I was waiting until you came around again. In fact, I was wrangling for another dinner, but the show tickets came first. I like it when a plan comes together." He chuckles.

"Don, you could have just called me and asked me to come by. I would have been scared to death, but I would have still shown up."

"Son, I'm a rather good judge of character. You passed the first time. The truth is I didn't want Helen or

Pam to know what I was once involved with. Helen only knows I was part of a special unit which flew missions all over the world. She thought I was a pilot, nothing more. Sometimes I was so busy I could hardly keep my flying status current. I know your world David. I was there too."

I sit back, take a long pull on my beer and shake my head. "Such a small world. When I met Pam, I had no idea how intertwined we would all become. Unbelievable."

While I am still processing all of this, Pam glides into the room.

"I'm ready. I hope Dad kept you amused while I was changing." She says as she leans down and gives me a kiss.

She looks gorgeous. Her auburn hair, which is usually pulled back, is now flowing onto her shoulders. She has on a sparkly white, form fitting dress with long sleeves, modest scoop neckline and tan high heels. Well maybe they are sandals with all the straps, but *high heels?* The woman wears combat boots at work. How can she walk on those things?

I stand up and stare like a fool. "Wow, you are so beautiful." Then I realize her parents are still here, so I add, "You clean up nicely."

Everyone laughs.

We go off to Las Vegas. We knew there wouldn't be time to eat before the show but that's all right. Vegas has a plethora of fine places to dine.

"You and Dad sure looked serious when I came up. Everything okay with you two? Is Dad behaving himself?" Pam cautiously asks.

"My dear you cannot imagine how good it is with us." I answer impulsively.

I'm driving but I can feel Pam looking at me; I can feel the questions forming in her pretty head.

I refocus and add, "Yes he's a cool guy. We seem to have a lot in common. Enjoy talking with him." I sense her relaxing.

"I'm so glad. He does seem to like you. Right from the start he was asking if you could come over for dinner again soon. The military connection, I guess. Whatever. I could not be more pleased you two are bonding. He hasn't been too friendly with my past dates."

"Score one for me."

"Score two. Mom likes you too."

We arrive at the show… good seats with a great view of the stage. Headliner is an older singer, but he still has it together. I ask Pam if she had to buy the tickets off the other officer. She says he offered them to her if she would work his next two shifts at Area 51.

"I told him it would be a huge sacrifice, but I wanted to see this guy's show." She smiles at me. "I'd take every shift at Area 51 if I could, but I didn't tell him." She leans in and gives me a kiss.

Man, isn't there any air conditioning in here. I'm beginning to sweat.

When the show is finished we look for a place to eat. This town is all new to me. I ask Pam where she would prefer to dine.

"There is a seafood restaurant near here. I have a craving for crab. Haven't been out for a while." She smiles. "Been occupied at Area 51 you know."

"Let's go."

We do and have a wonderful time. The waiter is great and does not bother us too much. He gets a good tip.

On the way back to her place, I mention I was shown the Guest Room as the place for my stuff. I assumed, what it implied.

She giggles, "Yes I'm afraid so. It is my parent's home and we haven't been a couple too long, so you get it."

"Good with me. I mean actually it isn't, but I know what you are saying." My mind is saying 'holy crap, her Dad was a spook'. Any thoughts of sneaking down the hall are gone. The last thing I would see would be a flash from the end of the hall.

We get home and are greeted by the pooches. Parents are apparently in bed. After lingering good night kisses, we go off to our respective rooms.

Dog and Grizzie go off together toward the family room. What the hell? How does he rate?

CHAPTER FIFTY-ONE

I fall asleep with a hodgepodge of thoughts whirling thru my brain: Don is a retired intelligence man who wants to help me with my case, I want to be with his daughter, no these are two separate ideas, no they aren't, but yes they are. He is her father, I should not put him in harm's way, but he could be of great help to me. I drift off with ideas of how I can use him and be with Pam, at the same time.

The alarm on my phone goes off, jarring me from a fitful sleep. I have to go to work, but my mind is still shuffling between the two of them. I can't tell Pam about her Dad. Those are his wishes. He seems to like me so I will walk the line. Damn, this shit can be hard sometimes.

I wash up in the attached bathroom and after dressing, go out to the kitchen. Don is sitting at the counter reading the paper and drinking coffee.

"Good morning Dave. How was the show? Coffee? The girls are still asleep"

"Yes please. The show was great. Had a nice seafood meal after."

"Oh yes. Pam and her crab. She loves crab. We go down there every so often and she gets pissed if we didn't wait for her to be home." He laughs. "It's nice out. Why don't we go onto the patio so we can talk?"

They have quite the lovely back yard. It is an explosion of greenery. Palm trees, along with things I don't know the name of, and splotches of colorful flowers scattered throughout. It is generally warm in Las Vegas, so things grow here all year.

Dog and Grizzie are lounging in the sun on the lawn. Dog does manage to break away and come over to me. He gives me a shit eating grin; I know he does. Then he goes back to the lawn. Jerk.

"He sure is a watchful fellow. Checked out the whole house last night. He would follow Helen or me if we left the room. I can see why you feel safe with him."

Dog looked up from the lawn and gave me a quick nod.

"Look at that, he seemed to understand what I just said. I thought Grizzie was well trained, but he is almost human." More than you know, I think silently.

Then he asks if I have thought about his offer to help with my case.

"I assume you can come and go to Creech pretty much anytime you want?"

"Yeah, I can. What do you have in mind? You have an idea, I can see it in your eyes."

"Could you drop in on your old pal, Major Andrews and say hello?"

"I can, but you better have a damn good reason for me to see the bitch."

"How about to place a bug in her office?" I ask with raised eyebrows.

"Holy crap. You're after her? Hell son, I'll *live* there if it will help."

"No Don, just the bug. Well, maybe one other thing, but it will come after the bug."

"Come on boy, give me some meat. You know I'm hooked." He leans over the table.

I tell him the whole story about Cranston, Pierce and the Major. Of course, leaving out the aliens and the talking Dog. While I'm speaking, Dog has moved closer to us. He doesn't want to miss out on anything. Grizzie follows and lays next to him.

"Whew. Beats the crap out any of my old cases. How much does Pam know?" asks the concerned father.

"Pretty much what I just told you."

"Do you think I should tell her about my background in the service?"

"At this point, I say no. She would kill us both if she thought I was endangering you. She loves you. In fact Don, I'm still not sure I should even be involving you."

"Well you have. Let's get planning. Do you have a bug?"

"Uh, yeah, pretty much any type of electronic device we need. Don't ask any more right now. It will all come in time."

He sits back and drinks some coffee. "Who do you actually work for Dave? This is way beyond the DOD agents I've met."

371

"DOD with some help from old friends." I smile.

"Where do you want this bug planted? Apparently in her private office. I can do that. No problem."

"Let's trade cell phone numbers. I'll call you tomorrow or maybe even later today and let you know the timetable."

"Damn it feels good to be back in the game, even in a small way." He grins as he gives me his phone number.

Just then the door opens and a sleepy-eyed Pam wanders out and gives me a kiss. "You're up early. Oh yes, you have to go to work. Sorry," she snickers. "Breakfast will be ready soon. Mom got me up."

We eat and then I must leave.

Lingering goodbyes and Dog reluctantly jumps in my truck.

"Well you have been among the missing," I growl at him.

"Hey sorry you had to have your own room." He is mocking me.

"You and old Dad are going to work together, Good. I vouch for him. He likes you. The fool!" I try to slug him but he moves away. "Animal cruelty!" He yells out the open window.

"Shut up. Someone might hear you."

CHAPTER FIFTY-TWO

On the drive back to Area 51 I plug in and roust Michael. I fill him in on Don and tell him I need a bug. I also ask about the cell phone dump device.

"No problem with the bug and the device is ready for your approval. You have made good use of your time I see. Does Pam know about her father?"

"No and she is not to be told. At least not yet."

"We previously did a preliminary background check on Pam's parents. We now know he was a former USAF Intelligence officer."

"You were going to advise me of this, *when*?" I ask indignantly.

"Settle down please David." Michael cajoles me. "We just found that piece of information last night. It took some investigating to discover how involved he was in the covert world. Basic records only show him as a pilot. Burrowing deeper into their encrypted files we were able to discover he was indeed an intelligence operative. Seems he went on several assignments overseas, mainly Europe and occasionally the Middle East. Interesting man. Excellent reviews by superiors. He has the background to assist you. How much of your plan are you going to share with Pam?"

"Nothing yet. Don is going to make a visit to Creech, to see his old buddies. As a retiree he has a legitimate reason to be there. He'll check in with his old unit, say 'Hi' to a few people and when the opportunity presents itself, he will plant the bug in the Major's office. Since you have the phone dumping device perfected, he could linger there a few minutes, while you dump her phone. I mean, what could go wrong?" I say with skepticism in my voice.

"Is that as much as you will use him?" Michael asks in a concerned voice.

"Yes, Dad, that is all I plan on for the father of my lady."

"Good. We will have the bug and phone device ready when you want it."

After I finish talking with Michael, Dog looks at me and slaps his ear to turn off his 'device'. I turn off mine, look at the beast and say, "*What?*"

"You know he *IS* the father of your woman. I like him and Helen, so don't put him in harm's way."

"Dog, I am touched with your concern. You don't show much compassion for anyone, usually."

"Yeah, well I like them and if anything happened to him because of you, Pam would be pissed and then I might not be able to see Grizzie anymore."

"Ah ha! Now we get to the crux of your concerns. Self-serving. That's the Dog I know."

"Well you know it's true. You don't want to lose Pam. Right!?"

Fuzz Butt is right. Don offered his services because he misses the old world and saw a chance to keep his hand in. I definitely don't want to jeopardize my relationship with Pam or to put Don at risk. But this is an easy task for him. I must admit he might be helpful further on, depending on what we learn from the Major's phone.... Stop it David. You are sounding too much like the spy master and not like the suitor. Don's safety comes first. Yeah, the relationship I want with Pam is right up there too.

After checking in at the office, Tom and I go to the caves. Dog, of course, tags along. We meet with Michael and one of their techs. They show me the listening device or bug. It is like a peel and stick dot, a quarter inch, no bigger. It is literally peel and stick. It could be placed anywhere and not be noticed. Military equipment that regularly sweeps for listening devices will not be able to detect it.

"The bottom of the Major's desk telephone would be perfect." Michael advises. "Don will have to place another small item, the transmitter, within a hundred feet or so. Outside and facing our direction would be ideal."

The tech then holds up a small rock.

"Easily fits in the palm of your hand, or better yet, Don's," Michael declares.

Tom reaches for the rock, "clever, absolutely clever. One thing we have in Nevada is rocks. One more will not be noticed."

"You know what I do to rocks, don't you?" Dog ribs them.

375

"You can't hurt this. It could be in a place which gets watered regularly and not be damaged." The tech proudly declares.

They show me the phone-dumping device. It resembles two ultra-thin smart phones sandwiched together. Easily carried in a shirt or pants pocket.

Michael educates us on how to use the device. Nothing to it. Just point it towards the target and push a small button on one end when you are within twenty-five feet.

"Keep at it and you'll be able to dump it from your caves." I chide.

We take our toys and go back to the office.

First, I call Don. "I can go to Creech anytime you need me to go, Dave. Weekdays are when the Major works. What little of it she does." Don scoffs.

"I need her, or at least her cell phone, to be there. We have a device that will grab her data. All you need to do is be within twenty-five feet of her phone for it to work. You can keep it in your pocket. The bug is a small quarter inch dot you can stick on the back of her desk phone or some other item that won't be leaving the room. Oh yes, there is a small rock you need to place outside within a hundred feet."

"That's it? Who do you *actually* work for Dave? These sound like Star Wars gadgets."

"You're close Don," I mumble. "Closer than you know."

"So how do I get these items? You want to come to dinner tonight?"

"Uhh, yeah I'd love to, but so soon? Wouldn't it seem weird to the ladies?"

"Nah, I like you. The girls are thrilled. Not many of Pam's suitors have made the cut. You're the first. I did not like any of them, especially her ex. The asshole!"

"I'd be honored to come to dinner tonight, what time?"

"Hold on," Don says. Then I hear him open a door and call out. "What time is dinner? Dave's coming." I hear babble from the ladies. "How about six? Work for you?"

"I'll be there." I smile and hang up. It will be up to Don to explain how this occurred. Hope he tells me so I can be ready. Pam is nobody's fool. She'll begin to probe. Probably hitting up Dad right now.

Dog and Tom are sitting, looking at me.

"What? Don't either of you have something to do?"

"Nah, just listening to you is enough for me. How about you Tom? You have anything better to do?" Tom just grins and shakes his head.

"Bet you still have to have your own room."

"Dog. Shut up." I growl. No respect, I get no respect.

Smirking, Tom says he needs to check on something and leaves.

"Wait for me." Dog hurries out behind him.

"You can stay with the aliens tonight, jerk."

The dog spins and dashes back into the office.

"Aw come on, can't take a joke? You wouldn't make me stay, would you?"

"Of course not. But you are still a jerk."

CHAPTER FIFTY-THREE

As soon as my tires hit the driveway at Pam's house she is out the door and running up to me. She's typically happy to see me, but from the look on her face, I can tell this time is different. She sticks her pretty face into my open window.

"Okay Cloak and Dagger Man, what are you and my Dad up to?"

"Uh, no kiss?"

She reaches in and with both hands firmly around my throat, asks determinedly, "What are you two doing?"

Quickly deciding any answer, including the truth, would be harmful to my well-being, I choke out, "What did he tell *you*? He asked me to come for dinner."

Relaxing her grip on my throat, Pam lowers her head and stares piercingly into my eyes. "He said you told him a little about what you're doing and he just wanted to know if he could be of any help. Says he is missing having something to do, thought you might need someone who could come and go at Creech without any questions. Is that what this is about? David!"

Without breaking my gaze, I reply, "The truth is he wanted to help plan our wedding."

She just looks dumbfounded. Threw her for a loop.

I can see her mind click in, "Two peas in a pod." Reaching in again, she turns my face upwards and gives me a big kiss. "My Dad wants to be of some help, doesn't he?"

"Yes he does, but I don't want to put him in harm's way. I just told him I would think about it and see if I could come up with something."

"And *what* have you come up with, Mr. Spy Master?"

Without batting an eyelash, I respond, "Just going to have him drop by his old office and chat up his former co-workers. See what's happening. Sound safe enough?" I look up at her with the most sincerity I can muster.

Dog, thru out this interrogation, has been quietly sitting next to me. He now starts to squirm and whine.

"Oh poor Dog, he has been patiently sitting here and he wants to see Grizzie. Come on David, let's go inside. You're clear, for the moment.'' She is staring at me again, trying to peer into my soul. I am not out of the woods yet. This one is tough.

We go in, Helen is busy in the kitchen. She gives me a big hug. So far so good. The dogs jump around and then go outside.

"Don is outside puttering in the garden. Go and say hello David. Pam will help me finish dinner."

"Uh, thanks, sure I can't be of some help?" Always the gentleman.

"No, no. You go out. Don's been waiting for you."

I find Don sitting on a bench, under a tree, beer in hand. He holds up one for me. This is how he *putters in the garden.*

"How tough was my daughter on you?"

"I made it through unscathed, for the moment, how about you?"

"She was all over me. Pam is a smart cookie. Makes me proud. Don't let her into our world Dave. I worry enough with what she's doing now."

She is deeper into *our world* than you could imagine, I think to myself. What a mess I've made. The lady I'm getting serious about has accidently gotten involved in my top-secret world and now her father also wants in. I did not want either of them involved. She got there by accident and Don by offering to assist. I need his ability to freely get into Creech and to the Major, because I do not want to put Pam at risk. Now his task seems safe enough, but I am feeling uneasy about it all. Into my fog comes Don's voice.

"David, you in there? You look miles away."

Snapping back into the moment and taking a long drink of beer, I look at the person I hope will be my future father-in-law. "Don, I think you should not be involved with my operation. I do not want to take any risks with your safety." He starts to open his mouth. "No, let me finish, please. I could not live with myself if anything happened to the father of the woman I love. I know you are no novice at this game, but see it from my point of view, please." I am getting choked up.

Standing up he puts his arms around me. Don also is emotional,

"Son, God I love you for that. You have no idea how much your words mean to me." He gives me a big bear hug. Then, firmly taking hold of my shoulders and looking directly at me he states, "Be that as it may, I am still going to help you. Damn it. You need experienced help. Not someone who will say the wrong thing or tip your hand. This is a delicate matter and I'm your man. Period!"

Overwhelmed, I slump down onto the bench. Catching some movement out of the corner of my eye, I look up and see Pam coming out of the house. Freezing in her tracks, she looks at Don, then me, she doesn't know what to make of the scene. Before I can react, Don calls her to come over.

As she hurries toward us, questions are forming in her mind, you can almost see them: what just happened, is David alright, what did Dad say to him?

As I get to my feet, Don looks at his daughter and smiles,

"Get the worried look off your face Kid. We are fine. In fact, we are better than fine. This fine gentleman just asked for my approval to marry you. I said yes! As if there was any doubt."

She absorbs what her father has just said, looks at me, back at her father and throws her hands up in the air,

"Aughhhh! You two! Peas in a pod! Idiots, you are both idiots!"

Pam spins on her heels toward the house, stops, turns back to us and then puts her arms around both of us.

"You two are going to drive me crazy." She hugs and kisses us. "What am I going to do with you guys?"

"Love us?" I offer.

CHAPTER FIFTY-FOUR

Don excuses himself, mumbling something about beer and the call of nature, and heads to the house.

Pam looks into my eyes with tears in hers. Taking her in my arms, I gently kiss the top of her head. She responds by turning her head upwards, pulling me to her mouth and intensely kissing me. When we break for air, she wipes her eyes,

"You know I love both of you, but tell me what you guys are planning? You didn't really ask his approval to marry me, did you?"

"Well indirectly I did. I told him I didn't want anything to happen to the man I hoped would be my father-in-law."

Tears now are flowing down her cheeks, Pam holds me tightly, "That is the most beautiful proposal I've ever heard."

"I know we said we were going to take it slow, but with all that has happened, I've never felt closer to anyone or more truly in love. Yes woman, I want to marry you. If you will have me."

"Yes! Yes! Yes! Was there any doubt?"

"Well you just never know." I smile.

We decide going back to the house is a good idea right now. Left to ourselves who know what would happen in the garden.

"I had no idea what just occurred with you and Dad." Pam says as we are walking hand in hand. "I was coming outside and saw Dad grab you by the shoulders and then you collapsed onto the bench. I was scared. I know he likes you, so I had no clue what just happened." Looking up at me, "He is still going to do something for you, isn't he?"

"Like I told you, just going to pay a friendly visit to his old office."

"That's it. One visit?"

"One visit."

"You know I do love you, but I'm not so sure about your *professional* side. I think you could be scary. I'm glad you are on my side."

"I will always be there for you *and* your parents." I pledge solemnly.

As we are walking, Dog and Grizzie are right next to us. They have been the whole time. Dog has been listening in and Grizzie, she's just hanging with her Alpha.

As we get to the door Dog stumbles and holds up a front foot.

"What's the matter big guy?" I ask. He is giving me the 'I want to talk' look.

"Go on in Pam, he's probably just got something in his pad. We'll be right in."

After she closes the door, Dog asks, "Can I be the ring bearer?"

I grab him around the neck give him a big hug. "Of course, who else would I have? And by the way, thanks for breaking the mood out in the driveway. It helped a lot."

"Always glad to be of service. Grizzie will be the flower girl, right?"

We go in and I assure everyone Dog is fine. Just a stone, no damage.

Helen is beaming and comes over to me. "Is this true, you asked Don for Pam's hand in marriage? How sweet, no one does that anymore."

"Well, not in those exact words but, yes I did. I hope that meets with your approval as well?"

She hugs me, "I could not be happier. I hoped for this when I first met you. Welcome to the family." She hastily wipes her eyes. "Dinner is ready, everyone sit down."

After a lively dinner with plenty of laughter and wine, Helen directs the men to go outside and let the girls clean up. We do as we're told and after settling on the patio, Don looks at me, "So when do I start?"

With my back to the house I remove a small package from my pocket. Don leans over as I open the bug and the rock. Quickly I tell him what to do with them. He looks at the rock.

"The bug is obvious, but what's with the rock?"

"Just place it outside the office on the ground in some area on the northwestern side. Somewhere out of the way but within 100 feet of the office."

Don looks at it, shakes it and says, "I assume it is the transmitter for the bug. How far does it reach?"

"Far enough for my team to listen."

He cocks his head and gives me a quizzical look, "Come on David, you can give me more info."

"Okay, it reaches my office at Area 51."

"Holy shit! I cannot believe how the technology in our game has developed. That is out of this world."

"Yeah, Don, it kind of is." I smile.

The dogs have been on the grass behind us, Dog gives a snort.

I ignore him.

Now before the ladies join us, I produce the cell phone device and show him how to use it.

"Utterly amazing." He puts the devices in his pocket. "I can go to Creech tomorrow morning if you want. It's a weekday the Major should be there sometime."

Before I can answer the door opens and the ladies are bringing us some chocolate cake.

"I don't know if I can keep eating here," I joke, patting my belly "I will need to buy more clothes."

Genuinely nice family type of evening. I love it. Almost makes me forget about the world outside. After a while, Helen says she and Don need to retire and leave 'you kids' alone. We hug, kiss, and shake hands, Don and me that is. They go inside. Pam and I move to a cozy loveseat on the patio.

It is beautiful here. Most people don't realize Las Vegas is a real city, with homes, schools, grocery stores, the whole nine yards. Most of the world just knows about casinos, huge hotels and shows, the Sin City image. It is a desert, but with proper landscaping, it becomes a gorgeous, balmy place to live.

Area 51, not so much.

I could get used to living in a community like this. We talk and cuddle for a long time.

"Do you see what time it is?" Pam looks at a clock on the wall. "You have to go to work in a few hours, young man."

Apparently, the *approval* has been given and I am informed I may share Pam's room tonight.

"You have a couch for me?"

"No, smart ass. You may sleep in my bed, if you want."

"I want!"

After breakfast, Dog and I head back to the desert.

"Worked out for you didn't it?" The hound says haughtily as he is half leaning out the window so I can't hit him.

"Get back inside before you embarrass yourself by falling out."

CHAPTER FIFTY-FIVE

After checking in with Cranston and my cave dwelling operatives, I settle into my office. Tom is not here yet. No new messages. Good sign or not? I want things to happen now, come together, so we can get this whole mess mopped-up. Then Tom comes in, his plane just landed. Chuckling he explains, "Sorry I'm late, but the flight was delayed. Some aircraft called 'Air Force One' was due to land and we were put on hold. Imagine, the President is more important than the shuttle to the place which does not exist."

"Go figure, well it must be for a good reason. It is not election year."

"My FBI contact called me last night. He's been working on the case of the Major's *father*. He's using information from the agent handling the father. The sponsor for Major Kate Andrew's induction into the Air Force *and* for her move into the intelligence section was one Franklin Pierce. My FBI friend also knows Brad Young. Your friend, Howie's boss. Once he talked with Young all the pieces started coming together. Young, by the way, is in awe of the Intel you have developed."

I humbly nod. "With a lot of help from my team."

"My bud asked if we wanted him to wait a while before picking them up on espionage charges. I told him I thought so but would ask you. We don't want to spook them, do we? Taking the Major and her father would tip off Pierce, right?"

"If he could get the Germans at the same time, maybe. But that would leave Pierce free. I would sure like to get his ass involved. Beside I feel this goes beyond Pierce. If this is about a New World Order, then there are big names behind it. I've been thinking, this is not just Russia spying, its multi-national. There are no country allegiances for these people, only money and power."

"When are you going to get your father-in-law involved?" Tom asks with raised eyebrows.

"Future father-in-law, but hopefully today. He has the bug and cell phone dumper."

"May I ask what Pam thinks of all this?"

"She's cautious. For some reason she doesn't believe Don and I are levelling with her."
"Is she correct? Ah, I can tell from your expression you have not told her everything."

"Correct Tom. Those two have fed her a line." Dog pipes in. "He's *just* going to visit his old office and see how everyone is doing. They actually think she buys that."

"And why would you say that, my furry friend? What did you overhear?"

"Nothing!" He smirks and starts to leave.

"No you don't fuzz butt. Come on tell me."

"Steak and ice cream for dinner?" He cocks his head inquiringly.

"You know you get steak all the time. Too much ice cream and Grizzie will think you are getting fat. You wouldn't want that, would you?"

The hound lets out a sigh, "Okay, Pam was telling her mother she thinks Dad is pushing you to get him into the action. He's obviously bored being retired. Mom said Don used to fly some missions in the service he wouldn't tell her about. She always suspected he was doing more than just flying."

"What did Pam say?"

"She wouldn't be surprised. Dad has an edge about him. The same edge she sees in you, lover boy."

Tom goes to check on Cranston. It's important we keep up the charade. Tom baby-sits and keeps him thinking we have a handle on everything. The last thing we need is John going paranoid on us and calling Pierce.

My mind switches back to Don. He said he would get to Creech around eleven this morning. He can hang around with his old crew and go to lunch with them. If the Major is there, he will attempt to dump her cell phone. If she isn't, he'll plant the bug in her office. If her office is locked, he will come back after lunch and if she's there, hopefully complete his mission. Sounds like a lot of 'if's' to me. He will give me a quick text when he is on his way home.

There is nothing for me to do now but stare at the clock. I'm nervous, hell yes I'm nervous. It seemed like such a safe and easy mission for Don. But since he is the father of----yeah, yeah, I am distraught. I need to stop my mind from driving me crazy.

Then I feel something poke me in the ribs. It is Dog.

"Earth to David, come in David."

"Yeah, I'm here. Thanks, I'm can't help worrying."

"What is done is done. It will work or it won't. That's it."

"You're a big comfort."

"That's what I'm here for. Why don't we go over to the caves and see if the bug comes on line? It would be better than sitting here fretting."

"Why didn't I think of that? Thanks partner."

"Because you have your head up--well you know."

Why *didn't* I think of it? I'm just sitting around stewing. The personal aspects of this complex case are getting to me. I need a vacation.

I let Tom know what we are doing and head off for the caves.

Michael and George are in the control room watching the progress of Don's cell phone on a digital map. Creech's buildings are shown as if from a satellite photo. Most of them have labels showing their use.

"He's inside Creech now." George says as I enter. "He has stopped at the base intelligence office."

Looking at the display I see there is a blinking dot in front of a building. The dot moves toward the building and apparently goes inside. I don't know where the Major's office is, but the dot is moving around slowly, stopping then moving again. Greeting his former co-workers, I am guessing. Amazing. He stays in one place for over fifteen minutes, then moves toward the rear of the building. He goes near the outer wall for a few seconds and then goes back to the middle of the building and to another area. He stays there for two or three minutes then returns to where he was for a fifteen-minute period.

"Probably had to pee." Comments the hound.

"What was the trip to the wall?" I ask to no one in particular. "I wonder if it's the Majors' office."

The dot stays stationary until eleven forty and then moves outside to where he first stopped. Probably his car. Then the dot moves around the base and stops at the Officer's Club and goes inside. An hour and fifteen minutes later the dot goes back to Don's old office. It moves around the building for some time and then goes outside. This time it is thru the rear of the building. It slowly goes to the northwest and seems to just wander around, then goes back inside the office.

"We are live." Shouts one of the techs. We quickly gather around his equipment where there is a glowing green light. He points at his ear bud and smiles. "It is working perfectly. I can hear soft voices, like in another room." He then presses a button and we all hear the voices. I listen to laughter and what I'm sure is Don's voice.

The bug must be in the Major's office. Well done my future father-in-law. Now get out! Please. Oh wait, the phone dump. I guess the Major isn't in today. At this point I just want Don out and safely home. The talking stops. Next, I hear a female voice. "Good afternoon gentlemen. Oh Donald. How nice to see you. Come in and tell me how retirement is treating you." There is sound of footsteps and then a loud thump on the speaker.

"Probably put her purse on the desk." Speculates the tech.

Don starts talking to the Major. She tells him to sit and relax. She has to check her e-mails and then they can chat. I can hear chairs moving and cushions wheezing. Man, this device is sensitive. There is the clicking of a keyboard and in a few minutes she begins to ask Don how retirement is going. They make small talk for longer than I would have thought. Don may hate or at least resent her, but he carries on quite well. Then Don says he had better let her get to work and after more pleasantries he leaves. She asks him to please close her door on his way out.

Then all we hear is the clicking of the keyboard.

"Fricking amazing guys. Well done." I try to high-five the aliens, but we have an awkward moment in connecting. Different heights and all.

Since all sounds in the Major's office will be recorded, I leave and head back to my office. As soon as I'm outside I receive a text from Don.

"Good visit, heading home. Will call you later."

Whew. I feel better now. He was great. Maybe I can use him for----No stop it David. He is finished. No more.

Dog has been trotting beside me, then as if he could read my mind, oh yeah maybe he can, he stops, looks at me and says,

"If you do, I'll tell Pam." He glares at me and runs off ahead.

CHAPTER FIFTY-SIX

Tipping his head to one side with an inquisitorial expression, Tom looks up from his desk as I enter our office.

"It is done. Don will call later. The bug in the Major's office is operational and since he spent several minutes talking with her, I can assume he has completed the phone dump too," I report.

"Great news. I was worried something would go wrong. You know how these things can go south in a minute."

"Tom, he was brilliant. He BS'd the Major, as he was an old friend. She must have no idea he hates her guts. He talked about how life was good being retired, playing golf and so on."

"Did she ask him any leading questions, like she was at all concerned about him being there?"

"Man, you're good. You do know the game. No, I was worried when she asked him to come into her office and chat. She only asked basic stuff, like how he liked being free and having no schedules. He sounded relaxed and real. The man is no novice at our game."

"You are done using him. Aren't you Dave?" Tom asks, looking into my eyes.

"Damn, first Dog and now you. Yes. I am done using Don. I hated myself for doing it this time. I cannot go through this again. He and his family mean too much to me. He's not expendable."

"Unlike me?" Tom teases.

"You know what I mean. Don't make this any harder. You know how we feel about our ops team. We're all family. But Don's family-family." I sputter.

"Relax; I'm just messing with you. Yeah, I know how it is. The team is there to do a job. You hope to God everyone is still there at the end of it. Don is part of your future, but I don't blame you for using him. He wanted in. In fact, I would venture to say he worked it so you would need to use him. He's an old war horse who missed the action."

"You're right. He maneuvered himself into the position of being useful."

Since I had nothing else to do but anxiously wait for Dons phone call, I thought it would be wise for me to check in with John Cranston. I have just been giving him a wave and "how's it going" lately. Tom has been carrying out his baby-sitting duties.

"David, Come in. You seem so busy lately. Tom says you are making progress on who is making the threats on me." John gestures to a chair and settles back in his chair. He is much calmer than a few days ago. Thank you, Tom, for handling him so masterfully.

"Yeah John we are. A twisty trail seems to lead back to the DC area. We are getting closer, but not there yet. Be sure not to mention anything to your good buddy Pierce.

We don't need him setting off any red flags until we know for sure who is behind it all."

"No problem. The less I see or hear from him the better."

"He still on your case about the energy beam project?"

"Constantly. It's all he wants to know about." He sighs.

"And, what do you tell him?" I ask.

"We are making slow progress. Sometimes hit a blank wall but then find some progress. Jesus David, I hope you can get him off my back when you solve this whole situation. I can't take much more." He looks beseechingly at me.

"Uhh John, I thought I was just to find out who was threatening you and keep you safe. Not handle your personnel issues." I am pushing now to see how far he will go with this new admission regarding Pierce.

"I'm sorry David. I am concerned; no I am terrified, of Franklin Pierce. He is not the man I use to know. I don't know what he is into these days. He has always been a hawk. Well most of us were. But he has gone off the deep end."

"Like how? What's he saying?"

"Crazy stuff. He almost sounds like Hitler or Stalin. Rule the world stuff. '*We* should be in charge of the civilized world, not the politicians. The public doesn't know what is right for them.' I don't know David. I think the guy has gone wacko. He was always an ultra-right winger. You remember when he was in the administration of our warmongering President. Who always wanted to send the troops to invade some country. You know who I mean. I don't want to name names. I still wonder if the walls have ears. Well Pierce is much worse now. I sometimes wonder, listening to him, if he is working his own agenda."

"Trust me, John. There are no bugs in here. We have the safest office in the building."

"I believe Nixon said that too." John says with a roll of his eyes.

"Humor, I like it John. It's time for you to relax. You are in a good, safe position now. Please trust me."

"I believe Nixon said that also. Just kidding. I do feel much more comfortable with you around."

We talk some more and then my cell phone rings. It's Don.

"I have to take this John. Keep the faith; it's going to be over soon." I say as much for myself as for him.

I go into my office.

"Hi Don. Talk to me." I practically yell.

He is amused. "Calm down Boy. All is well. Both assignments completed. This old dog can still hunt. I have something of yours. Want to come by tonight?"

"Won't it upset the ladies? I was just there."

"Got it covered. I just happened to hear of this new Italian restaurant and suggested we all go there. A nice family outing. They are pleased as punch. Well Pam is giving me the evil eye, but I will handle her. She knows I went to Creech today for you. I'll take her aside and say I just visited the guys and nothing new was going on. You are on your own after that. Six work for you? We have 7 o'clock reservations."

"I'll be there."

That old son-of-a gun.

I check in with Michael. He relays the gist of the Major's afternoon. Seemed routine. Nothing of apparent interest. Good, it's time for me to get ready for my dinner date.

Everyone is waiting for me as I arrive at the house. Don has laid the groundwork nicely. Helen is her usual cheerful self. Pam is her usual suspicious self.

"Wait until I get you alone, Mister. We are going to talk." She whispers into my ear as she greets me.

"I can hardly wait." I reply. She gives my arm a firm squeeze.

"Ouch." I cry out.

"Shut up or I'll show you ouch." hisses the love of my life.

Helen looks inquiringly at us. Picking up on it all, Don quickly says, "Stop horsing around you two. We have to get going, you know how traffic is this time of day."

Dinner goes well.

After a fun outing we return home. Don and Helen retire and leave Pam and me to our own devices. I look like a beaten puppy. I can do that well if needed.

"Oh stop it!" She grabs me and leads me down the hall to her room. So far so good. Pam grabs me by the shoulders and stares into my soul,

"Is it over now. No more missions for my Father?" She is trying to be serious, but I see the sparkle in her eyes. Pulling her to me I wrap my arms around her, "No more missions for your dad. I promise. Remember I didn't want him to do this one."

"Yeah, but you dangled it in front of him. Didn't you David?"

"Maybe, but I tried to back out." I weakly say.

"I know, he smelled action and wanted in. Right?"

'Yes Dear."

She slugs me in the arm.

The rest of the night was less painful.

CHAPTER FIFTY-SEVEN

In the morning, Don slips me the phone dump device. This is the first time we have been alone.

"How was it? You sounded like the Major was your best friend. Great job Don."

"I assume the bug worked. I have been dying to ask you. But we weren't left alone last night. How's Pam with you? Give you a hard time?"

"The bug worked flawlessly. It is so good I could hear you in the other room laughing with your friends. Pam was trying to be tough guy to me, but she softened, thankfully."

"She's just worried I might do something stupid. I told her I just chatted with my old teammates, see how the Major was these days. None of them like her and they resent her being pushed in on them. She does stay to herself and leaves them alone to do their jobs. She only signs whatever she has to and meets with Cranston and Pierce. The guys don't know much about Pierce. Just think he is a DOD bigwig making a boondoggle trip to Creech so he can visit Vegas."

"What do they think of Cranston?"

"Oh, they have no qualms about him and the Major fooling around. No secret there. The guys could care less. She doesn't bother them, and they don't bother her."

"Maybe you should have stayed, if she's not intrusive to them."

"No. I couldn't stay being subservient to her. Especially her being a Major. It was made clear to me she was the head of the section. Not by her but by the Pentagon. I couldn't live under that arrangement. They knew it. But if I had known about your case I just might have stayed on."

"Oh no, Don, we both would be dead at the hands of your daughter by now."

"Probably true." He looks around furtively, "If you need me to snoop around anymore, just say the word."

"You do believe in living on the edge, don't you?" I laugh. "No sir, you are done, finished, laid off."

He looks slyly at me, "The offer is on the table."

Dog who has been there all along lets out a low moan.

"What's the matter big guy? You okay?" Don asks.

'He's fine, he probably gobbled his food too fast." I lean down and whisper, "Behave yourself'

We leave and head back to base. I get the phone device to the aliens as soon as I arrive. Michael greets me at the cave entrance and rushes off inside to see what secrets the device holds. It is kind of weird to see the little guys run. Everything works correctly but the large head makes it look scary. Also funny.

Dog watches Michael and snickers. "Be careful shorty, the center of gravity thing is not in your favor."

I go to my office and try to busy myself. This could be a big break for us. My nerves are at fever pitch. I feel my heart thumping.

Tom comes in and he too is anxious. "Can't we go over to the caves and watch? He asks. "I feel we are going to get the answers we need to finish this case."

"Leave them alone. The last thing they need is you two sweaty giants looming over them." Dog admonishes us as he goes out on his daily treat trek in the building.

Finally, Michael hails us on my ear implant. "What a treasure trove of phone numbers. Some we don't know about. Just give us a little more time to run them all down. It looks like we are getting to the heart of this. I think we may have a lead on Pierce. Be patient my friends."

I relay this to Tom. I don't know what my face shows, but I can see relief in his. Tom says, "I felt this would do the trick. We are going to break this wide open; I know it."

We settle into our chairs. I look at the heavens, "Please let it be."

Dog comes bouncing in. "I told you two to just leave the squirts alone and they would get it done."

Lunch time rolls around. "Let's go get something. I don't feel hungry, but it will pass the time." I suggest. Tom agrees. Dog is already heading out the door.

"You're going to get fat and Grizzie won't like a tubby boy." I call after him.

We pick at salads. Neither of us can even make small talk. We sense this could be a defining moment for us. Dog is only nibbling at his burger.

"What's the matter, too well done?" Tom asks.

"No, you guys are getting to me. How will this end?" He sticks his nose toward me, "David, we will still be together, won't we? I mean you will stay with Pam and me, right?" His brown eyes are imploring.

"Of course, you goof. I told you early on we would not part, ever. What's wrong Dog? I thought you could read our puny minds."

"Not as much as I made it seem. I never thought much about things ever changing but now that this may be coming to an end, I am getting a little scared. You and me, we are pack." He moves over and puts his head in my lap. There are tears welling up in his eyes. Tom is choking back tears.

I scratch Dogs ears. "Buddy, we are a pair, partners. A pack. Why are you worrying now?"

"These are evil people we are dealing with and I don't care so much about me, but I couldn't stand to lose you. Plus, I kind of care for Grizzie and Pam and Don and Helen. All of this is a real family to me. The little guys are okay and Mickey is great, but I feel connected to all of you too." Turning his head toward Tom.

That's it, we are all bawling like babies. Fortunately no one is close to our table.

CHAPTER FIFTY-EIGHT

We are now just taking in the *moment* with Dog. I have wiped his eyes and mine. I am hugging the furry beast. Tom keeps wiping his eyes and is gazing off at nothing.

In my ear, I hear a clearing of the throat and Michael softly says, "Pardon me for interrupting, but I think it is time for us to get together. We have sorted out the phone numbers. You need to see it all."

This jars me back. "Yes Michael, we'll be right there."

Dog straightens up, shakes his head. "To the bat caves." He is back too.

George meets us and we go to the control room. Michael has all the phone numbers the Major has called and the ones who have called her listed on a large screen. Dates and times are shown. These guys never cease to impress me.

Pointing to each number, Michael identifies the location or name of each one. "If the Major has the number in her directory then we have the name. The others we have only a location." He uses a laser pointer. "This is John Cranston's burner phone. She calls it daily. Sometimes for only a few minutes, other times for much longer. This one is his office number, but she has not called it since he got the burner phone." He sweeps the pointer over a half a dozen numbers. "These are Air Force administration locations. Mostly in the Pentagon & D.C. Some of them call her off and on. Our guess is these are official calls in line with her supposed job. Now this one is listed as *Frankie*. Must be Franklin Pierce. He is located in the Arlington Virginia area. This is not an official phone number and appears to also be a burner phone. It is a cell phone as we can track it moving around the Virginia and D.C. area." Michael turns and looks at us. His face is beaming. He is properly proud of their work.

Tom and I are just shaking our heads in awe. Dog sits up and rather harshly says to Michael, "Good 'dog and pony show' Shorty. Who does Pierce contact? Who else is involved? You haven't told us anything we don't already know."

I start to scold the insolent mutt when Michael smiles and holds up his hand, "Patience my furry friend. We have more; I was just laying the groundwork."

Dog snorts and lays back down.

"We have detected Pierce periodically goes to a certain location in rural Virginia. It is not his residence. We have learned the owner of the property is a retired US Army general, Charles Lamar. He was Pierce's cohort during the weapons of mass destruction time frame and subsequent ill-advised ventures the government got into during that administration."

Tom lets out a low whistle. "Those two are still at it. Holy shit. This is more than scary."

"So how can we find out what goes on at those meetings and who else is present?" I ask no one in particular.

Dog slowly stretches and rises to his feet, "I can do it. Take me in the Dumb Car and let me loose. Put a camera on me and I can roam around and watch."

"Buddy, no! They could shoot you. There may be guard dogs already. No. You are not going, period." I am panicky about losing Dog.

The hound comes over to me and rises up putting his front paws on my chest. Gives me a lick. "Thanks partner, but do you have a better idea?"

George jumps in, "The Smart Car *is* the answer. Just not like that. We could still do a good surveillance without anyone being in harm's way. You went to Sedona and got the goods on the Germans."

"I like it. I do think it should be Dog and me. Michael can drive. We can still use Dog's senses, after we check out the place."

Tom looks at Michael and George. "Can you teach me to safely operate the car? I do not think you fellas should be far from here. Either of you. If something goes wrong, it will create a monster of a public panic. Besides, the colony needs your leadership, now more than ever."

I just look at Tom. "I can't let you put yourself at risk either. You are retired and alive. I want you to stay that way."

"David, you and I both swore to uphold the security of our country. I'm in." Tom looks at me with a sharp nod.

I just dumbly look at everyone. They are staring at me.

Michael speaks up, "He makes a valid point, David"

Resigning myself to their logic, I acquiesce. "All right, let's plan it and see how it might work."

George puts a satellite map of the area in Virginia on another screen. He zooms down so closely we can see the license plates of the cars in the driveway.

"This is NSA level technology, guys." Tom admires.

"That's who we got it from. We do not have our own satellites you know. But as long as we can access theirs, we don't need any." George adds with a smirk.

The location appears to be a large farm. There is a huge house and several outbuildings including a big barn. There are acres of fields and orchards that seem to be worked. Tractors, pickups, and other pieces of equipment are evident throughout the property. The General has retired well, as would be expected.

Michael has been writing down the license information of the various vehicles. He gives them to one of the techs.

After checking out the property, George begins to zoom in on trees around the house. Shakes his head and keeps zooming in here and there.

"What are you looking for George?" I ask.

"A suitable location for a remote camera so we can watch the driveway and the house. Somewhere no one will be going. Power poles are not a good idea. They have storms and wind back there and if the power goes out a service member will find the camera. The trees are too full.

412

Ah there." George smiles. "An old windmill. The blades may still work but there are no wires hooked up, so it is just a nostalgic yard decoration. Perfect."

Tom's mouth is agape. "You're a clever devil, you are thinking like you have been in our business."

George smiles conspiratorially. "In the distant past, perhaps."

Dog groans.

After much discussion, we decide to place a camera in the windmill. We could do this just as we did with the German's house in Sedona, using the Smart Car. Due to the size of the main house, trying to place any listening device would be of questionable value. Michael says they can make a weatherproof camera to transmit pictures using an encrypted cell phone.

"So how long would the battery last?" I ask.

"Probably a month or so, while transmitting 24 hours a day."

"I can barely get a day out of mine." I grumble.

"Superior technology." Michael proudly replies. "Will not work on your primitive devices, sorry."

The short but clever people are to construct their device and Tom, Dog, and I will fly out at night to Virginia and install it. Tom is to get flying lessons. Hey me too. Why should he have all the fun?

Since we can only fly at night, Tom will have to stay late a few evenings. I can go anytime. No wife. Oh yes, well sort of I do, but I do not go home every night.

The thought really hits home.

Yes, Pamela, I am hopelessly head-over heels in love with you.

CHAPTER FIFTY-NINE

Tom is staying a few extra hours tonight to begin his flying lessons. I go into the control room and start listening to the Major's daily activities. There was nothing unusual until she called John Cranston in the afternoon using her cell. They engaged in some small talk and then she asked him, "So how is your project coming? Did you solve the power drain problem yet?"

John answers firmly, "Yes, as a matter of fact we did. It is looking quite promising at this point. I expect to get the first test results by the end of the week. I was waiting until tomorrow night to tell you."

Major Andrews coos back, "I'll be here waiting."

He has no idea I can hear this conversation or I even know of Major Andrew's existence. Wow, John is laying it on thick. He is playing the game just as I coached him. I wanted him to keep optimistic with Pierce, but he is playing the game with her too. I wonder if he knows she has a connection to Pierce. If he does not, then John is revealing top secrets. Does not make sense to me. It would be out of character. How can I find out what is going on without showing my hand?

George comes into the room. He has listened to the Major's tapes today. I tell him my concerns.

He smiles almost smugly, "You need to keep listening. Your questions will be answered in due time."

Fine, don't be the grand oracle to me.

As if he read my mind, which I'm not sure he can't, George says, "I had the same concerns when I first listened. But please continue, all will be explained."

I put the earpieces back and hit the play button. As soon as she hangs up with John, the Major uses her cell phone and places a call.

"Hello my doll," answered Franklin Pierce. "How's our boy coming along?"

"Much better. Actually sounded confident. He said they had solved the power drain issue and were expecting some test results by the end of the week. I told you I could get him motivated."

"You certainly motivate me baby," Pierce softly answers.

Gag, I cannot bear much of this crap.

George is smirking. "I told you. Keep listening it gets better or worse, depending on how you take it."

Pierce and the Major keep talking for several more minutes. Basically, it looks as if Pierce sent her to motivate John, however she could. From the conversation John Cranston knows the Major works with Pierce and as a result, she is his conduit. This makes sense now that I piece the time frames together. John has not been talking with Pierce as often as he once did. This would coincide with the Major's arrival at Creech. The pieces are beginning to fit together.

"Tomorrow night is the rendezvous for the lovers, I take it." George says.

"So it would seem. Wonder when Pierce gets his turn?"

I listen to the rest of the Major's day. Nothing eventful.

Tom and Michael return from the training. "Well, how'd he do?" I ask Michael.

"A natural. He'll be ready with another lesson or two."

"Only a lesson or two? My life hinges on *a lesson or two*?"

Tom looks offended and then bursts out laughing, "I guess I never told you I flew before, even had a pilots' license."

"Begs the question, why did you stop flying?"

"After I joined the DEA, I never had time. You know how it goes. Sent here, sent there, and never stayed in one place long enough to put down roots. When I met Gina, I decided she was going to get all my free time, what little there was. Never got back to flying. Gina frets enough because of my job. I couldn't make it worse."

"I take it we won't be mentioning the Smart Car in the future?"

"No, probably not, I still worry her enough. But it is incredible. You cannot get into trouble. It's foolproof. Even Dog could fly it." Tom chuckles.

In my ear device I hear a loud, "I heard that. Dave tell smarty pants to watch his mouth."

I repeat the pooch's comment.

"Sorry Dog, wasn't a criticism of your abilities."

Dog snorts in my ear.

CHAPTER SIXTY

Since it will be another two hours before the next Janet Airlines shuttle flight to McCarran, I tell Tom he can take my truck home. He will get home a lot quicker.

"Just bring it back in the morning."

"Yes Dad. Full tank of gas and no dents"

"Just go. No flying class tomorrow, you'll go home to Gina at the regular time."

"You're going to be with John on his *date*, aren't you? At least when he goes to her office. Too bad you don't have a wire in his cell phone."

My mind clicks. Shit. How did we miss that? I look at Michael and George. Before I can form the words, Michael says, "We could put a chip in his phone, then you could listen to him and everything that goes on around him. Can you get it for thirty minutes? Bring it to us and we can insert a transmitter."

"I never thought of it before. Now I feel stupid. We listen in on his office, but we don't hear what goes on when he is out of his office."

"Don't feel bad, we missed that too," George says. "None of us thought we needed to wire him personally. Tracking his cell phone and listening to his office conversations seemed sufficient.

"Who is he playing? Tom askes. "The Major and Pierce or us? I will bet on the former. I think he is in over his head with the Major and doesn't know how to handle her or Pierce. She has him wrapped around her little finger. He wants to get rid of Pierce, but not her. My opinion, for what it's worth."

"I agree with you, Tom. I just do not feel he is lying to me. He is very conflicted. When he finds out the Major is working him, who knows what he will do. The old *honey trap* has got him ensnared. The part that worries me is the fact he has never mentioned her to me."

Tom shakes his head, "I'll bet the affair thing has him too ashamed to tell you. He probably thinks if you make Pierce go away, the Major will still be his. There is no fool like an old fool."

"We will see after tomorrow night. Getting his phone should be easy. I'll tell him we are doing a routine search for bugs. I'll ask for his phone and his car keys, and then run the phone over here to you guys," I say nodding toward the cave dwellers. "Regardless of what happens with him and the Major, the next morning I will have a heart to heart conversation with John. It is time for him to know, what we know. I did not want to involve him until we had the camera in place in Virginia. Now with the revelation he *already* knows his girlfriend is aligned with Pierce; we have to see what he has to say."

Everyone solemnly nods agreement.

Dog, who has joined us in the control room yawns and offers, "I can sense people better than all of you. John is an old fool, but he is not scamming you. He is caught in the web of his screwed-up life. He owes Pierce for saving his career. He is dead set against the whole beam weapon project. He was doing a good job of dangling Pierce along until the Russian woman came into his world. She hooked him and now he is more screwed up than ever. You Dave, are his only hope of salvation."

We all just stare at the K-9 psychologist.

Looking at us he stands up, "Well am I right or not? Don't just stand there like the dummies you are, say something"

We all stumble at saying something. "Uh, yeah well, maybe, I don't know, he may be right."

The dog just scoffs, "It's getting late. I am tired of having to do all your thinking. Everyone go home and get a good night rest. We continue in the morning. Come on Dave." He saunters for the door.

We do as the Alpha has instructs.

CHAPTER SIXTY-ONE

Back at our apartment, Dog jumps onto the couch and settles down contentedly. I pour a healthy dose of Crown Royal and collapse in my chair. He is staring at me. I take a long pull on my beverage. "What?"

"Am I right? You have not said one word since we left the caves. I'm entitled to my opinion since I'm in this too."

"I've been mulling over your dissertation; quite a lot from such a small brain. But I am inclined to agree with you."

"Quality over quantity." He retorts.

"I want to trust John. He is pathetic, but basically a decent human-being who admits his past mistakes. Now he's embroiled in a dangerous mess. Just wish he had revealed something about the Major to me."

"I agree with Tom, he is embarrassed to tell you. He has a deep respect for you Dave. I can tell. You are his protector. He will do whatever you tell him."

"Yeah, pat him on his head and say, 'good boy'. What's he going to do when I take his *cookie* from him?"

"The Major? He will be fine. You are his alpha. Trust me, he will follow your commands. He knows he is lost without you. He needs a pack. Everyone does, not just dogs and wolves. In the CIA he was a pack member. He was fine until Pierce started to go on a tangent. Now John is lost, no pack. The Major is a distraction, not pack to him."

After listening to the canine Socrates, I finish my drink. "The more I am around you, the scarier you get. Where does all this come from?"

"Wolfgang was always reading out loud to me. He was alone and I could talk. So, we would discuss various topics. It was fun for me. Gave me a *broader intellect*. Close your mouth David. Your mouth agape is not attractive. Pamela would laugh."

I pour another whiskey.

"If you don't mind, I'm kind of parched from lecturing. May I have a beer?"

The next morning, I have no problem getting John to relinquish his cell phone and car keys.

Tom has arrived with my truck. "It has a shimmy at ninety-eight but settles down after a hundred and ten." He advises while handing me my keys.

"That's an improvement, use to shimmy at eighty. I have John's phone. Let's take his car and go to the caves."

Michael has the transmitter ready and installs it in just a few minutes. I take it back to John and assure him all is safe, including his Benz. The rest of the day goes by quickly. John announces he has a meeting at Cheech and will be leaving early.

As I drop Tom off at the airstrip he says, "I'm dying to know what happens tonight. If it's good--call me!"

Dog and I go to the control room to listen to the night's main event. Instead of going off to find Mickey, the pooch settles on the floor.

"I don't want to miss anything. This is big." He nods his huge head.

There is a palpable tension in the room. We are all aware this could be a defining moment with our mission. We want to know actually what happens when they're together. The consensus is to trust in John, but the fact that he never mentioned the Major is disconcerting.

We track Cranston as he goes to the base intelligence office. He has been nervously humming to himself the entire trip. This is new to me. Even in his office when he thought he was by himself; we were monitoring him. I don't remember him humming. The little spooks agree. He has not shown this apparent nervousness prior to tonight.

Wonder why?

He is let into the building by the Major. We can hear a kiss and a soft "missed you" from Major Andrews. John mumbles incoherently. They walk into her office, a door closes, and then there's the sound of chairs moving.

"You ready for dinner?" She says. "It's prime rib night. One of your favorites."

John clears his throat, "No, I'm just going home. I can't do this anymore Kate. I do love my wife and this all makes me ashamed of what I've been doing to her. I am a better man than this. Tell Pierce nothing has changed. I'll still keep you informed regarding the project but no more meetings. I'm sorry."

In the control room we all are staring wide-eyed at the speaker. Michael whispers, "Oh my."

There is a long quiet spell, then Major Andrews says in a low, hesitant voice, "John, I – I don't know what to say. I care for you---yes, I love you. I did from the start. When I met you, I thought you were just some agent of Frank's- uhh- Pierce's. I was just to keep checking with you on the project that was all. But I wanted to spend time with you. He never knew about our—our relationship. Please John, what has happened? Can I do or say anything to get you to reconsider." She sounds distraught.

A chair slides. "I'm sorry Kate, but I've made up my mind. This has been troubling me for some time. Actually, from the first time you took me to your apartment. I admit I loved the intrigue, the sneaking around to be with you. I knew it was an immature and irresponsible thing to do, to you and to my wife. She deserves better and so do you."

There is some moving of chairs, sniffling, the sound of clothing rubbing on the phone, and then, "I am truly sorry to have misled you Kate. I am going home now. I am so sorry." There is the sound of his walking out of the room and then the door closing.

"God damn it!" Spits out Kate Andrews as we hear her pressing a button on her cell phone.

"What's going on?" Franklin Pierce asks. "Didn't he show up?"

"Oh he showed up alright! He got all moral on me! Says he can't do this to his wife or to me. Said I deserve better than him. Can you imagine?" she is barely able to

426

enunciate due to her rage. Sounds like she is slipping into her native Russian tone.

"Hey, hey Baby, it's all right, no harm. I didn't like him messing with my woman anyway. Is he still going to keep in touch with you on the project?"

"Yes Frank. He said he would. Is that all you care about? Not that he hurt my feelings. Is that how you think of me? You still have a wife too! Am I just another part of the project? Frank, am I?" Major Kate Andrews then disconnects the call.

She storms out of the room and slams the door.

Dog breaks the stunned silence in the control room. "A woman scorned is a woman scorned, even if she was just playing Cranston along. Wow, some ego."

Pandemonium breaks out. Everyone is talking at once. After we settle down, Michael offers, "John Cranston has become ethical. We never saw it coming. I am guessing you didn't either, David?"

"This came to a head today. He seemed pre-occupied. He was staring at his desk calendar when I went to get his phone and keys. I asked if he was all right and he waved his hand and said he was fine."

Brian, the tech, is on duty in the control room. He has heard all the night's happenings. Poking at his computer he calls out, "I've figured it out." On his computer is John Cranston's personal file, the one compiled by the aliens. Brian is pointing to one entry. "Today is his wedding anniversary. Twenty-five years today."

We collectively gasp.

Brian continues, "Actually, *I cheated*. Just after he left Creech, he phoned his wife and asked if he could take her to dinner. She started to cry. 'You remembered John. You remembered.' I thought it was pretty neat." Brian smiles.

CHAPTER SIXTY-TWO

Leaving the caves, I call Tom and fill him in on what occurred.

"Did not see that coming. What happened to cause him to do it now?"

I tell him about John's twenty-fifth anniversary.

"He's been feeling guilty all along, I'll bet. Seeing the date on his calendar slapped some sense into him. You still going to talk with him tomorrow?"

"I don't know. Let's mull it over tonight and talk about it in the morning. How soon do you think you will be ready for our flight?"

"At least one more session. That thing is just like playing a video game. You need to learn too. It is a hell of a lot of fun. Besides if anything goes wrong you might have to fly us back. Always have a back-up plan you know."

"Maybe I should learn." Dog offers.

"You have the smarts but the opposable-thumb thing would hold you back." Tom answers.

"Discrimination," Dog grumbles

In the morning Tom and I, and of course our leader Dog, meet to discuss our next move. George and Michael are listening from the caves.

Michel speaks first, "My suggestion would be to wait to confront Cranston until we have footage from the Virginia location. Then we can determine if there is more to this connection between General Lamar and Pierce."

"My thoughts exactly. Depending on Tom's learning curve, we should be able to get the camera up in the next night or so. Has Mr. Pierce made any more trips to the farm?" I ask.

"No. He has been staying in the Arlington vicinity. Another thought….While you are in the area of the farm, why not fly to Pierce's home and see what it looks like? We have found what we think is his residence. At least he goes there most nights. Having been a pilot, Tom is a quick learner. He should be ready after another class."

Since Dog and I are the only ones with implanted hearing devices, I repeat all of this to Tom.

"Told you. Okay if I come over for a flying lesson tonight? I told my wife I would be late."

"Yes of course, come over. Why don't the three of you dine with us? Dave you should get some time in the car too."

"Sounds good. I can get my first lesson tonight."

Cranston comes to the office shortly after we finish talking to the aliens. John stops in to wish us a "Good Morning Men."

"You're in good mood John. Any special occasion?" I inquire.

'Well, yes. Last night was Doris's and my twenty-fifth anniversary. We went to our favorite restaurant and had a wonderful night. We have not done that for far too long. I have been much too involved with this wretched place and have been neglecting my wife. Those days are over." With that, he briskly walks into his office.

Tom and I just smirk. Neither of us says a word.

Dog on the other hand, "I guess he got some huh?"

"Dog shush. His door is open." I close my door.

A couple of hours later, my phone rings. It is Eddie at EG&G. This is *not* a coincidence.

I take a deep breath, "Eddie, how are you----" I don't get another word out. He is growling into my ear, "Did you tell Cranston about us, Doris and me? You said you didn't care and would not tell him. Manning why did you tell him, after all I've done for you?"

"Eddie, Eddie, calm down." I am trying not to laugh. "Ed, listen I have not said anything, and I would not, I keep my word. Why? What made you think I did?"

"Because Doris just told me we were done. She and Cranston have worked out their problems and she is staying with him."

Keeping a straight face and serious tone I say, "Did she say why, what happened?"

"That's all she said. 'Thanks for the good times. *Don't call me.*' What was I supposed to think Dave? You're the only one who knew. What's Cranston doing these days? Has he been there?"

"Yes, he's been here. Nothing out of the ordinary. Well he was in an unusually good mood this morning. All I know Ed."

He utters something unintelligible and slams down the phone.

"Rude." Now I'm laughing.

Tom says, "I could hear him over here. He is pissed. Two dumped consorts in less than twenty-four hours. Maybe Ed and the Major---no, wouldn't work." Now he is laughing.

John then comes in the door. "What's the joke? You guys are having too much fun this morning. I can hear you in my office."

"Reliving old war stories John. Sorry if we disturbed you." I say with a straight face.

"The way it has been around here, it is grand to hear some laughter. It's almost lunch time. Come on, I'll buy. All three of you."

At lunch John says how much safer he feels since we have joined him. Says he has faith we will take care of the problems. We assure him we are very close to solving everything and will keep him in the loop.

After work we dine with the little people and when it is dark, Tom and Michael head off into the night skies. I go down to the control center to listen to the Major's day at the office. Brian is on duty. "She was a no-show today, David. She turned her cell phone off after leaving the building last night. We have no way to follow her until it is turned back on."

"She is still pissed. Can you tell if anyone tried to call her?"

"Not until she turns it back on. But her office desk phone rang off the hook. No one left any messages."

"We never got a chance to dump Pierce's phone. Damn! Just keep watching where he goes. That's all we can do for now. Maybe he'll hop a plane and come here. She is too vital a link to Cranston and Pierce's pet project for him to take this lightly."

Brian nods agreement. "The Germans have been well behaved. They are working away on their project. Pierce did get them quite worried. They are also concerned Brandon hasn't contacted them lately."

"Can you understand German?" I ask.

"Ja, I haf been studing jusing their tapes as practice." He jokes, "It fills in the mostly quiet time around here."

"I hope you understand it better than you can speak it."

'Yes, I do well with the comprehension. No so good with the speaking. Harsh sounds. Michael and George just roar when I try to speak German."

I ask Brian how Mickey is doing, what with the whole thing about her father and then her brother. "She is extremely optimistic, visits Brandon regularly. He feels stupid for getting involved with the outside world. Mickey is proud of being involved with you and Dog in keeping the colony safe."

"She is a smart kid, her head is on straight," I say, "I can understand the frustration of the youth here. They are just like teenagers everywhere, curious of the world and yet they are not allowed to come out of the caves. Tough for them."

In an hour or so, Tom and Michael come back from their flight and call me to meet them in the hangar bay. Oh Boy my turn.

Tom has a huge grin on his face. "It is so damn fun Dave; you will love it."

Tom takes my truck and heads home, as I get in the Smart Car with Michael. He has me sit behind the wheel or where the wheel is supposed to be. It has controllers, much like a video game. He points out each control, and then has me lift the car upwards. "Gently, just pull back ever so gently. Now let it just hover."

The car rises vertically about ten feet and when I let loose, it just stays in place. I am hovering. Cool.

Then Michael gives me several small movements to try. So far so good. Next, he has me slowly flying around the hangar. I don't hit anything and stay away from the walls.

"Alright, now we open the hangar doors and start some real flying."

He pushes a button on the dash and the side of the cave opens enough for the car to pass. I squeeze it thru and out into the night I go. Michael has me gaining altitude and executing turns and then range wider and wider from the caves.
This is so damn neat. I love this thing. Before long I am

434

over the test range and then go toward Tonopah, a little town on the edge of government land. He has me turn east and fly higher and faster. Then he lets me just go where I want to.

"Do not worry, David, you cannot crash this vehicle. If you let go of the controls, it will just hover. Try now."

We are going at a surprisingly good pace. I have no idea what the speed is. "Now?"

"Yes, just let go of the controls. Trust me."

Well, I think, he is up here with me, so he must know what he is doing. I release the control levers. Yup, we come to a quick halt and are hovering. I don't know our altitude, but any lights below are pin pricks.

"Wow, amazing Michael. Uh, just how high are we?"

He points to the screen in the center of the dashboard. I have been so focused on flying I hadn't looked anywhere but in front of me. The screen has a gps map of the land beneath us. On one side are some numbers. Twelve thousand, two hundred, fifty-three feet! That's over two miles straight up. I am truly awestruck.

"Not that it matters, but how fast were we travelling when I let go of the stick?"

"Just under six hundred miles per hour."

"Frickin' unbelievable. I know I've been with you doing far more, but to fly myself is amazing. Maybe Tom will be the passenger."

Michael is just roaring with laughter. "I knew you would be hooked. It is enjoyable, is it not?"

"Enjoyable! Michael you always understate everything. This is a blast!"

I make the instructor indulge me for another hour. This car, bird, plane or whatever it is, has seduced me. I could fly all night. It *is* safe. When we are anywhere near an airplane, or potentially crossing paths, a warning is flashed on the screen showing the other object.

"The car will not allow you to strike another object, unless you override the sensor." The aeronautical professor states.

"Yeah, then how did it strike me in the street that fateful night?"

" An unforeseen circumstance, it has been addressed." Michael says stiffly.

"Meaning George doesn't fly anymore, that it?" I am lighthearted with him, but I vividly remember the collision.

"Yes, along with a software enhancement."

CHAPTER SIXTY-THREE

I take mercy on Michael and we go back to the hangar. He claims he needs his sleep. The little guys run down quickly; I could have stayed all night. This *means of transportation* is one amazing piece of technology. I'm going to be flying a lot. Michael even told me I could solo, after more practice. He might have just been humoring me.

Dog is not impressed. "Oh great, I have to put up with you driving that thing? Don't I get a say in any of this?"

"You can always stay home." I say bluntly.

"No, somebody has to look after your ass. Grizzie and Pam would be pissed at me if I let anything happen to you."

The next morning after Tom arrives, the three of us make our way to the caves to huddle with Michael and George. Michael pronounces Tom ready to fly us to Virginia.

"Does he even know where it is?" asks the Dog.

"Yes I do. We went there last night." Tom retorts.

"You weren't gone that long. Virginia is on the east coast. I know my geography."

"Yes Dog, but with the speed our vehicle is capable of achieving, we could have gone to Virginia and back three- or four-times last night." Michael enlightens.

"If you guys went to Virginia, why didn't you plant the camera while you were there?" I ask.

"We did not have it with us, and we only overflew the state. We did not engage in any low-level work. That will be for you gentlemen to do."

"I'm ready. How about you Dave?"

"You're the one with the wife who has to be wondering what the hell you are doing staying late and driving my truck home every night. You call it."

"Gina is fine. We've been thru so much in my in my career she could not be happier with me in this job. A couple of late nights compared to the days and weeks I would be gone, no problem. Besides, she likes you and Dog."

"I'm the one who seals the deal." Dog throws out his massive chest.

"Then how about tonight?" I ask.

"Let's do it." Tom says.

"Don't I get a vote?" asks the canine.

"It's two to one. You lose no matter what you vote."

"Fine!"

It is set. We will begin our operation as soon as it's dark. George shows us the camera and describes how to attach it to the old windmill. Michael gives us the coordinates of the farm and Pierce's residence. Nothing to do now but wait until night fall. Oh yeah, we better show up around John and make a show for him. I am anxious to see if he is still as ecstatic as he was yesterday.

Just as we are leaving for the office, George receives a call from the control room informing him Major Andrews has turned her phone on and appears to be heading for Creech. They acquired a fix on her location when she turned on her phone. Maybe her residence? Good, the FBI will have no problem picking her up when the time comes. No, not there, they're too showy. They will get her at Creech and drag her out of her office in handcuffs. I would like to watch that show.

George assures me he will keep tabs on the Major. We go back to our office and find John, still in an upbeat mood. Good. We do not need any complications at the moment.

Pam calls just before lunch. She will be working area 51 tonight.

"Off at midnight, as usual?" I ask.

"Yep, you going to be around? I would like to see you if you're not too busy being a secret agent."

"Actually, I will be doing some secret agent stuff at the caves, but I should be done by midnight. I'll make a point of being done. I miss you too, you know."

"As long as it doesn't involve my father, I'm good."

"Cross my heart, you dad is done working for me. In point of fact, he was working for his country, the country he has sworn to protect."

"You are so full of it, David. Part of your charm, I must admit. See you at your place at twelve?"

"Absolutely. Love you lady."

"Love you handsome."

Of course, my teammates hear all this.

"Boy you better make sure your ass is back here." Smirks the Dog.

Tom exhales and looks at the ceiling.

"Yeah, praying would help." I say. "We should be okay on time, we'll have almost four hours after night fall. It's only a few minutes to get there. Yeah, we'll be fine."

Dog looks at me as only he can, "Yeah, what could go wrong?"

I throw a pen at him, "Get out of here before you jinx this."

The rest of the day drags by.

After dinner, Dog, Tom, and I head for the caves. As we are driving, I see an Air Force Police vehicle approaching from behind. The emergency lights come on and dutifully I pull over. It is Pam.

"Oh good, Tom you can finally meet my lady."

Pam walks up to my side and I roll down my window.

"Was I doing something wrong, Officer?"

"Having driven with you before, it was one of the only times you haven't."

"Pam meet Tom, Tom this is Pam."

"Hi Pam, so glad to finally meet you. You are as beautiful as Dave says you are."

"I see you are as full of BS as he is." She reaches past me and extends her hand. "Nice to meet you, too. David has only praise for your help. Please keep him out of trouble."

"I promise." Tom says as he shakes her hand.

Giving a quick look around, Pam sticks her head in and gives me a kiss. "See you at mid-night."

She drives off and we continue to the caves. "I can see why you're taken with her. She is a keeper." Tom says.

"She should have let Grizzie out. I could have used a kiss too. Who knows if I will live thru the night with you two idiots?" Whines the pooch.

At the control room, George says Major Andrews appeared to carry on a routine day. When she listened to her phone messages, they were all from Franklin Pierce. Yelling, threatening, cajoling, and finally begging her to answer. She did eventually call him and said she was fine, and the project was the important matter at hand.

"The conversation was short and business-like," George says. "Pierce seemed to be relieved at her attitude and tried to make amends, but she cut him off curtly."

"Tonight is more vital than ever. We need to get the camera installed so we can identify all of the players in this game." Michael interjects.

Tom and Dog both look at me. I ignore them.

"What am I missing?" asks Michael. "Tell me, please, we are all in this together."

"Lover boy has a hot date at midnight. He better be back or his ass is grass." Dog answers.

Michael and George break out in wide grins. My face is flushing, I can feel it!

"Don't worry David. You will have ample time to get there, attach the camera and observe Pierce's residence. *Piece of cake* for the Smart Car. You will even be able to stop by Sedona and scrutinize the Germans." George says with a sly smile.

"No, no, the one mission is enough." Sweat is forming on my brow.

Everyone is enjoying my anxiety.

Michael, ever the calming leader, assures me, "You will have an adequate amount of time. Worst case scenario, you could call your lady and have her come here. We would entertain her until your return."

"Oh sure. HI honey I am in Virginia, go over to the caves. The people who tried to kill you will take good care of you." I hear myself. I'm embarrassed now. "I'm sorry guys that was poor of me, bad humor. Let us just be sure I get back on time."

Michael comes over, reaches up, and puts a hand on my shoulder. "Please relax David, it will all work out. I know you care deeply for her. You are trying have a normal relationship during abnormal times. But everything will all work out. I am confident."

CHAPTER SIXTY-FOUR

Dusk is upon the high desert of Nevada. We all go to the alien's hangar and make our final check for the mission. Michael double checks our in-car communication with the control room. "Just talk and we can hear you. It is hands-free."

When we are ready, Dog climbs between the seats onto the rear of the car.

"This is not going to work. With your two fat asses up front, there is no room for mine. It was tight when Michael drove. Now it is impossible."

Tom tries to move his seat up a little. He must be able to handle the controls. I have more room, so I can scoot forward some. My knees are up to the dash. "That's it. Can you fit now?"

"It'll do. "Grumbles the canine.

"That or stay home."

"I said it will do! Now let's get this done."

After a quick check outside, Michael opens the hangar door and waves us on.

Tom smoothly lifts off, eases the craft thru the opening and into the night. He immediately attains an altitude of fifteen thousand feet. I set the coordinates of the farm into our on-board guidance system and off we go. It is somewhat cloudy part of the trip but after we cross the Mississippi the sky is clear.

"Beautiful. Just magnificent," I say gawking at all the incredible open sky. The stars are bright, and the half moon is glowing. "Lucky it's not a full moon. We may be stealthy, but we're not invisible. Our silhouette would be seen against the moon. We don't need to be spotted."

In a few more minutes, the screen on the dash advises we are close to our target.

Tom descends until we can see streetlights, roads, and buildings. He is using night-vision goggles the aliens fabricated. "It is like daylight out there. Amazing technology."

I put on my goggles "Wow, Tom this is far better than anything the military has, at least when I was there. I can see colors, not the green and black we had."

The guidance system shows we are quickly approaching the farm. Tom drops down to seventy-five feet. The site is dead ahead. We spot the driveway and follow it to the main house. It looks exactly like the satellite picture. All is quiet around the darkened house. There are outside lights on, but no vehicles parked in the front. It is almost midnight here on the east coast, only nine at home.

Tom soundlessly cruses the area. We see several outbuildings. About three hundred yards away from the main farmhouse is a much smaller home. It too is dark. Possibly an employee. Someone must work all this land. Tom eases toward the windmill. So far, so good. There are a few clouds around the moon. That's in our favor.

I lean out the window and talk Tom toward the windmill. "Damn, I can't touch the frame." The slope of the structure does not allow us to get close enough for me to reach it. Even stretching further out the window, I can't touch it.

"Wait, I got an idea." Tom says. "Michael showed me how to bank the car. Let me try this. Get back inside and hold on."

He tips the car toward the windmill. We are now parallel to the windmills frame.

"How's that?"

"Hey guys, my ass is jammed into the side of the car. Hurry up Dave, this is not comfortable."

"Be quiet Dog. Give me a minute. I can reach it now. Up a foot if you can Tom."

He moves us up. I can reach the framework and begin to mount the camera. It is quite compact and fits on the inside of the windmill's frame. We check with Michael on the setting of the lens. He gives me the ok and I tighten the screws on the mount.

"Picture is perfect", says Michael. "Now, will you go to Pierce's residence? It is only a couple of minutes away. You have the coordinates. David you still have ample time to make your date."

"Yes Dad, work before play. I know."

Almost instantly we are at Pierce's residence. A typical southern-style two story mansion on a large plot of land. Neighborhood is upscale. Large four car garage. No vehicles outside. House is dark and has numerous security lights around the premises. Michael confirms Pierce's cell phone is inside. So the assumption is, Franklin Pierce is also.

"Come on home my wandering humans, you have done well." Michael is actually making a joke.

Tom gains altitude and heads west for Area 51.

"What was the big deal about seeing Pierce's house?" Asks the crabby canine. "You didn't plant a camera or anything, so why come?"

"Michael just wanted us to eyeball it. Since we were in the area, why not? There might have been something going on there. It was worth a couple of minutes." I say, but this gets me thinking. Why was Michael so insistent on us going to Pierce's house? What does he have up his little sleeve?

In no time we are descending toward the cave hangar. The door opens as we approach, and Tom slips our vehicle inside.

"Well done, Tom! Like you do it all the time." I heap praise on my talented human partner.

"This thing is so simple. Except for almost killing you, it seems infallible."

"That's old news. Let it go, please." George pleads into the speakers.

CHAPTER SIXTY-FIVE

Smiling like a proud parent, Michael is waiting for us. "Well done men. It was a perfect mission. David you have plenty of time before your social engagement. I would suggest a celebratory drink. Tom, I know you have a drive ahead of you, so perhaps not."

"I'm only glad it all went so well. It felt good to be at the controls again. Dave you have one for me. I will take your fine truck and be on my way."

I give Tom a guy hug. "You were flawless. Sleep in tomorrow. Come in when you feel like it. Maybe take Gina to a nice breakfast. She deserves it."

"I'll take you up on that. Be in around one."

We see Tom off and then retire to George's office. Michael is *proud as punch* of what we have accomplished. He raises a toast, "Just a few short weeks ago we were facing an unknown threat. Now thanks to you, we have a grip on the situation. I realize it is not over yet, but I feel good about this. We are remarkably close to wrapping it all up. Do you agree, David?"

"Absolutely Michael, but we are not there yet. There have been plenty of surprises along the way so I wouldn't count our chickens before they hatch."

"Chicken! I'm hungry. See you guys in a while." Dog trots off to the kitchen.

"Don't forget we have a date in a little while. If you're not ready, I'll leave you." I call after him.

"You do and I'll start talking to Pam and you won't like what I say."

"Jerk. Just hurry back."

Michael bursts out in laughter. "He is such the comic relief we all need."

"Here's to Dog. He has been more assistance than we ever imagined." George takes a swig.

"Yes, I admit it too. He has been invaluable and yes, fun to have around, most of the time."

Dog and I meet the ladies at midnight. We are all relaxed and comfy in my apartment. "So, my super spy what were all of you doing at the caves? I saw Tom leaving in your truck. Kind of late for him wasn't it?"

"Why didn't you pull him over? He might have been stealing it."

"I did. He told me you were done and would be ready for out date. He seems so nice. Says you gave him a new lease on life with the job."

"He's a great partner. I am lucky to have found him."

Dog makes a low grumbly sound.

Looking at the hound I say, "*You* are my best partner and I am glad to have you."

Pam is wide-eyed, "That's not the first time Dog has acted like he understands you. Are you two that bonded? Grizzie and I are like one, but what you guys have is almost human."

Dog looks at me intently. I pause, "Well, to tell the truth, besides the aliens there *is* one more secret here at Area 51... Him. You needed to know *sooner* rather than *later*, so here it is." I nod at Dog.

He slowly stands, looks at Pam and says, "He really loves you Pam and I love Grizzie. I hope we can all stay together, forever. Oh yes, and I can talk. We didn't know how to tell you."

Pam just sits there, openmouthed, eyes unblinking. I reach to steady the wine glass in her hand. She blinks, grabs the glass, and downs it all. Sinking back into the sofa, she keeps looking at Dog.

"Honey, I didn't know how to tell you, but you did need to know."

Turning to me, "You are not a ventriloquist. He does talk, right? Is he an alien too?"

"No. My mother was an alien, my dad was a German Shephard."

Still looking at me, "You are not a ventriloquist, he does talk. I don't know if I should scream, run out of here or just have another wine."

"Have more wine, please. Just let it set in. His mother was Michael's pet. Their dogs are capable of speech. See... his tongue is more human-like than Grizzie's. He can form words. That is the only real difference. Grizzie would speak if she could."

Since Pam has not moved, I get more wine. She takes a sip, "David Manning, do you have any more secrets I should know about. If so, hit me with them now, while I am still too stunned to move."

Gently I put my arms around her. She doesn't pull away, good. "Baby, this is all. Finding out about the aliens was a shocker for you to handle I know, but you needed to learn about Dog too. I didn't know how, except to... just show you. You caught on to his perception of what I said, so tonight seemed like the right time."

Grizzie rises from the floor. She looks at Dog, then at me, and finally at Pam. Then lays back down and lets out a low sigh.

"How do we interpret that?" I ask Pam.

"Beats me."

"She is merely expressing her feelings that this is not a big deal," Dog states.

Pam keeps talking with Dog. Can't blame her, this is a whole new weird world to her. He is good and answers her questions. Finally, he looks at her, "Look Sweetie, I like you and all, but Grizzie is my date. Talk to David. He moons over you all the time. Give him a break."

"Dog." I scold, "Behave yourself. This is new to her. It took me awhile too."

"It's alright, David, he's right. It's just so, so..."

"Weird, Yeah I know." I say, putting my arm around her. She cuddles into me.

"You moon over me all the time, huh? This could work out for me. He is like your little brother, after all."

Dog and I both let out groans at that thought.

CHAPTER SIXTY-SIX

The following morning, Pam and Grizzie go back to Creech while Dog and I head for the office.

"Sure was quiet in your room partner." Comments the hound.

"She was whispering because she was afraid you might hear, now she knows about you."

"With my hearing, I've heard you two all the time." He snickers.

"Please, don't tell her. She is having enough trouble wrapping her head around all of this as it is."

"No problem."

John is not here yet, so I check in with the short ones. It is three hours later on the east coast so there may have been some new activity.

"Anything going on over there?" I inquire.

George says Franklin Pierce has been burning up his cell phone. "He's been at it all morning. We are not able to hear his calls, but we do know when he makes them. Something is stirring."

"Too bad we couldn't tap his phone instead of just tracking it. By the way, why was it so important we fly over Pierce's house last night? You planning anything I should know about?"

Michael breaks in, "We just wanted a positive lock on the location. You flying over it gave us confirmation. Nothing sinister." He pauses, "Yet."

Hastily George adds, "We know all the pieces have to be put together, we have no plans for Pierce. We have complete faith you will diligently track down all of the entities involved."

Now I am worried. Can't say I blame them; their very existence is being threatened.

"Changing subjects, so is anything else happening? The Major, the Germans, anything I should know about? If you feel like telling me."

"David," Michaels sounding very father-like, "we are not withholding any information from you. You are our front line. We need you. We do believe in knowing our enemies. We have Major Andrews located, Cranston seems to be no threat now, but Pierce is a real concern. We need to use our technology to stay ahead of everyone."

"I can buy that. When you figure out what Pierce is up to, give me a shout."

Dog and I both turn off our earpieces. "Can't blame them for trying to be ahead of the game." I say.

"Yeah, but what would they do? Send a missile into his house? I guess they could. The little shits are smart enough."

"I believe they could. But only as a last resort. They aren't animals, like you."

"I'll tell Pam you are being mean to me."

"I knew I would regret her knowing about you."

A refreshed Tom shows up just before one o'clock.

" Did I miss anything?"

"Only the fact Pam knows about me." Dog says.

"How did that go over?"

"Better than I thought," I say.

"Well, after being attacked by aliens, could have gone either way." Tom says. "Tough little gal."

My cell rings. It's Michael. "Would you turn on your ear devices, please? We have updates for you."

"Uh, sorry Michael, we got distracted. Tom's here too. What's up?"

"The major is in her office. Routine day so far. It looks as if Pierce is heading toward the farm. Pierce called the German's and repeated his threats to have them extradited if they didn't make progress soon. They are quite agitated over his threats and are concerned Brandon has not called. They are discussing possibly leaving the country and going to Brazil. We cannot afford to let them get away. They have too much knowledge about the beam device."

"I agree, Michael. But it would be best if we could snare them all at once. Taking just the Germans would spook Pierce and anybody else involved in this plot. We

457

have to stay on top of this. Since Pierce is going to the farm, we can see if any others are involved. You say he goes there quite often. Hope it's just not poker night."

"With all the activity he had on his cell phone today, along with pressuring the Germans, I would venture a guess this is all connected." George offers.

"Keep us informed. I'll come over later, after Cranston leaves."

"I don't know if I should leave tonight or not." Tom says.

"Go home while you can. We won't be able to do much but collect information tonight. When this hits, then it will be all hands-on deck. Paws too."

"Funny" Dog snorts.

Tom leaves at five o'clock. It's now eight o'clock in Virginia. Michael advises several cars are gathering at the farm. He is trying to make out license numbers, using our newly installed camera. Dog and I grab a quick dinner and head over to the control room.

"Just in time David," Says George. "It is starting to get interesting. We have some familiar faces on the camera."

"Familiar like how?"

"Political, governmental and businesspersons. Here, take a look." He shows me some screen grabs from the farm camera.

"Him? No shit, him too? I thought he was dead. Her! No way, she's in on the new world order too?" I am astonished. The faces I see are past and present big wigs. Government and business. So far two men and the one woman. "So where is the Russian connection? There must be some link between Major Andrews, her father and the GRU. Is Pierce here?"

"Yes," Says Michael. "He was the first to arrive. The others came chauffeured, in separate cars. Apparently Pierce is not high enough up to warrant a driver."

A limousine pulls into the driveway. We all stare at the screen anxiously. The front seat passenger gets out, looks around the area, and then opens the rear door.

"That's a bodyguard, if I ever saw one." I state. "Looks eastern European to me."

A gray-haired man slowly gets out, he is followed by a somewhat younger looking male. The two head toward the entrance to the house. The bodyguard keeps scanning the area.

"There is our connection." I announce.

"Who is he?" Michael asks. "He does not look familiar to me and I have kept abreast of world events ever since we arrived."

"He is old guard--KGB. The intelligence service for the former government. He did not make the cut when the current Russian president came to power. He was thought to have been purged. But apparently not. Has been in a comfortable retirement I would say."

"Pulling the strings from behind the curtain?" George asks.

"I don't have any idea. He may be on his own. I do remember he was at odds with the present leader over the direction the country should take. That's when he disappeared. Tomorrow I will have Tom check in with his FBI pal. If this old player had a part in the defection of the Major's father, then we have some answers."

"Or more questions." Michael wisely adds.

CHAPTER SIXTY-SEVEN

I give Tom an update on last night's revelations.

"All of those people and General Groskinshev too. He was a big-time rival to the current Russian regime. Everyone assumed he was purged. Where has he been?"

"Not purged, apparently. How about the lady, Marlee Grabo, how did she get into this mix? She was the head of a couple of big Fortune 500 corporations. Tried her hand at politics. Didn't fare well there."

Tom thinks a moment, "I try to follow the markets, because of my meager investments. Seems to me she was booted out of those companies. Was hailed as a turn-around wiz and only made them worse. Had a massive golden parachute for every separation. So how are all these people connected? Especially with Groskinshev?"

"I'm afraid to speculate, especially considering all we know about Pierce and his desire for the beam weapon. I think a call to your FBI friend is in order."

"Absolutely, I was already thinking he needs to know about all this."

As Tom dials his contact, Dog says, "I haven't been around as long as you guys, but I can smell a rotten egg here."

"I'm afraid it's a whole carton, Pal."

"Somehow we have to get a bug on Pierce or some of those individuals. We need to know what they are planning."

"Well, listen to you. You are more than just a pretty face. I couldn't sleep last night thinking of that, but how is the question. It's not like we have access to them, like we do to John and the Major."

"Think! You are the black ops specialist. I can't think of everything," lectures the all-knowing hound.

"Wait a minute, I've got it. Tom, put your bud on hold, I've got a question for him."

"Here, you ask him. He is all ears and open to ideas. We got his attention." He hands me the phone, "His name is Greg."

I talk with Greg. He is one hundred percent in this now. "Jesus Christ, I won't be able to sleep until we get this cleared up, or we are all dead. This is huge."

"*I* couldn't sleep last night."

"We have had concerns about some of those individuals in the past. Never had any clue they were hooked up. And Groskinshev, how the hell did they all get together? Mind boggling!"

I ask Greg if there are any locations back there in DC or Virginia where Pierce might go and need to relinquish his cell phone. He says there are several places Pierce goes where it is the security protocol.

"You're looking to plant a bug in his phone, right? I can handle it. Since my unit is basically internal investigations, we pretty much have a free rein, so no one can influence us. As far as this matter is concerned, I can justify being involved since there is the possibility of the complicity of the agent who first dealt with Major Andrews's father. I can have Pierce tailed and try to see where and when he goes to these locations. Then if I know beforehand, I will be there and after he hands his cell over to security, I will insert the bug."

"I will never say a bad thing about the FBI again. I'm impressed Greg."

"Sure you will. Everyone is jealous of us." He says with a smile in his voice.

"I assume there is no problem with the security personnel involved?"

"No, not at all. They serve at our pleasure. You may have heard of them, Wackenhut. The company handles government facilities."

"Wackenhut, of course, they are all over Area 51. They and EG&G seem to be the unofficial caretakers of our government facilities.

"Don't get me started on EG&G. That's for another time." Greg snorts. "Have you told Brad Young at the CIA yet?"

"No, we wanted you to know first."

"I'll call him right now. If he's in, we'll make it a conference call. We need to be coordinated so none of these creeps get away."

Brad is in his office, so Greg hooks us all together. After the usual pleasantries we bring Brad up to date.

There is silence on the line. "Brad are you still there?" I ask.

"I'm just wondering if I have enough time in service to retire yet." He responds. "Holy shit, what a clusterfuck this has turned out to be. First, we have a couple of two-bit spies and now we have a threat to world peace. Groskinshev and the rest of those clowns, who'd of thought they would find each other?"

Greg says, "My view also. We could arrest Pierce, Andrews, her supposed father, and the Germans, but that would tip off the top dogs. We cannot move until we get some evidence, hard evidence, against those public figures. This is getting so complicated I might have to start a spread sheet."

"We already have one." I say self-righteously.

We all kick around various ideas. In the end it comes down to FBI Greg getting his hands on Franklin Pierce's cell phone.

Tom pipes in, "Why stop at Pierce? The others are more public. Maybe someone can get into their office or home and plant a bug. Possibly see an opportunity to get the phone. Maybe they go to a gym? Just a thought."

"Tom's the man." Dog pipes up.

"Who was that?" Greg asks. "Who is on the line?"

Coughing, I choke out, "Just me guys. I was drinking some coffee and swallowed wrong." I glare at Dog, who is sinking to the floor.

"Had me worried, this is supposed to be a secure connection." Greg says. "Actually, Tom, you are correct. We have other players involved. Since the people involved are all on the east coast, except for Groskinshev, it would be best for me to handle this. Everyone agree?"

"Always comes down to the FBI, doesn't it?" Brad pokes.

Greg comes back, "What about Groskinshev? He is not a citizen and is involved in some seemingly subversive activities. Sounds like a CIA job to me."

"Last we heard of him, he was living in the Swiss Alps. He would be more difficult to approach than Pierce." Brad retorts.

I jump in, "Guys, guys, let's not start an interagency battle. We have a common enemy. I would agree Groskinshev is not a viable target. But I do have to say, it always come down to the almighty FBI to save us. Is there any way Tom and I can help? We do have resources."

"You all never quit, do you?" Greg says. "Yes, speaking of resources, how in the hell did you know who was at General Lamar's farm?"

"Sorry, ultra-top secret, which is way above either of you. I'm sorry guys, but we cannot divulge our source."

"Come on, Manning, what do you do at Area 51? How did you get there?" Brad queries.

"I came on Janet Airlines."

"He's not going to say anything, Brad. Maybe when we are all retired, we can sit on the porch and have drinks at the *old spooks home* and swap stories." Greg says. "And Tom, how did a nice DEA fellow like yourself wind up with him?"

Smirking Tom replies, "I came in on Janet Air also."

"Fuck both you guys." Greg snorts.

CHAPTER SIXTY-EIGHT

During the great 'meeting of the minds', it was agreed the FBI will try to put a bug in Pierce's cell phone, follow General Lamar and the other solid citizens who were at the farm and try to tap their phones. Hopefully, a few days of observing these people's activities will give us some idea of how they are connected. Brad, of the CIA, is delving further into the Major Andrews affair, looking for any connection to General Groskinshev. Tom and I are racking our brains for ideas on how we can assist, since we have *top secret* resources.

The cave snoopers are already hard at work digging thru any news accounts of these *persons of interest*.

"We need more to work with than media reports," George complains. "I hope your friends can give us some insightful information."

"Hey, we are only lowly humans, what can you expect from us? We don't travel at light speed." I retort.

"Michael is checking the video you took of the farm and its surroundings. He thinks there must be some way to get more reconnaissance. Other than just watching who comes and goes." George says, motioning toward Michael as he works at a computer. "He is looking for a way to get sound from inside the house. It is so large though."

"Yeah, not a little cabin like Schultz's place. That was too easy. However, there was no sign of any external security guards at the farm. There must be some type of security system. Maybe the General just feels safe way out there. Being an upstanding citizen and all."

"David, that is it," Michael almost shouts as he turns toward us, "The security system, of course! If he has any type of system, it will be wired to a panel inside the house. There is a gated entrance, so logically there will be a call box for visitors to use. If we can gain access to the box, we can set it to feed a live audio from the house to the unit on the windmill. Why did I not think of that resolution before?"

"Yeah Shorty why didn't you? You guys are the brains, after all." Dog answers.

"None of us are getting enough sleep lately." Tom says.

"I need to see what the gate speaker looks like, so I can create the proper device to accomplish our task." Michael looks at Tom and me, "You gentlemen up to a flight tonight?"

"Uh, yeah sure, Tom?"

"I'll be here."

"Call your wife and we'll fly again. Exactly what are we going to do Michael? Just take a picture of the box?"

"You two go about the rest of your day with Cranston and come back here after dinner. I will look at various systems on the internet and devise a unit or two which should work in whatever is being sold today. With any luck one of them will be compatible and can be installed. You know, actually I should go with you and do the work myself."

"We can't risk you out there, Michael. We have already discussed it."

"I agree, but neither of you have the background in electronics. This is a sensitive task and we will not have much time. Beside I am smaller and have less chance of being noticed."

"Yeah, no one will notice a glowing blob in the dark." Dog adds.

"I can wear dark clothing and a hood." Michael says indignantly.

Brian, the control room tech, speaks up, "I could do it Michael. That way, you as our leader will not be at risk. I do that level of work all the time."

All of us look at Brian and then at Michael.

"He makes a valid point." I say.

Michael looks irritated, then sighs and says, "Thank you Brian. You are correct of course. It just has been so exceptionally long since I was in the heat of a battle, I guess the old warrior wanted to get in the action again." He looks at all of us, "Yes Brian has the skill and the youth for the assignment. He should be the one."

Tom starts to speak, and I cut him off, "I will fly. Tom doesn't need to be risked any more than necessary either. Dog will need to come also."

"Fine! You can always risk the dog."

"Wanna stay home?"

"No."

It is settled. Tonight Brian, Dog and I will fly to the farm in Virginia and reconnoiter the area, looking for any gate security panels, plus anything else that looks like an electronic gateway into the big house. Before we leave, Michael will give me a refresher lesson on the Smart Car. Tom has had more time behind the controls, but he reminds me the vehicle is fool proof. Michael agrees I will not have a problem. Dog is less optimistic.

"You kill us and Pam and Grizzie will haunt you."

Regardless of the pooch's concerns, he agrees to go along.

"Someone has to watch over your ass."

I pass my refresher course to Michael's satisfaction. The time comes and we load up the vehicle with the bags of devices, which take up some of Dog's area. He is less than pleased, but then again, he is never actually *pleased*. Eating and being with Grizzie being the exceptions.

I look at Brian as he straps himself in. "You ready?"

"Absolutely," Is his composed response.

We take off. I ease the craft thru the opening and ever so tenderly, move the controls to gain altitude, then speed.

"Wow, I love this thing. Absolutely amazing." I blurt out.

Brian also has a broad grin on his face. "I have never been in one of these. We had transporters back home but not like this. I feel as if I am in one of your jet fighters. I have always been fascinated with flight. Perhaps, when the situation we are facing is resolved, I may be allowed to fly."

"I am sure Michael would go along with allowing you to fly. It's a brave thing you're doing by volunteering to come along."

"It is a matter of duty, both to our people and to yours. We are your guests and quite appreciative of the accommodations your government has made for us."

"Honestly Brian, if it were me, I would be highly pissed at our government for allowing someone like Schultz, the latitude he was given. I appreciate your graciousness."

"It is the way it is. As the hero of one of your western movies said-You play the hand you are dealt."

"I'm quite impressed Brian. My favorite line was not quite so philosophical-Do you feel lucky, punk?"

"I always liked that one too." Brian chuckles.

We cruise along enjoying the view of America by night. I ask Brian how Mickey is doing, "Haven't see her lately, been busy."

"She seems just fine. Now that her brother has been reined in, she can go back to being a kid."

We reach our destination and I expertly, well cautiously, guide the car down to tree top level. The farm is in front of us. I ease around the house, which has a few lights on upstairs. It is 1:00 am in Virginia. No cars in the driveway. The caretaker's house is dark. So far so good.

We scan the area with the heat sensors we used in Sedona, looking for any warm bodies, human or canine. Nothing showing in the grounds. Two subjects are in the upstairs of the house in the same room. Probably the General and his wife. I unhurriedly float over the road leading to the gate. No lights are nearby so I set the car onto the roadway about two hundred feet from the gate and move toward the entry. There is a six-foot-high stone wall running on each side of the gate. Michael and George are watching the camera feed at the caves. "You are close enough," Michael instructs. "Brian, walk gradually toward the gate. Let us look at what you are seeing. Stay close to the wall."

Brian is dressed in a black jumpsuit with a balaclava over his head. He has a communication device around on his head with a wire down to one ear. It is a camera and radio. He gets out of the car and walks toward the entrance.

"He looks like a short, fat ninja." Dog snickers.

"I can hear you," Brain whispers.

He gets about twenty feet from the gate, "I can see a panel like one we looked at today." He moves closer. Michael says to stop and look up and down around the gate and wall.

"The only camera I see is the lens in the panel. Don't worry, I won't push the button and activate it," Brian says.

Michael has him move closer. Michael and George study the panel and after cross-checking the name and numbers on it, tell Brian, "It is the second one we saw on the internet. Do you remember how to access it?"

"Yes I do. Dog could you bring me the bag with the 2 marked on it?"

"Roger that." answers the canine. He picks up the number 2 bag and jumps out the open door. He has been sniffing the air the whole time we have been in the area. He continues cautiously toward Brian, handle of bag in his mouth and nose quivering. Brian takes the bag and begins to open the panel.

Dog is still taking in the scents. His jowls are flapping as he takes in smells, assesses them, and simultaneously passes them out. It has always amazed me, all the sensory abilities dogs possess. His sensors are processing hundreds of scents all at the same time. Suddenly his body tenses, "Hurry up Brian, there is something in the field behind us. Not a human, it is dog-like, wolf or coyote."

I pivot the car toward the open area. The heat sensors show an object low to the ground quite a distance from us and moving in the opposite direction.

"What a nose, Pooch, it is leaving the area. I'll keep an eye on it."

Brian has opened the panel and Michael is guiding his steps to install the device that will connect to the house. It seems like an eternity to me, but it is actually only a couple of minutes until Brian announces, "It is in. I am closing. Can you tell if it works, Michael?"

After a pause, "Yes it does. We can hear distant noise, like a television. Good work son, now get back to the car." Father Michael intones.

Dog and the little ninja climb back in and we lift off. My heart has been racing. This is worse than doing the mission, just sitting and watching. I reach and give Brian and then Dog high fives.

Brian is pumped. "What a sensation. I have never felt like that before. The adrenaline rush your people talk about, I imagine."

Dog throws back his head and lets out a hellacious howl.

"What happened? is he alright?" George asks worriedly.

"Yes, not to worry, that is his battle cry."

CHAPTER SIXTY-NINE

A quick flight back and we are all still 'pumped' as Brian says. George and Michael greet us and invite us to George's office for a celebratory drink. Brian starts to walk away, and Michael stops him, "You too Brian. You are the man of the hour. I honestly do not believe I could have done the work as quickly as you did. You made me proud. The colony shall know of your heroics!"

Brian blushes, which is kind of weird to watch, colorless to bright pink. *Fascinating*, as Spock would say.

After a couple of drinks, I go home and try to sleep. I am still excited. I cannot wrap my head around what we just accomplished, in less than an hours' time. Dog is snoring away. He does not impress easily, I guess.

Tom bursts through the office door in the morning. Eyes searching my face for emotion. I calmly look up from my desk, "Good morning Tom, sleep well?"

"You butthead! Don't play all calm with me. What happened? Did it work? Come on man, don't mess with me."

I can't hold back any longer, breaking into a broad smile, "Yes, it was a textbook success. In and out in minutes. The cave now has audio feed from inside the farmhouse. It went flawlessly. Those little squirts know what they are doing."

Tom wants to hear all the details.

"what's next? Wait on the FBI, I guess?"

"Unless we can come up with some other idea. I admit Tom, I could fly the craft every night. What a blast."

"You should take up flying, in human airplanes. But, after the Smart Car, flying will never be the same for me. Such limitations on our planes." He shakes his head.

That day and the next are boring. The farmhouse contains only the General and his wife and they're acting like a normal couple. He deals with a man who seems to be the foreman of the farm operation. He must live in the second house. The General's wife talks on the phone to her friends. Routine elite gossip. No indication or mention of Pierce or any of the other actors we are aware of. But as Michael pointed out, General Lamar could be using a phone upstairs or even a cell outside and we wouldn't be able to hear him.

FBI Greg advises us he is getting a basic pattern of Pierce's activities. Hopes to accomplish the phone trick soon. Brad from CIA has nothing new for us.

Pam and Grizzie took a shift here in Area 51, so I had a pleasant diversion from my growing anxieties. We have been talking each day, sometimes several times a day. After the initial shock about Dog, she seems to have come to terms with it all. I greet them as usual. Pam saw thru me right away.

"Somethings' going on…. isn't it David? I can feel it in you."

"Yes, my baby, I can't hide anything from you."

"Better not." She threatens. "Can you tell me?" She gives me a come-hither look. "After learning about the aliens and your talkative friend, I can handle almost anything."

"Let's pour you some wine, get comfortable. But first, I must remind you of the secrecy oath we all took, even though you have already seen more than most military personal ever will."

She gives me a *look* only a woman can.

"I had to say that, now I will tell you all."

And I do, all of it. The farm, Pierce's associates, the FBI and CIA's involvement. Oh, and the Germans too, hadn't covered them before. Do not want to miss any details now. Time to get it all out.

A puzzled look grows across her beautiful face. "Sedona? In Arizona? You poked around the German's place and planted a listening device there? I hadn't met you then, but the farm is in Virginia. You have been there and hooked up a tap on the gate. I saw you the night you said you went to Virginia and yet you were here at midnight. I do know my geography. Am I missing something else?"

Clearing my throat, I take a drink, "I was coming to that part next in this tell-all. We traveled in the Smart Car. Which is a real Smart Car except the little guys have modified it with their technology, so it flies. You have to see it. I could take you for a flight if you want to." I weakly add.

Pam bursts out laughing, "Are we still being serious or are you trying to lighten the mood?"

Dog, who has been curled up with Grizzie, looks up and says, "It is real Pam. I ride in it all the time. David is an okay pilot, Tom is better, but *never* go with George."

Quickly finishing her wine, Pam looks at the ceiling, "Mom told me not to get involved with a serviceman. But I did and here I am entangled in a world power struggle, aliens, a talking dog and," She turns toward me, "a man I dearly love."

"There are exceptions to every rule, even Mom's."

CHAPTER SEVENTY

The following morning starts off quietly. The *cave* reports Major Andrews seems to be going thru the paces of her normal duties, whatever they are. No contact with John Cranston since she came back after her hissy-fit. John is seemingly happy to be back with his wife. Tom and I are drinking coffee and trying to think of something, anything we can do to expedite this case. Dog, of course, is roaming the building mooching.

Just before noon, Greg from the FBI calls, he also has Brad from the CIA on the line. Greg is bursting with pride, "I got Pierce's phone this morning. The card is in place. You should get a feed now."

"Hold on Greg, let me contact my listening station." My implant is on and I hear George in my ear "We are on it David, wait, wait, yes we have feed. We got him."

"Greg, we have feed from his phone. Good job. Now we will see where this leads us."

"You amaze even me. I won't ask how you do what you do. You wouldn't tell me anyway." Greg says.

Brad pipes up, "Can I come work with you David? If you have the FBI in awe, then I want in."

We have a good laugh at Greg's expense, then Brad gets serious, "I have been able to connect General Groskinshev with General Lamar. They were involved in behind-the-scenes talks after the Soviet Union break-up. Neither government talked about it but there was some movement between conservative factions in both countries to attempt to work together to keep the peace and stabilize what was left of Russia. It didn't work out and the present regime prevailed. Groskinshev then slipped out of sight. The interesting part, not only the two Generals were involved but also Franklin Pierce and Henry Marlowe. He was one of the visitors to the farm that night. Former high-level diplomat in the same administration as Pierce. Now he is CEO of Defenus, a Pentagon favored defense contractor. Got the connection now?"

"I'm all ears." I say.

Greg continues, "The lady, Marlee Grabo, she is on the Board of Directors for the Defenus, as are the gentleman, including Lamar. Pierce is a consultant."

In my ear I hear Michael, "Mind boggling, absolutely mind boggling."

Greg says, "Keep us in the loop of what goes on with Peirce's phone and I'll keep checking on the others."

"We will do guys, and to keep you updated, we have installed an audio link inside the General's house. Nothing of interest so far."

"How the hell------oh never mind, you won't tell anyway. Why do you need us anyhow? To share the blame if it all blows up?" Greg asks rather indignantly.

"Settle down, we can't do what you two can. Besides somebody has to arrest them eventually." I say. "And Brad, you get to catch two Russian agents and probably the Germans. Sounds fair to me."

After they hang up, we confer with Michael and George.

"I suppose I should not be shocked at all of these conspiracies, but I am." Michael says. "I guess it is the magnitude of the plot that overwhelms me. This is beyond mere political influence for a friend or cause. This is treason. No other word for it."

"Stupidity comes to mind." Dog offers.

.

CHAPTER SEVENTY-ONE

Now is the hard part, just waiting for something to break. We have bugs, taps, cameras and whatever else we could think of, in place. The cave guys are hovering over their monitors, continually. George says they have put all the control room techs on to the task.

Pam is coming over tonight, "If you are going to be in town." She giggles. "Or do you have to fly to the North Pole or some place?"

"At the moment I plan to be awaiting your arrival."

And I do. I don't tell her about the latest on the *involved persons*, she has had quite enough for now. We need some together time. We have a quiet night.

That should have been a warning to me. The next day the manure hits the fan. Michael calls my cell at six a.m., "Pierce is on the phone, he is setting up a meeting for tonight at Lamar's place. I'll keep you advised."

"Michael, at six o'clock? Couldn't he wait until you got to the office?"

"It's nine back east. Looks as if things maybe happening. Go back to sleep."

I lay back down but my mind is already racing. Pam cuddles next to me.

"You aren't going to sleep. I can feel your anxiety from here. If you must leave, please call me. You don't have to say where you are going, but please call."

"So you can worry? That doesn't sound wise." I wrap my arms around her.

"Because if I don't hear from you then I know you are here and safe. If I know you are gone, then I will pray for your safe return to me. It might seem silly to you, but please humor me."

"I promise."

We then entwine our bodies in sweet love. Finally, I do have to go to the office. We linger at the door. Touching my cheek she whispers, "Promise you will tell me if you leave."

"Promise." I kiss her gently and then again passionately.

I leave and drive to the office. Dog is unusually quiet.

"Is this the day things are going to happen?"

"I don't think so pal. But I feel it is the beginning. If there is a meeting tonight, hopefully we will be able to learn what the group is planning and when."

"Grizzie felt it too. Probably picked up on your vibes. She was really nuzzling me before we left."

"We'll be fine Buddy. We aren't on the front lines. We are in the HQ, planning and pulling the strings. At least that's how I hope it goes."

"I'd gladly be on the front lines with you Dave. We are an awesome team."

"Yes we are." I reach over, ruffle his soft hair, and give his head a squeeze. "Best partner ever."

He swallows and looks out the window. "I love you David. You are like a litter mate to me. I'd gladly die to protect you." Then he wipes his eyes with a massive paw. I pull over to the side of the road. Sliding over to him, I wrap both hands around his large body and burrowing my face in his fur, "I love you too, brother."

Tom is already in the office, drinking coffee. He says John is happily ensconced in his office.

"Let's go to the caves." I fill him in on the way.

The control room is the busiest I have ever seen it. Little people scurrying around, listening, watching, and recording.

Michael and George are overseeing it all. They are in their element. Both greet us and bring us up to date.

"Here is what is happening. Franklin Pierce called the Major first thing this morning. He was all business to her. Asked how Cranston was doing. She tells him Cranston isn't taking her calls. Side note here, she has not called Cranston as far as we can tell. With the bugs we have on both, phones and offices, we have heard no calls from her. She must be lying so as not to have to talk with Cranston. Pierce is quite agitated at this news. He slammed down the phone and called John Cranston a few minutes ago, while you were on your way here. Cranston tells him progress is slow, but he has hopes of having a functioning model by the first of the month. Pierce, still angry, tells John he must produce results soon or else, John will be replaced. John says he will keep pushing the scientists. They are struggling with the storage device for the energy, he says. They can make the beam device function but have not been able to design a large enough capacitor to hold the power and still make it portable as Pierce desires."

"Good boy John. Exactly what I advised him to tell Pierce when he called. I never let on we knew about Andrews."

Michael goes on, "General Lamar has Pierce calling everyone in the *club* to have a meeting at the farm. Pierce must be the social secretary. Lamar wants it for tonight, preferably. All of them are coming except General Groskinshev. He has responded it would be *inconvenient* for him to come tonight."

"Inconvenient, wow, he must think he is the all-important member to this caper." I say.

"General Lamar said to Pierce, and I quote: 'Fuck the Ruskie. We don't need him anymore. We will proceed without him. Franklin, pull his visa so he can't come back into this country.' Pierce said he would do it immediately."

"Shit, things are moving now. Keep your eyes and ears open guys. Anything we can do?" Tom asks.

"Just stay available, if we need to confer with you all."

"You all? Shorty are you from the south of your planet?" The insolent hound asks.

"That is why we like you Dog, your humor is appreciated, especially during these times." Michael smiles.

I conference call Greg and Brad to alert them to the planned meeting.

Brad says, "Groskinshev is ejected? He must not have enough influence remaining to serve the group's purpose. He will be a raging bear when he finds out his visa has been pulled."

"Why did they include him in the first place," Greg asks.

"Probably because initially he had a strong following among the old KGB. Time has passed and most of those old agents have been retired or left the country. London is where many of them now reside. If they get too critical of the present Russian leaders, they seem to have accidents." Brad answers. "The General has plenty of illicit funds to keep him safe in his Alpine redoubt. His motive was revenge for being ousted."

"So now we just wait and see what these plotters have in mind. The failure to develop a beam weapon is hindering their plans. Tonight, we'll see if they have a Plan B." Brad says. "Wish we could listen in."

"It will all be recorded. But will it be admissible? There is no court order for the surveillance, is there?" I inquire.

"Greg proudly says, "Not a problem. This involves national security. I covered it initially with our Department of Justice AG. We are on solid ground. It will, I am sorry, come out the FBI managed to plant these various devices, but our cause will be served. Before you all get bent out of shape, this is how it has to be."

"Personally, I don't have a problem, but I must say, *it's always all about the FBI.* There, now we may proceed." I say.

Brad just grunts, "Yeah, of course. We all knew that was how it would go. I will get some great stats though. How about you Dave?"

"Pat on the back and hopefully a permanent job. I like it here."

CHAPTER SEVENTY-TWO

All of us are on pins and needles the rest of the day. Tom and I just sit around the office looking busy. Dog even hangs around more than usual.

"What's the matter, treats run out?" Tom asks.

"No, I just feel better if I'm close, in case something happens."

George or Michael check in with us periodically with updates. It seems tonight's meeting at General Lamar's farm is still a go. All concerned will be there except the Russian. Probably just a well, the government would have paid hell trying to extradite him from Switzerland. With his visa now cancelled, he is of no concern to us.

The meeting will be at seven-thirty tonight, Eastern Time. That is four-thirty here in Nevada.

Tom says, "I am going to call Gina and let her know I'll be late tonight. I can't miss any of this."

"You just want to drive my truck again. But yes, you do need to hear all of this too."

Michael tells us, "Come over to the control room, we will provide food-service during the evening's performance."

489

"Michael, a spot of levity, I like it." I respond.

"I'm trying to keep us all upbeat now. The rest of the colony has not been advised of the present situation. Just the elders are aware and of course the techs. We are with you in this, David. It is vital to all of us this threat is abated."

At four o'clock, we all settle in for the 'show'. As promised, there was food available and front row seats. We watch the camera at General Lamar's farm as the guests arrive. We can hear some small talk as they enter the house. The link into the house is good. Mrs. Lamar is of course the gracious hostess, making sure all have a libation and hors d'oeuvres.

"Bet they have better goodies than we do," Dog says.

"Bet they don't feed their dog in the meeting," I rebut. "In fact, has anyone heard any dog in there?"

Michael advises he has seen Mrs. Lamar walking a Chihuahua occasionally in the yard.

"Ugh, they're mean little suckers," Dog proclaims.

When Pierce arrives, we are able to hear everyone much better. He is right among them. All the guests are present by seven p.m. We can tell by the tone of their voices; they all are nervous. Wasting no time, General Lamar has everyone sit down.

"This is all business tonight. We must make hard decisions, now. Franklin, please bring the others up to date."

Clearing his throat, Pierce starts in, "The project at Area 51 is making no headway. The team cannot design a proper storage unit to enable the beam weapon to be portable."

There is a furor in the room. A woman's voice barks, "After all this time, what have they been doing? Franklin you were supposed to keep the pressure on Cranston or whatever his name is, to make this happen."

"Marlee, calm down. Let him finish." Lamar admonishes. "Go on Frank."

Pierce continues, tension showing in his voice, "thank you Charles." He clears his throat, "we all know the beam was developed by the German scientist Schultz while he was at Area 51. He made a powerful weapon but was unable to contain the electric charge and it blew up as he fired it. The government at the time cancelled the project. I was involved with Schultz and reporting to General Lamar. We could see the value of this weapon, if it could be made into a field piece, mobile you know. We told Rich, who was on the Senate Intelligence Committee at the time about it. Rich, you were able to get the project re-authorized. I convinced the program manager to retire," Pierce snickers, "and put John Cranston in his place. Keeping Schultz on black ops payroll, I arranged for his old partner, Herr Hoffman, to come over from his retirement in Switzerland. They have rebuilt the original design but still need the storage unit or capacitor to make it feasible. The aliens had such a device and it was apparently destroyed in the crash of their vehicle. By great fortune, Schultz was contacted by one of the younger aliens, who wants to help finish the program. The German paid little heed to the alien, fearing he might be a trap or something. Anyway, since I have been putting pressure on the two, they now want his assistance."

"So how do we get them together?" Asks a male voice.

"Apparently the young aliens say they can get to the highway on the east side of Area 51. Honestly, Rich, I have no idea how anyone could get out of there. The security is intense. We know how intelligent the aliens are, they must have a way. Schultz says when the young ones have the design completed, he will pick them up on the highway and bring them to Sedona. There they will perfect it."

"Is there anything we can do? You can get in Franklin; couldn't you just take them out yourself?" Another male voice asks. "You're the spooks spook, right?"

"Henry, when I said the security was intense, I meant it. No.... I could not take them out."

General Lamar speaks up, "If we could expedite this we would. The aliens are our only hope. Pierce will make sure the Germans are encouraging them."

There is a scattering of comments, then the woman, Marlee Grabo, drowns them all out, "Franklin, what about the Russian woman you have overseeing Cranston? You have not mentioned her. Why?"

Clearing his throat yet again, Pierce says, "John Cranston has broken up with her. He will not answer her calls. She is now a useless connection."

"Then she must be removed before she tries to do something stupid. Like burn you and Cranston." Grabo says.

"How do we do that?" Pierce asks.

"She should be eliminated. You have done it before Frank, for the cause, do it now. Before she gets religion."

"Kill her? Is that what you are saying, Marlee?"

"It is the only solution. She may not know much of our ultimate plans, but she knows enough to cause great damage. At this stage of the game, are you getting soft Frank? Perhaps you were too chummy with her?"

"Uh, no, no, I just went to Creech once a month. I agree we must keep her quiet. I'll get on it immediately." Pierce's voice is wavering.

General Lamar speaks, "I think she does have to be taken out of the plan for all our sake. What about the rest of you? Thoughts? Comments?"

The Rich voice says, "How did we get her anyway? Wasn't she a Russian defector?"

Grabo answers, "General Groskinshev and Lamar pulled it off. Got her supposed father to defect and he brings along his make-believe daughter. The two Generals though she would be an asset in our plans. Frank took her under his wing. Exactly how did that all work, Frank?"

Lamar interrupts, "Marlee save it for another time. We have a more important question now. Our plans to stage a coup of the United States government is dependent upon our having superior weapons and plenty of them. When our unsuspecting stooges stage their massive attack on Washington we will rise and blow them to hell, along with all the D. C. Administration. Of course, we will be sure it appears *they* are responsible for destroying the administration. We then will be hailed as the saviors of our great nation. The military will be on our side. It is choreographed to be swift and stunning."

"Do we have enough of the General Staff on our side to pull this off?" The Henry voice asks.

Lamar answers, "We will when we are ready. I have one or two more to convince. We are close to who we need. Now back to the matter at hand. What to do with the Russian?"

"Can't we just deport her? She is a fraud." Pierce asks hopefully.

"Out of the question, Frank. You know better. Perhaps Marlee is correct; do you have feelings for her?" Lamar demands. "She must be eliminated. If you cannot do it, then I will arrange it. Let's all take a break. Refresh your drinks, eat something. We need to breathe and relax. No discussion until we are all back."

There is the sound of people moving, glasses tinkling, and footsteps on hard flooring.

We all look at each other. No one speaks at first. Finally, Tom says, "My God, they really are serious. This is no two-bit operation this is real. Freaking scary."

"Who exactly are these guys, Henry and Rich? Do we know?" I look at Michael and George.

George answers, "Henry Marlowe, former highly placed official in several administrations and now CEO of

Defenus, the defense company we mentioned earlier. Remember, all our players are on the Board of Directors. Richard Henley is another past governmental figure of some notoriety if you remember. They, along with Miss Grabo and the General are ultra-right-wing conservatives."

Michael's face turns ashen, "Frightening enough by themselves and absolutely terrifying together."

CHAPTER SEVENTY-THREE

Franklin Pierce has said nothing during the break. He has not moved. We would have heard material scratching against the microphone if he had gotten up. The others have obviously moved away into the background. After a few minutes there is the sound of footsteps approaching, then General Lamar says in a quiet tone, "Frank, we have no choice in this matter, you do realize that, don't you? Personal feelings have no place in our world. You of all people know that. Remember the woman in Berlin several years ago? We believed she might have been a Russian agent. You were quite enamored with her, yet you did the right thing. Come on Frank, you going soft in your old age?"

In a quaking voice Pierce says, "Charles, I know you are correct. Yes, there are feelings involved, I admit. But couldn't we still use her in a different area? She could be our contact with those libertarian idiots we're using for the attack on D.C. None of *us* can afford to be directly connected with them."

"Frank, it would not work. They believe a woman's place in the home. No way would they deal with her. Besides, we already have the young punk Henry uses. It is his contact, so no. I see no alternative. We are in this operation too far to take chances now. That's final."

"Yes general," Pierce says solemnly.

Lamar calls the others back to finish the meeting. "Frank and I agree as to the elimination of the Russian woman. I will see to the matter. Frank, your focus should be on the Germans. Do whatever is necessary to get them working with the aliens. We cannot afford to waste any more time. Those **Freedom Now** assholes are chomping at the bit to make a statement. Henry, your man is still in good stead with them, right?"

"Yes, but he tells me they are getting antsy. They are hot headed and plain wacked. He doesn't know how much longer he can keep them waiting."

"We are financially backing them; doesn't that give us some control over them?" Grabo asks.

"My man says some of them are getting spooked and are worried their mysterious backers might be the FBI. He is doing his best with them. No guarantees on how long he can influence them. We need to get moving before they do some stupid act on their own and get busted. Then we will have to start over with another group."

"The way our project is going, perhaps we should cut them off and find another bunch. Lord knows there are enough crazies out there," Rich says.

"We may have to but let us give this a little more time. Frank, you get on the two Germans, and Henry, you keep close contact with your man. If no one has anything more, I say let's call it a night," Lamar declares.

There are no objections and the group begins to disperse. We watch them leave on the outside camera. They get in their vehicles with no more conversation and drive off. Pierce included. Lamar goes inside and says to his wife,

"Don't give me that look. I never said it would be easy. But it is coming together."

"Frank Pierce is your weak link Charles, you know it. Everyone else knows it. Can he carry it off with the Germans and the aliens?"

"What choice do I have? He is loyal, just not what he used to be. Maybe none of us are. I will have to keep checking on him."

They walk away and the voices are fading.

"So General Lamar is going order a hit on the major, sounds logical to me," says Dog.

"Dog, you ought to be ashamed of yourself," George admonishes him.

"For that group, it is logical," I say. "The end justifies the means. Nothing can interfere with their scheme."

"The FBI and CIA are going to love this. Can't wait to hear their reaction," Tom says.

"We'll call Brad and Greg first thing in the morning. We need to move quickly, before the Major has an accident," I caution.

"Why bother?" Dog pipes up. "Let the group do the dirty work. Save the taxpayers money."

"Dog you are incorrigible. Beside she could be a witness for the government. She does need to be picked up and held incommunicado until this is resolved," Tom says. "Or before Pierce tips her off."

"You think he would?" George asks. "What would he do with her?"

"Every agency has safe houses at their disposal. He could hide her in one. I'm sure he has access to plenty."

"When she disappears won't the General get suspicious?" Michael asks.

"He'll just think Pierce got to her first. Pierce will think the group got her," Tom says. "They both will deny any knowledge of her disappearance to the others."

Brian says, "I'll keep an ear open on Pierce's phone, just in case he tries to warn her."

"Great Brian, we are moving quickly now, and we have to keep on top of *all* of them. Michael, George, I have an idea and I need your input."

"We are all ears," George says.

Dog snorts, "Ears, you call those ears?"

Michael chuckles, "Dog you are in a mood today. Go ahead David, what is your idea?"

"We will need Greg and Brad in on this also. What if you get Brandon to call the Germans and say he has found his fathers' papers and can construct the capacitor? Then hopefully we can maneuver them here, to ostensibly pick up Brandon."

"And the authorities will arrest them, I like it. Yes, very clever. Brandon will cooperate. No question," Michael says. "How about Franklin Pierce, the General and the others? They must be stopped, or they will continue their atrocious plans."

"The FBI and CIA will snare them, along with the Major's Father," I reply.

"Wonderful, tell me what you want Brandon to say and when."

"We'll know better after we talk with Greg and Brad. In the meantime, just keep monitoring everyone, Major Andrews too."

We leave the caves and Tom is excited. "This could all come to fruition—finally! If the feds have enough evidence to arrest everyone, which I think they do. The tapes show conspiracy for treason, among other crimes."

"Yeah, I think the evidence is solid, but it will be the prosecutor's opinion that matters. There are some heavyweight politicians and business executives involved. The media will have a feast when this story breaks. The only concern I have is the existence of the aliens might come out. Yet, that has been a rumor for years and no one can prove it. I wouldn't want anything to cause them any more trouble."

In my ear Michael softly says: "Worry not about us my friend, we will be safe."

CHAPTER SEVENTY-FOUR

Tom doesn't hear Michael's comment. Dog looks at me and I subtly nod my head...no. Let it go for now, I'm thinking.

Tom leaves for home and we head back to the apartment. "What did Shorty mean by: don't worry about us?" Dog says after slapping his device off.

I shut mine off. "I haven't the faintest idea, pal. A few weeks ago, they were frightened to death of the threat to them, now *they will be safe*. Apparently, something has changed in their world. I will press the issue tomorrow. No secrets--that was our agreement."

"He wouldn't have said nything if he didn't want you to know, right?"

"I hope so. But everything has become so damn convoluted I'm beginning to wonder; *how many plots are there*?"

"Whatever happens, it's you, me, and the girls, Right?" He extends a paw toward me.

"Absolutely." I grab his paw and give it a squeeze.

Sleep is fitful, too much is going on, and my mind is overworked trying to figure everything out. The revelation from Michael is a new ball game. He sounded conspiratorial, rather than just trying to ease my mind.

Morning finally comes and I head for the office. No surprise, Tom is already here. "Ready to call the guys?"

"You bet, let's do it."

We get both Greg and Brad connected and relay the tale from last night.

"I have to go now, I think my mother is calling me," Brad mutters. "Seriously, could this be any worse? A coup against the government? Destroy Washington and the Administration? My God, this is South American or Eastern European stuff, not America. We have to pick up Andrews, that's for sure. How about the Germans?"

I speak up, "Before we get any further gentlemen, it is time to hear the rest of the story since this is a secure line. Without question you cannot speak of this to anyone."

"I've always thought you were holding something back on us, what is it?" Greg asks. "You definitely have advanced technology out there in Area 51, we don't have, correct?"

"Yes, we do. We have highly advanced technology to be exact."

"Don't try to say there really are aliens out there and they are helping you." Brad says with a snicker.

"I won't......but it's true. They have been here since Roswell. Remember Roswell? Well it was true, basically."

The silence on the line is deafening. I give a brief rundown of the story up to the present. Still no sound. "You guys still there? Brad? Greg?"

They both acknowledge, faintly. So, I tell them our present plan.

Greg offers. "Are you *sure* the young alien will cooperate?"

"Absolutely. Since he learned the truth about his father's death, he has done a complete turnaround. I have been thinking we could possibly get all the collaborators to come out to Area 51. Use some ruse. Say something like, 'Brandon is now the leader of the aliens and he wants to meet with the leaders of the coup.' Those people don't know how old any of the aliens are. It has been quite a few years since they arrived. It might work."

"You mean a pact between the aliens and the plotters? It might be feasible. Obviously, they hold the aliens in high regard intellectually. I say it is worth trying. We could grab all of them at once." Greg declares. "But first we must arrest Major Andrews, for her safety. Probably pick up her 'father' to keep him from wandering off."

"Brad, your thoughts?" I ask since he has said not a word.

"I'm still at Roswell. I have always believed there was more there than the weather balloon story the government put out. The Russians have constantly alleged we were hiding something *huge* at Area 51. Much more than new aircraft."

"Not exactly *huge*, they are smaller than us," I chuckle. "But they are here and trapped. No way to get back home. Their technological advances have been a great help to us. In return, the government has been secretly providing them with all they need to enjoy life as much as possible, in their underground world."

We talk more, but they need a few minutes to work this new information out in their heads. After they sound more settled, we agree to follow thru with the plan to arrest all involved out here, at Area 51. Next step will be getting Brandon to entice the group out here.

After the guys hang up, I ask Michael if he is listening.

"Of course, you knew I would be. I can assure you Brandon will tell them whatever we want him to. He is quite anxious to ensnare his father's killer and protect the colony. Come over and we will work out a script for him."

Checking on John, we find he is busily working in his office, still in a happy frame of mind. Good, now the three of us go to the caves.

George takes us to Michael's office. We come up with the scenario that Brandon is the leader of the aliens now, since the elders are either too old or have died. He is to propose to the humans, they work with him. He has now developed the weapon and wants to share in the new government. The aliens wish to be a part of the outside world and have much to offer the plotters.

"Can he carry this off?" I ask.

"Oh yes, certainly. He does have the 'gift of gab' as your people say. He can pull this deception off. We will be with him and you will also be beside him. That would be best," Michael says. "You could coach him as it unfolds. You do need to meet him first and get your own feeling for his state of mind. He is not the same young man you heard on the tapes. I assure you. He asked to meet you, in fact."

"Good idea. I would like to talk with him first."

"How about right now?"

"Let's do it."

Michael places a call and in a few minutes, there is a knock on the door.

George opens the door and Brandon cautiously walks in. He does look like a teenager compared to even Brian. Taller than Mickey, but definitely has a youthful face. He is nervous, looking down at the floor then at his Uncle Michael.

"Brandon, this is David and Tom." He gestures toward each of us. "You know Dog."

Brandon looks quickly at both of us and then takes a deep breath, faces me and says in a quivering voice, "Mr. Manning, I'm sorry. I never meant to harm your girlfriend or anyone. I was messed up. We were getting high on stuff we found outside. We-uh-I thought I could be all powerful and you humans were inferior. Please forgive me. I was stupid, ignorant! I am so ashamed of myself and for the shame I brought to my father's name. I am no better than the German who brought our ship down. He thought he was above the law and so did I. I will do anything to help the colony. Please do not hate me, I am **not** the person I was. I was like your Hitler. I thought I could rule the world. So stupid." There are tears in his eyes. "Please forgive me. Let me help if I can." He looks over at Tom and then back to me.

Dog, bless his soul, gets up, goes to Brandon, and nuzzles his arm. "He means it David. I can feel his pain."

I swallow, stand up and offer the boy my hand. "I do forgive you Brandon. I was young and full of big ideas once. Maybe not quite that big, but I can't imagine how hard it is on you kids being stuck here, through no fault of your own."

He takes my hand with both of his, tears streaming down his pale cheeks. "I am so sorry; we are better people than I have shown. Thank you for helping us. Uncle Michael has told me some of what you have done for us. Without your help we would be in grave danger."

Tom gets up and reaches his hand out to the boy. "Brandon, it takes a man to admit his mistakes." Leaving one hand on mine he takes Tom's in the other. "Thank you sir."

We all sit down and fill Brandon in on our plan. He says he can do it.

"You must be firm. You're in the driver's seat, they need your assistance. Tell the Germans you will only speak to with General Lamar. I don't think they even know about him. That should get the group's attention," I say. "We'll be right there with you, if needed."

Brandon swallows hard, "I can do it. Whatever you need, I can do it." He turns to Michael, "I will not let you down, ever again, Uncle."

Michael gets up, goes over to him, and gives the boy a hug.

"Welcome back Brandon."

CHAPTER SEVENTY-FIVE

Michael looks around the room, "Well, what do you say? When do we make the call?"

"As soon as possible, let's get this ball rolling," I proclaim.

George agrees, Tom nods affirmative, Dog lets loose with his war cry. "Aaaarrroooo!"

Brandon steps back, "I have never heard Dog do that before. What does it mean?"

"It means 'Gird your loins' kid. We are going into battle."

Brandon laughs, "Dog you have always talked funny. Where did you learn all the information you have?"

"From Wolfgang, he was always reading old books to me."

"Alright, the history lesson is over. Let us get to work." Michael asserts.

We go over our plan, work out any kinks we can think of and then it's time to make the call to Schultz in Sedona. We all enter the control room. This telephone will leave no trace. Brandon has never been in here. He looks around at all the equipment and monitors, with wild-eyed awe. "I had no idea what was in here. I foolishly thought you would have no awareness of what we were planning. At one time I would have resented the intrusion but with our present situation, I now understand why you elders had to keep track of us."

"It was not so much keeping track of *our* people, but more the need to keep our secret safe from the outside world." Michael says quietly.

Little does Brandon know the elders would not have become aware of his plans if it hadn't been for Mickey. His concerned little sister was the one bright enough to alert me. Thank goodness for Agent Mickey.

There is a table with a phone, and we all grab a chair and gather around. Brandon is in front of the phone.

"Anything going on with our various friends, Brian?" Michael asks.

"No. Pierce has not called Sedona yet. Lamar is pushing him to get the ball rolling. Major Andrews has not come into work yet, but it's still early for her. The Germans are constantly talking about leaving for Argentina. They are getting even more nervous."

Then my cell phone shows a text. It is from Greg. His people will be picking up the Major as soon as she hits the gate at Creech. Wow, no grass growing under his feet. That was fast. What has it been? An hour since we talked?

"Major Andrews will not be at work today," I announce.

"Impressive," says George.

"Show off FBI," grumbles Tom.

We make the call to Sedona. Schultz answers the phone.

"Ya hallo,"

"This is Brandon. I am ready to deal with your people. I have perfected the beam device."

"Ya, so, we come and pick you up?"

"No, I must speak with General Lamar and only him."

"Who is this Lamar? I do not know him."

"Franklin Pierce does. You know *him*, correct?"

"Ya Pierce, but not Lamar. Pierce I talk to."

"I will only talk to Lamar. You call Pierce and pass on this message. I will call you back in one hour. Understand?"

"Ya, but,"

"No, ya but, you tell Pierce if he wants the device, he will set up a meeting with Lamar. One hour." I take the phone and slam in down. Dramatic effect always sets the mood.

The Germans are beside themselves. Mostly in German, sometimes in English. George translates. Hoffman: "You must call Pierce, now. We have put too much work into this to lose it. Call him!"

Schultz is unsure but he does place the call. Pierce is frustrated with the information. "How did they find out about General Lamar?"

Schultz is sputtering, "I do not know who this Lamar is, do you Herr Pierce?"

'I'll call you back." Pierce hangs up.

Now we dial Franklin Pierce's cell phone before he has a change to call Lamar.

"Pierce," he growls.

"Hello Franklin Pierce, this is Brandon, the leader of the alien colony at Area 51. You know the place, I believe."

"How the hell did you get my number?"

"I know a lot about you, Franklin, also General Lamar and the rest of your conspirators. I am not dealing with your decrepit Germans. I will only talk with General Lamar and your group. I have developed the beam weapon and I want to discuss a business arrangement. You would be wise to call Lamar and have him set up a meeting, at his house in the country. Eight o'clock tonight your time would be perfect for us. I will call you at precisely eight tonight. You do have speaker option on your phone, I presume?"

"Of course. Now listen, how do I know you are who you say you are and have the weapon?"

"Foolish human! How do you suppose I have your phone number and know about your treasonous group? Because we are more intelligent than you. We are tired of living in this cave. The elders are no longer in power. I am! I will expect to talk to all of you, at exactly eight o'clock. If not, there are others who would be anxious for our assistance."

I nod at Brandon and he slams down the phone. We high-five him. "Great performance son, you are too good at this. Your Uncle Michael said you had the gift of gab. You sure do. Perhaps a career in acting, I'm just saying, never know."

He blushes. It is so cool to see them blush, it's instant pink.

"Do not encourage him, he is not out of the dog-house yet," Michael says gruffly.

"Hey 'dog-house' is a four-letter word. Shame on you Michael", says the Dog, equally gruff.

Good old Dog, always breaks a tense mood, when needed.

I text FBI Greg the Germans are his…. the sooner the better. He immediately responds his people are around the corner from their house, waiting for the go-ahead. He also says the Major is now in custody as is her supposed father.

"*More* showing off," mutters Tom.

It does not take Franklin Pierce long to place a call to General Lamar. The General is taken aback to say the least. They yell and scream back and forth for a while. Lamar blames Pierce for losing control of the situation and Pierce lamely asks, 'what else could I have done'? Lamar begrudgingly acknowledges Pierce was right.

"They had you by the balls, Frank. Damn it to hell we need the aliens and they know it. How do they know about me and about the rest of us? Obviously we need them on our side; their intelligence is frightening. Call everyone and get them here by seven so we can make some sort of a *strategy*. Though what the hell it will be I don't know. I need to think about it. Don't tell the others the aliens know about all of us. Just say you have arranged a phone call with their leader, who is willing to deal with you."

Pierce contacts the members of the group. They are excited and praise Pierce for pulling this all together so quickly. Pierce is properly humble. I know he is sweating the whole time.

"Well, that was a productive day's work and it isn't even lunch time." Dog has a unique way of summing up a situation.

CHAPTER SEVENTY-SIX

After congratulating ourselves, we now have nothing to do until five o'clock, our time, eight on the east coast. Brandon has rehearsed on how he will control the phone call to the plotters. He is getting into this character almost too easily. Good thing we stopped him before he was able to pull off his plan. He is allowed to leave and go join his family. He knows he cannot say anything about what he is doing.

Michael and George walk us out.

"Brandon is definitely gotten into the role. If I might suggest, you need to keep him busy in the future. Give him some important tasks but nothing critical, if you know what I am saying."

"We are way ahead of you, David. George and I have already discussed this. He needs to be molded, carefully. Like many famous men in history, he could either be a great leader or the devil incarnate."

"I'll second that," Dog says. "But right now, I do sense his awareness of how screwed up he had become. He seems to be sincere in his remorse."

"Thank you, Dr. Wolfgang. You have created a monster." I say looking toward the labs.

"Hey, sorry if the vocabulary is uncomfortable, but some of us have learned to enjoy the finer things of life."

515

Back at the office, all is well. John is blissfully unaware of what is churning around him, as he should be. There is time enough to bring him up to date. No need to disturb him.

I call Pam and we talk for a while. "What is going on my super spy?" You have carefully avoided any mention of what you are up to. Come on give. You can't fool me, even over the phone."

"Damn woman, you are just a smart as you are beautiful."

"I'm listening, still haven't heard anything but your BS."

"Wait until tonight Baby. I'll have a better idea of everything by then. You still coming here, aren't you?"

"That all depends on you." She says indignantly, then softly, "Of course I am. I had to rattle your cage. You aren't flying anywhere are you?"

"No I'll be here. Things are at a critical stage right now. I'll tell you what I can."

"I'm sorry David, I know you have a big weight on your shoulders, I just worry about you and whatever is going to happen. I love you and fear for your life. You are playing with evil people. Please just be careful."

"Right now, I am in the safest place possible…inside the most secure area, which does not exist."

"That is no comfort David, those people are capable of anything. Remember South America, you don't know who else may be secretly working for them."

"Thank you my love, for keeping me on my toes. That idea has always been in the back of my mind, because of South America." I had the concern someone here may be a sleeper for Lamar. He hasn't given any indication of an inside person, but he did say he would handle Major Andrews without Pierce. He must know some bad actors out there.

After we hang up, I say to Dog, "Extra alert Bud, too close to the goal for a foul."

"My thoughts too. So far no one has aroused any of my highly tuned senses. I'll be on *hyper alert status*."

"No one in the building has seemed any different or nervous lately?"

"No, most are typical government workers, putting in their time and waiting to go home. There have been no *new hires* since we've been here."

Tom agrees a mole may be around here, but none of our plans have been compromised. We caught Lamar and Pierce by surprise so if there is a spy, it is not close to us. There are countless personnel working around the area....EG&G, Wackenhut, other defense contractors and military, just to mention a few.

"The most secure installation on earth is populated by much more than the public is aware." Tom observes.

I go down to the security desk in the lobby. I have kept a good rapport with the officers assigned there. I make small talk and work around to any new arrivals that they are aware of. I am told there are no new persons in the building or the various labs nearby. I should feel better, but the thought is haunting me. Pam jarred me into the reality of this kind of work. I was too involved with the case and getting complacent in these surroundings. Thank you my Love.

The rest of the day drags by, as life does when you are waiting for an event of importance. Tonight, will make or break our plan. If Lamar's group buys into our scheme, it will be a victory. It needs to work, there is no viable Plan B.

To kill more time, I visit John. He is in a chatty mood. He tells me Doris, his wife, has asked him to bring Dog and me to dinner again. "She likes you, but she is very fond of Dog. It would make her happy. How about in the next few days? I know you have been seeing that cute Air Force gal, how is that coming along? If I'm not getting too personal." *No John not too personal since I know more about you and your wife's private lives than you will ever be aware of.*

"We would love to John. Doris is a great cook and fun to be around. As far as my dating goes, it is at the serious level. Quite serious."

"Well, then why don't you bring her along too? Doris would be thrilled. She said you are too nice and handsome to be alone. All of her friends are too old, but she asked around to find someone for you."

"Tell her I appreciate it but I'm good now. Exceptionally good. As far as dinner goes, I'll check with Pam and let you know."

I'll see what tonight brings before trying to make future plans. If all works according to our script, we should have a few days of quiet before the *coup de grace*. I hope and pray.

Mercifully the time comes. We all congregate in the cave's control room. Brandon is nervous.

"I hope I can pull this off. The last time it was fun, but I know how important this time is, to all of us." he looks at me, "Please David don't leave, I need your help for this. I do not understand how you humans process things. I do not want to say the wrong words."

"Hey kid, I'm not going anywhere. We will see this through together. You will be fine. We all are right here."

Just before seven p.m. Eastern Time, the group begins to arrive at Lamar's. We watch and all are accounted for, except the Russian. He is definitely out of the plan now. As soon as the last one arrives, General Lamar begins to talk. He lays out the true accounts of Brandon's calls to the Germans and Pierce. There is an uproar from everyone. Lamar must yell to settle them down.

"All of you, just shut up! It is not the time for blaming, bickering or finger pointing. It is what it is, period. The aliens have outfoxed us. They are much more clever than we thought. But, the leader, Brandon is his name, seems to want to deal with us. He wants them to be a part of the new world. They are tired of living in the caves. What we need to discuss is how we handle his request. We need his weapons. They have obviously superior intelligence and could be of great use to us."

"Or a great threat, if they decide to rule us." Declares Marlee Grabo.

"How many of them are there?" Henry Marlowe inquires.

Pierce answers his inquiry, "Only about fifty, probably less if some have died."

"If they become too big a problem, we could order a strike on them. Once we have the beam weapons of course." Lamar quickly adds.

"Jesus Christ, Charles, at least lets see if we can work with them. Sounds to me like they could be a huge ally if handled correctly." Richard Henley sputters, "We can't go around killing everyone. Isn't the President and his administration enough?"

"I'm just saying if they become too big for their britches. Besides, we are not killing the current administration, the libertarians are."

Marlee speaks up, "So we have to deal with these creeps as long as we can, is that what you are saying Charles?"

"That's it, unless someone has a better idea."

The room is silent. "Okay then, we will listen to what this Brandon has to say and try to work with him for the present," Lamar announces. "Let's get some refreshments and wait for the call."

Muttering ensues as they move to wherever the refreshments are located.

George laughs, "If they had any idea we heard every word they would all run for the hills. It would be hilarious if they were not so serious."

"Sounds as if they will go along with our ideas. Let us hope for the best. It is your show now Brandon." Michael says as he pats the boy on his shoulder.

Almost in tears, Brandon says, "I wish I had never called them in the first place. We would not be in this situation if I had not contacted anyone."

"No son, because you did, we have a solution to a problem, we already had." Michael says gently.

We all concur. Brandon seems convinced and is pulling himself together. It is finally eight o'clock on the east coast. It is time to make the call.

In Virginia, the group has settled down and is breathlessly awaiting the call. I can imagine the anxious looks on their faces. We can hear the clinking of ice in glasses.

"Hope they are sober enough to talk," Dog comments.

George dials Pierce's cell phone and gives the handset to Brandon.

"Hello, this is Franklin Pierce." He is nervous. Good!

"Franklin, it is good to see everyone is present. I assume the Russian is no longer part of your group?" Brandon says mockingly.

"How the hell do you know about him? Oh never mind, yes we are all here."

"So General Charles Lamar, since you appear to be the leader of this group, what do you have to say to my offer: I give you the weapons, assist you in your nefarious plot to overthrow the United States Government, in exchange for freedom for my people to come out of the shadows and join your society. We would of course want assurances we would be part of the ruling entity, whatever you plan to call it."

"We have already discussed this and we agree in principle. But what exactly do you mean by: *be a part of the ruling government*? A voice in decisions on running the country?"

"I assume all of you will have an equal voice in the decisions that govern. As a ruling junta."

"Uh, well yes that was our initial plan."

"That would be five of you. Correct? You, Ms. Grabo, Mr. Henley, Mr. Marlowe and Mr. Pierce. Correct?"

Marlee Grabo hisses, "How does he know all our names. This is scary."

"Oh please Ms. Grabo, do not get melodramatic. We are not children playing games here. This is the real world." Brandon looks at us and smiles. We give him a thumbs up.

Lamar gruffly, "Marlee, just be still. You are not helping matters. Uh, Brandon, one clarification, Mr. Pierce is not one of the ruling panel, he is our Chief of Staff."

Brandon smirks, "Oh sorry Franklin, I overestimated your importance in the group. I'm certain you will be a make a fine Chief of Staff. Alright then everyone, that makes four of you. I would make the fifth which would avoid any split decisions. Correct?"

"Uh, yes, well, I suppose it would." Lamar is stammering.

"Well lady and gentlemen, why don't we discuss it when I demonstrate the weapons to you."

"Oh, yes, wonderful. How would you do it? You are in Area 51 still, aren't you?

"Of course, where else would we be. Your government has kept us prisoner here for years. I would demonstrate the beam weapon right here for you. All of you are invited. The four junta members and the Chief of Staff."

"At Area 51? How would you be able to do demonstrate the weapon there? "Lamar is caught off guard. Perfect.

"We may be prisoners per say, but not helpless by any means. I expect among you, there is the availability of a business jet? Yes?" Gasps and unintelligible murmurings in the room. "Come now, don't be shy. Mr. Marlowe surely within your huge arms company there must be at least one plane available? Another point to consider Mr. Marlowe, we have produced a functioning prototype. Someone will need to manufacture them. I would expect it would be you and your arms factories."

"Yes, I do have a Gulfstream. But what does that have to do with anything. I can't fly to Area 51 in it. No way. It is a restricted base."

"Minor problem. Franklin, you have the necessary contacts to allow the plane to be given clearance, your man Cranston could arrange it. Right?"

"It could possibly be done, I'm not positive, but maybe." Frank is sweating now, I can tell.

"See, no problem we cannot solve together. Now, you tell me when you can make the trip and I will give you a demonstration you will not forget. We will even throw a party in your honor. A few days' notice is all we need. Franklin, you have Cranston arrange suitable transportation for the group from the airstrip and I will see they are brought directly to us."

"No way am I going to that barren patch of desert. You men go." Ms. Grabo is shaken.

"Now, now, my dear, I assure you this is not a barren patch of desert. The amenities are amazing. Franklin, tell her the facilities here rival the offices in D.C."

"Marlee the place is quite modern, you wouldn't know that because there are no pictures of this top secret area."

"I'm not going; I don't care what you say. The whole idea is crazy."

"Ms. Grabo, I insist. Your trip here will be unforgettable, trust me. I must have all of you who will be in power, here. I must convince everyone who matters to the new regime of the importance of the weapon and our commitment to you."

Lamar speaks, "we will all be there. Give me a few days to arrange the trip. Yes, Henry does have a suitable jet. How do I contact you when we are ready?"

"Oh, don't worry about contacting me. I will know and call you. I hope this is the beginning of a lasting relationship. Good night." Brandon hangs up.

"Masterful, my boy, just masterful." Tom says as he slaps Brandon on the back

CHAPTER SEVENTY-SEVEN

While we are celebrating in Nevada, back in Virginia, the mood is chaotic. Lamar is trying to keep everyone under control. Well, mostly Marlee Grabo. She is dead set against going to Area 51. The men are cautiously opportunistic about the trip.

Henry Marlowe says, "What could go wrong? We will be in a secure, well-guarded governmental facility. Frank can arrange for our passage to wherever they are and even provide guards. Right Frank?"

"There is no way they can do anything inside that place. They live in underground quarters, all very modern I am told. Besides, why would they harm their only chance to get out? They have a marketable product and are willing to bargain for their freedom." Frank answers.

Lamar clears his throat, "Frank, well put. Exactly what I was about to say. They need us. Yes, we need them, at least for the present. It looks like a win-win to me. Do not forget, they could offer their services to another country, like China. Scary thought, right? We need to firm up the arrangement and get those weapons. Besides Henry, as Brandon pointed out, someone must produce the weapons. Better you than Beijing."

"How would they make contact with China? That's bull, Charles," Richard Henley says.

"How did they find us, Richard? Their capabilities are overwhelming to say the least. Maybe not the Chinese, but hell they could contact the damn libertarian idiots. Or the mob. The aliens are not going to go away. We need to be their only customer."

There was still some grumbling and *what ifs,* but Lamar prevailed. He gave Henry orders to reserve his personal plane for the flight and told the rest of the group, to find a date in the next few days to be available for the trip. Everyone had to *check their schedules.* Lamar wanted answers by tomorrow morning. Franklin Pierce was told to contact John Cranston and make arrangements for a civilian plane to land at Area 51 and have transportation available for five to be taken to the alien's cave.

"I guess it's time to let John in on what we've been up to this whole time," I announce.

"Can I watch?" asks Dog, "I want to see the look on his face. Especially the part about Major Andrews."

"Promise not to laugh?"

"I'll try."

After their shift ends, Pam and Grizzie come over to my place. I give her a brief update...... Major and Germans in custody, meeting of the conspirators and the aliens is set for here in the next few days. In addition, to break the tension, I tell her about the invitation to dinner from John's wife.

"Will this be before or after you tell him about the case?"

"After, I have to get to him first thing tomorrow before Pierce does. I left him a text message not to talk to anyone until he sees me tomorrow."

"I assume I play dumb about all of this?"

"Just be your usual charming, personable self. You'll like Doris. It will go fine."

"I'll be curious how Cranston takes all the news."

"So will I Baby, so will I."

The next morning, Tom, Dog and I are anxiously awaiting John's arrival. He comes in early. Got my message.

"What's up guys? Sounds like something big."

"Pierce call you?"

"No, is he going to?"

"Here's some coffee, let's go into your office and I'll tell you a story."

Tom has already wisely told me it would be kinder to John if *I* were the one to tell him what we know. Dog comes in and curls up on the floor. John settles at his desk. I have his full attention. I give him the whole story, from what we have learned about the Germans, Pierce, and then the plotters. His mouth is agape. Leaning back in his chair, he looks as if he will pass out. I tell him about our plan with the aliens to lure the group out here and have all of them arrested, at one time. He is overwhelmed.

"How on earth did you uncover everything? You are amazing, David."

"I couldn't have done it without the aliens help. *They* are amazing."

"Is there anything I can do to make things better for them? I understand they can get almost anything they want already." John is sincere.

"Get them back home. Which of course we can't do. They are a great people. It is a shame the world isn't able to know and appreciate them."

I forgot my *device* was activated. "Thank you, David. Much appreciated." Michael says quietly in my ear.

"So, uhh, John, then is a little more to this plot I need to go over with you."

He gets a solemn look on his face. "You know about Kate Andrews."

"Yes, John, I do. I was quite pleased when you broke it off. Much better for you to get your marriage back together on your own. Makes me much more comfortable for what I'm going to say now."

He takes a long drink of coffee, sets the cup down and looks at me, "I was such an ass. Doris and I were drifting apart, mostly because of this damn job and the pressure Pierce was putting on me. After you came and got a hold on things, I was feeling guilty. I have loved Doris from day one. It was not right for me to ignore her, I know. She felt it too. She told me she had a dalliance also and never felt right about it. Getting back to together, talking it all out, was the best thing for us. We are back to where we started. I never even imagined you would find out about Kate. You were focused on Franklin and he was the source of my stresses. I do not even want to know how you found out. It is over. I haven't called her and have not heard from her since I broke it off."

"She was the conduit to Pierce, correct? He sent her here to encourage you to keep the project moving." I look at John and raise my eyebrows.

"Yes, what a fool. I did not even see it coming. With my years in the intelligence world, you would have thought I would have seen a *honey pot* scheme from a mile away. She was good. What has happened to her? Did Pierce move her on to some other job? What I'm really asking….is she gone from here? I do not want to ever have to deal with or see her again."

"She is guest of the government, courtesy of the FBI. She was a complete fraud." John just stares at me. I tell him the whole phony defector story about her alleged father. In addition, Pierce, and General Lamar, were involved from the beginning.

"They are all traitors! I never knew Lamar, but Pierce has been going off track on a lot of things. I was frightened of him. I know what he has been capable of, in the past. He will be arrested, right?"

"Oh yes, all of them will. Right here in Area 51. I am assuming between you and Pierce, clearance for the private airplane to land can be arranged?"

"Yes, we have done it for defense contractors in the past. The crew must stay on the plane until the guests leave. Heavy security will be present, of course."

"Good, when Pierce calls just listen and go along with it. I'm surprised he hasn't called by now."

As if on cue, John's phone rings. Looking at the number, John says, "It's him."

He answers and listens attentively, then he tells Pierce to give him the date and time and he will arrange everything. He then hangs up.

John smiles, "I can't tell you how good it feels to have that bastard on the hook. He is telling me if I want to keep my job, I had better make this happen. What a pompous ass!"

"You handled it perfectly John. When is the group coming?"

"In five days, Sunday morning at ten o'clock. Good choice since most of the workforce will not be on site. Work for you, Dave?"

"Perfect, when would you like Pam and me for dinner?"

John calls Doris and she tells him tomorrow night would be perfect. I already know that works with Pam's schedule. I mention Grizzie. John laughs, "The more the merrier, you know how Doris love dogs. Yes, bring her alone."

Now the date is confirmed. I conference call Greg at the FBI and CIA Brad.

Greg is noticeably awed, "Dave, I honestly did not think you guys could pull it off, at least not so quickly.

Sunday at 10 am. I will be there with a team by 8 am, so we can get the lay of the land. That work with you?"

"Absolutely, looking forward to it. How are you getting here?"

"We'll drive up in convoy from the Vegas office. I'll make all the arrangements"

"I would ask you to make it as confidential as possible. I am not sure if Lamar has any local friends, if you know what I mean?"

"Man, you are on top of it, you never know who works for who, do you? It will be just my team. We won't tell the Vegas office what we are up to. Just get some cars from them the night before. Since we are OPR they know better than to ask too many questions. The locals always think we are looking at them when we come around. Which of course we usually are. There are no friends when you get into internal investigations. Part of the job."

"Sounds good, see you Sunday. Brad, you are not coming, I take it?"

"No damn it, out of my realm. But do not fear I'm sure the glory boys will be able to handle it. Right Greg?"

"Here we go again, pick on the FBI." Greg chuckles.

"Guys, it is settled. Keep in touch."

I sit back and take a deep breath. Tom is grinning, "I will be here Sunday, I'm assuming?"

'Damn straight. To keep a watch on the feds. Left to their own devices they will probably get lost or arrest the wrong people. In fact, why don't you meet them at Mercury turnoff and lead them in? I would be more comfortable."

"Yeah, makes sense."

I call Greg back and he is relieved for the guide. Admits he wasn't aware of how big this place is until he just looked at a map. Gotta love 'em, almighty FBI assumed the gates would open and they would drive right into Area 51. Getting to the turnoff is only half the trip. Yes Greg, this is a huge place. Area 51 is only a small portion of the entire restricted area.

Michael and George have been like little kids, babbling in my ear the whole time. I finally had to tell them I would check in later. This is a big deal for them, actually it is a lifesaver, so I understand the excitement. I ask them to have Brandon make a quick call to Pierce and tell him he will be expecting their arrival Sunday at ten a.m.

However, I have things to do. What was it? Oh yes, I need to tell Pam we have a dinner date tomorrow.

CHAPTER SEVENTY-EIGHT

I have done all I can for now. Time for some fun. I pick up Pam at her parent's house and we drive to the Cranston's. Doris is her gracious self. "I am so glad to meet you, Pam. David is such a great guy, and the thought of him being alone always concerned me. Also, you two have a ready-made family," she says as she hugs Grizzie and Dog. "Your girl is beautiful."

Dog, being the jerk, he is, lowers his head and moans softly.

"Oh Dog, you know how handsome I think you are, don't be jealous." Doris looks at Pam and says quietly, "Sometime I think he can actually understand me. The looks he gives. He is quite special."

"Yes he is," Pam agrees, giving me a sly smile.

After a pleasant dinner, we are just sitting outside and chatting when Doris says, "Oh, David, I wanted to tell you about a friend of mine whose dog just had puppies. I had shown her a picture of Dog I took the last time he was here. She told me her Irish Setter had five pups, four of them look like the mom but the fifth is black and quite a furry boy, just like Dog."

I almost choke on my beverage.

"Uh, interesting. Where does your friend live? If I may ask." Dog looks at me and his eyes widen.

"Not too far from here, just a little south." I relax, so does Dog. Doris continues, "She use to live in north-west Las Vegas, but just recently bought near us."

Dog and I are again alert.

"Looks similar to my guy? That's interesting," I stammer. Pam gives me a.... where are you going with this? *look.*

"Yes, he is bigger that his litter mates also. The funny thing is, she says he seems to be mimicking her when she talks to him."

Dog is starting to get up. I give him a NO look. I down my wine.

"That's quite interesting Doris. You know I would like to see this pup, if it would be possible. I've never seen any other dog, that looks quite like Dog."

"Oh, I'm sure she wouldn't mind at all. Let me give her a call." She gets up and goes into the house. John offers to get more wine and also leaves.

"What is going on?" Pam asks, those eyes of hers boring into mine.

"It's a long story, I'll tell you on the way home."

She looks at Dog. "You seem to know about this too, *lover boy.*"

He is about to open his mouth when John comes back with wine. I gratefully take it. Doris comes back and says her friend would love to show me the puppy. Any time tomorrow would be fine with her."

"Could I have her address? Maybe I could stop by in the morning."

I get the address and the rest of the evening is a lot more relaxed. We say goodbye and get into my truck.

As soon as the door closes, "What is the story, David, or Dog, whoever has the courage to tell me?"

Dog just stammers, "Uh well you see, sometimes, well you know, there are certain, uh moments, oh shit Dave, you tell her."

"Coward. Okay, let's just say there is a remote possibility Dog may have met an Irish Setter the first time we were on our way to Area 51. It was in the northwest and near the highway."

"I had to, uh, relieve myself and well, she just appeared, like a vision of loveliness."

Pam looks at me, disapprovingly. "Hey, he wasn't my dog, then. I had a head injury, remember? Yes, he did wander into the bushes with an Irish Setter. That's all I know."

"So why are you going to see the dog? He won't be liable for child support?"

"Think about it Baby, if this is his puppy and he can talk, that is a huge problem. Where did he come from, why can he talk? Too many questions. He would only produce more talking dogs. Science would eventually find some unknown DNA and the whole alien theory would surface again. No, he needs to be given a new home and I know where."

Pam thinks about it, then her face breaks out into a smile, "Mickey, that's who. Right?"

"Yep."

Dog smiles, as only he can. "If he is my son, then Mickey is the only choice."

We spend the night at Pam's parents and in the morning, since Pam has the day off, we all drive to the *puppy's house*. Grizzie is happily hanging her head out the window. Dog is apprehensively staring out the windshield while standing on the console. "Hey, I can't see, get in the back." I grumble.

It is a fashionable neighborhood, not quite up to the Cranston's, but nice. Doris's friend is outside when we drive up and is excited to see Dog. "The puppy looks just like him. I told Doris, it could be his son. Come in and see for yourselves."

Pam and I go in. Dog and Grizzie stay in the truck. Dog is a nervous wreck.

We enter the room with the dogs. There are four little red puppies crawling on each other and one larger black, furry pup chewing on a toy.

"My word, he does look like a *little* Dog," Pam whispers.

"I don't know how to explain him," says the lady. "We did have her bred to a pedigree Irish Setter. He had a perfect bloodline. However, she did get out of the yard one day when she was in heat. That's the only explanation we can come up with. It is going to be difficult to sell the others with him as a litter mate. He is so sweet though. It's like he is older than the others. He listens to me and tries to mimic me. It's cute. I remembered Doris showing me the photo of your dog. I couldn't help but think of him when I looked at this puppy."

I go to the pup, lean down, and extend my hand for him to smell. He looks up from his chewing, inquisitively. "Hey big guy. How are you doing?" I say quietly.

Looking at me, he opens his mouth, "Hey big guy," He says in a high-pitched tone. It is not perfect, but I have no doubt what he is saying. That does it. He is Dog's son. No question. I ask exactly where she lived previously. She tells me. I punch in the address on my phone and when it comes up, I look at her, "I do believe my dog is the father." I relate the 'potty stop' story and that it was the vacant lot alongside her house.

"My heavens," she laughs. "What a coincidence. What are the odds you would be there and also be friends of the Cranston's?" She is fanning herself. "Unbelievable."

"I agree. Would you consider selling him to me? I know a special girl who would love him."

"Absolutely not." She says firmly. "I insist on giving him to you. Please, he needs to be in his own place, with someone who would appreciate him. My snotty world of purebred breeders is not right for him. I love my Setters, but that little guy is special."

I ask if Dog could come in, to see how he reacts. She is not sure how the mother will respond to him but says to bring him to the door of the room.

I get Dog and tell him what I think. "Want to go in?"

"Yes I do, but leave Grizzie here. Her coming in wouldn't work too well."

"Yeah, I know, the other woman thing." I snicker.

I bring Dog to the entrance of the room. Mom stands up and starts a low growl, then stops. Dog makes a soft sound. She cocks her head and wags her feathery tail, then runs up to him. They dance around a bit and rub noses.

I have never seen anything like it." The lady says. "She actually remembers him and apparently fondly."

"He is unforgettable, that's for sure." I say.

We take the pup to Dog and he smells him all over. Then looks at me and nods. That did it. We carry him to the truck and show Grizzie. She is all over the pup, Licking and nuzzling him. Pam just smiles. After chatting with the lady at little more, we thank her profusely and drive off. Pam is now holding the pup on her lap and Dog is making soft noises to him.

"Well Dad, you did well. Fine looking son. Are there any more out there we need to rescue? Now's your chance."

"No, I didn't get out much you know." He says sheepishly.

CHAPTER SEVENTY-NINE

After driving Pam back to her parent's home, she has to work tonight and will see me after her shift, I continue on to Area 51. On the way I call Michael and tell him about Dog's indiscretion and ask if I can give the pup to Mickey.

"I think that is a grand idea, David. Wonderful. Perfect timing. I will let you surprise her. She will be thrilled."

I then let Tom know what I'm doing and I'll be there soon. He is laughing, "Dog's son, I'm not surprised. How many more are out there?"

"Shut up, this is the only one." snarls Dog.

As I am approaching the caves, I begin to think about Michael's recent remarks: first, *not worrying about them* and now the *perfect timing* comment. He is telling me something—without actually saying it.

At the caves Michael calls for Mickey to come to the lounge. I am holding the puppy. Dog is proudly sitting beside us. He is softly murmuring to his son.

Mickey comes in the room and squeals with delight when she sees the pup. "Oh Dog, is it yours? Looks so much like you. Were you ever this small?"

I let her hold him. She is in heaven, kissing, petting and just loving the little one.

Michael smiles approvingly.

"Mickey, would like to have him, for your own, since I took Dog away from you?"

"Oh David, I can't believe it," then she looks at Uncle Michael. He nods affirmatively. She starts to squeal again. "I love him. He is just a little Dog. Look at him, he is so cute." She kisses the puppy and says, "I love you."

The puppy looks at her and says in a squeaky, garbled voice, "I love you."

Michael is beside himself, "my word, he talks. He is Dog's son. Unbelievable."

Mickey hugs me, hugs Dog and hugs her Uncle Michael, all while clutching the little one. Michael has her go back to her quarters so she can enjoy the new addition to her family.

"I hope you told her mother," I say.

"Of course. She said it was the best thing that could happen to her right now."

"Michael, is there anything you want to tell me?" I ask pointedly.

He sighs, "Yes, but not yet. It is good news so do not be concerned. When I am certain then I will tell you all about it." He rests his small hand on my shoulder. "Soon, I hope."

I start to say something more, then stop. He will tell me when he is ready. I leave to go to the office and Dog comes along. "Don't you want to stay?" I ask him.

"No, I think it's better if Mickey has some time to bond with him. I'll be around, but for now just let them get to know each other."

"Quite mature of you and out of character, I must say."

"We have a big job coming up Sunday, we need to keep focused." He's staring out the truck window.

I reach over and give his big, furry head a rub. "You will always be my partner, you know that."

He nuzzles my hand, "You and me pal. I know it." A single tear rolls down his face. That does it. I'm bawling now. "Hey Dave, I'm okay, this has just been a very emotional day. I'll be fine."

At the office, I check with John. He has made the necessary arrangements for the private plane to land on Sunday. "When do they get arrested?" He inquires. Good question. I guess that will be Greg's choice. Then in my ear, Michael says, "we have a better idea. Let them come to the caves and meet Brandon."

I excuse myself from John and go into my office.

"Michael are you crazy? Why would you want that? It makes no sense." I'm indignant.

"Brandon promised them a party. They expect to be feted. Indulge us on this point."

"How can we ensure your safety if they go in your quarters? Explain yourself Michael. This is illogical."

"Hear me out, please. After all the grief they have caused us, I would like a chance to address them. It will be in the antechamber, just inside the cave. The entrance to our complex will be closed. We are a proud people and would like to face our enemies. Let them know they cannot master us. It will be perfectly safe for me. I will confront them when they enter and have my say. Then I will step into the complex and secure the door. Your people can then take them in to custody. There is no way out for them, except the door they came in. I just ask that your people stay back, until I have had my say. Then do your job. I will have fulfilled mine."

I argue with him, but he is adamant. I do understand he wants to have the last laugh at these fiends, who have caused them such anxiety. It is true, the foyer or antechamber is just that, you cannot get into the complex except thru the next door. Telling Michael I will get back to him, I shut off my device and tell Tom Michael's plan.

"He has got a right to vent at these ass-holes. I can understand. He will be safe if he just speaks and then exits into his area. Keeping the FBI back is, I guess, a way of protecting their existence. The group will be more concerned about their ruination at that moment. There will be some immensely powerful folks going down the tubes. That will be their main worry."

Dog looks up, "He's right. Where can they go? When Michael slams the door in their faces, what will they do? Turn around and there will be the feds. Game over."

Their arguments are logical, but I have an uneasy feeling. I don't know why. True, the room is large enough for Michael to stand in the rear when the group enters, speak to them, and then exit into his area. There will only be six of them at most. He can have his say before they are even halfway into the space.

I tell Michael I will consider his plan. Greg is to call me tomorrow when he is in Las Vegas. I'll go over it with him.

Today is only Friday, which means I have today and tomorrow to fret over this. Wonderful.

Tom and Dog are both in the same frame of mind.

"Nothing else to do until Sunday. Are we just going to tag along with the FBI or what?" Tom asks.

"Of course, we will be at the plane when it lands. John will have a shuttle bus for our guests. Security will stay at the plane and baby-sit the crew. We will lead the bus to the caves. If we go along with Michaels' idea, we will point out the door and stand back while they enter. The FBI will be close but not in sight. Maybe a car or two in our parking lot and any others around the hill by the old bunker. When the guests enter, we signal the feds to pull up and grab them. All I can think of."

"You are not comfortable with this are you?"

"Shit no!"

"How about we have security pat them down for weapons when they disembark. It is our right in this secure area."

"Tom, I knew there was a reason I liked you. Good logical idea. I would feel better. Besides why would they want to harm an alien until they get their hands on the beam weapon? I'm just trying to make this more complicated than it needs to be."

I am trying to relax and just savor the fact we will beat the crazies.

Later in the afternoon, I get a call from good old Eddie at EG&G.

"Still mad at me pal?" I ask.

"No, it wasn't your fault. I was getting uncomfortable about the whole affair anyway. Doris was too, I could tell. It just wasn't right. But that's not why I called. I had an unusual request come in today. One of the contractors working on a project up there wants to send one of their techs in on the Saturday afternoon plane to Area 51. It strikes me as unusual. Most projects don't work weekends. They claim he is needed because of some technical problem just discovered. Given the unusual events involving you I thought you might be interested."

"What is the contractor's name?"

"Defenus LLC. They are involved with an old project that has been all but finished, from what I can learn. The best part is he will not be returning on our plane. He will have another ride out, they said. You interested?"

Defenus, holy shit. That is Henry Marlowe's company. I'll bet he is coming here in case anything goes wrong on Sunday.

"Eddie, not only lunch but dinner is on me. Give me the particulars on this gentleman and put him on the flight. We will see he gets the royal welcome."

"If you say so. Sounds as though he won't be getting a ride out," Eddie snickers.

The man's name is Alfred Barlow. His plane will arrive tomorrow at four-thirty pm. Eddie has full ID info on Barlow, DOB, physical description and even a photo the company provided. He faxes it to me.

I check with John about any projects Defenus might be involved in here. He checks with the base office. They only have one project involving the company. John calls them and is told the project is completed and they are about to leave the area. They further tell John no Defenus personnel have been involved for several months.

I advise Greg at the FBI. He runs file checks and finds the man does not exist. Phony ID he advises. Greg asks if we can hold him until Sunday and then he will arrest him along with the others. Not a problem I reply, we have a holding facility up here. Brad's former snoop was detained there. We will be happy to give him a room for the night.

Tom quips, "Feel better now? You knew someone would crawl out from under a rock, didn't you?"

CHAPTER EIGHTY

Michael has invited Dog and me to dinner tonight. That will pass some time at least. Dog is anxious to see his son. After John and Tom leave, we go to the caves. There is a tension in the air. Understandable since their foes are coming in less than forty hours. George is nervous. Michael on the other hand is outwardly quite calm.

I ask George if he approves of Michael's idea to confront the plotters. "Oh yes, I heartily agree with him. It needs to be done. We appreciate your concern but there will be no threat to him. He will be just outside the door and will step back in when he is done speaking. We will immediately secure the door. He will be fine. Not to worry my friend. You may do as you wish with those people when we close our door."

"I still don't like it, but I do understand." Yeah, right.

As we enter the dining room, it is already full of the residents. They all stand up and cheer when Dog and I enter. I look at Michael, he turns toward us. "We all want to thank you for what you have done for us and your country. You have been brave and resourceful. We just wanted to show you our appreciation." He is handed a glass of wine and raises it in a toast. "To our earthly comrades. May we continue to have a long and lasting friendship." Everyone yells and claps. Dog gracefully bows and I blush.

We are seated and I am handed my own wine, which I happily accept. "To our friendship and bond. I love you all." Where did that come from? Well I do mean it.

The rest of the dinner is relaxed, and the little people are having fun. Seem relaxed. Some even giddy. How soon did they begin drinking?

After dinner Mickey takes Dog to play with his son. Michael and I relax in George's office. We go over the plan for Sunday morning.

"You have all the work David, we will just stay back behind our door and leave it to you and your friends." Michael says quietly. "You are not expecting any problem from them, are you? Most of them are too old to cause much trouble."

"You never know about the old ex-military guys," I say. Then I tell them about the 'visitor' who will be arriving tomorrow and our plan to take him into custody as soon as the plane lands.

"What would be the grounds to arrest him," George asks.

"Basically, he is using a false identification to gain access to a restricted governmental facility. The FBI will sweat him after the others are in custody for the true reason for his visit. With his boss in jail for treason, he will probably tell all."

George shakes his head, "Too much drama. We gave up on that eons ago. Hopefully Earth will too, before it is too late." He raises his glass. We follow in agreement.

Dog and I leave in time to greet the ladies at my place. Pam is just pulling up as we arrive.

"And where have you two been? Carousing with the little ones I suppose?"

We all go in and settle down. Pam is excited, "Guess who will be here tomorrow and Sunday?"

Dog immediately stands up, "You don't mean you and Grizzie will be here when the traitors come?"

"Yes, we will. The base was requested by the FBI to have extra security here on Sunday. So I volunteered Grizzie and me."

Before I can speak, the hound says, "Not a good idea, Pam. We don't know what will happen. You two should not be here. Not safe."

"I agree. We don't expect any problem, but you don't know what might happen with this bunch of crazies." I chime in.

Undeterred, Pam says, "Too late, it is a done deal. No one else wanted it anyway. You are stuck with us."

I tell her about the man coming in tomorrow. "Honey, we don't know what Lamar and his associates are capable of doing. Can't you at least be at the other end of the area, not right here?"

"Nope. I am assigned to be at the landing strip." Putting her arms around me she says softly but firmly, "David, if you are in any danger, I need to be here. Someone must look out for you. You are too gung-ho sometimes. I won't interfere, just be on the side. Just in case."

"Baby, I love you, but security will also be at the strip. We will be fine."

"Wackenhut. Give me a break, just a bunch of wantabees and some burned out ex-military types."

"Like me?"

"No. Not like you. You know what I mean. Most of them were discharged dishonorably anyway." She slugs me in the arm, "God, you are so, so, touchy. I love you David, damn it."

"I give. You love me." I take her in my arms and kiss her. "I worry about you too, hot shot."

"Make sure Grizzie stays close to you." Dog says as he licks Grizzie's face.

The remainder of the night passes without any further drama. Dog looks at me a couple of times with worried eyes. I smile weakly and nod back. We did not need more to worry about, at this point. Damn FBI, why didn't they leave the Air Force out of it?

Morning comes and since Pam works tonight and tomorrow, she can stay here. We all go to breakfast and then to my office. She has not seen it yet. The security on the door greets me with a sly smile. "Morning Dave. Adding to your staff?"

I tell him Pam is Air Police and will be working the weekend here to assist us.

He gets a twinkle in his eyes, "Welcome to the place that doesn't exist, Ma'am. You have a beautiful dog too. May I --." He reaches his hand toward Grizzie, she lets out a low growl. Dog steps forward and makes a soft sound to her. Grizzie then wags her tail. The guard looks amazed, "He told her I was okay, right?"

Pretty much," I answer.

Pam says, "She is quite protective of me, has been since Afghanistan."

"Afghanistan? God bless you lady. I thought Viet Nam was rough, but what the troops have to go through in Iraq and Afghanistan... just horrendous."

We go to my office. Dog takes Grizzie on a tour to see if anyone left out treats.

"This is it? I pictured some stars war command center." She jokes.

"That's over in the caves. With them on my side, I don't need anything else."

"Is Tom coming in to help you greet your special visitor today?" Pam asks.

"Tom will be on the plane, with the visitor, seated right behind him. Clever plan we worked out. The poor chap doesn't have a chance." I smugly say.

"Be careful, *pride goeth before a fall*, remember?" Is her response.

Tough woman. Keeps me on my toes. Love her!

When the time comes for the Janet plane to land, Pam, the two dogs and I are waiting. Pam and Grizzie are back on duty. There are workers from day shift waiting to travel back to McCarran. I have them form a line to one side and away from the stairway.

The jet pulls up to the spot and the ground crew pushes the stairs up to the door as it is opened. Per my instructions they also move aside. There is a skeleton crew on weekends. They emerge and walk down the stairs, then our *man* emerges with Tom right behind him. The guy is hefting a duffle bag. As he reaches the bottom step, I step up and confront him.

"Alfred Barlow?" I ask.

"Yes, that's me." He answers, still holding his duffle.

"Set you bag down please." He does, a confused look on his face,

"Is there anything wrong?" His eyes are darting all over.

Tom is right on him.

"Sir you are under arrest for entering a restricted government installation."

"But I have authorization. Ask Defenus. I work for them."

"Yeah, you probably do, but the FBI says Alfred Barlow is not your real identity. That's another charge." Tom has quickly grabbed his wrists, placed them behind him and clicked on the handcuffs.

"You've done this before," I remark.

"Couple of times," Tom responds.

We take Mr. Barlow or whoever he is, to the detention facility and book him in. A search of his person turns up nothing unusual, but when we open his duffle....it is a different story. What appears to be tools rolled up in a Snap-On imprinted cover, is a Mac-10 fully automatic pistol, along with several loaded magazines. There is also a sleeping bag, cell phone and some MREs, military field rations. Apparently, he was going to hide out and wait until the plane arrived tomorrow. He would provide cover for the group, should anything go wrong. He doesn't look over at us as we unwrap it all. He asks for an attorney. I tell him the FBI will be along sometime tomorrow and he can discuss it with them. He is led off, sputtering about his rights. "You lost them when you entered Area 51," I call out as he goes thru the door. It closes with a solid, metallic clank.

After inventorying his duffle and its contents, they are placed in an evidence locker.

"Dinner anyone?" I ask.

CHAPTER EIGHTY-ONE

Pam gets a meal break and can take it whenever she wants, so she joins Dog and me. Tom is going home for the night. In the morning, he will oversee herding the FBI agents to the designated area.

"Make sure you have all of them," I caution. "Don't want any loose agents wandering around."

After we dine, Pam goes about her patrolling. I call Michael and ask if he could use some company. I have until midnight to kill until *my love* gets off duty.

"Uh, no, sorry David, but we are uh, having a meeting tonight and it's going to run late. So let us, as you people say, take a rain check. If you do not mind. All is ready for the morning, correct?"

"Yes. Sure." I answer. This is not like them, but in all fairness, tomorrow is a big day...their archenemies arrive. Michael is going to jeopardize his personal safety by speaking to them, against my better judgement. I can envision there is a group session or prayer like meeting tonight. They are a very close-knit group, after all.

Dog is disappointed; he was looking forward to playing with his son.

"After tomorrow everything will settle down and we get back to a normal routine."

"We have no *normal* routine, Dave. We have been on edge the whole time since you got here."

"Thanks, Pal, like it is my fault?"

"No! You know what I mean. This whole caper has been our *normal*. What do we do after tomorrow?"

"I expect you and I will stay on with John and be bored to death with nothing to do. Sounds good to me. Maybe Pam and I can get married and live a real life together, with you two pooches, of course."

"Sounds great to me. Where are we going to live?"

"I think some nice community, like Don and Helen's. Not a snotty place like John's".

"I could deal with that. Can we still see Doris occasionally? She loves me you know."

"You sleaze, you just like her treats. Don't try to fool me."

We watch boring television until the girls come over at midnight. Opening the door for them, I am blown backward by a strong gust of wind, as Pam and Grizzie rush inside.

"Where the hell did that come from?" I ask, as I strain to push the door closed.

"It just came up, as I was pulling into the parking lot. It has been clear and calm all night, then this monster dust storm just blows in from nowhere, typical desert. So glad I don't have to go out anymore tonight."

We snuggle in for the evening, while the wind howls outside. We are up early the next morning, and thankfully, the wind has died down.

Tom calls and advises, *"The FBI has arrived,* and we are on our way to the office."

I greet the caravan and lead them to the club for coffee. "You have this up here?" Greg asks, "Not too bad."

"Try living here 24-7. This is all there is."

"Oh yeah, I get it. Nice for a visit, but not to live here."

I go over the plan again with Greg while his agents drink coffee. He does not like the part about letting the group into the caves either.

"As you and I agreed I haven't told them about the aliens," gesturing toward the others. "I didn't think they have a *need to know.*"

"Agreed. If it works as planned, your people will never see the little ones."

Greg calls the others over. There are four male and one female agent. Greg outlines the plan; Tom will lead them to their assigned positions. I drive Greg to our parking lot.

Pam and Grizzie are just getting out of their patrol vehicle. She is looking damn sexy in her crisp uniform with her partner by her side.

"No coffee for the hired help? Come on Manning you can do better."

"Greg, I would like you to meet Officer Disrespectful, from the Air Force."

Greg looks back and forth at us. "You know each other, I assume." He smiles cautiously.

"Yes we do. I will marry this woman one day, after you remove those treasonous bastards from here. Pam this is Greg, Greg meet Pam."

The formalities over, we go to my office. John Cranston is already waiting for us. After more introductions, I ask if he has heard from Pierce.

"He called earlier and said they were on the plane and would be here around ten. What do you want me to do, David?"

"Greg and I have worked out the plan: when our guests deplane, security will check for weapons or contraband, then you and I will get them on the shuttle, with Tom as the driver.... Security will stay with the plane and its crew. Pam will follow us in her Air Force patrol vehicle. We stop about twenty-five yards short of the entrance and tell them to walk to the doorway. It will be open, and they will enter and meet Michael. He will speak them and exit into the main complex, locking the door behind him instantly. Greg and his team will swarm into the chamber and arrest them.

"Why do they have to enter the cave?" John asks with a puzzled look.

"Because Michael, as the leader, wants to tell the group what he thinks of them. Sounds unnecessary to me but he insists. He does have a right after all; those egotistical assholes have made his life a living hell."

"Yes I suppose, but I don't like them being out of sight, even in the foyer. Should I go with them?"

"No John, I would suggest you stay outside with the rest of us. We don't want you to become a hostage."

John visibly shutters. "I'll stay with you two."

Greg says, "Sounds good to me. I will stay here in the parking lot until you get to the caves. There is the outside chance Franklin Pierce might remember me. We have crossed paths in the past. Don't want to spook him."

We all sit around making small talk, trying not to be nervous. This is a huge deal. Major government and political movers and shakers are going down. We cannot afford any slip-ups.

Finally, it is time to head to the landing strip. Greg drives to each of his agents and gives them a final briefing. Tom, John, Dog, and I get in the bus and Pam follows.

We position our vehicles at the strip and greet the security officers and ground crew. Everyone knows his or her job. At three minutes after ten, the radio of the ground crew crackles, the plane is approaching.

Showtime.

A mid-size Gulfstream business jet circles the field and comes in for a landing. Nice and smooth. The ground crew guides it to the parking spot. The pilot cuts the engines and as they whine down, the plane's door opens. Franklin Pierce surveys the area. Satisfied, he nods to the others inside. They begin to come down the stairs. Everybody is here, even Marlee Grabo. There is another woman also present. General Lamar helps her, must be his wife. So be it, she had full knowledge of the plan.

As each one reaches the tarmac, security makes a cursory check. Lamar is affronted, but Pierce quiets him. "It is standard procedure here. Relax Charles."

Once the check is completed, John greets everyone, and we lead the group to the bus. There is quiet babbling during the short ride. Some seem nervous while others like Lamar are excited.

We pull up short of the cave entrance and tell them to go through the open area. Lamar leads the way, "Come on, this is what we have been waiting for." He shouts. As the group heads toward the open door, Pierce turns back, "John, come on, you don't want to miss this."

John hesitates, looks at me. I shake my head firmly.

"Be right there Frank. Go on, I'll catch up." John calls.

"Smart John." I say.

Pam and Grizzie have come alongside us now. Dog is intent on the group as they reach the cave. He looks at me. I reach down and pat his head. "Patience." He wants to be with the feds as they make the bust. Cannot say I blame him, but our job is done. It is Greg's show now. If there is a problem, we will assist.

The group reaches the doorway and Lamar looks in. He motions the rest to follow him. He enters as do the rest.

The door slams shut, with a loud thud!

"What the---- it was supposed to stay open." I say, "Why would they close it?"

"Maybe one of the idiots accidently hit the button," Tom suggests.

"No," I say, "The door switch is in the rear. The aliens did it."

CHAPTER EIGHTY-TWO

Greg, who has been loitering in the parking lot, immediately races up, screeches to a halt, and jumps out of his car, "What happened! What happened? I though the door was going to stay open!"

I tell him the aliens must have shut it. But I don't know why.

"I can't even see the opening; it looks like the rest of the hillside."

I explain to him that is how the entrance was designed. The opening slides aside for access and when it is shut, it disappears.

"What do we do now?" Asks the bewildered agent.

"Beats me." I respond. Because I have no clue what the aliens have it mind. I tell Greg to bring his people up to us. He does and they stand around looking at him for guidance. I stare at the hillside, looking for any clue.

I step away from the others and call for Michael, George... anyone inside to answer me.

Nothing.

Then Pam calls out, "David, look over to the west side of the hills, the dust storm is coming back."

As I turn, I can see a swirling cloud of dust. It is growing and then becomes so dense you cannot see the sky. We get heavy winds out here, but not like this, and not suddenly in a clear, calm day. The little extra-terrestrials are behind it. I know it. But, what are they doing?

Then I remember Michael's cryptic comments: *do not worry about us, we will be fine* and the, *perfect timing.*

Son of a bitch. They have found a way out!

Then the ground begins to rumble.

Earthquake?

Then one of the agents yells, "Look at the top of the hill."

There is smoke pouring out into the sky from one point, and then other places along the hill begin to pour smoke upwards.

That would be from the ventilation shafts for the caves.

The rumbling and tremors increase in intensity and frequency. Then a portion of the hill collapses into itself. Next another collapse followed by many more.

"They blew up the caves," Tom yells.

"Look at the dust storm, it is rising upwards," Greg points to the dark mass of swirling dirt. "What the hell is going on?"

Pam, Grizzie and Dog are all around me. The others have not moved.

Tom comes over to us, "What have they done? Blown up the caves and killed the conspirators?"

Then in my device I hear, "Not to fear, my friend. The traitors are safe. That chamber was made to withstand an assault, remember David."

"Michael, are you in the cloud? How did you build a ship? What is going on?"

"Calm down. One thing at a time my boy. We told you we learned our ship had not failed but was shot down by the German. We informed our people back home. They began to immediately construct a second vessel. We may be advanced, but somethings still take time. We were notified a short time ago the ship was completed, tested and on its way to rescue us. I had them time it to coincide with the visit of the group. Once we knew the ship was on its way, I devised the plan to have Brandon lure them here, so you could arrest them."

"You sly devil, you never let on until the 'do not worry about us' line."

"I could not take any chances David. Surely you understand?"

"Yes I do, but still. This extravaganza you just created, why? Couldn't you just slip away in the night? Quietly?"

"It was a bit of showmanship, I will acknowledge. We did have to remove anything of value and destroy any evidence of our presence. Oh, and about the traitors, they are still safely *locked* in the chamber. When you are ready, I will send a signal to open the door. You can do as you see fit with them. Long prison terms, I would suppose?"

"Absolutely. Wait a minute and I'll tell the FBI to gather around the door."

I yell to Greg to surround the area with the door and the prisoners will be released. He just looks dumbly at me for a minute, then yells at his agents to follow him. He runs up to the area and when they are in position, I tell Michael, "Okay, open the door."

He does, and the mountain slides opens and the group staggers out into the waiting arms of the feds. They seem none the worse for wear.

"Michael, they are out. Is this goodbye? I guess it is. I will miss you all. You made me feel like family."

"David we will eternally be grateful for all you did to help us. Without you, that pack of wolves might have gotten to us before our people could. We will be in touch with you periodically, thru your device. Just to see how you are. Remember, if needed, we now will have the means to come and assist you. Dog, we have not forgotten all you did for us too. I am glad you and David have found partners. You both deserve future happiness."

"Thank you, Michael. Uh, I'm sorry about all the little shit jokes and such. I really do love you all. Especially Mickey. She has my son, right?"

"Yes Dog I have him right here. I love you too Dog. We had such fun." Mickey says. "Say 'I love you' to your daddy."

A high-pitched voice says, "I love you Daddy."

Dog is bawling, "I love you to my son. Wish we had more time together."

Mickey says, "I named him Dog Junior. Goodbye Dog and David. You be nice to Pam."

Michael comes back, "We have to leave now David, but first George wants to talk to you."
"David, I am so glad I did not kill you that night. To try to make up we have bequeathed the Smart Car to you. Small token for what you have done for us."

"Thank you George, but the caves are still blowing up. Where is it?"

Michael says, "We have placed it along with some other items you might use in our warehouse. You know the one where we would pick up our requisitioned items. We changed the locks last night. The key is tied under the seat of your truck."

"You guys, I am awestruck, with all that was going on, how did you manage to pull that off?"

"We had all night remember? No one was out in that storm. It was our ship landing by the way. As soon as it landed, we had everyone loading their personal items and any equipment we needed. Piece of cake as you folks say. Plenty of time to take care of our friends. Well, we must lift off now. We will be doing hyper-drive or whatever your science fiction writers call it. Goodbye my friends, we will be in touch."

"Goodbye everyone. We will miss you too."

The dark swirling cloud began to rise higher and higher in the sky. Then there was the biggest, brightest flash of lightning I have ever seen.

The cloud dissipated and the sky was clear again.

CHAPTER EIGHTY-THREE

When the sky exploded in a flash of light, everyone was stunned. Quickly relaying what occurred to Pam and Tom, I look toward the others. The FBI agents, John Cranston, and the prisoners are frozen in their tracks. I call out to everyone all is safe. "It was just a freak storm. Sheet lightning, they call it." Satisfied with the explanation, the feds continue to place their arrestees into cars. John hurries over to us.

"Tell me that was not the aliens." John pleads.

"It was not the aliens John, there are no aliens at Area 51, remember?"

"That was them leaving, wasn't it? How did they manage to get a ship built here?"

Greg is running up now, breathlessly he looks at the now clear sky. "That was them, right? The aliens."

"Greg, there are no aliens at Area 51." I firmly say.

"Not anymore, I get it. How did they get out, why didn't they leave before? I thought you said they were trapped here."

I ask Greg if the traitors had seen anyone in the chamber.

"No, apparently not. They claim as soon as they entered, the door slammed shut. Scared the crap out of them. They were in total darkness until it opened again, and we were kind enough to *rescue* them."

Then I relate to Greg and John, my conversation with Michael. "They are on their way home, so once again I say: there are no aliens at Area 51, period."

Greg is glad he never mentioned them to his people. Tom leads him to the lock-up to gather up Mr. Barlow. He can join his employers on their trip to jail. Pam goes about her patrolling, so Dog and I head over to the office. John has already gone back to his office and asked us to come over when we are done. When I enter his office, he tells me to have a seat. "David, it may have been Pierce's idea to hire you, but you have been my savior. I can't begin to thank you."

"Just doing my job," I humbly reply, "But I do have some questions. What comes next? Do you still have a job and what about Tom and me?"

John sits back in his chair, his face reflects the strain of the day, "I just got off the phone with the Director, to inform him of today's events. He was dumbstruck Pierce would be involved in such activities. I asked the same questions, David, and the answer is yes to all. I am the new Franklin Pierce. I get to stay here, manage the legitimate programs, and officially close the Beam Weapon Project. You and Tom will have positions as long as you want. The Director wants to give you both special medals for exemplary service to the Department. Since I will be Chief of all DOD projects at Area 51, you will be the Special Agent in Charge and Tom will be your Assistant Special Agent in Charge. I believe the terms are SAC and ASAC. How does that sound?"

"Couldn't ask for more John, thank you. I can't speak for Tom, he'll be here soon. He may want to retire for real now. I would like to keep him on somehow."

"Maybe he can do it part-time, give you a break so you can marry that lady." He smiles. "I'll do whatever I can for you two, I mean it. You saved me, not to mention our country. Heaven forbid their horrific plan had come to fruition."

"How about you John? Maybe you and Doris should take a vacation and enjoy being with each other again?"

"Great idea David. You and Tom can watch the ship while I'm away and we will do the same for you on your honeymoon. Sound like a plan?"

"Deal."

The whole time, Dog has been anxiously sitting and listening. He goes to John, put his gigantic paws on John's lap, and gives him a big slobbery kiss.

John is surprised, "Dog, you act like you understand. You are something else. You had better stick around too. The office staff would be heartbroken without you to spoil."

"He's my partner, he's not going anywhere."

Tom comes in then and I let John tell him the good news.

Tom is stunned. "You want me to stay on, even part-time? I figured I would be retiring for real this time."

"You do what is best for you Tom," John says. "David and I would like you to stay. You two are a great team. I owe my future to you guys."

Tom is quiet for a bit. "Let me talk it over with Gina. I wouldn't mind staying on part-time. Dave needs guidance now and then. It would be best for him."

John roars. I just give Tom a *look*, "You just don't want to be stuck home all the time. All those honey-does and such. You don't fool me."

"You'll find out soon enough." He smirks.

"Now that the world is again safe, I am going home." John says. "I would like to have both of you, and your ladies over for a celebration. We all need to relax. How about next weekend?"

"Sounds great to me," Tom says.

"Me too. I'll check with Pam on her schedule. She is due some time off after her double back shift today."

"Be sure and bring the dogs. Doris would insist."

John leaves and Tom and I just kick back and relax.

"First time in weeks with nothing to worry about. Hope I can take the lack of pressure."

"Where did you say they left the Smart Car?"

"The Smart Car! It is mine now! Let's go check out the warehouse."

We go down to my truck and, as promised, under my seat is a high security key.

"I though you always kept it locked? Oh yeah, no small problem for them, right?"

"Apparently not."

We drive to the warehouse and sure enough, the key works. Just inside the door is the Smart Car, still dressed in its' stealth flat-black paint. We open the doors. The seats are now on the factory brackets. Tom and I can sit comfortably, no more knees in the chest.

"They even took the time to human size it," Tom remarks. "Nice touch. Those guys have class."

Dog says, "I'll just watch. Unless you find me more room, you guys have a good trip."

"It will be simply fine for two of us Dog. Tom probably isn't going to be flying around at night. But we could."

"You will be flying Pam. What about Grizzie and me?"

"I'm sure you can amuse yourselves."

We leave the car and look around the warehouse.

"Looks like they moved the control room in here." Tom says.

"You're right. Look at all the cool stuff they left us. I don't know how to operate most of it, do you?"

"Let's find some twelve-year old, they can teach us."

"Sad but true. This generation is so far ahead of us."

575

"Scary."

Dog alerts, then runs to the open door. Pam and Grizzie walk in.

"Gentlemen this is a restricted government building, Can't you read the signs?" Pam says in a firm official tone.

"It is mine, now." I announce with a sweep of the hand. "The former tenants willed it to me."

"You're kidding; they just can't give it to you. It's government property, isn't it?"

"The contents were given to the aliens, courtesy of the government project. Since the aliens have departed, the remaining items are still project property. Tom and I are taking inventory of what may be of use in the future, for the project, of course."

Pam shakes her head. "Why did I even ask? By the way, do you two still even have jobs?"

"Yes my love, we do. I am the SAC and Tom is my ASAC. How is that? I can afford to marry you now."

She bursts into a grin, "Thank goodness, I have been worried you might have put yourself out of a job when this was solved."

"The thought did cross my mind also," I admit. "Now I can get a real house, not a base apartment. Care to go house hunting?"

"Speaking of marriage and house, may I leave now and go to my wife in our house?" Tom asks.

"Oh, yeah, go on, Tom. Take the next two days off, you missed your weekend because of this escapade. Nothing much is going to happen for a while now, I hope."

Tom heads home and Pam is almost off duty. "Say Officer, if you aren't doing anything would you care to join me for dinner?"

"I though you would never ask." She smiles.

RJ Waters

CHAPTER EIGHTY-FOUR

The week goes by quickly. Nothing much to do anymore. Tom and I continue to look over the cache of treasures the little ones left us. If we ever need to run a similar operation, the equipment is here. We are able to figure out most of it. If need be, we can find some electronics expert around here or even at Creech.

John has been learning about the projects he now has under him. Some are super-secret and quite interesting. He has on-site project managers, so he has only to check status reports and keep DOD advised on progress.

"Did Franklin Pierce have all these projects answering to him?" I ask John one day.

"He did, but the managers tell me, he paid little attention to them. Getting the Beam Weapon completed was his sole concern."

"How are they taking to having you right here and not in DC?"

"Actually, they seem to be pleased. Most of them felt no one cared if they made progress or not." John says. "Sad, because some projects are potentially more dynamic than the Beam. The managers are concerned about security for their areas. I assured them you would be meeting with them and assessing their needs. So, don't worry about not having anything to do."

"That's reassuring because I don't want to be bored. Maybe Tom and I can stir up some action." I wink at Tom.

"Don't chase shadows, I am enjoying the calm. However, I know if there is something there, you two will find it." John smiles and leans back in his chair. "You guys gave me back my life. We're still on for dinner with the girls Saturday, right?"

"Absolutely," Tom answers.

"You bet," I say.

We have a fun time at John and Doris's. The weather cooperates and we eat outside in the patio. Doris is in seventh heaven with Grizzie and Dog.

As we are just relaxing after dinner with some wine, Doris sits up, "So when is the wedding, you two?"

"Uh, well, we haven't set a date yet. But soon." I stammer.

"We did look at some homes today." Pam says, giving me a sly glance. "Even found one we both liked."

John sits up, "Where? You must be careful in this town. There are some *not so good* areas."

I tell them where we were looking. John smiles, "a great area, close to Hwy 95 for both of you to get to work. Gated I hope."

"Yes, gated, not guarded like yours but a nice, quiet development. The house is about five years old and the interior has just been repainted. Perfect choice of colors for us."

"It is available right now; the owners have already moved to the east coast." Pam gushes, "It is beautiful. I love the house and the yard; it even has a small swimming pool with a hot tub."

John asks about the price. I tell him and he says with today's market, it sounds like a good buy.

Tom and Gina also agree it is a smart move for us. "We can even carpool, if you're up to it." Tom asks.

"You are getting tired of commuting to the airport, I bet. Sounds fair to me. Now I will have to commute, but the upside is who will be waiting for me." I give Pam's hand a squeeze. "She has put in for day shift, since she has some seniority now."

Tom laughs, "You won't have anyone to run around with at night anymore, since your friends have left." He then pales, realizing the reference to the aliens.

Gina and Doris both look inquiringly at me. Dog stops his romping with Grizzie and looks at me. Damn he has great hearing.

"It's just as well. The guys were fun to hang out with, but they transferred, and I have someone to stay home with now." I cover the subject, hopefully. Tom, Pam, and John all relax and smile. Dog resumes playing.

That is as far as the secret needs to go.

Doris then says, "We would love to have your wedding and reception here. We have the perfect setting. If you would let us."

Pam looks at me, smiles, "We didn't know where to have it. My parents place only has a small park. We thought about that, but it is kind of public, if you know what I mean."

"Yes, there will be consumption of adult beverages." I advise.

John laughs, "We would be honored to host it. Doris and I owe you. Please allow us, as long as it is alright with your parents, Pam."

"I'll ask them, but after paying for my first, I couldn't let them anyway." She smiles at me.

"Yeah this one is on us. We already agreed."

"We will provide the party, please let us," Doris insists, "I have a good friend who caters. We would love to do it."

John stands up, looking authoritative, and declares, "There will be no further discussion. We will have the wedding here, our treat." He raises his glass.

"I love it when you talk like that, John." Doris exclaims, "It's kind of sexy." She then blushes.

"Well what can we say? Thank you very much, Doris and John, we do appreciate it." I reply.

Pam gets teary and hugs Doris. "Thank you two so much, it is so sweet."

The Cranston's will host the wedding. Gina will help Pam and her Mom with her planning and Tom, Don, and I will just sit back and offer moral support.

Well, it does not work that way. You knew it would not. The three men have a multitude of errands assigned. John is good about giving us some slack on being away. After all, we are over an hour away from Las Vegas out at Area 51. In reality, poor Don gets the bulk of the assignments.

With the wedding still a month away, Don whispers to me one night, "You sure there isn't anything I can do at Creech for you? These ladies are running me ragged."

I pat him on the shoulder, "Sorry guy, this is the curse of retirement."

We have a good laugh.

The guest list is simple. Pam's side is her friends and relatives, while mine is somewhat shorter. My best buddies are light years away by now. No family alas, and my friends list is short. Military friends are spread out around the globe. There is Greg from the FBI, he already told me he wanted to come. I would not expect Brad from the CIA but after filling him on the case, he also wanted to come out and meet me in person. There is good old Eddie from EG&G, wait no that will not do. Scratch him off the list. Dwayne the Vegas PI is not exactly a friend, so he is off the list also.

Eddie did call me one day before the wedding and said he was transferring to the EG&G main office. He said he would advise his replacement I deserved any help I requested. I told him I appreciated it.

"You still owe me lunch, Manning"

RJ Waters

CHAPTER EIGHTY-FIVE

We are now married and on our honeymoon in Hawaii. The wedding was perfect. Doris out did herself. My bride was sunning, absolutely beautiful. Dog in a custom tux with Grizzie in a cute bridesmaid frock were the stars. After an evening of revelry with family and friends, we left the next day for a whole week by ourselves.

Enjoying first class accommodations, sleeping late, and kicking back being normal tourists.

After the tension and pressure of the last, few weeks we can at last relax and enjoy being together, planning the future and all the things couples normally do. No conspiracies, threats, or unknown dangers to district our time together.

On the final day, we are lying side by side on the beach, soaking up the sun. Soft tropical breezes flowing off the water cool our now tanned bodies. My brain is calm, enjoying the lack of any pressing worries. As I begin to drift off to sleep, I hear a voice. Opening one eye, I see Pam is fast asleep. No one is near us.

What the hell, I wonder?

"David. David can you hear me?"

Made in the USA
Columbia, SC
08 October 2022

69036750R00320